RR

P9-BZD-878

Ralph Compton

THE KILLING SEASON

BERKLEY
New York

BERKLEY
An imprint of Penguin Random House LLC
1745 Broadway, New York, NY 10019

Copyright © 1996 by Ralph Compton
Penguin Random House supports copyright. Copyright fuels creativity, encourages
diverse voices, promotes free speech, and creates a vibrant culture. Thank you for buying
an authorized edition of this book and for complying with copyright laws by not
reproducing, scanning, or distributing any part of it in any form without permission.
You are supporting writers and allowing Penguin Random House to continue to
publish books for every reader.

BERKLEY and the BERKLEY & B colophon are registered
trademarks of Penguin Random House LLC.

ISBN: 9780451187871

Signet mass-market edition / June 1996
Berkley mass-market edition / August 2019

Printed in the United States of America
29 31 33 35 37 36 34 32 30 28

Cover art © Hiram Richardson
Cover design by Steve Meditz
Logo art by Roberto Castillo / Shutterstock

Ralph Compton Westerns

This work is respectfully dedicated to Loretto Academy of Our Lady of Light—home of Loretto Chapel—in Santa Fe, New Mexico.

Special Thanks To

John Ed Willoughby, a Birmingham, Alabama, radio personality, who first told me about Loretto Chapel and "The Inexplicable Stairs."

Richard Lindsley, of Loretto Chapel, who was kind enough to send me the story in its entirety. Mr. Lindsley took the time to supply me with the names of all those at Loretto at the time the famous spiral stairs were built. With the exception of Nathan Stone, all the persons referred to are authentic.

Rev. Hugh Feiss, OSB, library director/archivist, Mount Angel Abbey Library, St. Benedict, Oregon. The Rev. Feiss granted me the use of "The Inexplicable Stairs," which is copyrighted material.

PROLOGUE

Newton, Texas. March 5, 1873
Astride a grulla and leading a packhorse, Nathan Stone rode in a little more than an hour before sundown. His hound, Cotton Blossom, trotted alongside. The procession passed several saloons, and that alone was enough to draw attention. Few men just off a long trail would pass up the first saloon, and it was enough of a curiosity to tempt some of the patrons away from the bar to have a look. Seemingly unaware of the spectators, Nathan reined up before the mercantile. Dismounting, he looped the reins of the grulla and the lead rope of the packhorse around the hitch rail. He then paused, as though allowing the men from the saloons an opportunity to size him up before he entered the store. While he didn't wish to be recognized, he dared not seem fearful.

Just a few weeks past his twenty-sixth birthday, his dark hair was well laced with gray. A dusty gray Stetson was tilted over his cold blue eyes. His polished black boots with pointed toes and undershot heels would have been the envy of any cowboy, but the buscadero belt with its pair of tied-down Colts said this hombre didn't earn his bacon and beans wrassling cows. His trousers were black with pinstripes, while his shirt was almost the gray of his Stetson. There was but little to liken him to a man of the range except the red bandanna around his neck and the unmistakable effect of sun and wind on his hands and face. A long sheepskin coat tied behind the cantle of his saddle suggested he might have come from the high country. Stone entered the mercantile, and without command, the dog remained with the horses.

Nathan Stone preferred larger towns where he was less likely to be recognized, stopping only in the villages to re-

plenish his supplies or to buy needed grain for his horses.
When he left the mercantile, he purposely carried only a
sack of grain under his left arm, for it was a situation he
had come to expect. Men from the saloons had congregated
across the dusty street, and one of them stepped forward.
His right thumb was hooked under the butt of his Colt. He
wasn't drunk, but he'd had enough to respond to the taunts
of his comrades. He spoke.

"Ain't you Nathan Stone, the killer?"

"I am Nathan Stone," Nathan said coldly.

"Well, I'm Vern Tilton, an' I think I can take you.
Draw."

"Tilton," said Nathan, just as he had tried in vain to
reason with other foolish challengers. "I have no argument
with you and I have no reason to draw. Now back off."

"By God, Vern," one of the onlookers shouted, "he's
scairt of you."

"Damn you," Tilton bawled, "you ain't a-gonna cheat
me out of provin' I'm faster'n you. Pull your iron."

He emphasized his angry words by jerking out his Colt.
He was clumsy, painfully slow, and Nathan waited until the
last possible second. He finally drew his right-hand Colt as
Tilton was raising his weapon to fire. Tilton's Colt roared,
blasting lead into the ground, as Nathan's slug ripped into
his right shoulder. Tilton stumbled back and would have
fallen, if one of his companions hadn't caught him.

"Take him," Nathan said quietly, "and get the hell out
of here. I could have killed him. I had every right, and next
time, I will."

They backed away but they didn't leave, for though it
was nothing more than a village, there was a sheriff, and
he arrived on the run. Taking just one look at the bleeding,
swearing Tilton, he turned on Nathan.

"I'm Howard Esty, sheriff of this county. Now you shuck
them guns."

"No," said Nathan. "I only defended myself, and any
man that disputes me is lying."

"Speak up, damn it," Esty said, turning his attention to
the townsmen who had begun edging away. "Who started
this?"

"Vern pulled iron first," one of his companions said
grudgingly.

"Then take him to the doc and git him patched up," said

Esty. "And you," he said, pointing to the injured Vern, "be thankin' your lucky stars you're still alive."

They drifted away, some of them casting sour looks at Nathan and Esty. The sheriff was showing his years, gray hair poking through a hole in the crown of his Stetson. He was lean, his hands, face, and neck as leathery and weather-beaten as an old saddle. When Vern and his disgruntled friends were well beyond hearing, he spoke.

"There'll be no charges, an' I'm thankin' you for not saltin' Vern down for keeps. You'd of been within your rights. I'd not want you takin' this personal, but I'd be obliged if you'd finish your business at the store and ride on."

"I aim to," Nathan said.

He loaded the sack of grain on the packhorse, and returning to the store, brought out the rest of his purchases. He tied the neck of the sack, divided its weight behind his saddle, mounted, and rode out. Sheriff Esty watched him out of sight, sighing with relief. Nathan rode warily, for he didn't know where the bunch had gone who had prodded Vern Tilton into drawing. It was a town he wished to leave behind, and Cotton Blossom felt the same, for he had forged on ahead. Nathan rode a good ten miles before finding a decent place to make camp for the night. There was water from a seep that had pooled at the foot of a ridge, concealed by a heavy growth of willows. First Nathan unsaddled his grulla and unloaded the packhorse, allowing the weary animals to roll. He then quickly gathered wood, knowing it would be dark before he could boil coffee and broil his bacon, but he needed the food and hot coffee. Whatever the reason, a fire after dark—in Comanche country—could be the death of a man. Nathan chose a low place in the ground, kept the blaze small, and doused it when the coffee was hot and his rashers of bacon ready. He shared the bacon with Cotton Blossom and drank the coffee from the pot. There was little else to do except turn in for the night, so Nathan rolled in his blankets, his head on his saddle, a Colt near to his hand. He could count on Cotton Blossom alerting him to any approaching danger, but weary as he was, sleep wouldn't come. His mind drifted back to the afternoon shooting, to Vern Tilton, and he recalled something Wild Bill Hickok had once told him.

"When a man pulls a gun on you, always shoot to kill.

Let him live, and the first chance he gets, he'll show his gratitude by shootin' you in the back."

"Bill was right, Cotton Blossom," Nathan said. "Even if he fails to bushwhack me, he can always claim that my hand wasn't steady or that I was afraid of him ..."

As he had done so often, Nathan allowed his mind to wander back over the years, to that bleak day in January 1866. Ragged, hungry, afoot, he had returned to his fire-ravaged home near Charlottesville, Virginia, following two long years in Libby Prison in Richmond. Old Malachi, an aged Negro, had lived long enough to describe and name the seven renegades who had murdered Nathan's mother, father, and sister. Swearing a vow of vengeance on his father's grave, Nathan had taken the trail of the killers, following it west. His constant companion had been Cotton Blossom, the only living reminder of a past that had been lost to him forever. Reaching St. Louis, Nathan had become involved with young Molly Tremayne, only to lose her when he had again taken up the vengeance trail. While he had never gotten over Molly, he had never tried to reclaim her, for their parting had been bitter. So he had never learned that pretty Molly had died less than a year after his leaving, having given birth to his son. . . .

In a little Missouri town, Nathan had found and had killed the first of the seven men on his death list. In Waco, Texas, dealing faro, he had found himself in an uncomfortable position when the three unwed daughters of the saloon owner had set out to trap him. He had escaped, only to find himself pursued by Eulie, the eldest of the trio. Unable to rid himself of her, he had made the best of it. Eulie had dressed as a man, had called herself Eli, and had proven her ability to ride, rope, and shoot. Nathan's manhunt had led him to New Orleans, and there Eulie had so impressed Barnaby McQueen with her horse savvy that McQueen had persuaded her to remain at his ranch, gentling a horse. Nathan had begun spending his time in New Orleans saloons, seeking some word of the men on his death list.

On a New Orleans street, Nathan had gone to the aid of a stranger, and as a result, had gunned down two killers employed by Hargis Gavin, owner of a New Orleans gambling empire. Byron Silver, the stranger whom Nathan had befriended, had been associated with French Stumberg, owner of his own gambling houses and archenemy of

Gavin. Stumberg, from what Nathan had learned, harbored two of the killers on Nathan's death list, so when Byron Silver had persuaded Stumberg to hire Nathan, Nathan had taken the job. But Nathan quickly learned three things. The first and most disturbing had been Stumberg's involvement in white slavery, the selling of young women in Mexico. Second, Nathan had found Stumberg intended to win a horse race—a race in which Eulie was determined to ride a McQueen horse—by ambushing certain riders. Finally, Nathan had learned Byron Silver was an undercover agent from Washington, seeking to trap French Stumberg. The day of the horse race, Eulie had been shot out of the saddle and had died. Byron Silver had been wounded, leaving only Nathan to prevent the escape of Stumberg and his killers, and Nathan had accomplished that by blowing up Stumberg's steamboat, with the gambler and his killers aboard.

Nathan had left New Orleans, having learned that one of the killers he had believed was with Stumberg was riding with the notorious Cullen Baker. Baker and his gang had been reported in Arkansas, and Nathan had ridden to Fort Smith. Offered the badge of a deputy U.S. marshal, Nathan had accepted it, awaiting Baker's next foray into Arkansas. Eventually he had confronted the Baker gang, killing two of the outlaws. One of them was a killer from Nathan's death list.

Returning to Texas, five men still to be found, Nathan had paused in Lexington, where he had become friends with Viola Hayden and her father, Jesse. Viola had been set to ride Daybreak, her big gray, in a race with odds against him of twenty-to-one. On impulse, Nathan had bet five hundred dollars on the horse, but after collecting his winnings—ten thousand dollars—had been forced to shoot his way out of an ambush. While in Lexington, Nathan had met Texas Ranger Captain Sage Jennings. From the ranger, Nathan had learned that two of the killers he sought had left Texas, apparently bound for Indian Territory. Following, Nathan had gunned one of the men down, taking from him a young girl, Lacy Mayfield. From Lacy Nathan had learned that the man he had killed had been on his way to Colorado. Nathan, taking the girl with him, had ridden to Colorado. Reaching Denver, he found that the killers he sought had ridden south to Ciudad de Oro, a mining town. Leaving Lacy at a Denver boardinghouse, Nathan had ridden south, finding and gunning down one of the killers on his death list. There, however, Nathan had been given a false lead that had taken him to Austin, Texas, while the killer he sought had gone to Fort Dodge and eventually to Denver.

Reaching Austin, Nathan had found Viola Hayden working in a saloon, destitute, her father dead at the hands of the man who had lost ten thousand dollars to Nathan just a few months before. Despite Nathan's efforts to save the girl, she had shot the man who she believed had killed her father and had then shot herself. Returning to Colorado, Nathan had found Lacy Mayfield involved with the owner of a saloon, a man Nathan had learned was one of the killers on his death list. In the fight that followed, Lacy had been gunned down by the outlaw when she had come between him and Nathan's gun. Thus it had been a bitter victory, the killing of this fifth man, for he had taken Lacy with him. While in Denver, Nathan had become friends with Wild Bill Hickok, and when Hickok had ridden east to Hays, Kansas, Nathan had ridden with him. Nathan had spent a few days with Hickok, until he had been elected sheriff. Nathan had then ridden to Kansas City, uncertain as to how and where he would find the last two men on his death list.

In a Kansas City newspaper, Nathan had seen a reward dodger that had been widely circulated by the Pinkertons on Frank and Jesse James. Among the names of men who had ridden with the infamous outlaws, Nathan had found the name of one of the killers he sought. Following a bank robbery by the James gang, Nathan had found the hideout of the outlaws and had led a sheriff's posse to it. While Frank and Jesse had escaped, Nathan had confronted the man he had sworn to kill and had forced a shootout. At loose ends, not knowing where he might find the seventh man, Nathan answered an advertisement in a Kansas City newspaper and took a position with the Kansas-Pacific Railroad between Kansas City and Hays. It had been his duty to repair telephone lines torn down by Indians or outlaws and to warn train crews of damaged track. After serving with distinction for a few months, Nathan had resigned because he had seen nor heard nothing of the seventh and last man he had sworn to kill. Riding south into Indian

Territory, he had been taken prisoner by the ruthless El Gato and his band of thieves and killers.

Nathan had soon learned that the killer he sought was not among the renegades, and as he plotted his escape, he had learned that El Gato had a girl he planned to sell into slavery, in Mexico. Talking to her, Nathan had learned that her name was Mary Holden, that she longed to escape. But before Nathan could make a move, he had been forced to ride with El Gato and his outlaws on a winter raid into Kansas. Slipping away during a blizzard, Nathan had returned to El Gato's camp, overpowering the two men El Gato had left behind. He had then taken Mary south, to Fort Worth, Texas. Nathan had been in Texas often enough to have become friends with the post commander, Captain Ferguson, and the officer, assuming Mary was Nathan's wife, had assigned them a cabin. By the time Nathan and Mary had left Forth Worth, riding north, Nathan Stone had done the very thing he had vowed never again to do. He had become involved with a woman, more committed than he had ever been, but still burdened with his oath to kill the last of the seven renegades who had murdered his family in Virginia.

While at Forth Worth, Nathan had learned by telegraph that Texas outlaw John Wesley Hardin had been involved in shootings in several south Texas towns and was believed to be riding north. One of several men who had been riding with Hardin had been identified as Dade Withers, the seventh and last man on Nathan's death list. He and Mary had ridden to Fort Dodge and then to Hays without finding a trace of Hardin. Fifty miles east of Hays, on their way to Abilene, they had ridden into a holdup involving a Kansas-Pacific train. As he had traded lead with the outlaws, Nathan had been seriously wounded. But the train crew had remembered him from his Kansas-Pacific days, and taking Mary and the wounded Nathan aboard, had reversed the train and backed it to Abilene. The railroad, grateful for Nathan's daring, had paid all his medical bills and presented him with a reward. When he had recovered, he had been offered the task of taking a posse after the outlaws, for they had become an expensive nuisance, destroying track and stopping trains bearing army payrolls. But Nathan had declined, determined to find that seventh man, so the Kansas-Pacific had hired other men to trail the train robbers.

Again Nathan had taken Hardin's trail, and he had found evidence that the outlaw and his companions had reached Wichita with a trail herd. But there the men had split up, and Nathan had trailed Dade Withers west, knowing only that the man rode a horse with an XIT brand. Reaching Fort Dodge, Nathan and Mary had learned that a lone outlaw had robbed the mercantile at Dodge City, just west of the fort. At the mercantile, Nathan had learned the outlaw had ridden south on a horse bearing an XIT brand. He had not been followed, for he had struck exactly at sundown, so when Nathan had taken the trail the next day at first light, it had been easily followed. But the lone rider had traveled less than a mile when he had been surrounded by others. He had ridden away with the larger band and Nathan had followed them all south until they had crossed the Cimarron, into Indian Territory. Thus the seventh man on Nathan Stone's death list had become part of El Gato's band of renegades.

Riding to Kansas City, Nathan had agreed to pursue the outlaws on behalf of the Kansas-Pacific Railroad, but learned something that stopped him in his tracks. Mary Holden was expecting his child, and he had set aside everything else to marry the girl. But Mary had refused to remain safely in Kansas City, insisting on staying at Fort Dodge until Nathan and his posse had captured the band of renegades. But the outlaws always escaped into Indian Territory, leaving Nathan frustrated. Unknown to Nathan, El Gato had been sending a man to Fort Dodge to look and listen, and the outlaw chieftain had learned that Mary—his former captive—was there. Nathan had become fed up with railroad methods and had ridden to Hays. From there he had taken a train to Kansas City to resign from the railroad posse. Awaiting just such an opportunity, that very morning El Gato's men had stolen Mary away from the fort and had taken her into the wilds of Indian Territory, to the outlaw stronghold. Only Cotton Blossom, Nathan's hound, had followed.

Learning that Mary had been abducted, the post commander at Fort Dodge had telegraphed the Kansas-Pacific office in Kansas City. Nathan immediately had engaged a locomotive and tender for an emergency run to Hays. From there, he had ridden to Fort Dodge, arriving after dark. He had learned that a party of soldiers had gone after Mary, only to be ambushed. Nathan had then ridden out alone, to find Cotton Blossom awaiting him near the Cimarron. With the dog guiding him, he had ridden into Indian Territory and had found the outlaw camp. In the darkness of El Gato's cabin, he had killed the outlaw leader in a knife fight, only to learn that the renegades—a dozen strong—had already ravaged and murdered Mary. Grief and rage had taken control of Nathan Stone, and he had burst into the outlaw bunkhouse, his Winchester blazing. He had gunned down ten of the outlaws—including Dade Withers—but had been so severely wounded he had been in danger of bleeding to death. He had been saved only because Cotton Blossom had returned to the fort and had been able to attract the attention of the soldiers.

Healed in body but sick to his soul, Nathan had ridden to Kansas City, only to learn the newspapers had created him an unwanted reputation as a fast gun, a gunfighter. The Kansas-Pacific had released an etching of him, and his reputation seemed to have spread throughout the frontier. In one town after another, he had been forced into gunfights to save his own life, with each new killing adding to the deadly legend. Finally, in the fall of 1872, he had managed to drop out of sight. Riding south to New Orleans, he had found refuge with Barnaby and Bess McQueen, who had befriended him and Eulie so long ago. There he had remained until the last week in February 1873. Finally he had ridden away, hopeful of escaping his past, only to find it stalking him like the pale horse. There in the street of this little Texas town he had been forced to face up to the awful truth. He was a marked man. While he had fulfilled his promise to his dead father, it now seemed a hollow victory, as he thought of what it had cost him. His vendetta had led to a bitter parting with Molly Tremayne, in St. Louis. He had been hell-bent on going to New Orleans, and it was there that Eulie had been shot. His winning—and taking—ten thousand dollars had cost Viola Hayden her father, driving her to murder and suicide. Lacy Mayfield had been gunned down trying to save one of the very men Nathan had sworn to kill. Poor Mary had suffered a horrible death in Indian Territory only because she had wished to be near him. He groaned, for their faces seemed to have been burned into his mind with a hot iron, and he couldn't escape them. Sensing his anguish, Cotton Blossom came near. He scratched the dog's ears, thankful for his faithfulness, feeling even that was more than he deserved.

For a long time Nathan lay looking at the silver stars in the purple of the sky, until he finally slept. Sometime after midnight something awakened him, and he realized it had been the rattle of dry leaves, as Cotton Blossom had gotten to his feet. It was in the small hours of the night, when every sound was magnified many times, and it was all the warning Nathan Stone had. With the snick of an eared-back hammer, he was moving, rolling away from his saddle, palming a Colt. There was a roar from the surrounding thicket and two slugs slammed into Nathan's saddle. He fired three times. Once at the muzzle flash, once to the left, and once to the right. There were no more shots, and there was a rustle of leaves as Cotton Blossom trotted toward the thicket. Nathan followed, and taking the dead man by the ankles, dragged him out into the clearing. The moon had risen, and with the starlight Nathan had no trouble identifying the man.

"Damn you, Vern Tilton," Nathan said bitterly. "Damn you . . ."

CHAPTER 1

Lampasas, Texas. March 18, 1873

Nathan Stone had ridden halfway across Texas without again being forced to resort to his deadly revolvers. Within him was the desperate hope that his dismal luck might be about to change. He had ridden all day in a cold, steady rain, and his horses plodded along with heads down. A lank and sodden Cotton Blossom looked as though he had been skinned and his hide again stretched over his bones. Nathan's eyes roamed the muddy, deserted street that was Lampasas, seeking a livery, for his horses were done. Then he would find a hotel with a dry bed, and finally a cafe with hot food for himself and Cotton Blossom. Reaching the livery, his horses trotted gratefully under the roof of an open shed that faced the street. With total darkness but a few minutes away, a lighted lantern hung from a peg driven into the wall. Nathan dismounted, and from somewhere within the livery, a horse nickered. Nathan's packhorse answered, alerting the liveryman to their presence. He came limping out, looking like the stove-up cowboy he probably was.

"Howdy," he said. "You reckon she's a-gonna rain?"

"The way it's been threatenin' all day," Nathan said, "I wouldn't be surprised. My horses are as used up as I am. A double measure of grain for each of them, and there's an extra dollar for you, if you'll rub them down."

"*Bueno hombre,* thinkin' of yer hosses. I'll see to 'em."

"I'm obliged," said Nathan. "Where's the hotel?"

"Down the street, way you was headed. It ain't no *caravansera.*"*

"Good," Nathan replied. "All I want is a roof over my head."

The Colorado Hotel had obviously taken its name from the nearby Colorado River. It had two floors and Nathan

*Fancy place.

took a room on the first. Cotton Blossom was accepted without question. There was a cafe beside the hotel, and thanks to the continuous rain and chilling wind, the eatery was virtually deserted. A bored cook leaned on the counter while a man sat at a back table eating a steak.

"Amigo," said Nathan, "I'm gaunt, and my dog's a notch or two below that. Is he welcome?"

"Mister," said the cook, "business has been so god-awful bad, I'd welcome a tribe of hungry Comanches. The dog's welcome to leftovers, and there'll be plenty. What with all this rain, I'll be closin' early."

"Bring me the biggest steak in the house," Nathan said, "thick, cooked through, and sided with whatever else you got."

"You got it. While it's on the fire, I'll feed the dog. He looks like he's missed a few meals."

"We both have," said Nathan.

A chair scraped as a man got up, and Nathan found himself face-to-face with Texas Ranger Captain Sage Jennings. Grinning, Jennings put out his hand and Nathan took it. He hadn't seen Jennings since the ranger had joined him in the burying of Viola Hayden in Lexington, many months ago.

"Come on back to my table," Jennings said.

Nathan did, taking a chair across from Jennings. Cotton Blossom had followed the cook to the kitchen, and after he had fed the dog and put Nathan's steak on the fire, he brought the coffeepot and a tin cup for Nathan. For a moment Nathan just sipped the hot coffee, reluctant to discuss the painful past. But Jennings already knew it, minus the details. He spoke only of Nathan's work on behalf of the Kansas-Pacific Railroad, allowing Nathan to comment if he chose. Silent at first, he soon learned that he needed to talk, to unburden himself. So he told the sympathetic ranger all of it, up to and including the shooting in Newton, a few days before.

"There's no end to it, Cap," said Nathan. "One damn fool after another, they pull their guns, and I have to shoot them to keep them from shooting me. Hell, I'm ready to stop the world and get off. How do I escape this reputation I don't want, never wanted?"

"You don't," Jennings said somberly. "This is the killing season, and the only law is a fast gun. You, my friend, are living under a blessing and a curse. The blessing is your fast gun that's keeping you alive, while the downside is the curse. Your deadly reputation. Perhaps it's time you consider my earlier suggestion and become a lawman."

"Legalize my killings? I've seen what's happened to Wild Bill Hickok and I don't want it said I'm just a killer behind a badge. I know you mean well, and I'm obliged for your concern. Now, if it's any of my business, what are you doing this far north?"

"I'm only a day's ride from Austin," said Jennings, "and there's nothing I can tell you that you couldn't learn in most any saloon. Texas is after a killer name of Clint Barkley. He's also known as Bill Bowen, and he's brother-in-law to Merritt Horrell. That won't mean a lot to you until you know something of the Horrells. The Horrell-Higgins feud has been going on for God knows how long. There's five of the Horrell boys. Benjamin, Martin, Merritt, Samuel, and Thomas. They fought together through the Civil War and they've raised hell to a lesser degree ever since. The state of Texas has pretty well shied clear of the feud between the Horrell and Higgins clans, but the word's out that the Horrells aim to defend Clint Barkley with their guns. For that reason, we're expecting Clint Barkley in these parts."

"And you're here to welcome him," Nathan said.

"I wish it was that simple," said Jennings with a sigh. "The man Barkley killed was a friend of mine, and I'm here only because I raised hell for the privilege. The governor has commissioned a state police force, and I'm waiting for a Captain Tom Williams and deputies to arrive from Fort Worth. I was told Williams is in charge, and I'm not to make a move unless so directed by him."

"By God, that's a slap in the face, an insult," Nathan said. "You don't aim to accept that, do you?"

"I do," Jennings replied. "This whole affair has been conducted with about as much secrecy as a sod-buster barn raising. Had I been in charge, I'd have ridden in, waited for Barkley to show, and taken him without going up against the Horrells."

"Now," said Nathan, "you'd have to fight the Horrell clan just to get at Barkley."

"Exactly," Jennings replied. "I aim to stay at the hotel,

waiting for this Tom Williams and his men to arrive. They're supposed to be here tomorrow."

"I have no particular place to go," said Nathan, "so maybe I'll just hang around and see how this turns out. Not that I expect you'll be needing help, of course."

"No way," Jennings said. "If I buy into this without specific orders, I'll likely be reprimanded by the governor."

The cook brought Nathan's steak, along with onions, potatoes, bread, and a whole dried apple pie. Cotton Blossom waddled out of the kitchen, seeking a place to lie down. When Nathan had finished his meal, he and Jennings left the cafe and returned to the hotel. As it turned out, Jennings had the room adjoining Nathan's.

"I'll see you at breakfast," said the ranger.

Nathan let himself and Cotton Blossom into the room, locking the door behind them. The dog curled up on an oval rug beside the bed, and Nathan tossed his hat on the dresser. Removing his buscadero belt with his Colts, he hung them on the head of the bed. He removed his boots and then his sodden clothes, spreading them on the floor to dry. He then blew out the lamp and eased himself gratefully into the bed. More than ever, he was thankful for a roof over his head, for the wind was slamming sheets of rain against the windows.

Nathan awoke before first light, aware that the rain had diminished or ceased. Taking an oilskin packet from inside his hat band, he removed a match and lighted the lamp on the dresser. He then poured water from a big white porcelain pitcher into a matching basin and, with a bit of soap, shaved. Cotton Blossom got up, walked to the door, and stood there wagging his tail.

"Come in, Cap," Nathan said, unlocking the door.

"That's some dog," said Jennings, stepping into the room. "If he's ever the daddy of pups, I want one."

"We stayed a spell with friends in New Orleans," Nathan said. "He ran with a couple of their female hounds, but I reckon he didn't get that involved. Anyhow, he's a mite old. He was grown when I came back from the war, and he's been with me seven years."

The rain had ceased during the night and there was blue sky visible through patches of gray clouds. The wind was chill, but there was a hint of early spring, for occasional tufts of grass had begun to green. Nathan and Jennings had breakfast, washing it down with plenty of black coffee. Cotton Blossom again ate in the kitchen, emerging as well-fed and satisfied as a hound ever gets. Nathan and Jennings returned to the hotel, to Jennings's room. Nathan took the chair while the ranger sat on the bed.

"So these newly appointed Texas lawmen arrive today," said Nathan. "Do you reckon they'll come looking for you, or just take the bit in their teeth and go with it?"

"It depends on whether or not they've been told I'm here," Jennings replied. "Unless I'm asked to take part, I aim to mind my own business."

Jennings was not wearing the famous silver star-in-a-circle. Few rangers did when working alone, especially in hostile territory, for they were feared and respected to the extent that outlaws took no chances. Rangers were shot in the back or ambushed.

"I reckon you have some idea as to where to find this Clint Barkley," said Nathan.

"Him bein' brother-in-law to Merritt Horrell," Jennings said, "I reckon I'd cat-foot it out to Merritt's ranch. If he wasn't there, I'd call on the rest of the Horrells until I'd rousted him out. He could be with any of them. These feuding clans are generally so bound up with one another, when you cut one, they all bleed."

"So these lawmen you're waitin' for could ride into a hail of lead from five outfits," said Nathan.

"They could," Jennings said, "unless they use some common sense. These Horrells know Clint Barkley has a price on his head. Any jaybird ridin' in with intentions of arresting him had best come prepared to sling some lead."

As the day wore on, it became unseasonably warm. The wind died almost entirely and the sun began to suck up the water from the muddy street. Even with the windows open, the hotel rooms became stuffy and uncomfortable.

"God," said Nathan, "in Texas, you're always soaked to the hide. Either from a three-day rain or from your own sweat. Makes me lonesome for the high country, where you can enjoy blizzards right on through April."

"There's a saloon down the street aways," said Jennings. "Let's mosey over there and have us a beer."

"Suits me," Nathan said. "We're two hours away from

sundown. Maybe your visiting badge-toters aim to arrive after dark, so as not to attract too much attention."

There was little to distinguish the Matador Saloon from thousands of its kind on the western frontier, and the barkeep had every right to be as bored as he looked. The place was as deserted as a cow camp on payday, and only one of the hanging lamps had been lighted to dispel the gloom. There were plenty of tables, but Nathan and Jennings leaned on the bar.

"Beer for each of us," said Jennings.

When the barkeep brought the beer, Jennings paid. Cotton Blossom crouched at Nathan's feet, his eyes on the door, for he didn't like saloons or the men who frequented them. Nathan and Jennings had been in the saloon only a few minutes when seven riders reined up outside.

"Oh, God," the barkeep groaned, "it's the Horrells."

"Who are they?" Nathan asked innocently.

"Trouble," the saloon man answered. "There's Tom, Mart, and Sam. I ain't sure who the others are."

"They'll likely be bellyin' up," said Jennings. "We might as well get us a table."

Jennings led the way, Nathan and Cotton Blossom following. The ranger purposely took a table off to the side, as near the swinging doors as possible. The seven men trooped into the saloon, and they were a hard-bitten lot. Every one was armed with a Colt, and as they entered, each man allowed his eyes to linger long and hard on Nathan and Jennings. Cotton Blossom's hackles rose, and he growled deep in his throat.

"Bring us a bottle," one of the men demanded of the barkeep.

"Hell," said another, "make that two bottles. Clint's buyin'."

They all laughed. Nathan and Jennings studied the man who paid for the whiskey. Cotton Blossom growled again, louder this time.

"What's that damn dog growlin' at?" one of the men at the bar shouted.

"What does it matter?" Nathan asked mildly. "He's not bothering you."

The exchange ended as sudden as it had begun, when four riders reined up outside. As the men dismounted, Captain Jennings groaned, for the evening sun glinted off the badges they wore.

"It's the law, by God," said one of the men at the bar.

As the seven drew and cocked their Colts, the barkeep disappeared behind the bar. Despite the ranger's vow not to involve himself without invitation, Nathan could tell by the look in Jennings's eyes that he wasn't going to allow the foolish state policemen to walk into a trap without warning. At the thump of the lawmen's boots on the porch, Jennings made his move.

"It's a trap!" Jennings shouted. *"Cuidado."*

As he shouted the warning, Jennings upended the table. But it wasn't much of a shield for two men, and Nathan seized the leg of a second table, dropping it on its side between himself and the gunmen at the bar. But the surprised lawmen hadn't acted swiftly enough. The Horrell clan had cut loose a veritable hail of lead that tore through the batwing doors. Running for the door, they fired at Nathan and Jennings, their slugs slamming into the wooden tabletops. But Nathan and Jennings returned the fire, wounding two of the men before they were free of the saloon. The seven had mounted their horses and were galloping away before the frightened barkeep crawled out from behind the bar.

"God Almighty," he asked in a trembling voice, "what brought that on?"

"From what I hear," Jennings said, "your friends the Horrells are siding a man wanted by the law. I expect there are dead men outside."

Nathan and Jennings, followed by the fearful barkeep, stepped through the shattered batwings. Three of the lawmen lay dead, while the fourth sat on the edge of the porch, his head in his hands.

"My God," said the barkeep, "they was gunned down like dogs."

"A shame," Jennings said, "but maybe some good will come of it. You don't send sheep after a pack of curly wolves."

"Who *are* you, mister?" the barkeep asked.

"Nobody who matters," Jennings replied. He crossed to the other side of the street, bound for the hotel. Nathan and Cotton Blossom followed. Reaching the hotel, Jennings paused until Nathan caught up. Then the ranger spoke.

"It's near suppertime. Join me if you like. I aim to get an early start in the morning."

Nathan nodded, and they entered the cafe, Cotton Blossom following. He sloped into the kitchen and the friendly cook fed him his supper. Nathan and Jennings ordered their meal, seated themselves, and were drinking first cups of coffee before either spoke.

"I reckon you're ridin' back to Austin," said Nathan.

"I am," Jennings replied. "Why don't you ride with me?"

"I will," said Nathan. "I'll stay a few days, and then I aim to ride to Fort Worth and see if my old friend Captain Ferguson is still there."

Austin, Texas. March 21, 1873

Nathan visited some of the saloons in Austin, carefully avoiding the one where young Viola Hayden had gone to the bad. The second day following their arrival in the capital city, Captain Jennings invited Nathan to his office.

"I have something to show you," the ranger said.

Reaching the office, Nathan followed Jennings into a back room where the arms and ammunition was stored. From an open wooden crate, the ranger took a pair of new Colts, tossing them to Nathan butt-first. Nathan caught one of the weapons in each hand.

"Army-issue .44-40 rimfires," Jennings said.

"I've heard of them," said Nathan. "Metallic cartridges."

"Yes," Jennings said. "Now put them aside for a minute and take a look at this." He handed Nathan a new Winchester, still coated with grease from the factory.

"The new 1873 Winchester," said Nathan, "and it takes the same shells as the Colts."

"Exactly," Jennings replied. "We got ours when the army got theirs. The Colts and the Winchester are yours. I can spare you four hundred rounds. Any trading post or sutler's store should have ammunition by the time you're needing it."

"I'm obliged, Cap," said Nathan, touched by the ranger's generosity. "I'd hoped that eventually . . ."

"Eventually might be too late," Jennings replied. "You need them now, if for no other reason than to save your hide. The Indians have pulled out all the stops, and for the next few years, it'll be hell with the lid off. Quanah Parker's got near seven hundred braves. Lacking firepower, get that bunch on your trail, and you're on a one-way ride to the *campo santo*."*

Nathan spent the next few days in his hotel room familiarizing himself with the new Colts. Eventually he would have to find a secluded area and practice firing the weapons; he needed to know if they pulled to the right or the left. After almost two weeks in Austin, he felt it was time to ride on, north to Fort Worth. He again thanked Captain Jennings for the new weapons, loaded his packhorse, and rode north. Half a day out of Austin, his packhorse slid a right front hoof off a ledge of rock and came up lame. He was not more than three or four miles south of Georgetown, and there was but one thing he could do. Removing the heavy pack saddle and the lead rope, he set the animal free.

"I hate to leave you, *amigo*," Nathan said, "but it'll take you a while to heal, if you ever do. But at least you'll have a chance."

Nathan then loaded the packsaddle atop his own saddle, securing it with rope. Leading the grulla, he set out for Georgetown. The packhorse nickered, and Nathan tried to shut out the sound. If the animal healed, it would find a home, being near Georgetown. If it didn't heal, it would become food for coyotes and vultures. He tried not to think of that grim possibility. It would be near dark by the time he reached town. He was forced to consider the possibility he might have trouble buying another horse, for this wasn't much more than a village. In many a small Texas town, few men owned more than one horse or one mule, while those with two animals needed them to pull a wagon. By the time Nathan reached Georgetown, his feet were killing him. The liveryman was a thin old fellow with a piece of straw hung loosely between his teeth, and he eyed Nathan's overloaded grulla curiously. Finally he spoke.

"I ain't never seen that a-fore."

"You have now," Nathan said shortly. "Do you have some place I can leave this packsaddle for a while?"

"Tack room, I reckon. They's rats as big as possums, though."

"I'll risk it for tonight," Nathan said grimly. "Will you unsaddle and rub down my horse? He'll need some grain, too."

*Cemetery.

"Costs extry fer rubbin' down an' fer grain. Don't cost you nothin' fer unsaddlin', though."

"Well, thank God," said Nathan. "Tomorrow I'm going to need a packhorse. Do you have a horse or mule for sale?"

"Yeeeee doggies," he cackled, "that's by-God funny. I ain't had a hoss er mule fer sale since I disremember when."

"Do you know of anybody with a horse or mule for sale?" Nathan asked.

"Nary a hoss, nary a mule," he said, seeming to relish his negative reply.

"Then unsaddle, rub down, and grain this horse," Nathan said.

"Can't git to the saddle, with all them fixings you got roped to it."

Striving mightily to control his temper, Nathan untied the ropes so that he could lift the loaded packsaddle from the horse.

"Yeeeee doggies," said the exasperating old coot, "you figgered that out right snappy. Now I can git to that saddle. You wanta tote that load of truck to the tack room, I'll hold the door fer you."

"I'd appreciate it," Nathan said through gritted teeth, "as long as you don't strain yourself."

He lugged the heavy packsaddle into the tackroom, noting that the slatted door was secured only with a drop latch. Anybody with the brains God gave a *paisano** could get in. The old hostler looked at Nathan, his eyes crinkling at the corners, but Nathan didn't allow him to say more. Leaving the livery, his saddlebags over his arm, he set out for the hotel. Cotton Blossom trotted at his heels. The hotel was a single-story affair, and Nathan paid two dollars for a room for the night.

"Where's a good place to eat?" he asked the desk clerk.

"Down next to the jail. Around here, it's the only place to eat. But you'd best get your grub and get away from there. Mart Horrell and one of the Horrell hands, Jerry Scott, is in jail. We're expecting the whole hell-raisin' bunch of Horrells just any time."

"I've heard of them," Nathan said. "Why hasn't your sheriff just raised a posse and gone after them?"

*Roadrunner.

"A week ago," said the clerk, "our sheriff turned in his badge and rode out. He said there was just too damn many Horrells. They gunned down three lawmen over to Lampasas. Our lawyer, A.S. Fisher, is wearin' the badge until we elect another sheriff. If we can find one."

Nathan and Cotton Blossom found the cafe. Cotton Blossom had been fed and Nathan was drinking a last cup of coffee when all hell broke loose outside. Nathan got up and started for the door.

"You'd best stay off the street," the cook warned. "It's them no-account Horrells, likely here to bust their kin out of jail."

There were seven riders. They all dismounted, and the man carrying a sledgehammer advanced toward the jail. He was the man Nathan had decided was Clint Barkley. The cook stood beside Nathan, looking out the window.

"Which ones are the Horrells?" Nathan asked.

"Them two holdin' back is just Horrell cowboys," the cook replied. "The gent with the hammer is a friend of the Horrells, an' I hear he's hidin' out from the law."

Barkley attacked the door of the jail with the sledge, while his comrades shouted encouragement. After he had broken through, Nathan could hear the clang of the hammer as he attacked the cell door lock. When he emerged, the freed men with him, the Horrells cheered. But their merriment was short-lived as a rifle spoke from across the street. One of the Horrell cowboys cried out in pain and the Horrells began returning the fire. Then came a shouted challenge.

"Put down your guns. I'm Fisher, acting sheriff."

"You want our guns," one of the Horrells shouted, "come and get 'em."

Fisher had guts. Clutching his rifle, he came in a zigzag run, trying to reach the protection of a giant oak. It would have brought him much closer to his adversaries, but Horrell fire cut his legs from under him and he fell, far short of his goal. Dust spurted from the ground around him, as the Horrells renewed their attack on the fallen man. Then there was a woman running toward him, crying as she came.

"No! No! Don't shoot!"

"My God," said the cook in Nathan's ear. "That's Fisher's wife and she's expecting."

Guns ready, the Horrells were advancing, ignoring the

pleas of the woman. It was the kind of one-sided fight Nathan Stone hated. When he left the cafe, he was behind the Horrells. Drawing his right-hand Colt, he fired once and Clint Barkley's hat left his head.

"The next one will be a mite lower," Nathan said. "Mount up and ride."

"Gun him down," Barkley shouted. "It was him shot Mart and Tom in Lampasas."

But Nathan had an advantage. Wounded though he was, Fisher began firing again, catching the Horrells in a crossfire. There was shouting as townsmen came to Fisher's aid, some of them firing at the Horrells. Nathan had the satisfaction of knocking Barkley down with a slug through his thigh. As the wounded outlaw crawled toward his horse, Nathan fired twice. The lead kicked up dust, spooking the horse, and it lit out. Barkley was given a hand up behind one of the Horrells and they thundered out of town, bleeding but alive. Nathan walked down the dusty street until he reached the wounded Fisher. Other men were helping him to his feet, while his concerned wife wrung her hands and wept.

"Damn it," said Fisher, glaring at Nathan, "we had them boxed. Why did you invite them to ride out?"

"Because it was just you and me against seven of them," Nathan said, "and you were wounded, belly-down, with no cover. You've got gravel in your gizzard, pardner, and I reckon your intentions are good. It's your judgment that's not worth a damn."

"Mister," said one of the newly arrived townsmen, "we're needin' us a sheriff. The job could be yours if you're wantin' it."

"Thanks," Nathan replied, "but I don't want it. I don't usually buy into somebody else's fight, but I won't allow a pack of yellow coyotes to jump a man when he's down." He turned away, returning to the cafe where Cotton Blossom waited.

"By God," said the cafe cook admiringly, "it was good seein' that bunch of Horrells tuck their tails and run. Come on in. The coffee's on me."

"Thanks," said Nathan, "but I've had enough. I'll see you at breakfast."

CHAPTER 2

It was almost dark when Nathan and Cotton Blossom reached the hotel, and Nathan paused as he listened to a horse cropping grass. He walked around the building, and where grass had begun to green, found Clint Barkley's saddled horse. It was a black, reminding Nathan of the valiant animal that had been shot from under him by outlaws in Kansas. The horse lifted its head, watching him, and he spoke to it in a soothing tone. It stood fast and he ruffled its ears. Surprisingly enough, there was no brand. Removing the saddle, Nathan took the reins and headed for the livery.

"Black horse," he said, "as of now, you belong to Nathan Stone."

When he led the black into the livery, the cantankerous old hostler just stared, silent, unbelieving.

"Rub him down and grain him," said Nathan. "I'll settle with you in the morning." He was in no mood for questions and was gone before the nosy old liveryman could gather his wits enough to speak.

Nathan arose well before first light, anxious to put Georgetown behind him. He wanted nothing more to do with the troublesome Horrells and their outlaw kin. When the cafe opened for breakfast, Nathan and Cotton Blossom were waiting. At the livery, the old hostler greeted them looking as though he had slept in the hayloft.

"Yer horses is been grained an' they're ready," he said. "That'll be four dollars."

Nathan paid. He was being overcharged and they both knew it, but he only wanted to be on his way. Quickly he saddled the grulla, but it took some doing to get the newly acquired black to accept the bulky packsaddle. Nathan placed an extra blanket under the rig, and even after he had it in place, the black snaked his head around, wondering what this thing was he was expected to carry. He shud-

dered a time or two, and Nathan had to laugh at the curious
expression in the animal's eyes.

"Packsaddle won't hurt you, black horse," he said.
"We'll take it easy till you get used to it."

Nathan rode out of town, the black on a lead rope, Cotton Blossom trotting on ahead. Unless he chose to avoid
Waco, he would ride right through it. He had once dealt
faro there, in old Judge Prater's saloon. When the deal had
gone down, he had sloped out in the middle of the night,
escaping Prater's three grown daughters. But the oldest—
Eulie—had followed him, becoming his companion until
her tragic death in New Orleans. After a lifetime of abuse,
the girl had gotten her revenge by taking her father's favorite horse and the gold from his cash box. Nathan grinned
to himself, wondering if he dared ride back through Prater's
domain. He decided to risk it. After all, it had been seven
years. How long could a man hold a grudge?

Nathan rode into Waco in the early afternoon. He was
a good eighty miles south of Fort Worth, and it only made
good sense to stay the night. Waco had grown some,
sprawling out along the south bank of the Brazos. The
enormous old house that had once belonged to Judge
Prater was still there, and so was the saloon where Nathan
had dealt faro, but its name had been changed to the Bullwhip. Nathan reined up, dismounted, and stepped through
the batwing doors. He might as well find out if old Prater
was still alive. Two men sat at one of the tables, a bottle,
glasses, and a deck of cards before them. Nathan ordered
a beer and the barkeep sloshed the overflowing mug down
the bar. Nathan sipped the brew, awaiting his change from
two bits. While he had the barkeep's attention, he spoke.

"Last time I was here, Judge Prater owned this place.
What became of him?"

"He's been dead near five years," the barkeep replied.
"His oldest girl run off with a gamblin' man and the two
youngest took to whoring with the Yankee soldiers that
occupied the town. When their daddy cashed in, the gals
sold ever'thing and nobody's seen 'em since."

Nathan sighed. That took care of any possible clash with
Judge Prater. But that was small consolation, since he
would likely have enough men gunning for him, as it was.
He left the saloon and rode on to the livery. There he left
his horses, with instructions to rub them down and grain

them. Across the street was the Brazos Hotel, built during the years he had been gone. There were two stories and he took a room on the bottom floor. It was still early, but having little else to do, he and Cotton Blossom headed for the cafe. Next to it, however, was a newspaper office, and Nathan was intrigued by its hanging wooden sign. Either as a joke or as a reflection on the town's intellect, someone had painted a single word, in large letters: NEWSPAPER. Nathan opened the door, confronting a young man about his own age. Printer's ink streaking his face and a question in his eyes, he looked up from his typesetting.

"I'll take a copy of your latest," Nathan said, dropping two bits on the counter.

"My God," said the editor in mock surprise, "what's that?"

Nathan laughed. "I take it you don't see a lot of cash money."

"You take it right. It's mostly turnips, potatoes, onions, corn, and chicken on the hoof. I'm Andy Partain. You're . . . . ?"

"Just passing through," said Nathan. "I was attracted by your sign."

"I decided *The Chronicle* was a bit highfalutin for these parts. Nobody seemed to know what a 'Chronicle' was."

Nathan took the four-page paper and departed before Partain was able to come up with bothersome questions. He and Cotton Blossom entered the cafe. It being early, there would be fewer people to wonder who he was, and it was easier getting the cook to feed Cotton Blossom if the place wasn't too crowded. Taking a back table, Nathan read the newspaper while he waited for his food. There was a fair account of the fight in Lampasas where the trio of lawmen had been gunned down by Clint Barkley and the Horrells. Nathan found little else to interest him in the skimpy newspaper. There was a brief article on a small-time gambler and hell-raiser in Dodge City, William L. Brooks. Nathan had heard of him, and read the article with some amusement. Brooks had gotten on the bad side of a buffalo hunter, and the man had gone after Brooks with a .50-caliber Sharps. Somehow the dispute had been resolved without injury to either party. By the time Nathan's steak was ready, a number of other men had filed into the cafe.

One of them was Andy Partain, and he immediately headed
for Nathan's table.

"Nathan Stone," he said, loud enough for everybody to
hear. "I knew I'd heard of you. It was you who gunned
down that band of outlaws in Indian Territory last year.
You brought El Gato and his renegades to justice."

It was a bad moment, and Nathan could have cheerfully
strangled the young editor. Men at other tables had forgotten their food and were openly staring. Two men looked
at each other, their eyes hard and cold. They well remembered the night El Gato had died, when only they had
escaped a vengeful Nathan Stone.

"Partain," Nathan said grimly, "I did what needed doing,
and there's been more than enough said about it. Leave
it alone."

"Sorry," said Partain. "It was in all the papers, but none
of it in your own words. I thought you might want to add
something ..."

"You thought wrong," Nathan said.

There was an uncomfortable silence as Nathan finished
his meal, and when he left the cafe, the eyes of every man
were upon him. They watched him enter the hotel across
the street, two of the observers paying particular attention.
He would be staying the night, and his fast gun wouldn't
matter, for darkness was an equalizer. . . .

Locking the door of his hotel room behind him, Nathan
shucked his hat, his gun belt, and his boots. He stretched
out on the bed, staring at the fly-specked ceiling. Cotton
Blossom sat on the rug beside the bed, his eyes on Nathan.
Finally Nathan sat up, thumping his sock feet on the floor.

"Damn it, Cotton Blossom, it's too early to hole up for
the night."

The last rays of the setting sun crept through the window,
dappling the floor with a patchwork of gold. Nathan
dragged on his boots, strapped on his Colts, and reached
for his hat. If there were men determined to challenge his
fast draw, then so be it. He was damned if he'd hide behind
closed doors, imprisoning himself behind walls of intimidation erected by his reluctance to use his guns. He was fed
up with damn fools seeking to gain a reputation at his expense. His skill with a Colt—his reputation as a fast draw—
he would gladly relinquish, but not at the cost of his life.
Much of his trouble, Nathan conceded, was a direct result

of his love for poker. Inevitably, that kept him in the saloons, among the hell-raisers who frequented them. But what else was a man to do, with time on his hands? He stepped out into the gathering darkness, bound for the Bullwhip Saloon.

While the Bullwhip wasn't the only saloon in town, it was the most prominent, and even at so early an hour, business was good. Leaning on the bar, Nathan ordered a beer. He needed a few minutes for his eyes to become accustomed to the light. All the hanging lamps were lighted, and already a smoky haze had begun to halo them. Most of the men were serious drinkers, gathered two or three to a table, bottle and glasses before them. A man who gambled, however, was more cautious, drinking little or not at all. While any man could call for a game, Nathan chose not to. Being a stranger in town, he would only draw attention to himself, and that was the last thing he wanted. Setting himself a limit of three beers, he waited. Halfway through the third, a trio came in and when they reached the bar, one of them spoke.

"A bottle, three glasses, and a deck, barkeep."

"Any objection if I sit in?" Nathan asked.

"Five card stud, table stakes, no IOUs," said the man who had called for the cards.

"My kind of game," Nathan replied.

Nathan followed them to a table beneath one of the hanging lamps, allowing them to be seated first. Nathan then pulled out a chair and sat down. Cotton Blossom crouched behind him, not trusting any of these strangers. Nathan observed his companions as they served themselves from the bottle. They were armed, dressed in range clothes, and might have been riders for the same outfit. The game opened with a dollar bet, and Nathan lost two hands before winning one. His companions had emptied the bottle and were working on a second one. Losing a fourth hand, Nathan withdrew from the game. Drinking men soon became careless, and losing, often questioned the honesty of their companions. Nathan had learned what any professional gambler must know: There is a time when—winning or losing—a man must fold. Once Cotton Blossom was sure they were leaving the saloon, he wasted no time heading for the door. Nathan tilted the brim of his hat over his eyes and stepped out into the night. Lessening the time he would be outlined in the light from the saloon, he stepped quickly aside, but not quickly enough. A slug ripped through Nathan's left arm, above the elbow, and he was thrown against the wall of the saloon. The shot had come from across the street, and so swiftly did Nathan draw his right-hand Colt, his return fire blended with that of the bushwhacker. Nathan fired three times. Once at the muzzle flash, a second time to the left and a third time to the right. Men boiled out of the saloon to find Nathan thumbing fresh cartridges into his Colt.

"What'n hell's goin' on out here?" somebody shouted.

"A bushwhacker cut down on me," said Nathan, "and I shot back."

The bloody sleeve of Nathan's shirt was evidence enough. Suddenly there came the sound of a running horse, and when it was reined up, the man who dismounted wore a badge. The lawman ignored everyone else, his eyes on Nathan.

"I'm Sheriff Lomax," he said. "I can see you've been hit. Do you have any idea who did it, or why?"

"No, on both counts," said Nathan. "I stepped out the door and he fired from across the street. I fired at the muzzle flash."

"Elmont," said the sheriff, "guide this gent to Doc Melton's place. Barkeep, fetch me a lamp or lantern. The rest of you, go back to whatever you were doing."

Nathan followed Elmont to a log house two blocks east of the saloon. Knocking on the door, Elmont waited until it was opened.

"Doc," Elmont said, "this feller was winged in an ambush. Sheriff Lomax sent him to you fer patchin' up."

Elmont stepped aside and Nathan entered the doctor's house. Without being asked, he removed his shirt. Dr. Melton said nothing. He turned to the stove, stoked the fire, and set a kettle of water over the open eye. He then went into another room, returning with his satchel. Waiting for the water to boil, he examined Nathan's wound. Only then did he speak.

"You're lucky. It missed the bone."

When the water was hot, the doctor cleansed the wound, sloshed alcohol into it for disinfectant, and was applying a bandage when Sheriff Lomax arrived. Nodding to Dr. Melton, he spoke the Nathan.

"You nailed the *hombre* that done the shootin'. Hit him twice. He's bein' laid out over at Potter's cabinet shop. I'd be obliged if you'd go by and have a look at him."

"I will," Nathan said. He paid Dr. Melton five dollars and followed Lomax out.

The sheriff was afoot, for it was only a short distance to Potter's. Nathan recognized some of the men from the saloon, leaving as he and Lomax arrived. The dead man was laid out on an old door supported by a pair of saw horses. Potter removed a dirty sheet from the corpse. Looking from Sheriff Lomax to Nathan, he spoke.

"Mighty fine shootin' in the dark. You the gent that got him?"

"Yes," Nathan said shortly.

"Nobody what's looked at him knows him, Sheriff," said Potter.

"I don't know him, either, Sheriff," Nathan said. "Maybe without the beard . . ."

"He wasn't alone," said Lomax. "The second man lit out, and it's safe to say he's here in town somewhere. What do you aim to do for the rest of the night?"

"Return to the hotel and stay there," Nathan replied, "and unless there's a need for me to stay, I'll be ridin' out in the morning."

"No reason I can think of," said Lomax, "but ride with an eye to your back trail."

"Thanks," Nathan replied. "I aim to."

Nathan found Cotton Blossom waiting outside, and the two of them reached the hotel without difficulty. Locking the door, Nathan then positioned a heavy oak chair with its back under the knob. Tossing his hat on the dresser, he hung his gun belt on the head of the bed and removed his bloody shirt. Finally he tugged off his boots and stretched out on the bed. Only then did Cotton Blossom lie down on the rug. For a long time Nathan lay awake. While his wound pained him, sleep was driven away by a realization that tonight's shooting had forced him to consider. For the better part of seven years, he had been the hunter, seeking men he had sentenced to die. For almost a year now, he had concerned himself with the glory seekers who wanted only to test his fast gun. Now it seemed they might be the least of his problems, as he—Nathan Stone—became the hunted. How many of the men he had slain had family or

friends who would consider it justice done if Nathan Stone
was shot dead?

Nathan arose at first light, his left arm and shoulder stiff
and sore. He had a difficult time pulling on his boots, and
he didn't need a doctor to tell him he had a fever. He must
have some whiskey, and that meant remaining in town until
the saloons opened.

"Come on, Cotton Blossom," he said. "We might as well
have breakfast."

Stepping out into the dawn, he looked carefully around.
Seeing nobody, he went back to the cafe where he'd had
supper. It was still early and the place was deserted, for
which Nathan was thankful. The cook was the same man
who had served him supper, and while he looked at Nathan
curiously, he said nothing. He took Nathan's order, fed
Cotton Blossom, and went about his business. Several men
came into the cafe before Nathan finished his breakfast, but
they said nothing. Nathan and Cotton Blossom returned to
the hotel. Removing only his hat and gun belt, Nathan
stretched out on the bed. Hopefully he could go to a saloon, get the whiskey, and reach the livery without any
bothersome questions. He had an eighty-mile ride to Fort
Worth, and it might take the whiskey that long to sweat
the fever out of him. He now knew that the man he had
shot last night had a companion who had escaped, and in
his feverish condition, Nathan didn't relish the possibility
of yet another ambush. He must keep an eye on his back
trail, while depending heavily on Cotton Blossom to warn
him of what lay ahead. After two hours, Nathan's impa-
tience got the best of him. He turned in his key and went
to the livery.

"Pardner," he said to the liveryman, "it's a bad day when
a man can't saddle his own horse, but I've got a hurt arm.
I have a packhorse and a packsaddle, too."

"I'll take care of 'em," said the hostler. "Glad you got
the sidewinder that give you that hurt arm."

He said no more, and Nathan rode out, the lead rope of
the packhorse dallied around his saddle horn. To his relief,
he found the Bullwhip Saloon open and the barkeep alone.
Nathan bought a quart of whiskey, mounted the grulla, and
rode north. Waiting until he was out of town, he drew the
cork with his teeth and took a long pull from the bottle.

He seldom drank whiskey, and the stuff threw him into such a coughing fit, the grulla snaked his head around and looked at him.

"God-awful stuff, horse," he said. "Nobody but a damn fool would drink it for anything but medicine."

Having ridden only a few miles, Nathan became dizzy, and the back of his hand to his forehead told him his fever had worsened. He reined up and took another long pull from the whiskey bottle. The sun was almost noon-high, and in his feverish state, he had no idea how far he had ridden. He had killed half the bottle of whiskey, and he dared not down any more, lest he become too drunk to stay in the saddle. He rode on, the westering sun seeming oppressively hot. Finally, clouds drifted over the sun and there was a light breeze from the northwest, touching Nathan's brow with cooling fingers. Relieved, he put the back of his hand to his forehead, feeling beads of sweat. His fever had broken. Kicking the grulla into a slow gallop, he rode on toward Fort Worth.

Fort Worth, Texas. March 24, 1873

"It's good to see you again," Captain Ferguson said. "It's been downright peaceful in Indian Territory lately. At least in the western half."

"I hope so," said Nathan. "I don't aim to ride there again, if I can avoid it." Deciding honesty was the best policy, he told Ferguson of the attempted ambush in Waco.

"You've made enemies," Ferguson said. "Why not have the post doctor take a look at your wound, and lay over a week until it heals?"

"I'll take you up on that. I can't saddle and unsaddle my horse, can't load and unload my packhorse, and it's a hell of a job gettin' my boots on and off."

With time on his hands, Nathan hung around the post telegrapher. Having learned the code while with the Kansas-Pacific, he read all incoming messages without difficulty. Clint Barkley was still loose in Texas, the James gang was still robbing banks in Missouri, while Ben Thompson and his troublesome brother Billy were involved with a saloon in Ellsworth, Kansas.

Nathan grew weary of Fort Worth, and thanking Captain Ferguson for his courtesy, rode out the second day of April.

Avoiding most of Indian Territory, he crossed the panhandle, forded the Cimarron, and rode to Dodge City, Kansas. The rails had reached Dodge in the fall of 1872, and when Nathan arrived there less than a year later, the town seemed overrun with gamblers, whores, confidence men, buffalo hunters, hidemen, and camp followers. Where once there had been a tent with cots, there now was a three-story hotel. Across the street from the hotel was a livery, and Nathan went there first. Unsaddling his horse and unloading the packhorse, he left instructions for the animals to be rubbed down and grained. Leaving there, he paused, amazed at how Dodge had grown. Cattle pens were strung out along the railroad track, and the bawling of cattle was a never-ending chorus. Just counting those alongside the track, Nathan could see no less than seven saloons. It being early afternoon, Nathan crossed to the hotel, Cotton Blossom following. Taking a room on the first floor, he paused in the lobby. Thanks to the railroad there were newspapers from Kansas City and St. Louis, as well as Dodge City's own weekly. Nathan bought copies of all three, continuing a reading habit he had acquired while tracking the killers who had murdered his family in Virginia.*

Gray thunderheads had rolled in from the west and a cooling breeze swept across the plains from distant mountains. Nathan's room was comfortable, and he decided to remain there until suppertime, reading the newspapers. Removing his hat, gun belt, and boots, he stretched out on the bed. He read the local paper first. It alternated between crowing about the town's progress while deploring the end-of-track and cattle town violence that had made it all possible. The paper reported that in the first six months of its existence there had been nine murders in Dodge. Nathan found more accounts of the James gang's thievery in the *St. Louis Globe-Democrat,* but little else to interest him. But when he turned to page two of the *Kansas City Liberty-Tribune,* what he saw brought him to his feet in a rage. Looking back at him was his own image. It was the etching prepared by the Kansas-Pacific, commending Nathan for his efforts on behalf of the railroad. But *this* advertisement was a reward notice, offering five thousand dollars for Nathan Stone, dead or alive! It was offered by the Limbaugh

*Book one, *The Dawn Of Fury.*

family and went on to accuse Nathan of murder, in the killing of Rusty Limbaugh, the year before. Nathan ripped the paper to shreds and sat down on the bed, his hands trembling. Cotton Blossom watched him, knowing something was wrong.

"Damn these people!" Nathan raged. "I did everything a man can do to get around killing the little varmint, but he wouldn't have it any other way. Come morning, Cotton Blossom, we're ridin' to Missouri. I aim to raise hell and kick a chunk under it."

Nathan ventured out for supper that evening and for breakfast the next morning. He then turned in his room key, saddled the grulla, loaded the packhorse, and rode eastward, toward Kansas City. He followed the Atchison, Topeka and Santa Fe tracks, for that was the most direct route. He might have taken the train, but he had no assurance there would be a boxcar, and he needed his horses. First he would learn why the Kansas-Pacific had allowed the use of the etching in a death sentence reward notice. Then he would ride on to Jefferson City, to the state capital. There he would demand that the state's attorney general wire the sheriff of Springfield, where the killing of Rusty Limbaugh had taken place. Nathan had acted in self-defense, and since the state hadn't pressed charges, the Limbaugh family's reward should put them in violation of the law. Nathan had little doubt he would be vindicated, but that would be small consolation if some bounty hunter gunned him down before the wrong could be righted.

Kansas City, Missouri. April 6, 1873
While Nathan was treated courteously at Kansas-Pacific, the nature of his complaint had him meeting with Miles Herndon, the railroad's attorney.

"You must understand," Herndon said, "that the Kansas-Pacific had nothing to do with the etching being used in a reward dodger. The *Liberty-Tribune* created the etching to complement the story the Kansas-Pacific supplied. The etching belongs to the newspaper."

"You're telling me this damn newspaper can use a likeness of me anyway it sees fit," said Nathan angrily. "Even in an unlawful wanted poster that could get me shot dead."

"That's what it amounts to," Herndon replied, "and attacking the newspaper will get you exactly nowhere. If this reward has not been sanctioned by the state, then it's illegal, and as such, could and should be withdrawn. You would do well to contact the state's attorney general, requesting that he contact the sheriff in the county where the reward has been posted. If the law agrees you acted in self-defense, then a cease-and-desist order from the attorney general could be served through the county sheriff."

Nathan left the attorney's office, convinced he had been given sound advice. However, he was a hundred and eighty miles west of Jefferson City, and Missouri was teeming with potential bounty hunters who would kill a man for a hell of a lot less than five thousand dollars. He bought a paper, replacing the one he had ripped to shreds. Placing it in his saddlebag, he began the long ride to Jefferson City.

Jefferson City, Missouri. April 10, 1873

"Ma'am," Nathan said, "I'm not here to see an assistant to the attorney general. I want to see the attorney general himself."

"Sorry," said the prim gray-haired receptionist, "but the attorney general will see you only if circumstances warrant it. His assistant, Charles Atchison, will make that decision."

After an impatient half hour, Nathan was shown to Atchison's office. He sat with hands clasped, looking at Nathan over the top of his spectacles. Nathan leaned on the desk, the newspaper under his arm.

"Mr. Atchison," he said, as calmly as he could, "I need the help of the attorney general."

"So does everybody entering this office," said Atchison, unruffled. "I suppose you are going to tell me why."

"I am," Nathan replied, spreading the page of the newspaper with the wanted notice on Atchison's desk. Without wasting words, he explained events leading up to the shooting in Springfield, renewing his claim of self-defense.

"If there are no charges against you," said Atchison, "then you are within your rights, demanding that this offer of a reward be withdrawn. It is indeed illegal. A telegram to the county clerk in Springfield should determine that. You are welcome to wait in the outer office."

CHAPTER 3

Uneasily, Nathan waited, considering the possibility that the sheriff in Springfield had yielded to pressure and made him a fugitive. Could Atchison, excusing himself to send a telegram, be summoning the law to arrest Nathan Stone? But within half an hour, Atchison beckoned Nathan back into his office.

"There are no charges against you in Springfield," Atchison said. "Court records call the killing justifiable homicide. This office will issue an order to the sheriff in Springfield, and he will notify the parties involved that their offer of a reward is illegal, and is to be withdrawn immediately."

"Suppose they refuse to abide by that order?"

"Someone will have to take them to court," Atchison replied.

"You mean I—Nathan Stone—will have to take them to court," said Nathan.

"Of course," Atchison said. "The state will prosecute, but only when formal charges have been filed."

"So if they ignore your order and refuse to remove the price on my head, it's up to me to file charges and take them to court. What will the court do, spank them?"

"Your sarcasm is not appreciated," said Atchison stiffly. "Found guilty, there would be a severe fine. At least fifty dollars, I'm sure."

"Then send your court order," Nathan said. "I'll go on keeping my guns handy and an eye on my back trail."

Nathan departed in disgust, returning to the livery where he had left the horses and Cotton Blossom. He had but one consolation, and that was that he had seen the notice of the reward only in the *Kansas City Liberty-Tribune*. But Kansas City was a "jumping-off place" for anyone heading west, and that damning reward notice might hound him wherever he rode. Nathan was only a few miles from St. Louis, and he decided to go there. While he was still miles away, he could hear the bull-throated bellow of steamboat whistles, and it brought memories of those pleasant days in New Orleans, with the McQueens.

Finding a livery, Nathan saw to the care of his horses. Then he and Cotton Blossom went looking for a hotel or rooming house. Nathan chose a rooming house not far from the riverfront, with several cafes and saloons nearby. He had no trouble finding copies of the *St. Louis Globe-Democrat* and the *Kansas City Liberty-Tribune*. These were a week later than the issues he had read in Kansas City, and he wanted to see if the reward notice appeared in either paper. First he fanned through the *Globe-Democrat* and then the *Liberty-Tribune* without finding the offending advertisement. However, in the Kansas City paper, he found a piece that grabbed his attention. One of the James gang had been captured and had sworn that neither the James nor Younger gangs had shot and killed Bart Hankins during the failed bank robbery of February 13, 1866, in Gallatin, Missouri. Now the Hankins family had hired the Pinkertons and had posted a ten thousand dollar reward. Hankins had been the first of seven men Nathan had tracked down and slain, keeping the oath he had taken on his murdered father's grave.*

"Damn it," said Nathan aloud, "the glory seekers were bad enough. Now this."

At first he could see no way the Pinkertons could tie him to the killing of Hankins, but his mind wouldn't leave it alone. By God, there *was* a way! The Pinkertons had enough influence to gain access to military records and thus might learn the identities of the other men with whom Hankins had returned to Virginia. Six men who, along with Bart Hankins, had died by the gun of Nathan Stone. With Pinkerton persistence, there was more than enough evidence to establish a pattern. While all Hankins's companions had been gunned down while trying to kill Nathan, there was nobody but Nathan Stone who could swear that Bart Hankins had drawn first. It was time for a decision. For the next two weeks, Nathan allowed his beard to grow, leaving his room only for meals and to see that the livery was properly caring for his horses. Finally, the mirror convincing him his appearance had been sufficiently altered, he made the rounds of various saloons, sitting in on poker

*Book one, *The Dawn Of Fury.*

games, but avoiding high stakes. Only once did he encounter a hint of recognition. During a game of five card stud at the Emerald Dragon, a thin man in town clothes put down his cards and stared across the table at Nathan. Finally he spoke.

"Ain't I seen you somewhere before?"

Nathan laughed. "I doubt it. I'd remember an ugly varmint like you."

His companions all howled with laughter, and the moment passed. Feeling a little more secure, having spent three weeks in St. Louis saloons, Nathan rode back to Kansas City. He had continued buying regular copies of the *Kansas City Liberty-Tribune* without again finding a reward notice with the etching of himself. Perhaps the attorney general's order had served its purpose, or perhaps the Limbaughs had just given up from lack of success.

Kansas City, Missouri. May 26, 1873

Reading the current *Kansas City Liberty-Tribune,* Nathan discovered something that intrigued him. Edward Beard, a saloon owner from California, had been attracted to Kansas by the cattle boom, and had established a saloon and dance hall in Delano, just outside Wichita. Beard advertised around-the-clock high stakes poker and was seeking house dealers. While with the Kansas-Pacific Railroad, Nathan had spent many months in various Kansas·towns. Having allowed his beard to grow, it was time to learn whether or not his changed appearance had made any difference in towns where he was most likely to be recognized. He rode to Delano and offered his services as a house dealer, and his first impression of Edward Beard was unfavorable. He had a quick tongue, cold green eyes, flaming red hair and beard, and little patience.

"Twenty percent of the take," said Beard shortly. "It's your game. I ain't responsible for slick dealing, card shaving, knife or gun work."

Nathan laughed. "So that's why you're in Delano instead of Wichita. No law out here."

"It's no business of yours why I'm here," Beard said. "If you can't ride the bronc, then stay out of the saddle."

"I can ride your bronc," said Nathan evenly. "Just don't get in my way."

Beard had a whorehouse upstairs, and he was anything

but gentle with the women. For some reason Nathan never understood, Beard's place was enormously popular with the military, and soldiers were there from as far away as Fort Dodge, Fort Leavenworth, and Fort Hays. While riding the vengeance trail, Nathan had often visited the forts, and during his first week at the tables, he was greatly encouraged when none of the soldiers seemed to recognize him. Nathan and two other dealers—Benton and Kinzer—worked the tables from three in the afternoon until eleven at night, and Nathan got the impression they were more hired guns than house dealers. The night of June third, Nathan had his suspicions confirmed. Two soldiers got into a violent argument with Emma Stanley, one of Beard's prostitutes.

"Damn you," one of the soldiers shouted, "you owe me change."

"I gave it to you," Emma shouted back.

One of the soldiers drew his pistol, probably as a threat, but Emma seized his arm and the weapon roared. Wounded in the leg, Emma screamed. The soldier dropped the pistol and raised his hands. Benton, the house dealer, drew his Colt and would have shot the soldier in the back, but for Nathan. He drew his Colt and shot Benton. That should have ended it, but Edward Beard cut loose with a Colt. The soldiers who had argued with Emma escaped, but Beard, firing wildly, gunned down two innocent soldiers. Private Doley took a slug in the throat, at the base of his tongue, while his companion, Private Boyle had his right ankle shattered. Every other soldier in the saloon went to the aid of their wounded comrades, taking them away. The Colt still in his hand, Beard stalked across the floor and confronted Nathan.

"Damn it," he shouted, "if you had to shoot somebody, why didn't you shoot the fool who shot Emma?"

"Because Benton was about to shoot an unarmed soldier in the back," said Nathan coldly. "You've just shot two men who had done nothing. I'd say you're in deep enough, already."

"I'll be the judge of that," Beard shouted. "Now you and Kinzer tote Benton out back. This is bad for business."

Nathan and Kinzer carried Benton out the back door and put him down. Kinzer wiped his brow and spoke.

"He's bought himself a mess of trouble. Hurt a soldier,

and the rest of them will come down on you like a pack of lobo wolves."

Nathan said nothing, but Kinzer spoke the truth. Wound or kill a soldier—whatever the reason—and his comrades were likely to show up with fire in their eyes and guns in their hands. It was but a matter of time, and for Edward Beard that time arrived quickly.

Nathan had taken a hotel room in Wichita, stabling his horses in a nearby livery. Each time he rode to Beard's saloon, he had taken to leaving Cotton Blossom at the livery, with the packhorse. The dog hated saloons, was ever on his guard, and was capable of biting some clumsy drunk. The night after Beard had shot the two soldiers, it was ominously quiet, with nobody at the poker tables. Two or three men were upstairs, but none of the soldiers had returned.

"They'll be back," Kinzer predicted, "and there'll be hell to pay."

"Just shut up!" Beard shouted, but he obviously was worried, for in addition to his Colt, he carried a Winchester under his arm.

"They'll come back and kill us all," Emma whined.

Nathan said nothing. He had no intention of being caught on the short end of a gun fight with the Union army. It started with the sound of a shot, the tinkle of glass, and a slug through a saloon window.

"Ever'body out," a voice shouted, "and nobody gets hurt. We're burnin' this place to the ground."

"Like hell," Beard replied. He cut loose with the Winchester, firing wildly through the windows into the darkness. "Shoot, damn it," he bawled at Nathan and Kinzer.

"There's nobody to shoot at, you damn fool," said Nathan in disgust. "You've played out your string. Don't make it any worse."

But Beard seemed not to hear. He continued firing into the night, and while he had no targets, the soldiers did. The dozen hanging lamps began exploding, scattering flaming coal oil everywhere. One of the lamps showered Beard with burning oil. He dropped the Winchester and threw himself on the floor, rolling, trying to extinguish the flames. There were screams from upstairs, as the attackers took aim at lamps through upstairs windows. Girls practically fell down the stairs in various stages of dress and undress, while men fought their way down, boots in their hands. But the vengeful soldiers were not depending on the shattered lamps and scattered coal oil. They had brought coal oil of their own, and soon flames were racing up outside walls and licking in through shattered windows. Smoke swept down the stairs as the second floor caught.

"You men outside," Nathan shouted, "hold your fire. We're coming out."

"Come on," came the shouted response. "We won't shoot."

"By God," Beard snarled, "when we go out, we'll go shootin'."

"I reckon not," said Kinzer, slamming the muzzle of his Colt against the back of the saloon owner's head. "Take the crazy varmint's feet," he told Nathan, "and we'll tote him out."

A hundred yards from the burning saloon, they left Beard under an oak. In a shower of sparks, the saloon's roof caved in, and there was a clatter of hooves as the vengeful soldiers rode out.

"I don't aim to be here when he comes to," said Kinzer. "Adios."

"Neither do I," Nathan replied.

The two of them went to their picketed horses, saddled the animals, and rode toward the lights of Wichita. Behind them came the frustrated cries of women.

Nathan had no idea what kind of stink Edward Beard might stir up in Wichita, and he had no desire to become embroiled in it. At first light he rode west, leading his packhorse with Cotton Blossom trotting ahead. He had a little more than a hundred dollars and a dead man to show for his two weeks at Edward Beard's saloon. Dodge City was a two-day ride, and he had left there hurriedly, thanks to the reward notice he had discovered in the *Kansas City Liberty-Tribune*. He had no particular reason for going there, except that he wanted the Beard episode behind him. Besides, being friends with the post commander at Fort Dodge, he could learn anything of importance that had come over the telegraph.

Dodge City, Kansas. June 8, 1873
Feeling more secure behind his newly grown beard, Nathan again took a room at the three-story hotel. It was convenient, for the livery and two cafes were within walking distance. He again bought the latest editions of the Kansas City and St. Louis newspapers, but found nothing of interest concerning himself or anybody he knew. The next morning, he rode to Fort Dodge, renewed his friendship with the post commander and was given permission to speak to the post telegrapher.

"Do you read code?" Corporal Henegar asked.

"Yes," said Nathan.

"I keep copies of all incoming messages for thirty days, but they're just like I took 'em off the wire. No military secrets, nothing classified."

"That wouldn't concern me," Nathan replied. "I have friends on the frontier, and all I want is to see if they're alive and stayin' out of trouble."

"Nothing there but routine stuff," said Henegar. "If you have contacts at other posts, I could inquire."

"I know Captain Ferguson, at Fort Worth," Nathan said. "Since you're not busy, tell him Nathan Stone wants to know what's happening in Texas, aside from the Comanches raising hell."

Corporal Henegar sent the message and waited for a reply. When it came, Nathan read it as Henegar took it down. When the instrument became silent, Nathan was gripping the back of a chair, his face deathly white.

"Bad news?" Henegar asked.

"Yes," said Nathan. "Captain Sage Jennings is one of the best friends I have in this world. Nothing could be worse than knowing he's been back-shot, lying there in Fort Worth and may never walk again."

"Well," Corporal Henegar said, "I'm sorry to have brought you this kind of news."

"Don't be," said Nathan. "I'm obliged to you. Otherwise, I might have been months, getting back to Texas. Now I can ride out today."

Nathan returned to Dodge City, turned in his hotel key, and paid his bill at the livery. He saddled the grulla, loaded his packhorse, and rode south. All he had was the barest of details, knowing only that Jennings had been ambushed and his condition. Captain Ferguson might not have known anything more than what he had telegraphed, but that was enough to send Nathan to Fort Worth. Assuredly, Jennings would be in no condition to go after his bushwhackers, but that wouldn't stop Nathan Stone. Riding steady, resting his horses hourly, he could reach Fort Worth—three hundred and eighty miles distant—within six days. He only hoped, if the ranger's condition was critical, that he would live until Nathan could talk to him, hopefully to learn who had done the shooting.

Fort Worth, Texas. June 16, 1873

"He's been here two weeks," Captain Ferguson said. "He was brought here because we have a post surgeon. He was hit four times and two of the slugs were lodged near the spine. Our medic, Lieutenant Carter, successfully removed the lead."

"But he still can't move," said Nathan.

"No," Ferguson replied.

"I'm obliged for what you've done, Captain," said Nathan. "I'd like to talk to him, if I may."

"You'll find him at the post hospital," Captain Ferguson said. "Speak to Lieutenant Carter first."

Fort Worth was one of the few frontier outposts with a full-fledged hospital, and it was obvious why Captain Jennings had been brought here. Lieutenant Carter proved to be a very blunt young man.

"His condition is still serious," said Carter. "He lost a lot of blood and he's still very weak. He's eating poorly, if at all. He just doesn't seem to care. Don't stay too long."

When Nathan stepped into the room, he could scarcely believe his eyes. Jennings lay silent, his eyes closed. His body seemed to have shrunk, graying his hair, transforming him into an old man.

"Cap?" Nathan said softly. "Captain Jennings."

"Nathan," said Jennings. "Nathan Stone. I'd take your hand if I could. But that's just one of ... many things I can no longer do."

The lump in Nathan's throat felt half the size of Texas as he moved a chair near the old ranger's bed. Swallowing hard, he sat down. When he finally trusted himself to speak, he did.

"Who did it, Cap?"

"I can't truthfully say," Jennings replied, "but I was trailing the Horrells and Clint Barkley. I rode into that ambush like a damn tenderfoot."

"You have every reason to believe it was the Horrells, then."

"Yes," said Jennings, "but I have no proof. It happened near Georgetown. A rancher heard the shots, found me, and hauled me to town in his wagon. The doc patched me up and had me brought here. The doc here—Lieutenant Carter—dug out the lead, but I'm hurt in two places near the spine. He says my chances are fifty-fifty. I may heal in time, and then I may be crippled for life. Just like them skunk-striped Horrells, leavin' just enough life in me so's I ain't worth a damn to nobody."

"You haven't had time to heal, Cap," Nathan said. "Did anybody trail the varmints?"

"No," said Jennings. "They still got no sheriff at Georgetown, and by the time the sheriff from Lampasas rode over there, the trail had been rained out. Later, when I finally could talk a little, Captain Ferguson telegraphed the ranger outpost in Austin. I asked for a man to be sent to the Horrell ranches, and they're deserted. They've quit the territory, taking Clint Barkley with them, I reckon."

"They gunned down three lawmen at Lampasas," said Nathan, "and now you. What does it take for the state of Texas to put a bounty on their heads?"

"I'm through wondering what the state of Texas will or won't do," Jennings replied. "I have been officially reprimanded by the governor for trailing the Horrells without authorization from the state, and after a review, my commission with the rangers may be revoked. I might as well just die, damn it, and get out of everybody's way."

"Listen, you old catamount," said Nathan, "you're not about to die. At least, not for a few more years. You're goin' to get up out of that bed, and when you do, you'll still be wearin' the star of the Texas Rangers. Now I have things to do, and I'll see you again tomorrow."

The old ranger managed a grin, and Nathan closed the door. Lieutenant Carter nodded at Nathan approvingly, for he had been listening. Returning to the post commander's office, Nathan spoke to Captain Ferguson.

"When time permits, Captain, I need the use of the telegraph."

"Get with the telegrapher," Ferguson replied. "As far as I know, the instrument's been idle all morning."

Nathan composed a telegram to Washington, to his friend Byron Silver, at the office of the attorney general. While Captain Sage Jennings might never rise from his bed, he wouldn't be stripped of his commission as a Texas Ranger.

The following morning, Nathan returned to the post hospital, where he found Captain Jennings in a better frame of mind.

"You don't aim to roost here until I'm on my feet," he said.

It was a statement, not a question, and Nathan laughed. "No," he said, "I reckon you can manage that without me. I aim to mosey around and see if I can find out where that bunch of Horrells went."

"I suspected as much," said Jennings.

"I like to think you'd do the same for me," Nathan replied.

"I would," said Jennings. "It means a lot, havin' you here. A man never knows who his friends are until he's down. I'm obliged."

"You'll be hearing from Byron Silver," Nathan said.

"You telegraphed him?"

"I did," said Nathan. "If I hadn't, he'd have skinned me like a coyote and hung my hide out to dry."

Jennings laughed. "He went to Washington to work among the Yankees, but he never stopped bein' a Texan."

"I'll be in touch with Captain Ferguson by telegraph," Nathan said, "and when I ride back this way, I want to see you on your feet. Maybe I'll spend Christmas with you."

"I'd like that," said Jennings. "Ride careful, *amigo*."

Before riding out, Nathan took the time to meet with Captain Ferguson.

"When you have access to the telegraph," Ferguson said, "get in touch with me and I will see that you get a progress report on Captain Jennings."

"I'm obliged," said Nathan.

He saddled his horse, loaded his packhorse, and with Cotton Blossom leading out, rode south, toward Georgetown.

Georgetown, Texas. June 22, 1873

Nathan didn't bother taking a hotel room in Georgetown. Instead, he began questioning people about the Horrells and where they might have gone after quitting the territory. He learned nothing of importance until he reached Duncan's Mercantile. There he spoke to Andrew Duncan, who seemed reluctant to talk.

"Damn it," Nathan said, "I'm looking for Clint Barkley and the Horrells. Nobody else. From what I've learned, they've quit the territory. Now I know the Horrells hired riders from around here, and I want the names of some of those men."

"No," said Duncan, "I ain't wantin' on the bad side of 'em. I got to live here."

"I won't name you," Nathan replied, "unless I'm forced to bring the law into this. Now speak up."

"Tobe Warner, Wat Iverson, and Bob McKeever," said Duncan, "and I ain't seen any of 'em in a month."

It was more than Nathan had expected. There was always a chance the trio had ridden away with the Horrells, but an equally good chance they had not. Most of the ranchers in south Texas had managed to get a herd to market, and so were able to afford a rider or two. For three days, Nathan rode from one ranch to another. Eventually, at a Circle J line camp he found a surly, uncooperative Bob McKeever.

"I told you," said McKeever stubbornly, "I quit the Horrells. I don't know where they went, and I don't give a damn."

When Nathan took a step toward McKeever, the rider went for his gun. His left hand moving like a striking rattler, Nathan seized McKeever's arm, forcing him to drop the Colt. Fisting his left hand, McKeever took an awkward swing at Nathan, only to receive Nathan's thundering right against his chin. Releasing McKeever's right wrist, Nathan let the man slump to the ground on his back. Shaking his head, McKeever sat up, looking for his dropped Colt. But Nathan had retrieved the weapon, had swung out the cylinder, and was punching out the shells.

"Damn you," McKeever snarled, "you got no right . . ."

"I reckon you still need some convincing," said Nathan. "Get up."

"I got no reason to fight you. I ain't done nothin'."

"You know more than you're telling," Nathan said grimly. "Thanks to those damn no-account Horrells, a mighty good friend of mine may not make it. By God, somebody's goin' to pay."

"But I didn't shoot . . ."

"I didn't say he'd been shot," Nathan replied, "but *you* knew, damn you, and you know who did it. Now you tell me what you know—*every* damn thing you know—or I'll beat your ears down around your boot tops."

"It was Clint Barkley shot the ranger," McKeever said. "That's when I quit."

"I believe you," said Nathan. "Now where did Barkley and the Horrells go?"

"The Horrells was goin' to New Mexico Territory. Barkley had a woman in Ellsworth or Hays. Said he was goin' there."

Nathan dropped McKeever's empty Colt, mounted his horse, and rode away, Cotton Blossom and the packhorse trailing behind.

Nathan rode north, spending his nights on the trail, avoiding towns. As unwilling as McKeever had been, Nathan could see no reason for him lying. He had implicated Barkley and the Horrells in the ambush of Captain Jennings, and the lot of them quitting the territory was characteristic of the back-shooting sidewinders they were. Barkley, having done the actual shooting, would want to get as far away as he could. Nathan wanted Barkley, and while all he had was Bob McKeever's word, he had tracked men with less. He had to consider the possibility that Barkley had remained with the Horrells, that he might find them all in New Mexico Territory, but suppose Clint Barkley *had* ridden to Kansas? By the time Nathan reached Kansas by way of New Mexico Territory, Barkley could lose himself in Colorado, Wyoming, Nebraska, or the Dakota territories.

"We'll try Ellsworth and Hays, Cotton Blossom," Nathan said. "If we don't find him there, then we'll look for him and those damned Horrells in New Mexico Territory."

Eighty miles north of Fort Worth, Nathan crossed the Red River into Indian Territory. It brought back unpleasant memories, for there he had found Mary, only to lose her to El Gato and his renegades. The second day after crossing the Red, Nathan was sure of what he had only suspected before leaving Texas. He was being followed. In the territory, death might come from any direction, and sometimes the back trail took priority over what lay ahead. Reaching a rise, Nathan always paused, looking back. The sun bore down with a vengeance, and at first Nathan thought it was distance, that his eyes were seeing the tag end of a dust devil. Topping the next rise, he saw it again. A telltale puff of dust, while not a breath of air stirred.

"I don't know who you are, mister," Nathan said aloud, "but I don't aim to ride across Indian Territory with you on my back trail."

CHAPTER 4

Reaching the bottom of the slope, Nathan dismounted and removed his Winchester from the boot. From much experience, Cotton Blossom knew this was gun work and remained with the horses. Nathan crept up the rise, keeping within the cover of underbrush and thickets. When he had a good view of the farthest slope, he bellied down, cocked the Winchester, and waited. The rider was bearded, and while Nathan couldn't be sure, he felt like he had seen this man in the cafe in Waco.

"That's far enough," Nathan said. "You're covered."

"You don't own this territory," said the stranger. "I got as much right here as you."

"Pilgrim," Nathan replied, "you've been on my back trail since I left Fort Worth, and whatever your reason, I don't reckon it's in my best interests. Using just your thumb and finger, ease out that Colt and drop it. Then step down from your saddle."

The response was what Nathan had expected. The stranger rolled out of his saddle on the offside, drawing his Colt as he went. He fired three times beneath the belly of the horse, but the slugs ripped the air over Nathan's head. He fired once, and his slug caught the gunman in the chest, slamming him on his back. Nathan was up and running, kneeling beside the dying man.

"Who *are* you, and why were you trailing me?"

"I . . . ain't . . . talkin'."

"El Gato," Nathan said, playing a long shot. "You were with El Gato, one of the two varmints that escaped. You murdered my wife."

"We all ... had ... her," he said. "Ever' damn one ... of us ..."

He tried to laugh, but it was choked off. Nathan had been about to smash his face in with the butt of the Winchester, but it was too late. The outlaw was dead. Unsaddling the man's horse, Nathan set the animal free, leaving the dead man where he lay. The buzzards and coyotes were welcome to him. Returning to his horses, Nathan mounted and rode on. Unbidden, his mind drifted back to that terrible night in Indian Territory when he had found Mary dead after having been violated by El Gato's outlaws. Nathan had gone after them with a blazing Winchester, killing ten. He had accounted for the eleventh man in Waco, and now he had gunned down the twelfth and last in the wilds of Indian Territory. But there was no elation, no joy, only the empty realization that gunning them down could in no way compensate for all he had lost. Then, from the forgotten past, drifting over the lonely years, came a Bible verse his mother had taught him.

"Vengeance is mine," saith the Lord.

"That makes sense," Nathan said aloud. "Kill a man once, and he's lost to you. Throw the varmint into the fire and let him fry forever, now that means something."

He rode on, unsatisfied, but knowing his limitations. He had avenged Mary in the only way he knew how.

Dodge City, Kansas. July 6, 1873

Arriving in the late afternoon, Nathan found himself looking forward to a bath, town grub, and a clean bed. Checking in at the hotel, he bought copies of the *St. Louis Globe-Democrat* and the *Kansas City Liberty-Tribune*. As Nathan left the hotel lobby, the desk clerk studied the register and then looked at the clock. His relief would arrive within the hour. Then he would talk to Sheriff Harrington. . . .

Following his bath and a change of clothes, Nathan headed for a cafe. Having been there before, the cook recognized Nathan and Cotton Blossom.

"Steak cooked through," said the cook, "sided with onions, spuds, pie, and hot coffee."

"That will do for starters," Nathan said. "After feedin'

Cotton Blossom and me, you may have to close up and restock. We've been on the trail for a spell, without decent grub."

Cotton Blossom headed for the kitchen while Nathan took a back table. Reading the St. Louis paper, he found little of interest, and finishing that, turned to the Kansas City edition. In an item from Wichita, Edward Beard had begun construction on another saloon and dance hall, vowing to have it in operation by October. Ben Thompson and his troublesome brother Billy had spent the night in jail, following a brawl in a Kansas City saloon. The unpredictable pair had left town the next day, traveling west.

When the door to his office opened, Dodge City's Sheriff Harrington looked up.

"Come in, Harley. Somebody rob the hotel?"

"Nathan Stone—the gent with the dog—checked in a while ago."

"He's at the hotel now?" Sheriff Harrington asked.

"No," said Harley. "After takin' a room, him and the dog went out. Do you reckon there's a reward?"

"I don't know," Harrington replied. "I had a telegram from the Pinkerton office in Kansas City, and all they asked was that I wire them immediately if Nathan Stone showed up. They made it a point to say he has a dog with him."

"No reward, then," said Harley, disappointed. "A man wanted by the law ain't likely to be signin' his own name on a hotel register."

"I wouldn't think so," Harrington replied. "While the Pinkertons trail bank, train, and stage robbers, they don't limit themselves to that. I expect folks with money can hire them to track missing persons, too. I'll telegraph them, tell them Stone's here, and we'll see what happens."

Receiving Sheriff Harrington's telegram, the Pinkerton office in Kansas City sent an operative with the message to a Kansas City hotel. Hate-filled eyes read the telegram and steady hands loaded a Colt revolver. The recipient of the telegram checked out of the hotel and took a hack to the Atchison, Topeka and Santa Fe Railroad terminal. The schedule said the next train to Dodge would depart within the hour, arriving there before dawn. . . .

*　　*　　*

The shriek of a locomotive whistle awakened Nathan. Cotton Blossom had reared up on his hind legs, looking out the window into the darkness.

"Just a train comin' in, Cotton Blossom," Nathan said. "With the railroad through town, it's like trying to sleep next to a steamboat landing. It's a good two hours before first light."

A single passenger stepped down from the train, and taking a seat on a bench, waited for the town to awaken.

With the first gray light of dawn, Nathan arose. Leaving his room key at the desk, he and Cotton Blossom headed for the cafe. Immediately after breakfast, they would strike out north, toward Ellsworth. But suddenly, from behind there came a command that drove all thought of food from Nathan's mind.

"Nathan Stone, this is Sheriff Harrington. I need to talk to you."

His hands shoulder-high, Nathan turned slowly around. Harrington's Colt was thonged to his right thigh and he looked all business. But the sheriff wasn't alone. The girl had short dark hair under a flat-crowned hat. Her boots were scuffed, her Levi's faded, and an old red flannel shirt looked too large. She looked maybe twenty-one or -two, and her eyes were brimming with hatred. Before the sheriff could speak another word, she drew from the folds of her shirt a Colt revolver. There was no doubt she intended to kill Nathan.

"Hey!" Sheriff Harrington shouted. Seizing her arm, he forced the muzzle of the Colt toward the ground, and the roar of the weapon was loud in the morning stillness. But the girl was resourceful and cat-quick. Facing Harrington, she drove a knee into his groin, and using his moments of agony, wrested the Colt free.

But she now had Nathan Stone to contend with, for he no longer had any doubts as to her intentions. Before she could cock and fire the Colt, he caught her wrist, and when she tried to knee him as she had the sheriff, he seized her ankle. Using that and the hold he had on her wrist, he lifted her off the ground and slammed her down on her back. She let go of the Colt and Nathan kicked it back toward the hotel. Sheriff Harrington had regained his composure and stood there waiting for the girl to get up. She ignored Nathan, turning her anger upon the sheriff.

"You *could* help me," she snapped, struggling to her knees.

"I *could* lock you up for attempted murder," Harrington said coldly, "and I might yet, you little catamount. You lied to me. You told me you only needed to talk to Stone."

She laughed. "Oh, I *do* want to talk to him, to tell him who I am. Then I aim to kill him, because he murdered my brother."

"You don't have to tell me who you are," Nathan said. "You're from Missouri, and you're one of the Limbaughs."

"Amy, by name," said Sheriff Harrington. "Do you know her?"

"No," Nathan replied, "but I know why she's after me. I had to shoot her hotheaded brother or he'd have shot me. There's just a hell of a lot she hasn't told you, Sheriff, and I aim to fill in the gaps. Then I want to know how she dragged you into this."

"Then we'll talk in my office," said Harrington. "We're starting to draw a crowd."

The three of them walked the short distance to the lawman's office. There were four cells, none of them occupied. Harrington pointed to the first one.

"In there, Amy. I aim to hear Stone's side of this. Then I'll decide what to do with you."

Harrington locked the cell door, took a seat behind an old desk, and nodded toward the only other chair in the room. Nathan sat down and started talking. When he had finished, Harrington got to his feet.

"What you've said has the ring of truth," the sheriff said, "but I aim to telegraph the attorney general's office in Jefferson City, Missouri. That's as much for your benefit as my own. I figure if they hear from enough lawmen, all of us raisin' hell, the state might get to the bottom of this, and clear you."

"I'm more interested in getting the Pinkertons off my trail," Nathan said. "They're after me so this female sidewinder can fill me full of lead, and she has no legal right. I'm of a mind to ride to Kansas City and pull some Pinkerton fangs."

"You would be more than justified," said Harrington. "Fact is, after I've telegraphed the Missouri attorney general's office, I'll contact the Pinkerton office in Kansas City. They should know what Miss Amy Limbaugh's intentions are, and that as a result of their being involved, you're in a position to bring charges against them. If they persist in

hounding you, then I'd suggest you do exactly that. Now
let's ride to Fort Dodge and send those telegrams.''

"He's a killer," Amy shouted, "and I'll find him without
the Pinkertons.''

"He could have shot you dead and claimed self-defense,"
said Harrington. "Instead, he disarmed you. That's not the
mark of a killer.''

Reaching Fort Dodge, Harrington sent the telegrams,
and in less than a quarter of an hour the Pinkertons responded. Harrington read the message and passed it on to
Nathan. The telegram was simple and to the point. Sheriff
Harrington was to detain Amy Limbaugh until a Pinkerton
operative could question her.

"I reckon it won't stop her from comin' after you," said
Harrington, "but she likely won't have the help of the Pinkertons. Won't be another train out of Kansas City until
tonight. That'll give you a head start.''

"Thanks," Nathan said.

They waited for almost an hour for the Missouri district
attorney's office to respond, and when the telegram came,
it satisfied Sheriff Harrington.

"You told it straight," said Harrington. "The shooting
was ruled self-defense and the state has no charges against
you. When that Pinkerton varmint steps down from the
train, I'll shove this in his face.''

When they reached the jail, Nathan dismounted. "Before
I ride out," Nathan said, "I have some advice for Miss
Amy Limbaugh.''

Unlocking the door, Sheriff Harrington went in, Nathan
following. Amy Limbaugh just stared angrily at them, gripping the bars.

"Well, Amy," said Harrington, "Stone told me the truth,
and the Pinkertons have asked me to keep you here until
they can talk to you. If you know how, I reckon you'd
better come up with some truth of your own.''

"Damn you," she shouted, "you can't hold me without
charges. What *are* the charges?''

"I don't know all the fine points of the law," said Harrington, "but we can always use attempted murder. The
Pinkertons may have some of their own. Without their
knowledge, you used them with the intention of committing
a crime. Legally, Stone can sue the socks off them, and
they know it. For that matter, when the Pinkertons are

finished with you, Stone can file charges of his own. I certainly wouldn't blame him."

"No charges," said Nathan. "When the Pinkertons have had their say, turn her loose."

"Damn you," she said. "I don't want any favors from your kind."

"You've had your first and last favor from me," said Nathan. "The next time you pull a gun on me, I'll kill you."

Nodding to the sheriff, Nathan stepped out the door, closing it behind him. Mounting, he rode to the livery for his packhorse. While he expected Sheriff Harrington to truthfully present his case to the Pinkertons, he still intended to confront them personally. With that in mind, he rode eastward, toward Kansas City.

Kansas City, Missouri. July 12, 1873

The Pinkerton Detective Agency was housed in a two-story brick building. As Nathan stepped into the lobby, Amy Limbaugh and a pair of hired guns observed him from their hiding place across the street.

"Find some cover and spread out," said the girl. "When he leaves the building, wait until he's down the steps and away from it. Then cut him down."

Nathan was shown into the office of Roscoe Edelman, a regional director of the Pinkerton Detective Agency. Edelman said nothing, waiting for Nathan to speak.

"There's a gun-totin' female name of Amy Limbaugh who aims to kill me," Nathan said, "and through Sheriff Harrington in Dodge, I've learned the Pinkertons are responsible for her being on my trail. Now I'm here to tell you the straight of it, that the Limbaughs have no legal case against me, and I can prove it. If just one more sheriff comes after me as a result of your damn telegrams, I aim to purely raise hell and kick a chunk under it. Do you understand?"

"I am not accustomed to being threatened," said Edelman coldly, "and I refuse to be intimidated by a mouthy gunman. We have acknowledged our mistake, and we will no longer concern ourselves with your whereabouts. That's all the consideration you're going to get from this office. Close the door on your way out."

Fighting his temper, Nathan turned and walked out, leaving the door wide open. There was little to do except return to the livery where his horses and Cotton Blossom waited. Nathan had left the building and was at the foot of the steps when the first shot rang out. Lead slammed into his left side above his pistol belt, throwing him back against the steps. There was no way he could make it back to the safety of the building, and he rolled off the steps, drawing his right-hand Colt. Belly-down, he had become a more difficult target, and for just a moment, his antagonist forgot his cover. Nathan shot him twice. A second man fired, his slug kicking dust in Nathan's face. He fired once and had the satisfaction of seeing the killer stumble and fall. But another slug tore into Nathan's left thigh, and he realized he was caught in a three-way crossfire. The third bushwacker was to Nathan's left and much nearer. He fired once and Amy Limbaugh screamed when the lead struck her under the collarbone. All three bushwhackers were down and Nathan was struggling to his knees when the sheriff and his deputy arrived. They stood facing Nathan, their Colts drawn and ready.

"I'm Sheriff Wilhelm," the lawman said. "Drop the gun. The party's over."

"I didn't open the ball, Sheriff," Nathan said. "Three bushwhackers cut down on me and they've all been hit."

"You're just hell on little red wheels with a pistol, ain't you?" the sheriff said. Then he spoke to his deputy. "Karl, see to them that's hurt."

"You that's been hit," Karl said, "hold your fire. I'm a sheriff's deputy."

Nathan staggered to his feet and Sheriff Wilhelm allowed him to keep his guns. The sheriff still hadn't holstered his weapon, waiting for Karl's report.

"He's right, Sheriff," said Karl. "There's three of 'em, and one's dead. The other two are wounded, but they'll live. One of 'em's a . . . uh . . . female."

Before Sheriff Wilhelm could react to that, a crowd had gathered, drawn by the gunfire. One young man, a press card under his hat band, spoke directly to the sheriff.

"Sheriff, I'm Brandon Wilkes, with the *Liberty-Tribune*."

"I know who you are," Wilhelm growled, "and I got no time to talk to you."

"I'm not here to talk to you," said Wilkes coolly. "I want a story from this gentleman who seems to have survived all the shooting. Mr. . . . ?"

"Stone," said Nathan. "Nathan Stone."

Karl, the deputy, arrived, his Colt cocked. Ahead of him stumbled a bearded man with the left side of his shirt bloody and a bleeding, weeping Amy Limbaugh. Nathan suspected the girl was playing on the sheriff's sympathy, and to his disgust, Wilhelm seemed to be responding.

"Ma'am," Sheriff Wilhelm said, "the doctor's office ain't far. Can you make it, or do you need help?"

"Sheriff," said Nathan angrily, "this is the second time this little hellion has tried to kill me. By God, if you don't take that Colt away from her, I'm going to."

"I tried," the deputy said sheepishly, "but she wouldn't give it to me."

"Ma'am," Wilhelm said, "you'll have to give me the gun."

Brandon Wilkes, the newspaperman, seemed to have lost all interest in everybody except Nathan Stone. He spoke directly to Nathan.

"Are you the Nathan Stone who once was a trouble-shooter for the Kansas-Pacific? The man who rode into Indian Territory and single-handed, gunned down a band of train robbers?"

"I am," said Nathan, disgusted with Sheriff Wilhelm's fussing over Amy Limbaugh. "I would be obliged if you'd point me toward the doctor's office. The sheriff has his hands full."

There was laughter from some of the crowd that had gathered, and an angry response from Sheriff Wilhelm. He turned on Wilkes.

"Damn it, Wilkes, you're interfering. All these people are in my custody and I'll see that they're given medical attention. Now get the hell out of here."

"Not so fast, Sheriff," said Nathan. "I want my position in this brought out into the open, and I don't like the way you're goin' at it. That female rattler you've cozied up to is responsible for this ambush, and I aim to see that she's charged with attempted murder. She has no legal grounds for comin' after me, and I can prove that with one telegram. I believe Mr. Wilkes, here, might be willing to send that telegram in return for how this all started."

"Damn right I will," Wilkes said. "Right after the doctor's seen to your wounds."

"Sheriff," said Nathan, "I want it understood, before witnesses, that I will be pressing charges against this woman and her hired killer. I can present enough state-sanctioned evidence to hang them both."

"Like hell," the wounded gunman shouted, speaking for the first time. "This woman, she paid me an' Turk five hunnert dollars apiece. She wanted this gent dead. It was all her idee. Me an' Turk, we just done what we was told."

Brandon Wilkes laughed. "Well, Sheriff, there's your witness for the prosecution. I expect he will sing like a mockingbird to save his own neck. Once I've heard Mr. Stone's story and sent his telegram, the three of us will get together and satisfy your curiosity as to how all this began and the reasons behind it."

Clearly, Sheriff Wilhelm didn't like it, but there had been too many witnesses to the hired gunman's hasty confession. Nathan limped along beside Wilkes, and men moved aside for them to pass.

"You are indeed fortunate," the doctor said, as he examined Nathan's wounds. "None of your vitals were hit and no bones broken. Just don't do anything foolish for the next three or four weeks, and there should be no complications."

As Nathan and Wilkes left, they encountered Sheriff Wilhelm and his two prisoners in the doctor's waiting room.

"Stone," said Wilhelm, "I'll expect to see you at the jail one hour from now."

"I have business at the telegraph office," Nathan replied. "When I'm finished there, I'll come to the jail to file charges."

Nathan had been given laudanum for pain, and while he limped, he was able to walk.

"For a man that's been shot twice, you manage remarkably well," said Wilkes. "You can always do your talking when you're feeling up to it."

"I don't aim to do another damn thing until this is settled," Nathan replied.

"Then you were serious about sending that telegram."

"Yes," said Nathan. "It's to be sent to the office of the attorney general, Jefferson City, Missouri. Ask for a report on the Limbaugh shooting in Springfield, May 18, 1872. I was forced to shoot in self-defense, and no charges were filed."

After the telegram had been sent, Nathan and Wilkes waited for a reply, and while they waited, Nathan talked.

"The way I see it," said Nathan, "your newspaper owes

me. I came out of Indian Territory shot all to hell, and by
the time I was on my feet, your writers had painted me a
yard wide and nine feet tall. Every damn wet-behind-the-
ears kid with a Colt and shells wanted to test my draw, but
it didn't end there. Taking the word of the Limbaughs, your
newspaper set me up as a killer on the run, with a price
on my head."

"Yes," said Wilkes, "I remember. We even used the
etching from your days with the Kansas-Pacific. But now
it's pay-back time. Just as the *Liberty-Tribune* falsely accused you, it can now exonerate you by printing your story
from start to finish. It can also turn public sentiment in
your favor and against the Limbaughs."

"I'm counting on that," Nathan said, "but it'll be a mixed
blessing. While I'll be rid of the Limbaughs, I look for a
whole new crop of young fools to challenge me, trying to
make themselves a name at my expense."

It was a dismal prospect, and Wilkes could think of nothing to say. They waited in silence until a reply came to the
telegram Wilkes had sent. He read it with satisfaction and
then he spoke.

"It's just as you said it would be. Now, if you're up to
it, I think we're ready to talk to Sheriff Wilhelm."

Wilhelm had his prisoners in cells, and Amy Limbaugh
glared at Nathan in angry silence. Wilkes handed the telegram to the sheriff and Wilhelm read it. When he spoke to
Nathan, he was all business.

"It appears you're justified in filing charges. The state
will prosecute, but you'll have to be present for the trial."

"When?" Nathan asked.

"It depends on what's ahead of you on the docket," said
Wilhelm. "Probably three or four weeks."

"You'll need a place to stay," Wilkes said, when they
had left the jail.

"I have a place," Nathan replied. "Eppie Bolivar's. I
boarded there while I was with the Kansas-Pacific. I have
a saddle horse, a packhorse, and a dog waiting for me at
the livery nearest the Pinkerton building."

"You'd better stay out of the saddle for a few days,"
said Wilkes. "I'll fetch a buckboard and drive you to the
Bolivar place. We can tie your horses on behind."

*   *   *

Nathan enjoyed the quiet days at Eppie Bolivar's boardinghouse, and he became more and more impressed with the thoroughness in which Brandon Wilkes wrote the story of Amy Limbaugh's vendetta to avenge the death of her brother. Wilkes asked for and got an in-depth report of the attempt on Nathan's life in Dodge City, as reported by Sheriff Harrington. In each edition of the *Liberty-Tribune,* Wilkes unfolded a little more of the deadly drama, portraying Nathan Stone as a man wrongly persecuted by a vengeful woman, aided by the powerful Pinkerton Detective Agency. To Nathan's surprise, men who had known him during his days with the Kansas-Pacific rallied around him. One of them was Joel Netherton.

"The railroad can still use you," said Netherton. "Outlaws are still robbing trains, but with you riding shotgun, your reputation alone would scare them away."

"Thanks, Joel," Nathan said, "but it's my reputation I'm trying to live down."

Kansas City, Missouri. August 3, 1873

Nathan's wounds healed, and by the day of the trial, he was ready to be done with the whole affair. He listened with disgust as a court-appointed defense attorney tried to convince a jury that Amy Limbaugh was a noble, courageous woman who had sought only to avenge her dead brother. But the jury deliberated only twenty-five minutes.

"Has the jury reached a verdict?" the judge asked.

"We have, your honor," the foreman replied. "We find the defendants guilty as charged."

"The defendants will come forward for sentencing," said the judge.

Amy Limbaugh and the surviving gunman, Simp Anderton, were led before the bench.

"Amy Limbaugh and Simpson Anderton, I hereby sentence each of you to five years in the state penitentiary," the judge said. "Court is adjourned."

Amy Limbaugh lost all her feigned innocence, flooding the courtroom with an array of swearing that would have made a bullwhacker envious.

"By God," said Brandon Wilkes with some admiration, "the woman has talent greater than her ability to fire a pistol. Nonetheless, Mr. Stone, in the interest of your continued good health, I'd suggest you be elsewhere when the state turns her loose."

"I aim to be," Nathan said. "I have business in Ellsworth."

Before returning to Eppie Bolivar's place for his horses and Cotton Blossom, Nathan returned to the telegraph office. There he sent a telegram to Captain Ferguson, at Fort Worth, inquiring about Captain Jennings. Captain Ferguson's reply was brief, and Nathan read it a second time, swallowing a lump in his throat . . .

Regret to inform you Captain Sage Jennings died two weeks ago.

"I swear before God, Cap," Nathan gritted through clenched teeth, "I'll gun down Clint Barkley if I have to follow him to the gates of hell and go in after him. . . ."

CHAPTER 5

Ellsworth, Kansas. August 14, 1873
Nathan took a room at a boardinghouse, and leaving Cotton Blossom at the livery with the horses, set out to make the rounds of the saloons. He could think of no more likely place to begin his search for Clint Barkley. The third saloon he entered—which was Joe Brennan's—he found Ben Thompson running a game of monte. Thompson flashed him that twisted grin he reserved for his few friends. Thompson had shed his frock coat, and as far as Nathan could see, the deadly little gambler wasn't armed. Aware of his obvious "nakedness," he seemed embarrassed.

"This is one of the few towns where I'm on good terms with the law," Thompson said. "Sheriff C.B. Whitney's a friend of mine. He has a gun ordinance. He'll be asking for your irons."

"He can ask till hell freezes," said Nathan. "My guns go where I go. I'm looking for a killer name of Clint Barkley. He may also use the name of Bill Bowen."

"It's unlikely he'd linger here, then," Thompson said. "He wouldn't be comfortable with the sheriff's gun ordinance. About all I've seen looked to be soldiers and rail-road men."

Ben's brother Billy entered the saloon as Nathan was leaving. The younger Thompson either didn't recognize Nathan or didn't consider him worthy of recognition, for he didn't speak. Nathan noted with approval the hotheaded little varmint was unarmed. Long before Nathan had made the rounds of the saloons, he encountered the sheriff. He was an older man, but he still spoke with authority.

"I'm C.B. Whitney, sheriff of Ellsworth. Are you aware there's a gun ordinance?"

"I am," Nathan replied. "I'm Nathan Stone. Are you aware there may be men in this town who would like nothing better than catching me unarmed?"

"I'm considering that," said Whitney. "I've been reading about you in the newspapers. I'm not one to meddle in a man's business, but under the circumstances, I need to know how long you aim to be here."

"Probably not more than another day," Nathan said. "I'm looking for a killer. His name is Clint Barkley, and he sometimes calls himself Bill Bowen. He back-shot a friend of mine in Texas. He carries a tied-down Colt, dresses like a cowboy, and might hire on with some ranch. He's an aggressive, short-tempered little varmint, remindin' you of an overgrown banty rooster."

Whitney laughed. "I know the type, and I reckon him and me would have had words if he'd been through here. Keep your irons. I'm trusting you not to use them unless it's shoot or be shot."

Nathan nodded. It was a fair offer, and the old sheriff was leaving himself open for criticism by making an exception to the town ordinance. After a fruitless day in the saloons, Nathan stopped by the livery for Cotton Blossom and they went to supper. There being little else to do, Nathan turned in for the night. Ellsworth was looking less and less like the kind of place Clint Barkley would hole up.

Ellsworth, Kansas. August 15, 1873

When Nathan and Cotton Blossom went to breakfast, Nathan stopped at the mercantile and bought three newspapers. One of them was a weekly, from Dodge City. Nathan went through the Kansas City and St. Louis papers first, finding little to interest him. But the Dodge City weekly had news from Texas, and although it was weeks' old, Nathan read it all with interest. The Sutton-Taylor feud was raging in Texas. William E. Sutton had shot up a party of Taylors in April, near Cuero, Texas. The Taylors had retaliated and there had been another shooting fray in June. John Wesley Hardin had been involved in shootings in July. Once in Cuero, Texas, and again in Albuquerque, New Mexico. Nathan looked in vain for some mention of the Horrells, but found nothing. He did find a death notice for Captain Sage Jennings. The old ranger had been buried at Fort Worth with military honors. There was no mention of any survivors. How many an old frontiersman had died thus, alone, not even a next-of-kin to mourn his passing? Angrily, Nathan threw the paper aside, those few words roaming the shadows of his mind like harbingers of doom. Would that not be his fate, his life's blood leaking into the sand of a lonely arroyo or into the dusty street of some lawless western town? Nathan returned to his room because the saloons wouldn't open for another two hours. Cotton Blossom sat watching him reprovingly. The dog hated the saloons, but it rankled him, being left with the horses at the livery. Making the rounds of the saloons, Nathan saved Brennan's until last. He would pause there only long enough to speak to Ben Thompson before riding out. Reaching the saloon, he found Thompson about to leave.

"I got some business with a gambler name of John Sterling," Ben said grimly. "I lined up some side bets with him, which we was goin' to split, but the bastard won a hatful of cash and sneaked out without divvying."

Thompson stomped out of the saloon, Nathan following. In a nearby saloon, Thompson found Sterling, drinking with Happy Jack Morco, a local policeman.

"You damn tinhorn thief," Thompson shouted, "you owe me money."

"I owe you nothing," Sterling responded.

Sterling swung at Thompson and Ben returned as good as he got. But that was when Happy Jack Morco bought in, drawing his Colt and holding it on Ben.

"That's enough, Thompson," said Morco.

"It looked like an even scrap to me," Nathan said, his cocked Colt on Morco.

"Who the hell are you?" Morco snarled.

"A hombre that don't like seein' an unarmed man prodded with a gun," said Nathan. "Put it away."

"I'm the law," Morco insisted.

"I don't care a damn who you are," Nathan said. "You don't need the gun. Ben's leaving. Aren't you, Ben?"

"Yeah," said Thompson, realizing he was up against the law.

"You're in violation of the town's gun ordinance," Morco said, glaring at Nathan.

"I have an understanding with the sheriff," said Nathan. "Put your gun away and back off. Get moving, Ben."

Morco holstered his gun and Nathan began backing toward the door. Not until he was outside on the boardwalk did he relax.

"Damn that Morco," Thompson said angrily, "that was between me and Sterling."

"You were about to play right into Morco's hands," said Nathan, just as angrily. "He wanted you to go after him. Then he could have jailed you for assaulting a lawman or shot you dead."

Nathan thought it was over, but by the time he and Thompson reached Joe Brennan's saloon, Morco and Sterling burst in, Sterling shouting.

"Get your guns, you damn Texas sonsabitches, and fight."

Ben Thompson was out the door on the run. Nathan remained where he was. He had no intention of being sucked into a gunfight with a lawman, even if the badge-toter was as biased and unfair as Morco appeared to be. On his way back, Ben was joined by Billy, his younger brother. Billy was staggering drunk and he had a shotgun. Billy stumbled, pulling one of the triggers, and a load of buckshot narrowly missed two bystanders.

"Damn it, Billy," Ben shouted, "let me have the scattergun."

Billy was too drunk to resist, and Ben took the weapon away from him, passing it to a bystander.

"Now, you damn sonsabitches," Ben bawled, "if you want to fight us, here we are."

At that very moment, Sheriff C.B. Whitney and a friend, John DeLong, tried to calm the Thompson brothers.

"Come on," said Whitney, who was unarmed. "Let's go to Brennan's. I'm buying the drinks."

"Look out, Ben!" somebody shouted.

Ben turned to see Sterling and Morco charging, guns drawn, Morco in the lead. Ben threw up his rifle and fired, but Morco had ducked into a doorway, and Ben's slug ripped into the door jamb. Before Ben could fire again, there was a deep-throated bellow behind him, and he whirled to see Sheriff Whitney stumble and fall.

"My God, Billy," Ben cried, "you've killed our best friend."

Everybody—including policeman Jack Morco—seemed stunned. Ben Thompson took advantage of the lull, hustling the now sober Billy toward a livery. There was a rattle of hooves and Billy Thompson was gone. Ben went to his hotel and barricaded himself in his room, daring anybody to come in after him. Mayor James Miller approached Thompson's room, ordering him to surrender. Thompson refused. Furious, Miller fired the entire police force. Finally, when Jack Morco was persuaded to surrender his arms, Ben Thompson gave up his gun and allowed himself to be taken into custody.

When all the shouting and shooting was done, sundown was not more than an hour distant, and Nathan decided to stay another night. From what he had heard, Ben Thompson would go before the court in the morning, and while the daring gambler had in no way been involved in the shooting of Sheriff Whitney, he had helped his brother Billy escape.

To Nathan's total surprise, Ben Thompson had only been charged with firing at Happy Jack Morco, and when Morco failed to show up, the charges were dropped. Ben Thompson caught Nathan's eye and winked. "Luck of the draw," said the dapper gambler.

Weary of towns, Nathan planned to pass Dodge City a few miles to the east, and long before reaching the tracks of the Atchison, Topeka and Santa Fe, he could hear the faint bellow of a locomotive whistle. A train traveled westward, bound for Dodge. But the whistle sounded no more. The next sound rumbled like distant thunder, shaking the ground. Nathan shucked his Winchester from the boot and kicked the grulla into a fast gallop. Soon Nathan could see the dirty gray of smoke against the blue of the sky, and when he came within sight of the train, it stood idle. Smoke still billowed from the blown express car, while the engi-

neer and fireman stood beside the locomotive, their hands
in the air. A lone gunman held them captive, and while
Nathan wasn't quite within range, he cut loose with his
Winchester. It had the desired effect, drawing the attention
of the outlaw, and the trainmen were on him in an instant.
But the firing alerted the rest of the robbers, and some of
them bellied down under the wrecked baggage car. Nathan
reined up and left the saddle, using each bit of cover to
advance. Near the far end of the train, he could see a rider
coming, trailing nine horses on lead ropes. Taking careful
aim, Nathan shot the rider out of the saddle, and he was
now close enough for several additional shots to spook the
horses. There were angry shouts from the baggage car, as
the outlaws saw their means of escape galloping away. Nathan now had the advantage. While he was outnumbered,
his adversaries had virtually no cover unless they retreated
to the baggage car, and that soon lost its appeal, for the
fireman and engineer had retrieved their weapons and were
adding to the woes of the train robbers. Finally they ceased
firing altogether, and scrambled under the baggage car, putting it between themselves and Nathan. Nathan reined up
and used the baggage car for cover, cutting loose on the
retreating outlaws. He brought down two more before they
were out of range. Nathan noted with approval that the
engineer and fireman were binding the captured outlaw
hand and foot. Finished, they came to meet him, grins on
their grimy faces.

"By God," the engineer said, "one cowboy in the brush
is better than two Pinkertons in the baggage car."

"We'd better go have a look at them," said Nathan.

There were three men in the baggage car, one of them
in the garb of a railroad man, and he regarded his two
companions with disgust. One of them had a bloody gash
above his eyes, and it was he who spoke.

"We drove them away," he shouted triumphantly.

"We, hell," said the brakemen. "You didn't fire a shot
till they was on the run, and it was you that said they
wouldn't dynamite the express car. They was goin' to blow
the safe, too, if this gent with the Winchester hadn't took
a hand."

"They got nothing, then," Nathan said.

"Nothing," the brakeman replied. "We're owin' you,
mister . . ."

"Stone. Nathan Stone."

"Why, I know you!" the engineer said. "The Kansas-Pacific would have been a gone beaver if you hadn't wiped out that band of thieves."

"My God," said the fireman, "I just wish the AT and SF had the gumption to hire you, instead of these damned Pinkertons."

"You have some track that needs fixing," Nathan said, uncomfortable with the praise. "We can't be more than a few miles from Dodge. Your dispatcher there should be able to get a repair crew out here pronto. I can ride that way and take him word."

"You tell him he'd better," the engineer replied. "We ain't settin' out here after dark with a busted open express coach and a safe full of government payroll. I'll put this old iron horse in reverse and back her all the way to Wichita."

Nathan rode west, following the tracks. Being so near Dodge, the bombers hadn't used dynamite to blow the rails. Instead, they had removed a single section of rail, enough to derail a train. Two men, Nathan judged, could repair the damage in a few minutes. He had considered suggesting that the trainmen make the repairs themselves, but that was akin to suggesting that a cowboy milk the cows. Reaching Dodge, Nathan rode to the railroad depot, where he told the dispatcher of the attempted robbery and the torn-up track.

"Them damn lazy Irish," the dispatcher groused. "They could replace that rail easy, if they would."

Nathan laughed. "The engineer said if they wasn't out of there before dark, he'd just reverse the train and take it back to Wichita."

"He would, too, damn it, makin' it look like I ain't doin' my job."

Nathan rode away. He had saved them a payroll, and it was up to them to repair their railroad. Someone called his name, and Nathan reined up.

"I'll buy your supper," said Sheriff Harrington, "if you'll tell me how you finally got that Limbaugh filly off your back."

Nathan didn't really want to talk about Amy Limbaugh, but Sheriff Harrington had been a friend to him. Anyway, his taking the time to ride through Dodge and make a report of the attempted robbery and destroyed track to the railroad had brought him very close to suppertime. Why not enjoy a comfortable bed and a hot meal, and then ride out in the morning?

"On one condition," said Nathan. "You'll have to feed my dog, too."

"On one condition," Harrington replied. "When was the *last* time he was fed?"

"Best I recollect," said Nathan, "it was the fall of sixty-six, just before we came west."

Nathan spent almost two hours with Harrington, and ended up telling the lawman not only of the Limbaugh trial in Kansas City, but of the train robbery he had thwarted.

"You're missing your calling," Harrington said. "Thieves are giving the railroads hell. You could name your own price, just doing what you did today. Locking Pinkertons in the baggage car with the payroll will accomplish just one thing. The varmints will dynamite the coach, like they did today. You and your horse traveling in a boxcar near the end of the train could stop these train robberies cold."

"It's something to consider," said Nathan. "But for now, I have another trail to ride, down into New Mexico Territory. A debt I have to pay for a friend."

"I understand," Harrington said. "If you ever decide you'd like to ride shotgun for the Atchison, Topeka and Santa Fe, the division boss is right here in Dodge. I'll see that he's told you saved him a payroll today."

Leaving Dodge, Nathan rode southwest. Before darkness caught up to him, he would be in northeastern New Mexico Territory. He was about to cross the Cimarron, into the Indian Territory's panhandle, when he discovered the wagon tracks. Three heavily loaded wagons, and on the flat Kansas plain he could see where they had crossed the Cimarron and veered south. There were tracks of at least nine horses, and the wagons were drawn by mules instead of oxen, which meant that somebody was in a hurry.

"Must be a valuable load, Cotton Blossom," Nathan said, "with nine men ridin' shotgun. They could have used the railroad as far west as Dodge, unless they're involved in some scheme that can't stand the light of day. As it is, they've likely come all the way from Saint Louis or Kansas City, keepin' to the plains and avoiding towns. That's a hell of a lot of extra work for honest bull whackers."

Crossing the Cimarron, Nathan found where the party

had made camp the night before. There was a scattering of corn where they had grained the teams. While oxen ate grass, grain had to be hauled to feed the mules. From the tracks, Nathan decided the wagons weren't more than two hours ahead of him. While common sense told him to avoid the mysterious caravan, his curiosity was prodding him to follow, to discover who these people were and what they were hauling. He rode on, but cautiously. While he had come upon this trail by chance, the men ahead—likely heavily armed—wouldn't know that. His very presence could be taken as a threat. At best, he was subject to being greeted by drawn guns; at worst, by a hail of lead. When he sighted the wagons, two of them were on the farthest side of a dry arroyo, while the third was stalled midway. The left rear wheel was missing and four men were using a pole to hoist the rear of the wagon. Large flat stones had been gathered, and two men were stacking them beneath the axle to support the disabled wagon. Six of the men were unoccupied, and when one of them saw Nathan, he alerted the others. Two of them reached in through the canvas pucker of the wagon and came out with Winchesters, while the others waited, their hands near the butts of their Colts.

"I'm friendly," Nathan shouted.

"Come on, then," one of the strangers replied, "but keep your hands up an' empty."

Nathan reined up a few yards from the crippled wagon. He had made no hostile moves and he kept his silence. If this bunch took offense and challenged his right to be here, then it would confirm his suspicions of them. They all wore range clothes and not one of them had the look of a bull-whacker. His eyes on them, Nathan found himself comparing them to El Gato's renegades. Finally one of the men with a Winchester under his arm spoke.

"You been followin' us. Why?"

"You talk like a man with a guilty conscience," Nathan said. "I rode out of Dodge City this morning, and I crossed the Cimarron where you did. Until I saw your tracks, I didn't know you existed."

"You got a smart mouth, mister," said another of the strangers. "I'll give any fool the benefit of the doubt once. Now you ride on and keep ridin'. Show your face again, and you'll be left for coyote and buzzard bait."

The bunch looked rattlesnake-mean, and while Nathan had no doubt that whatever activity they were engaged in was illegal enough to hang them to the last man, his becoming involved would only succeed in getting him shot dead. Nathan rode carefully around the wagon, and might have escaped them, had they not left the six mules in harness. Cotton Blossom followed Nathan, but growling deep in his throat. One of the harnessed mules drew a wrong impression, and cow-kicking, narrowly missed Cotton Blossom. The hound reacted with a full-blown snarl that sounded like a half-starved wolf on the hunt, and the mules spooked. The wagon shot out of the arroyo, and when the wheelless axle struck an upthrust of rock, the load shifted. The entire side of the wagon split, ripping canvas and snapping bows, as heavy wooden crates were flung to the ground. Each had been branded with the famous Winchester name, and while that was damning enough, some of the crates had split, each revealing a dozen brand new model seventy-threes, identical to the one that rode in Nathan's saddle boot. The implication of what he had seen struck Nathan with the impact of a club, and he kicked the grulla into a fast gallop. But nine of his adversaries had saddled horses, and he could hear them thundering after him, and it was just a matter of time until they rode him down. He quickly learned, however, that they had no intention of wasting time on him, for they were shooting, and lead sang dangerously close, like angry bees. He reined up, taking his chances. They still might gun him down, but at least he had a chance. To run would be to die. Turning his horse, he faced them, giving up any thought of resisting. There was six of them, and they all had him covered.

"Unfasten that gun belt," one of them said, "and do it slow. Then let it fall."

Nathan did so.

"Wilson," said the man giving the orders, "gather up that gun rig." When Wilson had done so, the next command was directed at Nathan. "Dismount and start walking toward the wagons."

Nathan dismounted and started walking, noting that two of the men were leading his horses. He had no doubt as to what they planned to do with him, the only question being when and how. A man rode on Nathan's right and another on his left, and when he was near the wagons, the rider to his right buffaloed him with the muzzle of a Colt. His hat saved him, and while his head hurt like blazes, he was conscious. Facedown, he lay still. Moving would invite another blow, and they might crack his skull. He listened.

"Hell," one voice complained, "why didn't you just shoot him?"

"Because out here on the open plain, a shot can be heard for twenty miles," another disgusted voice answered. "We're likely to be stuck here for a while, and the last damn thing we need is to invite any more attention."

"This peckerwood said he just come from Dodge," a third voice cut in. "One of us could ride there and buy another wagon."

"God, McCluskie," a companion groaned, "was you born that stupid, or did you go to school and study for it? You'd have to take the teams with you, and you'd have the town follerin' you back, hopin' to learn how a man can lose a wagon—wheels, box, bows, and canvas—on flat Kansas plain."

"Hell," McCluskie replied, offended, "it was just an idea. You got a better one?"

"Shut up, both of you," a third voice commanded. "We should have brought a fourth wagon, reducing each load instead of overloading three. The terrain south to the Canadian River is likely to become even rougher, and even if these remaining wagons can make it, can we afford to leave a third of our cargo behind?"

"Hell, no," they shouted in a single voice.

"Then listen to me," the commanding voice said. "We promised Quanah Parker and his Comanches four hundred and thirty-two repeating rifles and two hundred rounds for each, and we promised delivery on the north bank of the Canadian. Now there's no way in hell we can live up to our end of the deal, because we got no way to get the Winchesters there. There ain't but one damn thing we can do, and that's to persuade the war whoops to come here for their guns."

"That's near a hundred miles," somebody said. "Suppose they won't come?"

"We'll sweeten the pot," said the commanding voice. "Instead of a hundred dollars per rifle, we'll take seventy-five. And then there's four cases of dynamite. Why get your ears shot off trying to breach the walls of a soldier fort, when you can just wait for darkness and blow it up?"

There was laughter. "By God, Burke," McCluskie said admiringly, "you can't be beat when it comes to figgerin' things out."

"Just keep that in mind, all of you," said Burke. "We're still a week away from our rendezvous with Quanah, and if they agree to come here for the rifles, that's another two days. At best, you'll be stuck here nine days. Gather all the rifles and ammunition from that ruined wagon and divide it between the other two. It's maybe two miles back to the Cimarron, and you can make it that far, even with over-loaded wagons. I'll be back as soon as I can."

"What are we s'posed to do with this *pelado* here on the ground?" McCluskie asked.

"Rope him to a wagon wheel," said Burke. "He might be useful as a hostage if others come nosing around. If we haven't found a use for him by the time I return, we'll burn the wagons, and he'll be in one of them. Quanah and his boys can take the blame for that. Now get busy gathering those cases of rifles and ammunition. I want to see all of it in the two remaining wagons before I ride out."

"Git up, you." McCluskie grunting, hoisting Nathan by his belt.

On hands and knees, Nathan pretended he was barely conscious. Despite his throbbing head, he was elated, for he might yet escape. With Burke away for nine days, those who waited would become bored, and bored men became careless. Nathan allowed McCluskie to hoist him to his feet and shove him toward one of the wagons.

"Now git down there with that wheel to yer back," McCluskie demanded.

Nathan sat down, his back to the wagon wheel, and McCluskie bound his hands behind him, to the rim. Nathan could have shouted for joy, for instead of rope, the gunrunner was using heavy cord. After McCluskie had knotted the cord tight and left him alone, Nathan ran his fingers along the wagon wheel's iron rim. As he had hoped, the continual pounding of the iron against rock had left jagged burrs sharp enough to cut the skin. Or the bonds that imprisoned a man.

"Now," Burke said, when the crates from the disabled wagon had been forced into the remaining two, "take your time getting these wagons back to the Cimarron. Hide them in the brush along the river as best you can, and post a guard at each wagon from dusk to first light. If I ride back here and find that anything has happened to the teams, to either of the wagons, or to the rifles and ammunition, the hombre responsible will be almighty sorry."

After he had ridden away, the others began readying the wagons for the drive back to the Cimarron. McCluskie loosed Nathan from the wagon wheel, but left his hands tied behind his back, forcing him to follow the wagons afoot. With Burke's order in mind, both wagons were driven into heavy brush along the river. McCluskie forced Nathan down, his back to a wagon wheel, and tied him as before. McCluskie was a man of habit, for it was the first wheel to which Nathan had been bound, with the burrs along the edge of the iron tire.

Nathan's bonds were loosed long enough for him to eat his supper of bacon, beans, and coffee, and then he was bound again. He could see the horses and mules—his animals among them—grazing on the opposite side of the river, apparently unguarded. His saddle and packsaddle lay beneath the wagon to which he was tied, and he had seen Burke throw his gun rig into the back of the wagon. When the camp settled down for the night, Nathan Stone would be ready. . . .

CHAPTER 6

After supper, Nathan listened to the men talk, and decided they were more than just a band of renegades. Burke—the man who had ridden to meet Quanah Parker—obviously had connections and power. How else could he have negotiated a deal with a Comanche chief and raised the money for three wagonloads of weapons and ammunition? While Quanah Parker and his loyal band had wrought havoc with frontier forts, newspapers were reporting heavy losses. The Union army was slowly but surely crushing the Indian rebellion and as the threat diminished, more and more forces were being brought to bear against the youthful Comanche chief. This, Nathan decided, was do or die for Quanah Parker. With more than four hundred repeating rifles in the hands of the Comanches, they might hold their own indefinitely, even against the Union army. Somehow these weapons must be kept out of Comanche hands.

With every intention of freeing himself during the night, Nathan considered the possibility of riding back to Fort Dodge and laying the situation at the feet of the Union army, where it belonged. But the new post commander at Fort Dodge didn't know Nathan Stone, and being a spit-and-polish type, would be unlikely to send soldiers anywhere upon the word of a civilian. Byron Silver, associated with the attorney general's office in Washington, would take Nathan's word, but Silver might not be in Washington. Even with Silver's help, Nathan reflected, government's wheels turned slowly. Discovering Nathan had escaped, the gunrunners could ill afford to remain on the Cimarron, waiting for Burke's return.

Only one grim conclusion remained, and that was if the Winchesters and ammunition were to be kept out of Comanche hands, the responsibility was Nathan Stone's. He began sawing the cords that bound his wrists against the ragged edge of the wheel's iron tire, feeling the sharp burrs bite into his hands and wrists. A guard sat on the tongue of each wagon, and Nathan had to be careful lest his movement vibrate the wagon enough to disturb the guard. While the cord binding Nathan wasn't so thick, McCluskie had used a triple thickness.

By the time Nathan had sawed his way through a third of his bonds, the blood from his many cuts had slicked his hands. The moon came up and set. Nathan heard someone coming and ceased his activity until a new guard had settled down and lighted his cigarette. There was no sound except the horses and mules cropping grass and the far-off cry of a coyote.

Free of his bonds, Nathan rubbed his arms and wrists, restoring the circulation. Needing time for what he must do, he decided against overpowering his guards, for he would risk waking the rest of the camp. Better to draw them all away, and nothing would accomplish that more swiftly than stampeding the horses and mules.

Nathan crept away from the wagons and toward the grazing horses and mules, moving slowly so as not to interrupt the grazing. Catching up his own horses, with an arm around the neck of each of the animals, he led them upriver far enough so that any disturbance wouldn't spook them. Returning to camp, he found a dead, thorny branch that had dried to perfection, and this he took with him to where the horses and mules grazed. Mules being the easiest to spook, he swatted two of the animals with the thorny branch, and they brayed as though being slaughtered. Another swipe or two with the branch had every horse and mule on the run, hell-bent for election, down the Cimarron. Reaction within the camp was predictable.

"By God, somethin' spooked the horses an' mules."

"Your fault, McCluskie. That drifter you tied to the wagon wheel got loose. Now he's took his horses and run off the rest. After them, damn it. Burke will gut-shoot us all."

Quickly Nathan retrieved his guns from the wagon and lit out on the run for his horses. He saddled and bridled the grulla, secured the packsaddle just enough to hold it in place, and looped the grulla's reins and the lead rope of the packhorse around a wagon bow. The spooked horses and mules hadn't run very far, and he could hear the shouts of the men. One of the boxes flung from the wrecked wagon had contained dynamite, and the box had split. He hoped the outlaws had gathered the loose dynamite and placed it in the rear of one of the wagons, where he could get to it, for he had little time and dared not strike a light. Nathan found no loose dynamite in the wagon to which he had been tied, and hurried on to the second. If he found no dynamite there, he would be forced to ride away, saving himself.

Reaching the first wagon, the first thing he touched was a tangle of fuse. Some of the dynamite had spilled out of the broken box, and Nathan gathered four sticks. While he had no experience with the explosive, he had seen it capped and fused during his months with the Kansas-Pacific Railroad. With his knife, he slashed off what he hoped was a five-minute length of fuse. He capped and fused one stick, binding it to a second stick with the fuse itself. Quickly he cut a second length of fuse, and using two more sticks of dynamite, prepared his charge for the second wagon. Lighting the first fuse and waiting to see that it caught, he ran to the second wagon and repeated the procedure.

With both fuses burning, knowing not how much time he had, Nathan set out upriver, leading his horses. A fleeting

shadow ahead of him proved to be Cotton Blossom. Believing he was now far enough from the wagons, Nathan
mounted the grulla, kicking the animal into a fast gallop.
His mind had become a ticking clock and he gritted his
teeth in anticipation of the explosions. But there were only
the shouts of the men downriver. Thanks to darkness and
his inexperience, he had improperly capped and fused the
charges. Or perhaps the fuses had sputtered out. But no!
He felt the concussion, the trembling of the earth before he
heard the first explosion. The charges blew within seconds of
one another, and as the cases of ammunition detonated on
the heels of the dynamite, there was a conflagration such as
Nathan Stone had never witnessed in his life. It dwarfed the
hell that had been Gettysburg, as one after another, balls of
flame shot into the heavens. It seemed the earth had been
painted an eerie orange, and Nathan had to fight to hold his
skittish horses. There were screams from the men who had
gone after their stampeded horses, and Nathan wondered if
they had been close enough to have been caught up in the
explosions or perhaps felled by lead from detonated shells.
    Slowly the pillars of fire in the night sky diminished and
there was only silence. There was no doubt in Nathan's
mind that the fiery aftermath of the blasts had been seen
in Dodge, Wichita, parts of Colorado, New Mexico, and
Texas. Looking back, Nathan could see a fiery halo. Likely
a prairie fire, which he regretted, but there had been no other
way. He rode on, wondering what would be the fate of the
men who gambled their lives on the illegal sale of guns and
ammunition to Quanah Parker and his Comanches. For certain, the men who had survived the blasts wouldn't be around
when Burke returned. Nathan laughed.
    "Well, Cotton Blossom, I reckon it'll be a real test of old
Burke's negotiatin' skills, when he brings them four hundred
Comanches on a two-day ride for guns and shells that ain't
to be had. From what I hear, Comanches have scalped a man
and shot his belly full of arrows for a whole lot less."

Dodge City, Kansas. August 18, 1873
On the train from Kansas City, Byron Silver had arrived
just before dark. In his coat pocket were orders from Washington to the post commander at Fort Dodge, who was to
dispatch a company of soldiers to a destination to be named
by Silver. While changing trains in Kansas City, Silver had

heard about the Limbaugh trial. Knowing Joel Netherton, the division boss for the Kansas-Pacific, Silver had gotten the story from him. Netherton had been able to tell him only that Nathan Stone had ridden west. With that in mind, Silver went to the sheriff's office, inquiring about Nathan.

"He left here early this morning," said Sheriff Harrington, "riding south."

"He's a longtime friend," Silver said. "I'd have liked to see him again."

"Buy my supper," said Harrington slyly, "and I'll tell you how that Limbaugh gal tried to shoot him, right here in Dodge."

"Maybe I will," Silver said. "Is Stone a friend of yours?"

"I like to think so," said Harrington. "It was me that checked out the Limbaugh story and proved her a liar, sending Stone to the attorney general's office, in Jefferson City."

"Come on, then," Silver replied, "and let's have a steak."

It was already dark when Silver and Harrington left the sheriff's office, and following supper, they lingered for another hour over coffee, talking. Silver found himself liking the sheriff, and not just because he had befriended Nathan Stone. Silver and Harrington had just left the cafe when they felt the earth shake.

"God Almighty," said Harrington. "An earthquake."

"An explosion," Silver contradicted. "In the sky, to the south."

They watched in wonder as an enormous ball of fire erupted into the heavens. Almost immediately there was a second explosion, and another sphere of fire joined the first.

"What in thunder could have caused that?" Sheriff Harrington wondered. "Not a damn thing out there but sagebrush, tumbleweeds, and flat prairie. And, of course, the Cimarron River, if you ride far enough."

"I can think of only one possible cause," said Silver, "and if I'm right, my reason for being here has just been eliminated. Tomorrow, I'll take some soldiers from Fort Dodge and ride south."

Respecting Silver's position, Sheriff Harrington asked no questions.

The Cimarron. August 19, 1873
Accompanied by a sergeant and four privates, Byron Silver reached the Cimarron just before noon. Nobody had any difficulty identifying any of the debris from the explosions.

"Winchester rifles," said Sergeant Wilcox. "At least, they used to be."

Riding on, they found the remains of three men, five mules, and two horses. Reaching the actual scene of the explosions, there was nothing but enormous craters in the ground. Half a mile south, there was an iron tire from a wagon wheel.

"Assuming that somebody escaped," Silver said, "let's fan out and look for tracks."

There was the remains of the wagon that had broken up. Silver had known the gunrunners had left St. Louis with three wagons. Splitting a third wagon's load between the two remaining wagons would have created impossible overloads. Silver rode on upriver for almost a mile, not sure what he was seeking. Near a small tree, he found horse droppings and there he dismounted. The droppings weren't quite a day old, and Silver slid down the sandy bank to the water's edge. There, in the wet sand, were the front paw prints of a wolf or coyote. Or of a dog. But Silver decided the prints weren't quite large enough for a wolf and were too large for a coyote. Mounting, Silver rode south until he reached sandy ground, and then he began riding a half circle until he crossed the trail he sought. There were tracks of two horses and the paw prints of the dog. Silver mounted and paused, his eyes turned toward the southwest.

"*Vaya con dios*, Nathan Stone. I don't know the why of it, but your reckoning and sense of responsibility were ace-high, *amigo*."

Santa Fe, New Mexico Territory. August 25, 1873

The last few miles before reaching the town, Nathan followed the old Santa Fe Trail. The first building to catch his eye was a magnificent chapel, its gothic design reminding him of some of the cathedrals he had seen in New Orleans. Reining up, he admired the towering structure before riding on.*

"Cotton Blossom," Nathan said, "I like the looks of Santa Fe."

Finding a livery for the horses, Nathan and Cotton Blossom crossed a wide street to a hotel. The Spanish influence

---

*Loretto Chapel was built in 1852 and stands today on the old Santa Fe Trail.

was everywhere, and Nathan was reminded of the south Texas border towns of Laredo and Brownsville. Other dogs wandered the streets, and Nathan spoke sharply to Cotton Blossom, lest there be trouble. Suppertime being several hours away, Nathan took a room for the night and bought a local newspaper, *The New Mexican*. After Cotton Blossom and Nathan had entered the hotel room, Nathan locked the door, shucked his gun belt, removed his hat, and tugged off his boots. He then settled down on the bed to read the newspaper. Most of the front section was devoted to local news, none of it of any interest to Nathan. A second section, however, dealt with other matters, including a growing resentment between sheepmen and cattlemen. A Spaniard, Armijo Estrella was running sheep, while a crusty old ex-Texan, Colton McLean, had cattle. According to the paper, the two had been at each other's throats for years, fighting over range, water rights, and apparently just for the hell of it. Now the situation was worsening, for McLean's riders were shooting at sheepmen, while Estrella's sheepmen were firing at cowboys. Estrella had been the first to bring in hired guns, and Nathan sat straight up on the bed, for there before him were the names of the Horrells! Much of the fighting had taken place near the little town of Lincoln, in southern New Mexico Territory, and Nathan vowed to ride there just as quickly as he could. He read the article a second time and then scanned the rest of the paper without finding any mention of Clint Barkley, and that bothered him. He might bring down the wrath of the entire Horrell clan without finding a trace of Barkley, but he had no other lead.

Lincoln, New Mexico Territory. August 30, 1873
Nathan wasted no time. Asking directions, he rode directly to Colton McLean's spread and found it to be all he had expected. Riding down a winding lane for more than a mile, he reached a gate behind which stood two men with Winchesters. He reined up when one of them spoke.

"Who are you and what's your business?"

"Nathan Stone. I heard Mr. McLean might be hiring hands."

"He might be," said the second man, his eyes on Nathan's tied-down Colts. "Foller Jake on up to the house."

By the time the gate had been opened and Nathan had ridden through, Jake was in the saddle. He held his

horse back until Nathan was slightly ahead, and the two
rode on to the ranch house that sprawled in a distant
grove of oaks.

Nathan stood beside his horse while Jake entered the
house. At the far end of the long porch, two hounds barked
furiously. Cotton Blossom cast them a bored look and then
ignored them. When Jake opened the front door and beckoned, Nathan entered the house. At the end of a long hall,
Jake knocked on a door and was told to enter. McLean
stood before a fireplace that used up half of one wall in
the massive living room. His was the rough clothing of a
cowboy. He hadn't removed his hat, and on his left hip
was a tied-down Colt. He was gruff to a fault and wasted
no time.

"Who told you I was hirin' riders?"

"You'd be a fool not to," said Nathan smoothly. "Armijo
Estrella's hiring."

"Well, now," McLean replied, his brittle blue eyes boring
into Nathan's, "mebbe you'd ought to be talkin' to
Armijo."

"Mebbe I'd ought," said Nathan, adopting the drawl. He
took a step toward the door.

"Fifty and found," McLean said, "and I supply your
shells. Jake, show him to the bunkhouse."

Nathan followed Jake down the hall, and they were on
the porch before Jake spoke.

"Don't push your luck, mister. Mr. McLean don't take
no lip. He'll talk to you after supper."

Nathan said nothing. Mounting the grulla and leading the
packhorse, he followed Jake to a distant bunkhouse. It
being Saturday afternoon, the riders were preparing for a
trip to town. Several of them nodded to Nathan, and nobody seemed overly curious.

"The barn's over yonder," said Jake, pointing. With that,
he departed.

Nathan unsaddled the grulla and unloaded the packhorse, toting his saddle and pack into the bunkhouse. He
then led the two horses to the barn. After rubbing them
down, he stalled and grained them. Returning to the bunkhouse, Nathan waited for call to supper. When the bell
pealed, Nathan headed toward the cook's entrance to the
ranch house. While the dining room had benches and tables

enough to seat thirty men, there was only McLean, Nathan, and the Mexican cook.

"Set," McLean ordered. "The Mex, here, is Squid. He swum ashore from a French merchant ship, lookin' for work and a place to hide. He's the best cook that ever drawed a breath, but he ain't worth a damn for nothin' else."

Squid grinned as he brought in sizzling steaks from the kitchen. Nathan looked at the rancher, puzzled by the man's jovial attitude.

"Eat, damn it," McLean growled. "Steak's gettin' cold."

They were down to the coffee before McLean spoke again. "What do you think of the spread?"

"I think," said Nathan, "if I was having gun trouble, I'd have kept some armed men in the bunkhouse."

"What the hell for?" McLean demanded. "I'm here, and two of the boys are at the gate. How much sand you think a sheepherder's got, anyhow?"

"I see the Horrell clan's hired on with Estrella," said Nathan, "and I happen to know they're a bunch of Texas killers on the dodge."

"Are you after them? Is that why you're here?"

"No," Nathan said truthfully, "I'm not gunning for the Horrells. I just happen to know they're a hairy-legged bunch who have worn out their welcome in Texas. If they're around long enough, some of them will have to be shot on general principle."

To Nathan's surprise, McLean laughed. "You talk like a Texan," he said.

"I've spent some time there," Nathan said. "What do you aim for me to do?"

"Take your turn ridin' the range. You don't shoot at Estrella's riders unless they fire at you or try to stampede the herd. You don't bother the sheep unless the varmints are run on my range. Then, by God, you rimrock every damn one."*

"Estrella's trying to take land that belongs to you?"

"Well, hell, I ain't exactly got the papers on it, but my cows was grazin' that land when this damn Spanish *pelado* was on the south of the river, eatin' chili beans."

---

*"Rimrocking" sheep consisted of driving the herd off a cliff.

"Estrella is calling your bluff, challenging your right to free range, then," Nathan said.

"You're talkin' like them slick-tongued lawyers in Santa Fe," McLean growled.

"You're defying the courts?"

"Hell, yes," McLean shouted. "I took this land from the Injuns, when there was one of the varmints behind ever' tree and bush. You think I aim to lose it to this shirttail sheep nurse without a fight?"

"I understand your position," said Nathan. "Have you considered leasing the land from the government?"

"A hundred thousand acres and more, at a dollar an acre," McLean said. "If I sold ever' damn cow I own at prime, I couldn't afford that, and neither can Estrella. They ain't that much cold cash in all of New Mexico Territory."

"So the answer is a shooting war between sheepmen and cattlemen."

"I reckon," said McLean, shrugging his shoulders. "The law says Estrella's got the same right to free range as I do, but it don't give him the right to get at the grass by shootin' my riders and stampedin' my cows."

"That same law denies you the right to claim free range by gunning down Estrella's riders and rimrocking his sheep," Nathan replied.

"By God," McLean bawled, "I've had the law read to me backward and forward, and I ain't about to have it done by a varmint I'm payin' gun wages. If you ain't with me, then you're agin me. Saddle up and ride, 'fore I lose my temper."

It was Nathan's turn to laugh. "I didn't say I was against you. I want to know where I stand, where the law's concerned. I'll side you as long as I eat your grub and take your pay, but I won't kill without cause. As I see it, you and Armijo Estrella are both outside the law, and you have the right to defend your herd and to retaliate as a result of attacks on your riders. If it comes to bushwhacking and back-shooting, then I'll ride on. I won't end up with a price on my head, just so your cows can eat free grass. *Comprende*?"

"*Si*," McLean replied.

"Now," said Nathan, "what do you know about this Horrell bunch that's hired on with Estrella?"

"They're trigger-happy," McLean said. "There's five of

the varmints, and last Sunday they got drunk and shot up a saloon in Lincoln. They threatened to shoot the sheriff and a deputy if anything was done."

"So nothing was done," said Nathan.

"Not a damn thing. I halfway believe Estrella's encouraging them to raise hell, givin' me notice that I'm in for it," McLean said. "But these Horrells ain't the worst of it. I'd say Estrella's got a dozen *Mejicanos* he's brung across the river, ever' one wearin' a tied-down Colt and the look of a killer."

"It purely sounds like a challenge," said Nathan. "How many riders do you have?"

"You've seen 'em," McLean said. "There's Hugh and Vance at the gate, the nine men who rode into town, and you. Twelve. So you're outgunned."

"Maybe not for long," said Nathan. "Dispose of the Horrells, and the odds are even."

"But you're not after them."

"No," Nathan said, "but once they know I'm here, they'll be after me. I interfered in a fracas back in Texas, when they were shooting up a town and about to kill an innocent man. I wounded one and sent them all running with their tails between their legs. They're not likely to forget that."

McLean laughed, his good humor restored. "These Horrells can't do nothin' but help me. Another hell-raising day or two in Lincoln, and Sheriff Bowie Hatcher won't care a damn what we do. Since that bunch of coyotes has got a mad on for you, I reckon we'll keep you close to home for a spell. The more mischief they stir up, the less favorable the law's goin' to look on Armijo Estrella."

But things didn't work out the way Colton McLean had hoped, because the Horrells again rode into Lincoln, accompanied by six of Estrella's imported *Mejicano* gunthrowers. It became a bloody Saturday night that Lincoln would never forget. A few minutes before midnight, one of Colton's riders thundered into the ranch on a lathered horse. Nathan Stone sat up in his bunk and was buckling on his gun belt when Colton McLean and the wounded cowboy reached the bunkhouse.

"Stone," said the rancher, "this is Riley, an' he just come from town. Now Riley, you tell it all. Then I'll have Squid see to your wound."

"We didn't do nothin', Mr. Colton," Riley said. "Gus,

Will, Sandy, an' me, we was just leavin' the Rio Saloon.
The bastards bushwhacked us, killin' Sandy, an' they
wounded the rest of us. We holed up in the Rio, an' Gus
an' Will is still there. They was more shootin' down the
street, an' I reckon the varmints has got the rest of our boys
pinned down. I got out the back door an' lit a shuck here."

"Stone," said McLean, "saddle up and ride. Take Hugh
and Vance with you. Whatever you have to do, then do it."

"Leave Hugh and Vance to cover the ranch," Nathan
said.

"By God," McLean roared, "I'm givin' the orders. Take
Hugh and Vance with you. I'll be here, and Riley can shoot.
So can Squid, if he's got to. Now ride, damn it."

Anticipating McLean's order, Nathan found Hugh and
Vance waiting.

"Riley didn't tell us nothin', 'cept there's hell in town,"
Vance said. "What're we ridin' into?"

As they rode, Nathan told them what he knew, and long
before reaching Lincoln, they could hear the ominous rattle
of gunfire. . . .

Lincoln, New Mexico Territory. August 31, 1873

"We'll rein up shy of town," Nathan said, "since we don't
know what we're buying into. A man on a horse is a prime
target, even in the dark."

It was a sound argument, and Nathan's companions said
nothing. Cotton Blossom had no desire to venture into
what he recognized as a gunfight, and remained with the
horses. Recognizing the need for firepower, the three men
took their Winchesters and set out toward the nearest
building.

"That's the Rio," Vance said quietly. "They likely got
the back door covered by now."

"Then we'll uncover it," Nathan replied. "We must get
McLean's riders out of there. With the outfit split into twos
and threes, they'll be overrun and gunned down to the
last man."

Coming in behind the Rio Saloon, they could see muzzle
flashes as one of the gunmen poured lead in through the
open back door. Before Nathan could make a move, Hugh
fired twice, silencing the gun at the back door.

"Get in there, both of you," said Nathan. "I'll cover you
while you bring out Gus and Will. Move, damn it. Whoev-

r's covering the front knows something's wrong back
ere."

Hugh and Vance were barely through the back door
when Nathan saw a shadow creep slowly toward the rear
of the saloon. Near the wall, beneath the roof overhang,
he dark was most intense. Nathan waited, daring not to
miss, for his shot would reveal his own position. Firing his
left-hand Colt, he fell to his right, as a slug whipped over
his head. He returned fire, aiming for the muzzle flash, and
there was no response. The two riders Hugh and Vance
hustled out of the saloon were still alive, but it appeared
their wounds might limit their participation in the fight.
Hugh spoke quietly.

"Gus an' Will's been bloodied up some, but their vitals
ain't hurt. They're goin' with us an' liberate the rest of
the outfit."

"Two down," Nathan said. "The varmint shootin' from
the front got nosy."

"The rest of the sidewinders has got Joel, Tobe, an'
Quad trapped somewhere," Vance said. "Let's slip in behind and give 'em hell."

With that in mind, the five of them set out toward the
sound of gunfire. Somewhere ahead, a woman screamed,
and the gunfire became more intense. The building under
siege proved to be larger than a saloon.

"God," said Will, "they're holed up in the Rio de Oro
Dance Hall. There's women likely in the line of fire."

"But the varmints we want are outside," Nathan said.
"We'll move in behind them and shoot at their muzzle
flashes. Make every shot count. After the first, you're as
much a target as they are."

They crept toward the dance hall, fanning out, each man
aware they were dangerously outnumbered. The firing from
within the dance hall was all but drowned out by the roar
of the guns of the attackers. Then from the darkness came
a shout, and Nathan believed it was one of the Horrells.

"You McLean cow nurses has got five minutes to come
out. You don't, then we douse the place with coal oil and
burn you out."

To the dismay of Nathan and the McLean riders, the
attackers ceased firing, and there were no muzzle flashes.

CHAPTER 7

"Damn," Vance groaned, "we'll have to wait for them to make the next move, because we don't know where they are."

"It's time for them to learn the rest of the McLean outfit is here," said Nathan. "Get ready to fire."

"No, damn it," Vance argued. "There's likely a dozen of these varmints, and our boys inside won't be no help to us. Hell, we can't surprise 'em if they know we're here."

"If they know we're here," said Nathan angrily, "they'll cut down on us and we'll have some targets. After they've fired the dance hall, what's to stop them from standing us off while the McLean riders inside are burned to cinders? By God, use your head."

"He's talking sense," Gus said. "Get your guns ready. Challenge 'em, Stone."

"You Estrella varmints are surrounded," Nathan shouted. "We're the McLean outfit, and we're ordering you to drop your guns. Make any move to fire the building . . ."

Nathan's plan worked to perfection as Estrella's riders cut loose with their guns. The five McLean riders were belly-down with Winchesters, and while lead roared overhead, they laid down a deadly fusillade, firing at muzzle flashes. The defenders inside the dance hall understood what was happening, and when they began firing, some of the attackers were caught in a crossfire. There were cries of pain and groans of agony that trailed off into silence.

"To the horses," somebody shouted. "Git to the horses an' ride."

The attackers ceased firing and ran for their lives. There was a clatter of hooves as those who were able to reach their horses galloped away.

"You McLean riders," said Nathan, "this is the rest of the outfit. Are you hurt?"

"This is Tobe," a voice responded. "Joel, Quad, an' me is bloodied up some, but we're alive. We're comin' out."

While the trio had arm and leg wounds, they emerged on their feet. A rider came up the street with a lighted lantern, and when he dismounted, Nathan could see a star pinned to his vest. Sheriff Bowie Hatcher had arrived.

"Now," said Hatcher, with all the authority he could muster, "just who the hell kicked off this fracas?"

"Why don't you start an investigation an' figger it out?" Gus suggested.

"By God, I've had a bellyful of you mouthy McLean riders," Hatcher growled. "Come Monday, I'm telegraphin' Santa Fe for a U.S. marshal."

"Hatcher," said Will, "them damn Estrella riders cut down on us without cause. Sandy Bigler is layin' outside the Rio Saloon with a bullet hole in his skull. If you don't saddle up and go after them coyotes for murder, then I reckon Mr. McLean will want to know why. It'll be a good question for him to ask your U.S. marshal when he shows up."

"You expect a lot of one man," Hatcher said bitterly.

"The U.S. marshal won't be but one man," Gus said devilishly.

"Sheriff," said Nathan, "we're taking no responsibility for anything that happened here tonight. We defended ourselves and our outfit, and we'll do it again. Now you gents that's in need of a doctor, let's be finding one. Then we'll ride back to the ranch, because we may be needed there."

"My God, yes," Joel said. "It'd be just like the bastards to try an' burn us out."

"Those of you that needs patchin' up," said Nathan, "have it done. Since the sheriff is providin' a lantern, I aim to see if we salted down any of those coyotes."

"I ain't been hit," Vance said, "and I'm comin' with you. I'd like to see some of them varmints with blood leakin' out."

"No more than me," said Hugh.

"Just a damn minute," Sheriff Hatcher protested, "this is law business."

"So was the gunfight that got one of our boys killed and most of the others shot up," Vance said. "Where the hell was you when we could of used your help?"

Hatcher stalked off with the lantern, saying nothing. Nathan, Vance, and Hugh were on his heels. The sheriff circled the dance hall and found three bodies, all of them

Mejicano. Nathan was disappointed but not surprised that none of the Horrells had been killed. They were the kind to fight when they had the advantage, to run when the odds tilted the other way. Saying nothing to Hatcher, Nathan, Hugh, and Vance joined their comrades at the doctor's office. When the outfit was ready to ride out, Hugh and Vance roped Sandy Bigler across his saddle. The men rode in silence, and long before reaching the McLean ranch, they where challenged.

"McLean riders comin' in," Vance shouted.

Leading his horse, Riley stepped out of the concealing brush. When the outfit reached the house, McLean and Squid stood on the porch with Winchesters.

"How bad?" Colton McLean asked.

"Sandy's dead," said Gus. "Rest of us got shot up some, but we'll heal."

"Bring Sandy into the parlor," McLean said. "Then I want to see all of you in the dining hall. Squid, start up some coffee."

They sat on benches drinking hot coffee and waiting for McLean to speak. Finally he did, and his voice was grim.

"Riley tells me they laid an ambush and gunned down Sandy without cause."

"They done that," Will said. "Gus an' me, we was right behind him when he stepped out the door of the Rio Saloon. Sandy didn't have a chance. There was at least three of 'em cut down on us, 'cause it was the next two shots that nailed me and Gus."

"Stone," said McLean, "when Riley brought me word, I sent you, Vance, and Hugh back to town. Tell me what happened from the time the three of you arrived until the end of it."

Nathan knew McLean was testing him, and he supplied only the facts, without exalting himself. McLean's eyes were not on Nathan, but on the faces of the rest of the cowboys who had been with him. There was still some animosity in the eyes of Hugh and Vance, and McLean sighed with satisfaction. Nathan Stone had taken command. While Estrella's killers had gunned down Sandy Bigler, they had paid with the lives of five of their own, and it was the kind of vengeance Colton McLean understood. He got up and put down his tin coffee cup.

"You all done what you had to, and you done well," said

McLean. "It's Sunday, not more'n three hours from day-light. We'll have breakfast at eight and then we'll lay Andy away."

"By God," Vance said, "you ain't lettin' them bastards get away with this, are you?"

"I can't see they got away with anything," McLean re-lied. "They started a fight and we finished it. We lost one man and they lost five. They're likely bellied-down with their Winchesters waitin' for us, but we're not ridin' into their trap. As it stands, they wronged us and we're guilty of nothing more than defending ourselves. I aim to leave it that way as long as I can."

Reaching the barn, the cowboys unsaddled their horses, and despite the late hour they took the time to rub the animals down. Nothing was said until they reached the bunkhouse, and Vance turned on Nathan.

"You work fast, bucko. You rode in yesterday and al-ready the old man's talking to you and down to the rest of us. Hugh or me could have told him what happened in town."

"I agree," said Nathan mildly, "but he didn't ask you. He asked me, and I told him."

"Damn it, Vance," Hugh said, "back off. He told it straight, givin' us credit as an outfit. You was goin' to stand there and let Estrella's gun hawks burn that dance hall. Now you got a mad on because Stone challenged 'em and forced a shootout."

"So that's how it was," said Tobe. "Me, and Joel and Quad was in there, and we'd of been fried alive. We're obliged, Stone."

"There was no disagreement," Nathan said. "The five of us fired together."

But Vance glared at Nathan, all the more agitated be-cause his hesitation under fire had been questioned. No-body said anything more, but Vance's comrades looked on him with disfavor, and Nathan knew it wasn't over.

"Damn it," Sam Horrell complained, "they ain't comin'."

"Why should they?" Ben observed. "We cut down one of them, they kill five of us, and you expect them to ride into another ambush, all in one night?"

"Ben's right," said Martin. "We're wastin' our time layin' out here in the brush. It'll be daylight in another two hours.

Even them *Mejicanos* was smart enough to give it up an ride back to camp."

Tom Horrell laughed. "I wish we'd of gone with 'em. I' of liked to see old Estrella's face when he learned five o his border hellions was salted down in one fight. He playe up them varmints like they're so tough they wear out thei britches from the inside."

"You're almighty quiet, William," said Ben. "Cat go your tongue?"

"By God," Clint Barkley said, "if I was a Horrell, afte tonight, I'd change my name. I don't like New Mexico, don't like sheep, I don't like Mexes, and I especially don' like Horrells."

"Mount up, William," said Ben. "Time we ride back tc the sheep camp, it'll be first light, and you can listen to old Armijo cuss in Spanish. Then we'll have a big bowl of good old mutton stew for breakfast."

The McLean riders who had been wounded groaned as they tugged on their boots, and there was nothing said as they made their way to the dining hall for breakfast. Squid had the coffee ready and there was the tempting odor of frying ham and baking biscuits. There was a grin or two from the cowboys when Cotton Blossom poked his nose into the dining room from the kitchen, since he had wasted no time making friends with the Mexican cook. Colton McLean came in, looking none the worse for the long night. Squid handed him a tin cup of steaming coffee and the rancher took a seat at one of the tables. He eyed the men as though he knew there had been words among them, but he found himself unable to get to Nathan Stone. Here was a man, he decided, who had played some poker in his time and had been damn good at it. Finally he spoke.

"Those of you who didn't pick up any lead last night are elected to dig a grave for Sandy. Right after breakfast, before it gets too hot. Any of you too stove up to ride?"

Nobody spoke, and McLean continued.

"Comin' out on the short end of that shootout last night, I look for Estrella to try and get even, but not by attacking the herd. We'll graze 'em as close in as we can and avoid losing any more riders in ambush situations because of the herd."

"Hell," said Vance, "they'll scatter the herd from here
o yonder."

"Maybe," McLean said, "but I want every one of you to
eep this in mind. We're dealing with bushwhackers, and
ttacks on the cattle are a means of luring some of you
vithin rifle range. They'll use the cattle to trap you, to keep
ou always on the defensive. Wars are never won that way.
You must choose your own ground. We'll fight, but we'll
do it on our terms, not theirs."

"I like that," Gus said.

"It's the way wars are won," said Nathan. "Keep your
enemy on the defensive."

"That's what we done last night," Will added. "We
orced 'em to fight on our terms."

While Vance said nothing, he clearly didn't like the favorable manner in which Nathan Stone was being accepted,
nor did he like McLean's reluctance to take the fight directly to Armijo Estrella's sheep camp. Nathan Stone didn't
walk on water, and eventually he would draw a bad
hand. . . .

Lincoln, New Mexico Territory. September 20, 1873
Following the gunfight in Lincoln in which Sandy Bigler
had been killed, McLean split the outfit insofar as trips to
town were concerned. Four of the riders were allowed to
go on Saturday night, while the remaining five rode in on
Sunday night. No longer did they enter or leave saloons by
the front door, and they stayed together in twos or threes,
when entering or leaving any establishment. Nathan, Gus,
Will, and Quad were in town, and after supper, they headed
for the Rio Saloon. As had become their custom, they entered through the back door, Nathan in the lead. Suddenly
he froze, for Ben and Martin Horrell stood at the bar. The
Horrells turned, their hands hovering over the butts of their
Colts, and there was no mistaking the recognition in their
eyes.

"One move out of either of you," said Nathan, "and
you're dead."

"So you're the bullypuss that's sidin' McLean's cow
nurses," Ben said.

"I'm tempted to call you Horrells skunk-striped, back-
shootin' sheepmen," said Nathan, "but that's too good for

you. An egg-sucking dog would shy away from you low
down varmints."

"You ain't proddin' us into drawin' agin you, Stone,"
Martin Horrell said. "We heard you're a man-killer. We'
choose our time."

"I'll be careful not to turn my back on you," said Nathan

The Horrells sidled toward the door, careful to keep thei
hands clear of their guns. When they had gone, Nathan'
companions looked at him with new respect.

"I reckon you know them varmints from somewhere,"
Quad said.

"Texas," said Nathan. "An outlaw relation of theirs
back-shot a good friend of mine."

"I'd not be surprised if that outlaw relation follered them
here," Gus observed wryly.

"I'm hoping he has," said Nathan, "but he's not a Horrell. His handle's Clint Barkley or Bill Bowen. But I'll
know the no-account coyote when I see him."

"All these sidewinders goes by the name of Horrell,"
Will said. "There's the two that just slunk out of here—
Ben and Martin—and the others is Samuel, Thomas, and
William."

"William? I never heard of him," said Nathan. "He could
be Barkley."

"They look related," Gus said. "Like they was all cut
out of the same cloth."

Nathan said no more. In a way, he was glad the Horrells
hadn't had the sand to draw, for McLean had cautioned
them against further gunplay in town. Nathan well understood the rancher's reasoning. With just half the outfit in
town, they were subject to attack by the entire bunch of
Estrella riders, with no hope of assistance from Sheriff
Bowie Hatcher. That, and McLean still sought to shift the
blame for the continued violence on the troublesome Spaniard, Armijo Estrella. Nathan and his companions returned
to the ranch without any shooting, but on Sunday night, all
hell busted loose, and it started when Vance failed to obey
Colton McLean's orders.

Hugh, Vance, Riley, Joel, and Tobe headed for town.
It was Sunday afternoon and the sky was awash with big
gray thunderheads.

"Come on," Vance said, kicking his horse into a fast gallop. "Let's get there ahead of the rain."

Reining up in front of the cafe, they dismounted and barely reached the porch before the storm broke. Ordering supper, they weren't quite finished when the Horrells—Martin, Benjamin, Samuel, and Thomas—walked in and took a table.

"Well, by God," Vance said loudly, "there's enough sheep stink in here to gag a flock of buzzards."

"Vance," said Hugh quietly, "shut up."

"You ain't my daddy," Vance growled. "There's four of us and four of them. Ain't you man enough to shear at least one of the woolly varmints?"

The Horrells seemed not to hear, and to the relief of Vance's companions, they were able to leave the cafe without a fight.

"Damn you, Vance," said Tobe, "the old man told us not to start anything. Shoot off your mouth one more time, and I'm ridin' back to the ranch."

"I'll go with you," Riley said.

"So will I," said Joel. "It's like McLean said, we don't know that the whole damn lot of Estrella's gun-throwers ain't holed up here somewhere."

"Hell," Vance said, "you saw what's here."

"We saw what was in the cafe," said Riley. "Even a gun-slick *Mejicano's* got pride."

Lincoln being a small town, there was little to do when a man grew tired of the four or five saloons. The Rainbow Dance Hall offered some variety, for there were women. The place also had a bar and several billiard tables, and the McLean cowboys were there when the Horrells arrived.

"Damn," Vance said, "them sheep-stink Horrells is here."

There was uneasy laughter that died quickly, and Vance's companions silenced him with murderous looks. The Horrells made their way to the bar, apparently ignoring the five McLean riders. Joel and Tobe, with intentions of keeping Vance away from the bar, led the way to a billiard table that wasn't in use. Riley racked the balls, and that seemed to have defused what might have become an explosive situation, but it wasn't over. The very first time Vance leaned across the billiard table for a long shot, a hard-flung empty bottle struck him in the back of the head. After that, it was

Katy-bar-the-door, as the remaining McLean riders entered the fray. Billiard balls bounced off heads, shattered lamp globes, and toppled pyramids of bottled whiskey behind the bar. The McLean riders, swinging billiard cues, were advancing to meet the Horrells when the roar of a shotgun stopped every man in his tracks.

"The next load of buckshot goes right in amongst you varmints," shouted the little man standing on the bar. "You ain't bustin' up my place. I don't care a damn if you kill one another, but do it outside. Now git!"

Being nearest the door, the Horrells left first. The McLean riders, as had become their habit, left by the back door. Hugh stepped out first, and a shot from the corner of the building ripped into his thigh.

"Them damn Horrells!" Vance shouted. Drawing his Colt, he lit out in a run toward the position from which the shot had come. But the Horrells were not the problem. From across the street, four Winchesters cut loose, and Vance died on his feet. Hugh, Riley, Joel, and Tobe scrambled back into the dance hall, slamming the door shut behind them. The deadly fire continued, lead tearing into the door and log walls.

"Them damn Horrells set us up," Hugh cried.

"And Vance walked right into it," said Riley. "The varmints can keep us hunkerin' in here the rest of the night."

"That's what you think," the barkeep said, shotgun under his arm. "I want the lot of you out of here, and by God, don't come back."

"Mister," Tobe said, "I'd rather face one shotgun in here than four Winchesters out there. We're stayin' right here until it's safe to leave."

The remaining dance hall patrons had gathered around, and by the time Sheriff Bowie Hatcher arrived, he had to elbow his way through.

"Can't you damn fools spend one night in town without tryin' to kill one another?"

"It wasn't us that done the killin', Sheriff," Riley said. "Vance is lyin' outside, gunned down in another ambush by them damn sheepmen. What are you aimin' to do about it?"

"I've telegraphed Santa Fe for a U.S. marshal," said Hatcher. "Hell, I ain't standin' in the middle with killers on both sides."

"You're a county sheriff," Joel said, "and this is Lincoln County."

"A county sheriff ain't responsible for a range war, with killers bein' brought in from everywhere," said Hatcher.

"Sheriff," said the barkeep, "I want this bunch out of here."

"Bushwhackers don't stick around after the first volley," Hatcher said. "I'll side you until you get your horses and load up the dead man."

Taking only enough time for the doctor to see to Hugh's wound, the four McLean riders left town. There was no moon and the rain had ceased, leaving only a cool breeze from the northwest. Nobody spoke, for there was nothing to say. It was still early enough to arouse McLean's suspicions, so when they rode in, he would know something was bad wrong. They had to ride past the ranch house to reach the bunkhouse, so none of them were surprised to find McLean waiting on the porch. Even in the dim starlight, the grim burden roped across a saddle told its own story. The four riders reined up.

"Talk," McLean said.

They did, taking turns, telling it true. McLean sighed.

"Damn it," said the rancher, "I've bent just about as far as I aim to. Tote Vance into the parlor. We'll bury him, come first light, and after breakfast we'll talk."

There was more talking to be done when the four riders reached the bunkhouse. Gus, Will, Quad, and Nathan listened in silence to a repeat of what McLean had just heard.

"Vance disobeyed the old man's orders," Gus said, "and I reckon he asked for what he got, but we can't let this go. If McLean don't fight back, I'll take my roll and drift."

"I kinda feel the same way," said Riley, "but how do we fight back? We take to bushwhacking on our own, we're no better than the yellow-bellied coyotes that's squattin' over yonder in Estrella's sheep camp."

"This is one of them porcupine problems," Hugh said. "You just don't know where to take hold of the joker. What do you think, Stone?"

"I think I'll keep my opinions private until McLean has his say," said Nathan, "but I'm not of a mind to take this without some retaliation."

It was enough to draw them together, to meet McLean's argument with one of their own, if McLean's proved less than satisfactory.

*   *   *

Hugh and Nathan dug the grave before sunup, and the sad task of laying Vance to rest was put behind them. McLean was there in time to read the Word, and when the grave had been filled, they all headed for the dining room and breakfast. McLean avoided what was on all their minds until they had eaten. When they were down to final cups of coffee, he spoke.

"I'm not one to speak ill of the dead, and we don't know that what happened last night wouldn't have happened anyway, so blaming it on Vance gets us nowhere. I believe the bushwhackers would have cut down on you anyway, when you left the dance hall. The brawl involving the Horrells just brought it on a mite quicker."

"That's how I see it," Riley said. "The *Mejicanos* took their revenge."

"Like I told you before," said McLean, "you can't win by allowing the other side to choose the time and place. I realize a man needs an occasional night in town, but not at the risk of his life. Until this thing with Estrella has been resolved, none of us will ride into Lincoln except in daylight, and then only for necessary supplies."

"I see the need for it," Gus said, "but I don't like it. Hell, if we pull in our horns and don't do nothin', that puts *us* on the defensive."

"It appears to," said McLean, "but we're *still* forcing them to come to us."

"Come the dark of the moon," Hugh said, "they can sneak in and burn us out. Or in their case, bushwhacking bein' more their style, they can hole up within rifle range and pick us off one at a time."

"The most danger will be at night," said Nathan, "but if you're interested, I may have a solution to that."

"Speak up, man," McLean said.

"One man, me and my dog," said Nathan, "dusk till dawn. We'll work far enough out so that a rider can warn the rest of you we're about to have visitors. That'll give you time to arrange a proper welcome."

"By God," McLean said, "that reminds me of Mosby's Rangers. It's a powerful plan, Stone, but it'll be a burden on you, with never a night to rest."

"The rest of us could spell you," Gus said, "each man taking a different night."

"Thanks," said Nathan, "but you couldn't count on Cotton Blossom without me. You'll still be doing your share, because I'll need a different rider with me every night. Once we know they're coming, one of you can hightail it back here to set up a reception. Me and Cotton Blossom will be right behind them. When you gents open up, I'll show them what a real, honest-to-God crossfire is like. We'll cure that bunch from sucking eggs, if it kills them."

It was frontier retribution, frontier justice, and Nathan was rewarded with applause and laughter. Tobe rode with Nathan the first night, and they covered a continuous stretch of five miles across a plateau from which any attack must surely come.

"I ain't pokin' holes in your plan," Tobe said, "but suppose the varmints takes the long way around and comes at the ranch from the west?"

"We can't be sure they won't," said Nathan, "but the odds are against it. To begin with, they'd have to ride twice as far, and once in position, they'd have to leave the horses a good two miles out. McLean's horse barn is to the west of the house, and almost every night the wind's out of the northwest. Sound carries at night."

"You're a thinking man, Stone," Tobe said. "You and McLean are a lot alike. But he only knows what he *should* do, while you have the talent for doing it."

The McLean riders kept to the ranch, and for six weeks, nothing happened. When the attack came, it was on Saturday night, the first day of November. Gus and Nathan were resting their horses when there was a rustling of leaves. But for that, Cotton Blossom was as silent as a shadow.

"They're coming," said Nathan. "Lead your horse aways. Have the rest of the outfit fan out, holding their fire till I open the ball. Let the varmints think I'm alone, and when they cut down on me, the rest of you fire at their muzzle flashes. Make every shot count and don't give them a chance to return fire."

Leading his horse, Tobe vanished into the shadows. Nathan moved to the south. When the attackers had passed his position, he would fall back until he was behind them. Cotton Blossom growled low in his throat, and Nathan paused, listening. Finally he sighed with relief. They were afoot and he needn't worry about his horse giving him away. Silently he removed his Winchester from the boot and crept back the way he had come. Satisfied they were now ahead of him, he moved forward toward the clearing they would have to cross. He bellied down, and when he cocked the Winchester, it seemed loud in the stillness of the night. . . .

CHAPTER 8

As the men moved into the clearing, Nathan counted twelve. He disliked shooting from behind, but these killers were about to attack what they believed were unsuspecting cowboys. Nathan cut loose, firing as rapidly as he could jack shells into the Winchester's firing chamber. Two of the invaders took slugs while the others bellied-down and began returning Nathan's fire. But he had rolled away from his original position and ceased firing, allowing them no muzzle flashes as targets. Their firing had the opposite effect, as the McLean cowboys began throwing lead at the muzzle flashes, and the Estrella riders had but one alternative. They gave up the fight, scampering to right and left, seeking to escape with their lives. Nathan had reloaded and had resumed firing, but the attackers were gone.

"Come on in," McLean shouted.

Nathan met the rest of the outfit in the clearing. Three of the attackers were dead, and again, the Horrells had escaped.

"Them that got away didn't get off easy," said Riley. "We got some lead in the sidewinders."

"Despite all they've done," McLean said, "we still haven't made an illegal move against them. They've always come after us, and we've defended ourselves."

"That's good, up to a point," said Joel, "but this could go on forever. Nobody wins."

"I don't think so," McLean replied. "This has to be getting on their nerves, or they wouldn't keep coming after us. I look for Estrella to hire more men and then try to wipe us out, once and for all."

"The tactic we used this time may not work again," said

Nathan. "By now they know we've had a roving sentry, that we were expecting them. Next time, they may bring enough men to come after us from more than one direction."

"That means more sentries," Gus said, "and there's just eight of us."

"Not necessarily," said Nathan. "Instead of watching our camp, suppose we stake out a pair of riders and watch theirs?"

"When they ride out," Will said, "our riders light a shuck back here, and we'll all be ready to greet them."

"That's it," said Nathan, "except our men can't afford to get too far ahead of them. We need to know if they're comin' in from one direction or if they split up."

"I like the sound of it," McLean said, "because it allows us to remain on the offensive without going outside the law. I'm considering hiring more men, if I can find them."

"If we play our cards right," said Nathan, "we can make do with what we have. It's not how many troops you have, but how you use them."

Lincoln, New Mexico Territory. December 1, 1873
Cotton Blossom barked once, and Nathan sat up in his bunk. There was the distant clatter of hooves, two horses coming hard. The rest of the McLean riders were awake, for it meant just one thing.

"That's Riley and Tobe," Gus said.

The two riders slowed when they approached the ranch house, and one of them hailed McLean. Then they came on toward the bunkhouse at a fast gallop.

"The varmints are comin'," said Tobe, as he and Riley left their saddles. "Fourteen men, and they're splittin' up, some comin' at us from the east, the others from the west."

"We can't set up a crossfire this time," Nathan said. "That's spreadin' us too thin."

"We'd best wait on McLean," Riley said. "He's the boss."

Colton McLean wasted no time getting there, arriving with a Winchester under his arm. With him was Squid, the Mexican cook, who also carried a Winchester. Quickly, Tobe explained the situation.

"About what I expected," said McLean. "There are ten of us. I'll take Squid, Riley, Joel, and Tobe, and we'll meet that bunch comin' in from the east. Stone, take Hugh, Guss,

Will, and Quad, and take the varmints coming from the west. You'll only get one chance to even the odds, so make that first volley count."

They took their positions afoot, careful to utilize what cover there was, while allowing their adversaries little or none. The only fault Nathan found with McLean's plan—and it couldn't be helped—was that the defenders who fired first would alert the other group of attackers that the McLean riders were ready and willing to fight. But the two groups of defenders began firing almost simultaneously, and the battle lasted only a matter of a few seconds. After the first volley, both the attackers and the attacked were firing at muzzle flashes, with McLean's riders having the edge. After the final shots were fired, Nathan and his men waited awhile before venturing from cover. There were two dead men, one of them Benjamin Horrell.

"The Horrells will give us hell now," Nathan predicted.

The divided McLean outfit came together at the bunkhouse. McLean and his men had accounted for one of the attackers, a *Mejicano*. None of the McLean riders had been hit.

"If nobody objects," said Nathan, "for the next few days, I'd like to keep watch on the Estrella camp. It's time I had a look at the rest of those Horrells in daylight."

"No objection from me," McLean said. "I have a telescope you're welcome to use."

Bellied-down on a rise, using McLean's telescope, Nathan scanned the Estrella camp, as he sought to identify the remaining Horrells. It puzzled him that he had never seen the elusive fifth Horrell, William. While he detested the Horrells, he had no real quarrel with them, except for their defense of Clint Barkley. This running fight between McLean and Estrella might drag on for years, and Nathan was weary of it. If he rooted the Horrells out and found no sign of Barkley, he would ride on, but he wouldn't forget. Somewhere, somehow, he would find the man, and Clint Barkley would pay. On the fourth day of his vigilance, Nathan's patience was rewarded. The three remaining Horrells entered the barn, followed by a fourth man whose back was to Nathan. When the four emerged they were mounted, and Nathan almost dropped the telescope. The fourth man was Clint Barkley!

"Cotton Blossom," said Nathan, "we're about to begin a long overdue skunk hunt."

Nathan kicked his horse into a fast gallop. Suspecting the Horrells were heading for town, he paced himself so that he might fall in behind and follow them. As long as Barkley was mounted, there was a chance the Horrells could lay down enough fire for the outlaw to run for it. Nathan intended to wait until Barkley was afoot to force a showdown and that time was fast approaching. The four reined up before the Apache Saloon while Nathan rode around behind the building. Dismounting, leaving Cotton Blossom with the grulla, he crept between the Apache and the building alongside it. The Horrells and Barkley already had entered the saloon, but they wouldn't be going far without their horses.

"Barkley, this is Nathan Stone. You bushwhacked a friend of mine in Texas. You have until the count of five to come out and stand on your hind legs like a man."

But Nathan was denied the showdown for which he had waited so long. From across the street came the cold voice of the law.

"Stone, there'll be no more shooting in this town. I am U.S. Marshal Evan Taylor from Santa Fe. You men who just entered the saloon are under arrest."

Careful to keep his hands away from his Colts, Nathan turned to face the lawman and found himself facing six of them. Behind Marshal Taylor stood five Mexicans, each armed with a Winchester.

"Marshal," said Nathan, "one of the varmints in that saloon is Clint Barkley. He killed a Texas Ranger friend of mine."

"I'll have to see proof of that," Taylor replied. "Now mount up and ride back to the McLean spread. Tell McLean I want no more shooting. Based on what Sheriff Hatcher has told me, the Estrella outfit has instigated all the violence, and charges will be filed."

Nathan backed away, but didn't immediately return to his horse. He waited until the Horrells and Clint Barkley came out of the saloon and were taken to jail. Then he mounted the grulla and rode away.

"It's good news," McLean said, "if Marshal Evan Taylor can make it stick. Leave this Armijo Estrella loose, and he'll have hired a whole new bunch of killers before the marshal gets back to Santa Fe."

"I got the impression he would be riding out after Estrella," said Nathan. "Now that I know one of the Horrells is Clint Barkley, I aim to gut-shoot the sidewinder, if I have to bust him out of jail to do it. For that reason, Mr. McLean, I'll be sayin' adios to you and your boys. From what Marshal Taylor said, Sheriff Hatcher is laying all the blame for the shooting and killing on Estrella and his guntoters. So when I do whatever I have to do, I won't be riding for you. *Bueno suerte.*"

"Hate to lose you, Stone," McLean replied. "Any time you're in these parts, ride in for a howdy and some grub."

All the riders shook Nathan's hand and seemed genuinely sorry to see him go, and he was reluctant to leave. But he thought of the Horrells and Barkley in the Lincoln jail, and that was incentive enough. Reaching town, however, Nathan found everything had changed. U.S. Marshal Taylor had taken a posse and had ridden to the Estrella camp, but as soon as he was gone, the Horrells and Barkley had managed to break jail. Nathan found Sheriff Bowie Hatcher at the doctor's office, barely conscious. In a vile mood, Hatcher didn't want to talk, but Nathan insisted.

"Damn it," Hatcher said, "one of 'em pretended to be sick, and I got too close. They snatched my Colt and near busted my skull with the muzzle of it."

Hatcher would say nothing more, and Nathan left the jail. He rode on to the livery and inquired about the horses of the fugitives.

"They stuck a pistol in my face and took their horses," the hostler said. "They rode out toward the east."

Having broken jail, the Horrells and Clint Barkley rode out as though returning to the Armijo Estrella sheep camp. But as soon as they were out of sight of town, Barkley reined up. Facing the surprised Horrells, he spoke.

"This is as far as I go. You damn Horrells are a jinx."

"Merritt and his missus ain't gonna like this," said Martin. "What you want us to tell them?"

"Tell them to go to hell," Barkley said. He rode south, toward El Paso and the Mexican border.*

*In January 1874, the Horrells returned to Texas, resuming the Horrell-Higgins feud.

*   *   *

When Nathan reached the place where Barkley and the Horrells had parted company, he paused for only a moment before following the single set of tracks that led south.

"I may be wrong, Cotton Blossom," he said, "but I'd bet my saddle Clint Barkley and the Horrells have split the blanket. It's about time the chicken-livered varmint quit hiding behind the Horrells."

Nathan rode carefully because Barkley would expect pursuit. Knowing they were stalking a man, Cotton Blossom loped ahead, wary of danger. Nathan estimated Barkley had not more than a three-hour start, which meant he wouldn't catch up with the outlaw before dark. To ride at a fast gallop was out of the question, for at any time, Barkley might double back and attempt an ambush. Cotton Blossom had been down enough trails to know that a rider doubling back meant trouble for Nathan Stone. If Barkley left the trail, mounted or afoot, Cotton Blossom would turn back to meet Nathan. With Cotton Blossom scouting ahead, Nathan had only to stay out of rifle range. An hour before sundown, Nathan reined up beside a spring. He unsaddled the horses and quickly prepared supper for himself and Cotton Blossom. Dousing the fire, he moved well away from the spring. Near where the horses were cropping grass, he stretched out, his head on his saddle.

"Cotton Blossom," Nathan said, "I'm counting on you. He may come after us."

Barkley, Nathan decided, would ride all night, attempting to outdistance pursuit, or he would resort to bushwhacking. Being hunted was hell on a man's nerves, as Nathan could testify, and he fully expected Barkley to come hunting him in the darkness. He wouldn't be hard to find, for in the still of the night, keen ears could hear the horses cropping grass. While Nathan knew he could depend on a warning from Cotton Blossom, he found himself unable to sleep. For the sake of comfort he had removed his gun belt, but in his hand he held one of the deadly Colts Captain Sage Jennings had given him. Nathan dozed, and when he suddenly awoke, he wasn't quite sure what had disturbed him. Then he knew. In the starlight, the horses stood with heads raised, having ceased their rhythmic cropping of grass. Cotton Blossom growled low, slipping silently into the shadows. Nathan lay still, hardly daring to breathe, aware that any movement might draw fire. The sound, when it came, only the keenest of ears could have heard, for it was the snick of a hammer being eared back. Nathan rolled away from his saddle barely seconds before slugs tore into the ground where he had been lying. He returned fire, shooting at muzzle flashes, but a frantic sound of running feet told him he had missed. Seizing his gun belt, he sprang to his feet and went after the bushwhacker. Then there was only silence, and having nothing to guide him, Nathan took refuge behind the trunk of a huge pine. It was a risky situation. While he could goad Barkley into shooting and revealing his position, he didn't know where the gunman was. But again Cotton Blossom served him well. There was growling, a scuffle and cursing, but before Nathan could reach the scene, there was a yip of pain from Cotton Blossom and blazing gunfire from the darkness. A slug whipped past Nathan's ear while a second one tore into his left thigh. Firing at the muzzle flash, he emptied one Colt with a drum roll of sound. He had the second Colt ready, but there was no need for it. There was a soft sound somewhere ahead of him, but a low whine identified Cotton Blossom. He waited until Cotton Blossom reached him, and placing his hand on the dog's head, he felt a gash that still oozed blood. Cotton Blossom had been struck with the muzzle of a Colt or the butt of a rifle. Nathan's own wound was bleeding as he could feel the blood running into his boot. He had waited long enough, and he limped toward the shadow that was the body of Clint Barkley. He lighted a match and found that the outlaw had been shot twice.

"Captain Sage Jennings," said Nathan, a lump in his throat, "this yellow-bellied, backshootin' coyote could die a hundred times and it wouldn't even the score. But it's all I can do, *muy bueno companero.*"

Returning to the spring, Nathan kindled a small fire and put on water to boil. He must attend to his own wound and to Cotton Blossom's. Taking strips of clean muslin from his pack, he tied a strip above his wound, seeking to stop the bleeding. When the water had begun to boil, he soaked some of the muslin and washed the dried blood from Cotton Blossom's head wound. He then soaked clean cloth in disinfectant and placed it over the wound.

"Lie down and keep that in place," he said, "so the medicine can do its work."

Nathan then removed his trousers and cleansed his own wound. The lead had missed the bone, but there was a ragged, bloody exit wound that continued bleeding, despite all his efforts. Finally he took mud from the spring, and after applying a heavy coat to the bleeding wound, wrapped it tight with muslin.

"We'll ride out at first light, Cotton Blossom. I reckon we're still a long way from El Paso, and I'm needin' a doctor."

When Nathan awoke at first light, he knew he had made a mistake. He should have ridden all night, for his left leg was stiff, swollen, and so painful he could barely stand. He boiled water, washed off the mud, and applied disinfectant. Quickly he prepared breakfast for himself and Cotton Blossom, finding that the dog's wound probably wasn't as serious as he had at first thought. His own wound, however, was a different story, and he could almost feel the fever engulfing him. He removed from his pack a quart bottle almost full of whiskey, and hating the stuff, downed as much of it as he could stand. The rest went into his saddlebag. With difficulty he loaded the packhorse and saddled the grulla. Unable to put all his weight on his left leg, he mounted awkwardly from the offside. The horse watched him curiously, wondering what had come over him.

Nathan rode south, and with the sun beating down, it seemed unseasonably hot. But it was the fever, and although Nathan had consumed most of the whiskey, it seemed only to have made him drunk. Near sundown, reaching a fast-running creek, Nathan tried to dismount. His wounded leg wouldn't support his weight, and having drunk most of a quart of whiskey, Nathan fell. His head struck a rock, and with a groan he relaxed. The sun dipped below the horizon and twilight came. The horses cropped grass while an anxious Cotton Blossom waited, but as the first stars winked silver from a deep purple plateau, Nathan Stone lay unmoving. . . .

Far into the night Nathan awoke, his teeth chattering. His head throbbed like the beating of a drum, almost in time with the ache of the wound in his swollen thigh. There was no more whiskey, and hungover as he was, Nathan never wanted another drop of the stuff. He crawled to his horse and seizing a stirrup leather, managed to get to his feet. He again had to mount from the offside, failing three times before he was finally in the saddle. His head reeling, he tottered from side to side, knowing he must ride on. Knowing that if he again fell from the saddle he might die where he lay. He looped the lead rope of the packhorse around his saddle horn and headed the grulla south. The animal chose its own gait, pausing to graze along the way. Nathan slumped in the saddle, unknowing, uncaring. When he again lifted his head, the last star had winked out and the eastern horizon swiftly was changing from gray to dusty rose. Somewhere ahead a horse nickered and Nathan's grulla answered. The distant horse nickered again. Weary, thirsty, the grulla trotted ahead.

"I'll milk the cows, Ma," said fifteen-year-old Ellie Wells, "but it's Jamie's job to feed the horses. I whacked him on the head but he wouldn't get up, and he cussed at me."

"I'll tend to him," Myra Wells said wearily. Jamie was thirteen and inclined to laziness when Jubal Wells was away, but it was the only peace Myra knew, for Jubal was forever swearing at the boy. Except for the guzzling of rotgut whiskey, she reflected, Jamie was already acquiring his father's bad habits. She was about to go rip the covers off Jamie when Ellie came running to the house.

"Ma," Ellie cried, "there's two horses back of the barn. One's carrying a pack and a man's riding the other. He's all slumped over like he's asleep or sick. There's a dog with him and he growled at me."

"Stay here," said Myra, "while I wake Jamie. Turn the ham when it's ready and break half a dozen eggs into that bowl."

She took a tin cup, and dipping it into a wooden bucket of cold water, prepared to do exactly what she had been threatening to do. The door to Jamie's room consisted of only a feed sack curtain, and she peeked in, not wishing to embarrass him if he was out of bed and getting dressed. But he was snoring, the blankets over his head. With a sigh, Myra took hold of the blankets and ripped them off. Like Jubal, Jamie wore no nightshirt and took the cupful of cold water on his bare hide.

"Damn it all to hell," he exploded, leaping out of bed. Myra seized him with her left hand and with her right, laid her open palm on his bare behind with a force that sounded like a pistol shot.

"Ow," he bawled. "Damn it, Ma . . ."

Myra swatted him again, but he barely felt it, for an even greater indignity had fallen on him. His sister Ellie was peeking around the curtain, enjoying his predicament.

"Ma," he cried in anguish, "I . . . I'm . . . get her out of here."

"I told you to tend the ham," said Myra.

"The ham's done," Ellie replied, "and I took it off the stove." She smiled at Jamie and stayed where she was.

"We'll leave you alone," said Myra, "if you think you can get dressed quickly. There's a stranger at the barn, perhaps sick or hurt. We may need your help."

"I'll hurry," he said miserably, hunching over in an attempt to cover his privates.

"Shame on you," said Myra, when she and Ellie had returned to the kitchen, but there was no rebuke in her voice.

Ellie laughed. "I reckon he won't take a chance on that happening again," she said.

Jamie emerged in overalls, flannel shirt, and brogan shoes. His eyes were on the floor, his face was red, and despite herself, Ellie laughed. Jamie swallowed a mouthful of swear words, bit his tongue, and said nothing. The three of them headed for the barn. The two horses stood with their heads down, while Nathan Stone slumped over the saddle horn.

"He's been hurt," said Myra, her eyes on Nathan's bandaged left thigh. "Ellie, loose his feet from the stirrups. Jamie, you help me get him off the horse."

Once the girl had freed Nathan's left boot, he would have fallen off the offside had not Myra and Jamie caught him.

"We must get him to the house," Myra said. "Jamie, you take his feet."

"Pa's goin' to raise hell," said Jamie.

"He's been hurt," Myra said. "Helping him is the Christian thing to do."

"There's nothing Christian about Pa," said Ellie, "or that no-account Ike Puckett and Levi Odell that he rides with."

Myra Wells said nothing, for it was the truth. Three years before, her husband had been killed by Indians. Left with two children, she didn't hesitate when ex-buffalo hunter

Jubal Wells had asked her to be his woman. Wells had moved them to a godforsaken hard-scrabble spread in southern New Mexico, fifty miles north of El Paso. Immediately, Wells had become partners with Ike Puckett and Levi Odell in the selling and trading of horses. Occasionally, the trio drove horses to the Wells place, where they would remain for a few days before being driven away and sold. The last bunch had been gone only four days when a sheriff's posse rode in, seeking stolen horses. Since then, Jubal Wells and his companions had brought no more horses to the Wells corral, and that had pretty well told Myra where they were getting the horses.

"He's awful heavy, Ma," Jamie panted. "Let's put him down and rest a minute."

They lowered Nathan to the ground, and Cotton Blossom crept as close as he dared. After a brief rest, Myra and Jamie took up their burden and continued on to the house.

"We'll put him on my bed," said Myra.

"It's near time Pa was gettin' back," Jamie said.

"I'm aware of that," said Myra shortly. It wouldn't matter where they lay the wounded man, she thought. Jubal Wells wouldn't even want him in the house.

"Jamie," Myra said, when they had Nathan stretched out on the bed, "those horses must be exhausted. Unsaddle them, rub them down, and water them. Then stall them with our horses in the barn. Ellie, I'll need you to help me. Stir up the fire in the stove and put on a kettle of water."

Myra started to unbuckle Nathan's gun belt, only to have him seize both her hands. She found herself looking into cold blue eyes that sent chills up her spine. She spoke just as calmly as she could.

"I'm going to see to your wound, and the gun belt must be removed. I'll hang it on the bedpost where you can reach it."

She thought the hard blue eyes softened just a little. They closed again and he let go of her wrists. She removed the gun belt, fastened the buckle, and looped it over the bedpost. She then loosened his belt and unbuttoned his trousers.

"You're taking them off?" Ellie asked.

"I am," said Myra. "I'll manage. You don't have to watch."

"I'll help," Ellie said. "I'll take off his boots."

Nathan offered no objection, and since he was a dead weight, he seemed to have again lapsed into unconsciousness. When they had wrestled him out of the trousers, Myra Wells was shocked at the condition of his wound.

"Lord, Ma," said Ellie, "it looks awful."

"Awful enough that he could lose that leg, if not his life," Myra said. "I only hope Jubal hasn't drunk up all the whiskey on the place."

"There's most of a jug," said Ellie. "Last time he passed out, I hid it. When he come to his senses, he thought he'd drunk it all."

"Get it," Myra said. "This man may need it all."

Myra bathed Nathan's wound with hot water. When Ellie brought the jug of whiskey, Myra soaked two thick cloth pads with it. One of the pads she placed over the wound where the slug had gone in, and the other over the ugly exit wound. These she bound in place, and then soaked them with more of the whiskey. Ellie had brought a tin cup from the kitchen, and filling it almost full, Myra patiently got Nathan to drink it a little at a time. Even in his condition, Nathan fought the vile brew.

"Either he ain't a drinking man, or he's used to better whiskey," said Jamie from the curtained doorway. "The dog looked hungry, so I fed him the ham. It was cold, anyway."

Myra Wells continued forcing the whiskey down Nathan, and for all that day and far into the night, the fever wouldn't let him go. His fight had become theirs, and none of them slept. Finally, two or three hours shy of first light on the second day, Nathan began to sweat. Ellie and Jamie gave up and slept, while Myra remained beside Nathan. She dozed and when a slight sound awakened her, the first gray light of dawn crept through the window. She rubbed the sleep from her eyes and then she laughed, for Cotton Blossom peeked around the curtain, only his head visible.

"You can come in," she said, as kindly as she could.

Cotton Blossom took a wary step or two, pushing the curtain aside. He sat down near the foot of the bed, looking first at Nathan and then back to Myra.

"You're a faithful one," said Myra. "Make yourself at home."

"Cotton Blossom," Nathan said weakly.

"He's been concerned about you," said Myra, "and well he should have been. I've been pouring whiskey down you since early yesterday morning."

"I'm obliged, ma'am," Nathan said. "Where am I?"

"In my damn bed," said an angry voice from the doorway. "By God, somebody's got some talkin' to do."

Jubal Wells had come home.

CHAPTER 9

Cotton Blossom was the first to react to Jubal's hostility. He turned and was about to do some real damage if Nathan hadn't spoken to him. The dog retreated until he stood beside the bed.

"Sorry," Nathan said. "He didn't like the sound of your voice."

"And I don't like some damn drifter and his fool dog squattin' in my house, with my woman, when I ain't here."

"Jubal," said Myra quietly, "he's been hurt and would have died without attention."

"Woman," Jubal growled, "there's some settlin' to be done, but for now, there's a use for you. Ike and Levi are here, and we had no grub for two days. Git in the kitchen."

He turned away, and Myra sat with her face in her hands.

"I'm sorry to be the cause of trouble, ma'am," said Nathan. "You go ahead and do what you have to do. I'll get up and get out of here."

"You'll stay where you are until you're able to be up and about," Myra replied. "I've done no wrong."

Myra left him there, and he could hear her in the kitchen. Soon there was the aroma of frying ham, and Nathan felt the pangs of hunger gnawing at him. For more than two days there had been nothing in his belly but bad whiskey. He wondered where Jubal had gone, guessing that he and his friends were unsaddling their horses. This woman who had rescued him had courage, and she proved it by bringing him a tin cup of hot coffee and a platter of fried ham and eggs. She had brought a bowl with an assortment of ham scraps for Cotton Blossom.

"You need food," she said.

"I do," Nathan agreed, "but this is a bad time for you, Mrs. . . ."

"Wells," she finished. "Myra Wells."

"I'm Nathan Stone. Until I'm able to ride, I'll stay in the barn. I won't go on taking your and your husband's bed."

"He's not my husband," she replied, "and I'm through sharing this bed or any other with him. He took us in, me and my two children, when we were destitute."

"You have no family, then?"

"My parents live in Ohio," she said, "and I can't go back. I ran away when I was just fourteen, married my husband, and we came west."

"Ma," said a voice from the kitchen, "I'm fixing breakfast for Jamie and me before they come to the house."

"Please do," Myra replied. "That," she said, speaking to Nathan, "is Ellie. She's barely fifteen, and Jamie's thirteen."

"It's none of my business," said Nathan, "but are you ranching or farming?"

"Neither," Myra said. "Jubal, along with Ike Puckett and Levi Odell, claim to be buying and selling horses, I believe they're stealing and selling horses."

"That's a serious charge," said Nathan. "Folks have died for less."

Before she could respond, Jamie and Ellie came in from the kitchen. Now that Nathan was conscious, they were shy.

"Jamie, Ellie," Myra said, "this is Mr. Stone."

"My pleasure, Jamie and Ellie. My friends call me Nathan. This is Cotton Blossom."

"That's a funny name for a dog," said Ellie.

"I inherited him," Nathan said, "and by then he was used to it."

"I have work to do in the kitchen," said Myra.

"Ma," said Ellie, "do you want me to help?"

"No," Myra replied. "I want you and Jamie to stay here and talk to Mr. Stone until Jubal and his friends have had breakfast."

* * *

Jubal Wells had his suspicions about the man in the house, and when he reached the barn, had a serious conversation with Ira Puckett and Levi Odell.

"Hell," said Puckett, "it's your house and your woman. Throw the varmint out."

"That didn't grab me as bein' such a good idea," Jubal replied. "This hombre ain't just a down-at-the-heels drifter. There's a brace of Colts hangin' on the bedpost. I reckon he's been shot and is likely still weak, but when he looked at me, he was purely taking my measure. He could be some kind of lawman."

"Let's have a look at his saddle and saddlebags," Levi suggested.

The trio went to the barn and wasted no time in going through Nathan's saddlebags and his canvas-wrapped pack, still secured to the packsaddle. Finding the leather bags full of gold double eagles, they all but shouted.

"God Almighty," Ike Puckett said, "there must be near four thousand here. While this pelican's laid up, we'd have time to get to Arizona, or even California."

"Don't be a damn fool," said Jubal. "We got a sweet setup right here, and I ain't one to outlaw myself for a handful of coin."

"Haw, haw," Levi Odell cackled, "you reckon horse stealin' won't outlaw you?"

"Maybe," Jubal conceded, "but there's a matter of proof. Not so with this cold-eyed jasper with the brace of Colts. He's the kind who'd track you down, gun you down, and when he's takin' his gold off your cold carcass, consider it proof enough."

"You're scairt of him," Levi said.

"Hell," said Ike, "so am I. Look at all this."

From Nathan's pack he had taken copies of newspapers. Some of them had accounts of Nathan's days with the Kansas-Pacific and of the deadly showdown with El Gato's renegades in Indian Territory. There were references to Byron Silver and the attorney general's office in Washington, and finally the death notice of Ranger Captain Sage Jennings. Then there were copies of various telegrams Nathan had received, several of them from Captain Ferguson, at Fort Worth.

"Exactly what I was afraid of, damn it," Jubal Wells said. "Right here amongst us, we got some kind of special lawman. We can't just salt the bastard down and have him be forgot. Kill him, and he'll be missed. That's just what we need: some U.S. marshal from El Paso or Santa Fe, lookin' for him and lookin' at us."

"So what are we goin' to do?" Ike asked. "Let him squat here until he heals and hope he rides on? What about your woman?"

"There'll be other women," said Jubal callously, "unless I'm behind bars or at the business end of a rope. The less this legal coyote sees of us, the better. We'll eat and ride south. We'll hole up in Ciudad Juarez until we're ready to run a new herd of broomtails across the border."

Left alone with the Wells children, Nathan found himself in the midst of an uneasy silence. Finally he spoke.

"Jamie, do you and Ellie like New Mexico?"

"I ain't liked nowhere we've been since my pa was killed," Jamie said. "At first, I liked it here, 'cause there wasn't no school. But there's nothin' else here, either."

"It wasn't so bad, even here," said Ellie, "if it wasn't for . . . him. When he's here, he's nearly always drunk. The worst times are when he has Ike and Levi with him, and all of them are drunk together."

"If I had a gun," Jamie said, "I'd wait till they're passed out and kill them all."

"Whoa," said Nathan. "Killing is serious business. I'd think on that some."

"I reckon you don't carry them for show," Jamie said, his eyes on Nathan's Colts.

"No," said Nathan. "When you begin using a gun, you're forced to carry one to stay alive. I am forever defending myself against men who are determined to kill me."

"Why do they want to kill you?"

"To prove they're faster on the draw than I am," Nathan replied. "Or they want me dead because I've been forced to kill friends or kin of theirs."

"That's how you got hurt, then," said Ellie.

"Not this time," Nathan said. "A friend of mine was shot in the back. I went after the outlaw who did it, and when it came to a showdown, he shot me before I shot him."

"But you didn't shoot him in the leg," said Jamie.

"No," Nathan said.

The conversation ended abruptly when Jubal Wells and

his companions entered the house. Their laughter was loud, and they were drunk or trying to appear so.

"Damnation, woman," Jubal shouted, "where's our breakfast? We got ridin' to do."

"He ain't all that drunk," Jamie whispered, "and they never ride out again the same day they come in. They're up to somethin'."

Nathan silently agreed. The trio had taken entirely too much time unsaddling, if that was what they had been doing. Facing Nathan, Wells had been predictably hostile. Now his attitude seemed to have changed abruptly, and the trio was anxious to be on their way.

"Jamie," said Nathan quietly, "you and Ellie had best leave me alone. I must get up."

"But Ma said you shouldn't," Ellie protested. "Besides, she told us to stay here with you until they finish their breakfast, and they ain't finished."

"Then close your eyes," said Nathan, "because I'm getting out of this bed."

"You can't scare her," Jamie said devilishly. "She helped Ma take your britches off."

"Jamie!" the girl cried, blushing furiously. She kicked him in the shins and turned her back on them.

Nathan flung back the covers and got shakily to his feet. His wound hurt, but there had been some healing, and he could stand. Quickly he donned his shirt, and by sitting on the bed, pulled on his trousers. He had some difficulty with his left boot, for the pressure strained the muscles of his thigh. When he had his boots on, he stood up and buckled on his Colts. He then spoke quietly.

"All right, Ellie, you can turn around."

There obviously was no way out of the bedroom except through the kitchen. Nathan waited, listening, but there was no sound except the rattle of dishes. Whatever the trio had in mind, they had discussed it before coming to the house. Nathan kept his silence. If his thinking was sound, Jubal Wells would not return to the bedroom before leaving, and in that event, Nathan vowed they wouldn't ride away until he knew his gold was secure. When the meal was over, chairs scraped the floor as the men pushed away from the table.

"We got some ridin' to do," said Wells.

With the sound of their leaving, Nathan pushed aside the

curtain and stepped into the kitchen. Myra looked at him and spoke softly.

"You shouldn't have gotten up," she said. "They're leaving again."

"A mite sudden," said Nathan, "and cause for me to wonder why. I aim to see them on their way."

He stepped out the door, limping, taking his time. Jamie and Ellie at her side, Myra watched. As he neared the barn, Nathan Stone no longer limped, and his hands were near the butts of the deadly Colts. He didn't enter the barn, but waited until the trio led their horses out into the open corridor. The big door at the far end of the corridor was closed, so they couldn't evade him. When they saw him standing there, thumbs hooked in his pistol belt, they froze.

"You hombres are in an almighty hurry to be gone," Nathan said, "and I just want to be sure you don't make the mistake of taking something that's not yours."

"We ain't taking nothin' of yours," said Wells sullenly, "and you got no call to come stompin' out here like the bull of the woods. By God, there's three of us."

"I can count," Nathan said coldly, "and I've been to skunk shoots before. Mount up and ride out, and if I find cause to come after you, I'll kill the three of you."

Without a word they mounted and rode south, none of them looking back. Nathan waited until he was sure they were gone and then carefully examined his saddlebags and pack. There was a slight sound behind him and Nathan whirled, a Colt in his hand.

"Sorry, Cotton Blossom," said Nathan.

He didn't doubt they had been through his saddlebags and pack, for nothing had been repacked as neatly as he had left it, but nothing was missing. They had to have found the bags of double eagles, and that puzzled him.

"I believe they thought you were a lawman," Myra said.

She stood in the door of the tack room where his saddle, saddlebags, and the loaded packsaddle had been stored. He got up off his knees, groaning. The pain in his thigh was throbbing like the beating of a drum.

"They seemed mighty anxious to get away from here," said Nathan, "but you could be right. Maybe I was lookin' at the wrong reason."

"Perhaps you were right and I was wrong," Myra said, "and your confronting them led to a change in their plans.

I don't know what you have that would have interested them. Jamie unsaddled your horses and stored all your goods in the tack room. None of us bothered anything, but I could never say the same for Jubal and his friends."

"They had already gone through my packs before they came to the house for breakfast," said Nathan. "I'm not a lawman, but I have worked with the law on occasion, and in my pack there are some newspaper accounts."

"That's why they were in such a hurry to ride out," Myra said. "After they went to the barn to unsaddle their horses, Jubal never mentioned you again. Always, following his trips to El Paso, he's questioned me, wanting to know if riders have been here. I believe he's ridden away for the last time."

"Then you can't stay here," said Nathan. "How many horses do you have?"

"There should be three in the barn. Jubal kept six. I believe three of them were left here for relays, in case Jubal, Ike, and Levi had to outride a posse."

"I'll be riding on to El Paso," Nathan said. "Why don't you plan on taking Jamie and Ellie and coming with me?"

"That would be the sensible thing to do. I'm ashamed of myself for having sunk this low for a roof over our heads and food. I was a fool to take Jubal Wells's name for myself and my children. My husband's name was James Haight, and I think Haight will be our name from now on."

With Wells out of the picture, Nathan looked at Myra Haight. She had brown eyes and dark hair without a streak of gray. She couldn't have been a day over thirty, if that, and he found himself attracted to her. He had no idea what she thought of him, beyond the fact he had been hurt and had needed help. Reaching the house, she wasted no time telling Jamie and Ellie what she intended to do.

"I'm glad," Ellie said, "but what will we do in El Paso?"

"I'll find a job," said Jamie.

"You'll go back to school," Myra said.

"Damn," said Jamie.

"I hear El Paso's a right smart of a town," Nathan said. "Why not just wait until you get there? I'll help you get settled."

"Jiminy," Jamie shouted, "are you goin' to live with us? After Ma sleepin' with old Jubal nigh three years, you'd be . . ."

"Jamie," Myra snapped, "go outside and stay there until tell you to come in."

Her face flamed red and she turned away from Nathan, while Ellie tried her best not to laugh. Jamie, who seemed honestly uncertain as to what he had done wrong, made his way to the door.

"I reckon I'd better take my weight off this leg," said Nathan, "or it will never heal."

"Yes," said Myra, grateful for his having changed the subject. "Take a chair at the table and I'll make some coffee."

The rest of the day dragged. Myra devoted her attention to Jamie and Ellie, lest they again say the wrong thing, while they kept their silence for the same reason. Nathan wasn't looking forward to the night because the cabin had only two rooms besides the kitchen. After supper, he had a suggestion.

"I think Cotton Blossom and me will sleep in the barn tonight. I'd not be surprised if Wells and his friends sneaked back and tried to take those other three horses."

"Surely not," said Myra. "It will be cold tonight and you're still not well. You have no business staying out there."

"I have plenty of blankets," Nathan said.

"Whatever you think is best," Myra replied. Clearly, she wasn't in favor of it, but Jamie and Ellie looked as though they had suggestions for keeping Nathan in the house, and her agreeing with Nathan silenced them.

Nathan was slow in climbing the ladder to the hayloft, for his wound still pained him. Cotton Blossom settled down near the foot of the ladder. Nathan had slept so much during the past several nights, he now lay awake, thinking. What was he going to do with Myra, Jamie, and Ellie, once they reached El Paso? Tawdry as it seemed, he could see how a woman with two children might have cast her lot with Jubal Wells. Life on the frontier had to be hell on a woman, even with a man beside her. What must it be like when she was alone? When Cotton Blossom growled, Nathan sat up, a Colt cocked and ready.

"Identify yourself," he said. "You're covered."

"It's Myra," she said softly. "Don't bite me, Cotton Blossom."

Cotton Blossom was silent, having growled only to warn

Nathan of her coming. She quietly climbed the ladder to the loft, catching her breath before she spoke.

"You didn't have to sleep in the barn. Jamie and Ellie already regard me as a fallen woman. As Jamie was about to point out, anything you could have done would have lifted me higher than I've been for the past three years."

"The past three years are exactly what you called them," said Nathan. "They're in the past. You should leave them there."

"You're a strange man, Nathan Stone. You're a gentleman, and I'm not used to that."

"That being the case," said Nathan, "I should ask you to sit. There's a cold wind comin' in under the eaves."

"I noticed," she said. "I'm only wearing a nightdress. If I'd fumbled around in the dark, I'd have wakened Jamie and Ellie."

"I'd bet my saddle they're awake right now," he said, "and they will be until you're in your bed. Hadn't you better be going?"

"I'm not ready to go," she said. "Besides, I doubt they could think any less of me than they do already. How is your wound?"

"Sore," said Nathan, "and you leaning on it's not helping."

"Sorry," she said. "I'll move around to the other side. Will you share your blankets?"

"I reckon," said Nathan, "if you don't value your reputation."

It was near dawn before Myra slipped back to the house, leaving Nathan alone with his conflicting emotions. While she had asked nothing of him, he felt obligated, and to some degree, guilty. To his surprise, breakfast was a cheerful affair. If Jamie and Ellie were aware of Myra's absence during the night, they chose to ignore it.

"Another day," said Nathan, "and I think we'd better be on our way to El Paso."

He wasn't in the least surprised when Myra came to visit him in the hayloft a second time. Again he felt guilty, as though he were building an obligation he might regret. For a while there was no conversation between them, and he thought she had fallen asleep. When she finally spoke, it was with a question.

"Nathan, after all I . . . I've done . . . am I still worthy of a decent man?"

"Let's turn that around," said Nathan. "I reckon you'll have to look long and hard to find a decent man worthy of you. Most men don't want a decent woman. That's why, in every town west of the Mississippi, the second building to go up is a whorehouse."

"What's the first?"

"A saloon."

"That's strange," she said. "Why the saloon first?"

"So men can get drunk enough to go to the whorehouse," he replied.

"Have you . . . ever . . . been there?"

"No," he said. "I prey on decent women, usually after they've made up their minds I'm a gentleman."

"You're making fun of me," she accused.

"You've already learned more about me than any decent woman has any business knowing," he said. "It's time you were getting back to the house."

"When we get to El Paso, will you . . . will we . . . ?"

"I expect we will," said Nathan. "Man's been taking forbidden fruit for two thousand years, and some woman keeps handin' it to him. We feed our weaknesses and ignore our strengths."

There were no saddles for the three horses Jubal Wells had left behind, so Myra, Jamie, and Ellie had to ride bareback, each carrying their belongings in a bundle.

"We'll take it slow," Nathan said, "but there'll be some sore behinds by the time we reach El Paso. I have a tin of sulfur salve in my saddlebag."

The first day, Nathan judged they traveled twenty-five miles. He called a halt while the sun was still an hour high, for they had reached a spring where there was good graze for the horses. That, and his three charges were so wrung-out they couldn't have ridden another mile. They all wore Levi's and flannel shirts, and they practically fell off their horses.

"After dark," Nathan said, "all of you can strip and sit in the spring runoff."

"I intend to do exactly that," said Myra, "and I may not wait until dark."

CHAPTER 10

El Paso, Texas. December 23, 1873

Granny Boudleaux's boardinghouse was different, to say the least. But so was Granny herself. The boardinghouse consisted of an old mission—long abandoned by the Spanish—that sprawled along the north bank of the Rio Grande, no more than a stone's throw from Ciudad Juarez. A Cajun, Granny Boudleaux defied description. She had black hair, piercing black eyes, stood several inches under five feet, and wouldn't have weighed more than ninety pounds soaking wet. She spoke English, Cajun, and Spanish, and on occasion, a mix of all three. It was to Granny Boudleaux's Hacienda Grande Nathan and his charges rode in search of rooms. Business had been poor and they were greeted by Granny herself.

"A room for each of us," Nathan said. "You have a place we can stable our horses?"

"Of course not," she snapped. "This look like a horse barn to you?"

"No," said Nathan. "I've seen horse barns in better shape."

For some reason that struck Granny as hilariously funny she slapped her thigh with her old black hat, like a cowboy.

"Four room," she said, obviously in a better mood. "Dollar a day, five dollar a week, twenty dollar a month. Grub fifty cent a day."

"Here's a hundred and forty dollars," said Nathan. "That's a room for all of us for a month, including grub."

"You stay long?" she asked hopefully, her eyes on the seven double eagles.

"That depends," Nathan said, "on whether we can find a place for our horses close to here."

"Jernigan's," she said, pointing. "Two block west."

Nathan unloaded his packsaddle and saddlebags, taking them into one of the rooms. Myra, Jamie, and Ellie had only their clothes, tied in bundles.

"Get settled in," Nathan told them. "I'll see to our horses."

When Nathan returned from the livery, it was near suppertime, and he found all the inhabitants of Granny's place in the dining room, except for Myra and Ellie. They, Nathan learned, were in the kitchen, helping Granny bring food to the table. Nathan said nothing, and when the meal was over, Myra and Ellie returned to the kitchen. An hour later, when they returned to their rooms, Nathan was waiting for them.

"Damn it, we're paying for rooms and grub. You don't have to work in the kitchen."

"She didn't ask us to work in the kitchen," Myra said. "We offered to help. Nathan, that poor woman has no help. She's taking care of all this by herself."

Myra Haight had a sympathetic ear, and she soon learned that Granny Boudleaux was facing a problem that seemed insurmountable.

"She owes the bank twelve hundred dollars," said Myra, "and she can't pay. The bank is threatening to take this place away from her."

"Maybe not," Nathan said, an idea taking shape. "Suppose you put up the twelve hundred and buy a half interest?"

"I don't have twelve hundred."

"I do," said Nathan.

"Maybe you didn't hear. I said *I* don't have twelve hundred dollars."

"I heard you," Nathan said. "Damn it, I'm lending you the money."

"Suppose I can't repay it?"

"Then I reckon I'll have to spend as many nights as I can in El Paso, taking it out in trade."

"A dollar for the room and two dollars for me," she said. "That'll be four hundred nights."

"Damn it," he said, irritated, "I didn't mean it that way."

"I know you didn't," she replied. "Business is business, and this is my idea. You don't owe me anything, Nathan Stone, and I won't take your money to ease your guilt."

"Then by God," he said, "if I can't lend you money without you becoming a whore to repay it, I'll withdraw the offer. If money does that to you, I like you better when you're broke. I'll learn to live with my guilt."

She laughed, but when she placed her hands on his shoulders, there were tears in her eyes. "You're doing this because you're going to ride away. That's what hurts."

"Not for a while," he said, "and if I do, I'll be back Take the money, damn it."

"I must talk to Granny Boudleaux. She has until December thirty-first. Then the bank will foreclose."

Two days after Christmas the papers were drawn up, and Myra Haight officially had half ownership of Hacienda Grande. It was a move Nathan never regretted, for on the first day of the new year, his troublesome past caught up with him, and he was again forced to resort to the deadly Colts. . . .

CHAPTER 11

Nathan had time on his hands, and not being a drinking man, he began visiting various saloons and gambling. El Paso drew men from both sides of the border, most of them of a caliber that suggested they could be hanged on either side of the river. One of these was a Mexican of some status, Manuelito Birdsong. He was armed with a temper of considerable proportions, a Bowie knife, and a .31-caliber Colt pocket pistol. The game, draw poker, had been in progress less than an hour in the Star Saloon, and Nathan watched as the Mexican was again about to deal the cards.

"This time," Nathan said, "deal all mine off the top."

Birdsong shifted a cigar to the other side of his mouth and regarded Nathan coldly before he spoke.

"You are implying that I cheat, señor?"

"I'm not implying," said Nathan. "I'm accusing. You dealt my last card off the bottom of the deck. I allow a man one mistake, and you've made yours."

Men scrambled to get away from the table, but there was no gunplay. Birdsong's hand froze on the butt of his Colt, for Nathan already had him covered.

"I think," Nathan said, "for the sake of your continued

;ood health, you'd better be on your way. The next time
ou draw on me, I'll kill you."

Birdsong got up and left the saloon without a word, but
the hate in his eyes warned Nathan that the fiery little gambler wouldn't forget.

"You'd better watch your back, friend," said the barkeep. "That little sidewinder's poison mean."

Nathan left the saloon, the incident having soured him,
but a seed had been planted. A pair of men—Pike and
Bodie—had once worked for the Kansas-Pacific Railroad.

"By God," Pike said, after Nathan had gone, "that's Nathan Stone. He's deadly with a Colt, just forked lightning
with either hand."

"Yeah," said Bodie, "and he's done some fancy shootin'
since then. There was the gal from Missouri that wanted
him dead for killin' her brother. She hired a pair of fast
guns and they went after Stone with a three-way ambush.
He shot his way out, killed one of the hired guns, and sent
the other—along with the girl—to the Missouri state pen."

Thus the legend of Nathan Stone grew, and so did the
number of men who wished to gain a reputation by beating
his fast draw. . . .

El Paso, Texas. January 1, 1874
Artemus Stewart had built himself a financial empire in El
Paso, having founded the bank of which he was now president. He had fond expectations of Arlie, his only son, taking the reins when old age forced Artemus to step down.
But Arlie, just twenty-two, had a passion for women, whiskey, and cards. He carried a tied-down Colt on his right
hip and had gained a reputation of sorts, not for his skill
with a gun, but because of the power his father wielded. It
was an open secret that Artemus Stewart could make or
break any man in El Paso County. There were benefits,
being the son of the town's wealthiest citizen, and Arlie
Stewart took full advantage of them. He soon forgot that
men shied clear of him, not because they feared his gun,
but because they feared his father. The sun was noon-high
on the first day of the new year, when Arlie Stewart and
three of his friends found Nathan Stone in the Arcade Saloon, playing poker. Arlie tipped back his hat, approached
the table, and issued a challenge.

"Stone, I hear you're quick with a gun. Well, I think I'm faster, and I'm callin' you out. I'll be waitin'."

"You'll have a long wait," Nathan said quietly. "Killing isn't a game, boy. Go home."

"By God," Arlie bawled, "I'm not a boy, I'm a man, which is more than can be said for you."

Lowell Stark, the county sheriff, had entered the saloon in time to hear Arlie Stewart make his brash statement, and he issued a warning.

"Arlie, I'm the sheriff, and I can lock you up."

"You can," said Arlie arrogantly, "but then you won't be sheriff no more. I'll have your badge, and you won't find work in this town forkin' horse apples."

There was some nervous laughter that quickly faded. Sheriff Lowell Stark had proven himself, but Arlie Stewart's threat was real enough. Stark said no more, but he could see what Arlie apparently could not. This Nathan Stone wasn't a man to talk down to, not by a wet-behind-the-ears kid like Arlie Stewart. Stone got to his feet, his eyes cold, and when he spoke, his voice was brittle, deadly.

"Boy, you've got one more chance to turn around and walk out of here alive. I have no reason to kill you, unless you go for that gun."

Men fought one another to get out of the line of fire. A chill wind swept through the saloon's batwing doors, but there were beads of sweat on Arlie Stewart's brow. He cut his eyes to right and left, but he was alone. There was a sinking feeling in his gut, for he must back up his brag or be forever branded a coward. He made his play, elated as his hand reached the butt of his Colt, for Stone hadn't moved. Arlie had cleared leather and was raising the weapon, when a single shot shattered the stillness. He was flung back into a chair, his Colt clattering on the floor. Wonderingly, he stared into the deadly muzzle of Nathan Stone's Colt, as smoke still curled from it. Finally, his eyes met Nathan's, and he saw compassion there. He died, then, with the realization he was a fool. Nathan Stone had not wanted to kill him. . . .

There was chaos in the saloon. Nathan thumbed a shell into his Colt, holstered it, and approached the sheriff.

"You saw it, Sheriff. He left me no choice. Are there any charges?"

"Not as far as I'm concerned," said Stark, "but in case

you don't know, his daddy's the tall dog in the brass collar in El Paso. The kid never got into anything his pa couldn't get him out of. Until now. God only knows what the old man's likely to do. Unless you've got business here, you'd do well to ride on."

"Damn it," Nathan said, "he drew first. Every man in here saw it."

"And every man in here's afraid to cross old Artemus Stewart," the sheriff replied.

"That includes you, I reckon," said Nathan.

"It does not," Stark said. "I'll side you, if it costs me this badge, but old Artemus is a tyrant. He'll ignore anything I say, and with his money, he could have hired enough men to have whipped the Mexican army."

Sheriff Stark knew he wouldn't have to break the news of the shooting. Artemus Stewart would already know. Stark wanted to know what the old man planned in the way of retaliation, and hopefully, talk him out of it. With a sigh, he knocked on the door of Stewart's office, and was bid enter. It was even worse than he had expected.

"Damn you," Stewart bawled, "a drifter kills my boy and you let him walk away. Why is he not in jail?"

"I can't jail a man for defending himself," said Stark quietly. "Arlie forced the fight. He had a chance to back off, and he didn't. I tried to talk sense to him, and he wouldn't have it. He asked for what he got."

"By God," Stewart growled. "I'll see that you get yours."

"If you're referring to this badge," said Stark, dropping it on the desk, "I'm returning it, and you know where you can stick it. I'm through bein' froggie, jumpin' every time you stomp your foot."

Stepping out, he closed the door, but he could still hear Artemus Stewart shouting as he left the bank and mounted his horse. Stark rode back to the Arcade Saloon, but there was no sign of Nathan Stone. Men looked at him curiously since he no longer wore the sheriff's badge, but nobody questioned him, for they knew.

Artemus Stewart wasted no time. The three men he had sent for stood before him and listened as he told them what he wanted done.

"I want you to raise a posse," said Stewart. "I'm paying ten dollars a day, per man, plus shells and grub. I want

Nathan Stone dead, and the man bringing me proof that he is, gets a thousand dollars. Do you understand me?"

"Yes, sir," Jubal Wells said. "Me, Ike, Levi, and how many more?"

"A dozen, if you can find them," said Stewart, "and by God, I want him. I don't care if you have to follow him to the ocean in either direction, or Canada to the north."

"Well, now," Ike said, after the trio had left Stewart's office, "that do make it some better, fifteen of us after Stone's hide. Bein' as how we're headin' the posse, we ought to have first grab at Stone's belongings, after he's been shot dead."

"That's how I see it," said Jubal Wells. "We'll let the others fight over the bounty on him, while we snag the gold in his pack."

"Hell, we're gittin' paid by the day," Levi said. "After we catch up to Stone and cash in his chips, let's find us a town with a saloon and a whorehouse and hole up for another two or three weeks. We can tell old Artemus we had to chase Stone all the way to Atlanta, and he won't never know the difference."

The three of them laughed, savoring the humor, as they began making the rounds of the saloons, seeking men for their posse.

Nathan rode back to Granny Boudleaux's boarding-house. It had become virtually impossible to talk to Myra without Granny listening, so Nathan spoke to them all, Jamie and Ellie included.

"The sheriff advised me to ride on," Nathan said, "and the more I think about it, the more sensible it seems."

"The one you shoot don't be near as bad as his daddy," said Granny Boudleaux. "If you ride back to town and shoot that old hellion, your troubles be over."

Despite the seriousness of the situation, Nathan laughed.

"You don't know what the mood is in town," Myra said. "Let Jamie ride in and find out. You were justified in defending yourself. Maybe the sheriff can talk some sense into this Artemus Stewart."

"Nobody talk sense to him," Granny predicted. "Nobody."

When Jamie returned, they all listened in glum silence.

"The sheriff quit," said Jamie, "and old Mister Stewart's hiring a posse to kill Nathan. He's paying ten dollars a day, per man, with a thousand dollars to the man that does the killing. And just who do you reckon is hirin' and leadin' this bunch of killers?"

Nobody said anything, as they digested the brutal facts, and Jamie continued.

"Jubal Wells, Ike Puckett, and Levi Odell, that's who. I didn't see 'em, but everybody was talkin' about it."

"That tells me what I needed to know," Nathan said. "No law standing in Stewart's way, and he's got the money to pay a pack of killers to trail me from here to yonder. I'd better saddle up and ride, getting as much of a start as I can."

"But where will you go?" Myra asked.

"San Antonio," said Nathan, "but I don't aim to spend all my time running. I'll set up a few ambushes as I go, and even the odds some."

"Oh, I hate this!" Myra cried. "You will come back, won't you?"

"When I can," said Nathan. "They'll search the town, and the sooner I can get away from here, the better. When Jubal Wells and his amigos see Myra, Jamie, and Ellie, they'll know I've been here, and this is where they'll take my trail."

"Lak hell," Granny Boudleaux said. "They see nobody but me, and I tell them I never see you, never hear of you."

"Bless you, Granny," said Nathan. "When I can safely ride back this way, I will."

Nathan rode east, shying away from the Rio Grande and the border. His pursuers, he suspected, would be sufficient in number to ride him down in rough country, and below the border, he had no friends. Instead of running ahead, Cotton Blossom lagged behind, because Nathan had been watching his back trail and the hound had picked up on that. There was no evidence of pursuit at the end of the first day, but Nathan kept his supper fire small, extinguishing it well before dark. He spread a blanket on the ground, and while it was still light, cleaned both the Colts and the Winchester.

Without Jamie knowing, Levi Puckett had seen him when he had ridden in to learn the mood of the town for Nathan. Puckett had then followed the boy back to Granny's place, and the next morning after the shooting, that was where the fifteen vigilantes came looking for Nathan Stone. Granny Boudleaux tried her best to keep them off Nathan's trail, but it only seemed to make them all the more certain.

"You don't have to lie to us, old woman," Jubal Wells said. "We know he was here."

They rode away—fifteen strong—in the direction Nathan had gone.

"Oh, damn it," said Jamie, "he didn't even get one day ahead of them."

Myra Haight said nothing. She strained her eyes into the rising sun, watching the dust cloud grow smaller, knowing that Nathan was somewhere ahead of them. He was just one man, and there were fifteen killers on his trail. Knuckling the tears from her eyes, she turned back to the house. . . .

Jubal Wells, Ike Puckett, and Levi Odell rode at the head of the band of killers they had recruited in El Paso. They were in high good humor, with most of them being more than a little drunk. Artemus Stewart had been more than generous with money for food and supplies, and the vigilantes led three packhorses, one of them almost totally loaded with quart bottles of whiskey.

"I got it all figgered out," Levi shouted to an attentive audience. "It ain't the drinkin' that kills a man, it's the soberin' up. So you just don't never sober up."

"By God, that ain't nothin' but the truth," said Ike, "and we can stretch old Stewart's bounty hunt out for as long as his money lasts, stayin' drunk all the way."

"Stone's got a dog with him," Jubal said. "Let's be looking for dog tracks."

"Hell," one of the newly hired riders cackled, "I'm so drunk I can't see hoss tracks."

"No more whiskey in the morning, then," Jubal said. "Save it for after supper, so you can sleep it off. This ain't no shorthorn we're after. He could double back, belly-down with a Winchester, and ambush the hell out of us."

There was grumbling, but they couldn't deny the logic of what Jubal had said. Reaching a spring, they unsaddled and made camp for the night. The wind had a chilly bite, and far to the west, a gray band of clouds had swept over the setting sun.

"By this time tomorrow night," somebody predicted,

'there'll be rain. Then we got no hoss tracks, dog tracks, nothin'. How do we know we're still on his trail?"

"We don't," said Jubal, "but have you ever knowed it to rain all over Texas at the same time? We ride on till the rain lets up, and then we circle till we find the trail again. Damn it, don't none of you jaybirds know nothin' about tracking?"

Southeast Texas. January 3, 1874

Nathan arose at first light, built a small fire, and prepared breakfast for himself and Cotton Blossom. He loaded the packhorse, saddled the grulla, and rode out, reining up on the first rise. There he surveyed the back trail and found no sign of pursuit, but Stewart's band of vigilantes would be coming, and it would be they who determined Nathan's course of action. He would stay ahead of them, and over the course of a week or two, attempt to wear them out. If that failed, it meant old man Stewart wanted him dead, whatever the cost, and Nathan would take the offensive.

By noon, the thunderheads had moved in from the west on a rising wind, swallowing the January sun. When the rain came, it was cold, but Nathan rode on, taking advantage of the daylight. The farther he rode during the storm, the farther his pursuers would be riding blind, seeking to pick up his trail. With darkness just minutes away, he reined up beside a creek at the foot of a steep slope. There was enough of a rock overhang to provide shelter to Nathan and Cotton Blossom. Others had sought shelter here, and someone had thoughtfully gathered some firewood. Nathan built a small cookfire, extinguishing it as soon as possible, so there would be fuel for a breakfast fire. It promised to be a perfectly miserable night, as the storm grew in intensity.

"Damn it," said Byler, "we should of rode on until we found some shelter 'fore we laid up for the night."

"You ain't likely to find a hotel any closer than San Antone," Jubal said. "If a little rain bothers you, maybe you should of stayed in the saloons in El Paso. It ain't too late to ride back, and that goes for any of the rest of you."

"I ain't bothered by the rain," said Connolly, "but I'd as soon be ridin', as settin' here like a half-drowned rooster."

"By God, you'll be a dead rooster," Ike Puckett said, "if

you ride blind into Stone's camp. It ain't likely he'll ride on in a storm like this."

"Not the least bit likely," Jubal agreed, "and there's nothin' he'd like better than for us to come stumblin' after him through the rain, not knowin' where he is."

"You don't know ever'thing, Wells," said Mayberry, who was still drunk. "When the rain's done, we still won't know where the hombre is, till he starts makin' tracks again. He could hole up and us be right on him, 'fore we know he's there."

"I ain't denyin' that," Jubal said, "with all of you owl-eyed. No more whiskey except at suppertime, and the next scutter that ends up falling-down drunk gets booted out."

Nathan was three days out of El Paso before he eventually sighted the dust of the men following him. Lest they learn how close they were, he built his fire in daylight, with brush along a creek to dissipate the smoke. He then rode on another ten miles before he made camp. Waiting until it was dark, he left his packhorse picketed and rode back to scout the enemy camp. It was time he knew just how many men were on his trail. The wind was out of the west and so he was downwind from his pursuers. He left the grulla far enough away so that the animal wouldn't nicker and reveal his presence. Never knowing what might develop, he took his Winchester. The bunch had obligingly established their camp near a creek, along which there was abundant growth, and Nathan crept along it from the north. Cotton Blossom had crept on ahead, and when the dog didn't double back, Nathan was reasonably sure none of the vigilantes were on watch. He easily identified the troublesome trio from New Mexico, Wells, Puckett, and Odell, and counted twelve more men he didn't recognize. There were three loaded packsaddles, proof enough that Artemus Stewart was sparing no expense. The coffeepot hung over the fire from an iron spider, and that gave Nathan an idea. It never hurt to keep the enemy on the defensive, seeing to it that they slept uneasily, never knowing for sure where their adversary was. He waited until Levi Odell tipped a whiskey bottle and fired, shattering the bottle in Odell's face. His next shot sent the coffeepot flying, while a third and fourth sent the horses galloping in a mad run down the creek. He then retreated, while pandemonium broke loose in the camp. Men cursed, rifles and Colts roared, and several men who had sought the safety of darkness were drawing fire from their companions.

"Damn it," Jubal Wells roared, "hold your fire."

"Help me," Odell whined, "I'm bleedin' to death and I can't see."

"The hosses is gone," somebody shouted. "Let's go look fer 'em."

"It's so dark you can't see your hand in front of your face," said Ike Puckett. "We'll have to wait for mornin'."

It was the truth, for clouds had moved in, hiding the moon and stars. Nathan reached his horse, mounted, and rode back to his own camp, knowing he wouldn't be followed. In a showdown, they might surround him or ride him down, but in a war of nerves, he had a definite edge. All he had to do was stay ahead, ride back under the cover of darkness, and just worry the hell out of them.

Nathan's pursuers spent an uneasy night, awaking to a chill west wind and a mass of low-hanging clouds that promised more rain. Nobody was in a mood for breakfast until the horses had been found, and they set off on foot. With the cold wind at their backs, the animals had drifted more than two miles. Breakfast was late, for they had but one coffeepot, and some of the men had to wait for a second pot to boil. Before they were finished with breakfast, a drizzling rain had set in. Some of the men who had been into the whiskey the night before were sorely in need of some "hair of the dog," but Jubal Wells was in an even more vile mood than those with hangovers. In silence they mounted and rode out, wet, cold, and hating one another. More than one man silently vowed that Nathan Stone would pay, but there would be unpleasant surprises ahead beyond anything their limited imaginations might conceive.

As the drizzling rain swept in, Nathan Stone laughed. While there was little shelter in east Texas, one man could find a rock overhang, the undercut bank of an arroyo, or some means of sleeping dry. Fifteen men, however, would have no dry bed, perhaps no fire, and unless they had another pot, no coffee. As Nathan rode on, the rain became more intense. His pursuers had barely found his trail following the first rain, and now they were about to lose it again. Adding to their woes, after last night they would be forced to take turns standing watch, for they knew not when Nathan Stone would visit them again. Reaching a spring at the foot of a rise, Nathan reined up. There was a blowing rain out of the west, for the wind had risen. Nathan found shelter on the lee side of some rocks and built his supper fire. When he had eaten and fed Cotton Blossom, he put out the fire, saving some of the wood for the morning. He then rolled in his blankets with a square of canvas over them as protection from the blowing rain, and slept soundly.

Half a day's ride behind, however, his pursuers had no shelter, and for a lack of dry firewood, were chewing on jerked beef.

"Damn such weather," Ike Puckett growled. "I'd give a day's pay for some hot coffee."

"I'd give a day's pay if I didn't have to listen to all this crying," said Jubal Wells.

"Well, hell," Kendrick said, "with old Stewart footin' the bill, we should of bought us a tent. If I'd of wanted to set on my hunkers in the rain, eatin' jerked beef, I could of joined the Union army."

"If it'll make you feel better," Wells snapped, "I'll cut your pay to eight dollars a month and you can make believe this *is* the Union army."

Under cover of darkness, an overcast sky and continuing rain, Nathan again visited the vigilante camp. He ventilated the spare coffeepot and with some well-placed shots, again stampeded the horses. By the time the men on watch got their Winchesters into play, Nathan had already done his damage. While confusion reigned, he mounted his horse and rode back to his own camp. Twice he had shot up their camp, and either time, he could have killed two or three men. He had nothing against them, and he still hoped that if the trail proved treacherous enough, most of them would give up the chase. His shooting had been close enough until they had to know he had spared them. But how much longer could he continue to spare them? The weather cleared up, and after the tenth day on the trail, all his pursuers were still there. Obviously, some of them would have to be hurt or killed, to make believers of the rest. On the eleventh day, an unexpected opportunity presented itself in a most unusual manner.

Having seen no threat from the men on their back trail,

Cotton Blossom had taken to ranging far ahead. On this
particular day he doubled back, growling. The sun was several hours high, and if there was danger ahead, Nathan
wanted to face it before dark. Picketing the packhorse, he
rode warily ahead, following Cotton Blossom. After not
more than two miles, Nathan heard a dog bark. Reining
up, taking his Winchester, he dismounted. There was a rise
ahead, and using underbrush for cover, Nathan crept to the
crest of it. Below, he couldn't believe his eyes, for there
was an Indian camp. For the time and place, they almost
had to be Comanche. Obviously, they planned to remain
there for the night, and in Nathan's mind, a devious plan
was taking shape.

Returning to his horse, he rode back to his picketed
packhorse. There he waited until he could see a distant
plume of dust that told him his pursuers were almost within
striking distance. Leading his packhorse, he rode north
until he was sure the animal would be safe. He then rode
back to the rise that overlooked the Comanche camp. He
counted probably thirty Indian braves. Shucking his Winchester from the boot, he fired four times among the Indians, careful that his slugs didn't find human targets. His
shooting had the desired effect, for every man with a horse
lit out toward the brush from which the shots had come.
Nathan kicked the grulla into a fast gallop, back the way
he had come, toward the pursuing vigilantes. Once he had
some brush and undergrowth between him and the Comanches, he rode north. Before the Comanches reached the
point where Nathan had changed directions, they were able
to see the oncoming vigilantes. With a blood-chilling
whoop, they galloped ahead.

Reaching a rise from which he could see the drama, Nathan dismounted, resting his lathered horse. Even from a
distance he could hear the terrified cries of the vigilantes.
Making no attempt to fight, virtually falling over one another, they wheeled their horses and rode for their lives.
Nathan rode ahead to his packhorse. From there, he continued north until he was well past the Comanche camp. He
then rode east until he found a suitable camp for the night.

Far to the west, Jubal Wells and his vigilantes were trying
to evade the Comanches. Wells, Puckett, Odell, Byler, Connolly, Warnell, and Kendrick had escaped, but only because
of the darkness.

"My God," said Ike Puckett, "there must of been fifty of the varmints. I wonder if the rest of the boys got away."

"You know they didn't," Kendrick replied. "Hell, they was ahead of us, and they're the reason we got away."

"We ain't got away yet," said Jubal. "If they're Comanches, they may be right here at first light, beatin' the bushes and lookin' for us."

CHAPTER 12

Come first light, Jubal Wells and six nervous companions looked warily around before leaving the brush in which they had concealed themselves.

"Trouble with Comanches," Warnell said, "the varmints don't give up easy. Lose 'em, and they're likely to slope around for three days, huntin' you."

"We got more to worry about than our hides," said Wells. "Them three packhorses are loaded with all our supplies, and we're two weeks out of El Paso. Old man Stewart will have us drawn and quartered if we ride in with nothin' to show for all the money he's got tied up in this."

"God, yes," Levi Odell said. "We can't go back to El Paso empty-handed, and without grub and supplies, we can't go on. Either way, we're in a hell of a mess."

"We can't set here in this thicket," said Kendrick. "At least, we got our horses. Let's ride out and look for the packhorses."

The first thing they found were the scalped and mutilated bodies of their companions. All eight had been stripped of everything, including their boots.

"Lord, God," Warnell said, "I hope they wasn't alive when them varmints done this."

They rode on, anxious to be away from the grisly scene.

"We'll ride south," said Jubal. "Them packhorses was bein' led by Mayberry, Gruhn, and Paschal, and when they was hit, it would of spooked the horses. We rode north, and I don't remember seein' 'em ahead of us."

"I reckon it'll depend on whether them Comanches rode

out last night," Ike Puckett said. "They couldn't see them horses in the dark."

To their surprise, they found two of the horses almost ten miles south of where they had been attacked by the Comanches.

"Damn," said Levi, "they would find the one with the whiskey."

"I'm glad they did," Jubal said. "Maybe they'll stay drunk enough, long enough for us to leave 'em behind. A man can't live without grub, but he can do without whiskey."

"Speak for yourself," said Levi sourly.

Nathan arose at first light, and with the Comanches in mind, decided against a breakfast fire. He and Cotton Blossom shared some jerked beef and they took the trail. Nathan believed they had come more than five hundred miles. Unless he rode far south, to one of the border towns, San Antonio would be the closest. He was unsure as to how many of his pursuers the Comanches had accounted for, but he suspected he would still be outnumbered considerably. On the plains, they might eventually surround him, but in town, they would hardly attempt it. He could take them individually, or even two at a time, but not all of them at once.

"He's bound for somewhere," Jubal said, at the start of the thirteenth day, "and it'll be harder for us to gun him down where there's law."

"Yeah," said Ike. "Remember when we was goin' through his pack? That telegram was about a ranger friend of his. Hell, if he's friends with the rangers, we could all get shot down or strung up."

"I'm considerin' that," Jubal said. "There's bound to be rangers in Austin, and maybe in San Antonio. We got to salt him down before he gets there. There's nothin' much but cactus and sagebrush. I say we flank him to the north and south and cut him down in a crossfire while he's out here in the open."

"That makes sense," said Byler. "We ain't gettin' nowhere trailin' along behind him. He always knows where we are. If we're closin' in on two sides, he can't stand us all off."

"Byler," Jubal said, "you, Kendrick, Warnell, and Connolly flank him to the north. Ike, Levi, and me will cover

him from the south. Stay just out of rifle range, worryin'
him for a while. When we find an open stretch, where he
don't have a shred of cover, we'll all move in and close the
door on the varmint.''

Nathan soon discovered what his pursuers had in mind.
Surveying his back trail, he could see two rising clouds of
dust, one to the north and another to the south. They had
split their forces, planning to box him in on the open plains
ahead. He had no way of knowing how far he was from
the nearest town, where he had a chance to take a stand.
As far as he could see, there wasn't enough cover to hide
a prairie dog. His only advantage was that when they got
within range with their Winchesters, they were within range
of his, but he couldn't properly defend himself from two
attacking forces, even if he had cover. He rode desperately
on, only too well aware that his grulla and the packhorse
couldn't maintain such a gait for more than a few miles.
He had but one chance, and that was to swing due south.
There were the border towns of Del Rio and Eagle Pass,
but even they might be too distant. That left him only the
brush and *barrancas** to the south of the Rio Grande. If
he made it that far. One immediate advantage of his change
in direction was that the riders attempting to flank him to
the north lost their quarry. Eventually they might flank him
to the east, but only by hard riding, which would exhaust
their horses. He still had the riders who had been flanking
him to the south, and all they had to do was keep coming
because they had seen and understood his move. Slugs
began kicking up dust to his right, but soon they would be
within range. Another more serious problem arose when the
grulla slammed a hind leg deep into a hole. The animal came
to a dead stop, pitching Nathan from the saddle. There was
no time to see to the grulla, to see if the horse had been
lamed or its leg broken. Nathan got to his feet and snatched
the Winchester from its saddle boot, leaving the spooked
packhorse to shift for itself. Nathan wasn't sure where Cotton
Blossom was, but the dog couldn't help him. Slugs sang over
his head as he sought cover, and one found its mark, tearing
into his back, above the left shoulder blade. Going to his
knees, Nathan stumbled to his feet in time to take a second
slug above his left knee. There was no cover, no protection,

*Ravines or gullies.

so he bellied-down and began returning the fire. He had the satisfaction of seeing two of his attackers tumble from their saddles, and that had a profound effect on the third rider, Jubal Wells. He dropped back out of range, but the riders who had been flanking Nathan to the north had circled and were now coming at him from the east. Nathan dared not focus his attention on them because Wells would have a clear shot at him. But the four riders had barely begun to fire, when a deadly rifle cut loose somewhere beyond them. Three of them were shot out of their saddles, driving the fourth man straight toward Nathan, who cut him down with a single shot. Suddenly there was silence, all the more profound without the thunder of Winchesters.

Jubal Wells watched helplessly as the distant rifleman killed Kendrick, Connolly, and Warnell, and ground his teeth as Byler rode headlong into Nathan Stone's fire.

"Damn you, Stone," Wells said aloud. "Today you drawed all the high cards, but I owe you, and I pay my debts."

Not believing his good fortune, Nathan waited, his Winchester ready. A single horseman approached from the east, his Winchester across his saddle. Still out of rifle range, he reined up and shouted a greeting.

"You out there! Are you alive?"

"Mostly," Nathan replied, "thanks to you. I'm friendly most of the time."

The rider laughed and kicked his bay into a trot. When he dismounted, Nathan could scarcely believe his eyes. The man was young, slender, and well over six feet. His hair was dark, as was his sweeping mustache. His trousers were dark brown, matching his frock coat, beneath which was a red vest with gold brocade. His fancy red tie accented the flowing red sash that circled his lean waist. He carried a pearl-handled Colt on each hip, and the weapons were thonged-down low. Before conversing any further with Nathan, he went to the grulla, and back-stepping the horse, extracted the hind leg from the hole.

"That leg will be a mite sore for a day or two," said the stranger. "He's a smart one, comin' up short when his leg was caught. Many a jughead would have busted the leg. How bad are you hit?"

"Shoulder and thigh," Nathan replied. "I've been hit

there before, but it never gets any easier. I'm Nathan Stone."

"I'm John Fisher. My friends—the few that claim me—call me King. I have a range, about ten miles from here, near Eagle Pass. I also have an old *Mejicano* housekeeper who's good with bullet wounds. You need some patching up, my friend."

"I'd be obliged," said Nathan.

Fisher brought Nathan's horse, and with some difficulty, he mounted. As they rode south, Fisher caught up Nathan's packhorse. For a while they rode in silence, and it was Fisher who eventually spoke.

"Seems I've heard of you. Maybe from Ben Thompson."

"I know Ben," said Nathan. "I met him across the border, and we barely made it back to Texas, Mexicans shooting at us every jump."

Fisher laughed. "By God, you *do* know the little varmint. I see him maybe twice a year, usually after he's been cut or shot up and lookin' for a place to heal. We killed all of last night in a poker game in a Uvalde saloon. I tried to get Thompson to come to the ranch for a couple of days, but he wanted to ride to Austin. God only knows why. He has no friends there."

"Last time I saw him," said Nathan, "he was dealing monte in a saloon in Ellsworth, Kansas. There was gun trouble, thanks to his brother, Billy."

"He's a damn little fool that can't hold his whiskey," Fisher said. "He's not welcome at my place. Someday, when Ben's not around to save his worthless hide, somebody will fill the little sidewinder full of lead. I'd have done it myself, if he wasn't Ben's brother."

Despite his hurts, Nathan laughed.

Eagle Pass, Texas. January 17, 1874

When they reached a crossroads, a sign caught Nathan's eye. It said THIS IS KING FISHER'S ROAD. TAKE THE OTHER ONE. When they reached Fisher's ranch, a long slab of pine hung above the gate, and burned into it was the name, PENDENCIA. Next to it was the distinctive outline of a crown. The ranch house was of adobe, long and low.

"We'll go in and get Shaniqua started patching you up," said Fisher, "and I'll see to your horses. Can you manage?"

"Yes," Nathan replied, "but I'll be slow."

Fisher held the door open while Nathan limped inside. Shaniqua looked more Indian than Mexican, and without a word, she led them to a bedroom. Quickly she spread a thick blanket over the covers and pointed to the bed. Gratefully, Nathan sank down on it.

"See to his wounds, Shaniqua," Fisher said. With that, he was gone.

Shaniqua said nothing, but began unbuttoning Nathan's trousers. He didn't resist, and helped by unbuttoning his shirt. Thankfully, the slugs had gone on through, and it took but a few minutes for Shaniqua to cleanse the wounds with hot water and apply a fiery disinfectant. She then soaked thick cloth pads with more of the disinfectant, binding a pad tight against the entry and exit wounds.

"Gracias, señora," Nathan said.

Shaniqua nodded and said nothing. She covered Nathan with another blanket and left the room. He was half asleep when King Fisher returned.

"After supper," said Fisher, "Shaniqua will load you down with laudanum, so you can sleep. She'll look in on you during the night. You'll likely be running a fever before morning, and I keep a couple jugs of firewater for that purpose."

"You purely know how to welcome a shot-up hombre," Nathan said.

"You know how it is," said Fisher. "Friends come and go, while enemies accumulate. I've ridden in here pretty well shot-up, myself."

Shaniqua brought the laudanum after supper, and Nathan slept until noon the next day, with only vague recollections of having been given doses of whiskey during the night. Nathan was sweating, had a ravenous thirst, and his head thumped with the remnants of a hangover. Almost immediately, Shaniqua arrived with a breakfast tray that included a pot of scalding black coffee and a pitcher of cold water. King Fisher came in, himself with a cup of coffee, and straddled a ladder-back chair.

"I can't think of a single good quality in whiskey," Nathan said, "except that it makes cold water and hot coffee taste almighty good."

Fisher laughed. "Now dig into the eggs and ham, give it a few days, and you'll be up and around."

* * *

Frustrated, Jubal Wells followed King Fisher and the wounded Nathan Stone until he reached the crossroads and the sign designating "King Fisher's road." There, he reined up, because he had heard of the notorious King Fisher.

"Damn you, Stone," he said aloud, "you can't stay there forever." Wheeling his horse, he rode north, toward San Antonio.

"Shaniqua has adopted your dog," Fisher said. "While your were sleeping off the laudanum and the whiskey, he showed up at the back door looking like he hadn't had grub since the fall of the Alamo."

"He's a hound," said Nathan, "and they always look gaunt, but they're smart. Cotton Blossom has a way of making friends with the cook."

It was the second day following Nathan's arrival at Pendencia ranch. Thanks to plenty of rest, good food, and excellent care, Nathan was able to join King Fisher at the supper table.

"I was pretty used up when we rode in," said Nathan, "but I don't recall seeing any cattle. If it's any of my business, how do you survive?"

Fisher laughed. "It's none of your business, but it's no secret, either. I reckon it's hard to believe but *everybody* in Texas don't raise cattle. Me, I like fine horses, and they don't cause you half the grief of a bunch of cows. Three or four times a year I'll hire riders, but for only two or three weeks at a time. Then we ride across the river into old Mexico and return with a herd of broomtails. They make damn fine cow horses, and since the army has finally decided Texans don't aim to rebuild the Confederacy, the forts right here in Texas will buy all I can deliver. I sell some to the rangers, too."

"I'm partial to horses, myself," Nathan said, "but wasn't there some kind of deal made between the United States and Mexico, after the war, about respecting one another's borders?"

"I seem to recall something along those lines," said Fisher, "but that deal was struck between Yankee politicians in Washington and *Mejicano* brass in Mexico City. The average peon don't care a damn what goes on in Mexico City, just like it don't bother me what the politicians are doin' in Washington. Across the river, I can hire Mex *vaqueros* for a dollar a day, and they know where the horse herds are. Of course, we have to dodge the Mex border patrol, but they're spread almighty thin. Mexico's got one hell of a border."

"I've always wanted to be part of a wild horse hunt," said Nathan. "I don't know how much help I'd be, but I don't expect to be paid."

"Just before or during the foaling season is the worst possible time," Fisher said, "and that kills February, March, and April. I'm planning another hunt during the first two or three weeks in May. You're welcome to ride along."

"I'd like that," said Nathan, "but that's three and a half months away. How do I earn my keep here until then?"

"You're not expected to," Fisher replied. "That's one of the benefits of selling horses instead of cows. You work maybe three months out of the year, and the rest of the time, you're free to ride into town, playing cards, and raising hell. On Friday, I generally ride into Uvalde or San Antonio and buy into an all-night poker game. You play poker?"

Nathan laughed. "Among other things, I've been a house dealer off and on, for maybe seven years. I can make a living dealing an honest game."

"Well, by God," King Fisher roared, "an hombre after my own heart. If you're up to it, we'll ride next Friday and have us a couple days of town living."

"I'll be ready well before then," said Nathan.

"I'll breathe a mite easier, havin' somebody to watch my back," Fisher replied. "There are folks in these parts that'd gun me down, just because they consider me a friend to Ben Thompson, and they hate his guts. Then there's some who hate *my* guts."

"I can't say I blame you for ridin' in," said Nathan. "It'd be a shame to disappoint all those people."

King Fisher laughed. "Stone, if I'm any judge, I'm plumb goin' to enjoy your stay at Pendencia ranch. You don't have a troublesome, snot-nosed little brother that can't hold his whiskey, driftin' around, do you?"

"No, thank God," Nathan said, knowing who he was referring to.

"Next Friday, then," said Fisher. "We'll hit San Antone like twin bolts of lightning."

Nathan wasn't sure he liked the sound of that, although

he did like King Fisher and his wild horse hunts. While King Fisher would never replace Ranger Captain Sage Jennings, he would still be a friend, and Nathan had no other in south Texas.

During the next few days, Cotton Blossom became friendly enough with Shaniqua that Nathan believed the dog would remain with her while he and King Fisher rode to town. He spoke to Fisher about it.

"I reckon if you don't drink or play poker, a saloon ain't much of a place to spend the night," Fisher said. "Leave him here, if he'll stay."

San Antonio, Texas. January 23, 1874

Nathan and Fisher rode out just before noon, bound for town. Riding in, hurt and sick from his wounds, Nathan hadn't fully appreciated King Fisher's spread. Now he did. It was near enough to the Rio Grande to see the fringe of greenery that marked the course of the river, and as far as the eye could see, there was no other sign of human presence.

"I like your ranch," Nathan said, "but how do you protect it when you're away?"

"I have friends across the river," Fisher replied, "and for several reasons, they don't want anything to happen to me or my ranch. There's Shaniqua, and they respect her. Then there's the cold, hard cash two or three times a year, when I hire Mexican riders. Besides that, I buy fruits and vegetables from poor farmers. When I need beef, I buy from some of the *vaqueros* who ride with me hunting wild horses."

"With free range and mavericks, you could rope your own beef," said Nathan.

"I could," Fisher said, "but then, who would protect the Pendencia when I'm away?"

San Antonio had changed little since Nathan had last seen it. He and Fisher rode past the old house that had once been the headquarters for Roy Bean's freight line.

"Last time I was here," said Nathan, "Roy Bean was living there, hauling freight from Corpus Christi."

Fisher laughed. "They finally evicted him for not paying his rent, but the old buzzard beat them. He was there near two years, most of it rent-free."*

*Roy Bean operated a freight line from San Antonio for twenty-two years.

"I haven't been here in a while," Nathan said, "so I'll follow your lead."

"I generally hang out at the Alamo Saloon," said Fisher. "They're open all night on Friday and Saturday, and the Cattleman's Hotel is just across the street. I keep a running tab at both places. Sometimes when I'm between horse hunts, I'm financially embarrassed."

"I have money," Nathan said, "if you're up against it. I got lucky on a horse race at twenty-to-one odds."

"God Almighty," said Fisher, "with luck like that, maybe I'll just follow you around and place my bets behind you. Do you follow the races?"

"I don't go out of my way," Nathan replied, "but if there's one close by, I won't pass it up."

"There's one in Uvalde every July fourth," said Fisher. "Why don't you stick around for that? We had some Mex riders last year, and one of them took home some money."

"That was some hell of a war," Nathan said. "I reckoned you south Texans and the Mexicans would still be shootin' at one another across the river."

King Fisher laughed. "Can't. We're too busy. They got varmints in their own country that needs a dose of lead, just like we got some here in south Texas that's needful of the same treatment. Some Sunday we'll ride across the border for a *Mejicano* rooster pull."

"What in thunder is that?"

"They bury a bunch of roosters in the sand up to their necks," said Fisher. "A rider kicks his horse into a fast gallop, and leaning from the saddle, tries to snatch a rooster's head off."

"I've heard of games like that among the Indians," Nathan said, "but they generally try to pick up an arrow from the ground. Why do Mexicans use roosters?"

"Hell, I dunno," said Fisher. "Why do they hot up their grub with enough pepper to melt an iron skillet?"

"Thompson told me he once had a mess of *tamales* in Reynosa, and had to spend the next three days settin' in the creek."

"Get Ben drunk and he'll eat armadillo," Fisher said. "A man that ain't satisfied with steak oughta be run out of Texas and made to live in Cajun country, where they eat crab, alligator tail, and the like."

Nathan laughed. "Gettin' back to the horse races, have

you ever considered keeping a few of the captured horses and racing them?"

"Yes," said Fisher, "but I usually have buyers for all I can catch. But there is one I'd keep for breeding and racing, if I could catch him. He's a black that we've named Son of Satan, because he'll stomp the life out of you, if he can. For any man who brings him to me, I have a standing offer of a thousand dollars."

"The hell with the money," Nathan said. "How can a man put a price on an experience like that, of capturing such a horse?"

"I couldn't," said King Fisher. "If it became a matter of money, I'd sell the ranch to own him."

Leaving the horses at the livery, Nathan and King Fisher entered the Cattleman's Hotel, where Fisher took a room for them through Saturday night.

"That increases your balance to two hundred and twenty dollars," the desk clerk said.

"This reduces it to zero," said Nathan, placing eleven double eagles on the counter.

King Fisher said nothing until they reached their second-floor room, and when he turned on Nathan, his eyes were cold, his voice dangerously calm.

"Stone, I'm forgivin' it this time, because your intentions are good and you ain't a born and bred Texan, but by God, don't you ever do that again. If I'm needin' money, I'll ask for it."

Gritting his teeth, Nathan withheld an explosive reply. Fisher hung his hat on a bedpost, shucked his guns, and tugged off his boots. He then stretched out on one of the two beds. Nathan followed his example, and they dozed until suppertime.

The Alamo was the most imposing saloon in San Antonio, with two full-length bars and four to six barkeeps. Nathan and Fisher bought into a game of five-card stud. Bets were five dollars. Nathan and Fisher each lost sixty dollars before their luck changed, and when it did, they began getting angry looks from the other four men. With each pot worth a hundred and twenty dollars, King Fisher won three in a row, while Nathan took the next two. The diamonds kept coming, and Nathan couldn't believe his eyes. All he needed was a queen, and it came on the last draw.

He showed his hand and turned his hole card, the jack of diamonds. There was a shocked silence, for he had drawn a queen-high, straight flush.

"I'm out," said one of the gamblers. "I ain't never seen luck such as that."

"Me neither," said a second man. "I ain't playin' agin him."

"I'm wonderin' if it's all luck," a third man said darkly.

"It wasn't my deal," Nathan said. "You're welcome to look at the cards."

"Hell, no, they ain't," King Fisher snarled, "I've played with this bunch before. They'll take your money all night, but win some of theirs, and they're ready to holler cheat."

Fisher had kicked his chair back just enough, and his eyes dared any man to so much as move. Nobody did. Nathan broke the uneasy silence.

"Take a hand, gents. I'm not goin' anywhere. You have a chance to win your money back."

There were murmurs of approval, and the two disgruntled men who had withdrawn again took their seats. It was King Fisher's turn to deal, and he and Nathan quickly lost twenty dollars of their winnings. When it came Nathan's turn to deal, he and Fisher each lost another pot. They withdrew from the game and went to the bar for a beer.

"Time to fold 'em," said Nathan. "I won't have another decent hand all night."

"I've never seen a man draw a queen-high straight in five-card stud," Fisher said.

"The odds were with me," Nathan replied, "and that's what I like about five-card stud. In a six-man game, by the time you come to the last draw, you have more than half the deck in play, all but six cards faceup. The other three queens were on the table, and my chance of drawing the diamond lady was one in twenty. It's a game of numbers, my friend."

"I believe you," said Fisher. "You've had experience, and it shows. That was slick, the way you put down them poor losers. I thought we was goin' to have to shoot our way out of there."

"Again, you're playing the odds," Nathan said. "I've shot my way out of a few games, and that's doing it the hard way. The more often you rely on your guns, the greater the odds that you'll take a bad one, right between the eyes."

"By God, you're a good influence," said Fisher. "I

reckon I've played too much poker with Ben Thompson. The little varmint's got a hair-trigger temper. Say the wrong thing to him, and he's got just one answer, and that's with a gun."

"He's bucking the odds," Nathan said. "He'll likely cash in with his brains leaking out on a poker table."

Nathan and Fisher visited other saloons, buying into other poker games, then moving on. At midnight—having had an early supper—they found a cafe and ate again. Fisher emptied his pockets on the table.

"I'm more than two hundred dollars ahead!" he exclaimed. "You're bringin' me luck."

"Whether you win or lose at the table isn't nearly as important as staying alive," said Nathan. "The odds are always in your favor when you use your brains instead of your gun."

CHAPTER 13

San Antonio, Texas. January 24, 1874
Saturday morning, King Fisher and Nathan had just sat down to breakfast in a cafe when a stranger approached their table. Nathan believed he had seen the man before, and when he nodded his head, King Fisher relaxed. The stranger, dressed in range clothes, was about thirty and had a tied-down, butt-forward Colt on his left hip. He spoke to Nathan.

"You may not remember me, but I was with Captain Sage Jennings, at Austin. My name is Bodie West. The captain always spoke highly of you, and I wondered if you knew of his death."

"I do," said Nathan. "I last saw him at Fort Worth, and when I telegraphed Captain Ferguson to inquire about him, Ferguson sent me the bad news. Take a chair and join us for breakfast. This is my amigo, King Fisher."

West nodded, dragged out a chair, and sat down. Nothing more was said until they all had first cups of coffee and had ordered their breakfasts.

"We suspected the Horrells had ambushed him," West said, "but by the time we got our orders to question them, they had quit the territory. Yesterday, I got word they've all come back. But their outlaw kin, Clint Barkley, wasn't with them. Nobody's seen him."

"Nobody will," said Nathan. "I learned for certain he was the back-shootin' little sidewinder that ambushed Captain Jennings. I found him in New Mexico, and he'll stay there until judgment day. I promised Cap I'd find him, that he would pay."

Without a word, West extended his hand, and Nathan took it. The ranger swallowed hard, and finally he spoke.

"We're obliged, and I say that in behalf of the State of Texas. The next time you're in Austin, I think we'll have something for you. Something from the captain."

Breakfast was mostly a silent affair, and the ranger was the first to leave. Not until he had gone did King Fisher speak.

"Stone, I reckon I spoke out of turn last night, when I said you wasn't a born-and-bred Texan. You're as much a Texan as any of us, and maybe more so than some. It takes a big man to avenge a friend, and if I cash in with a bullet in the back, then I hope somebody cares enough to go after the varmint that done it."

Nathan said nothing, ill at ease, wishing he had met the young ranger at another time and place. Leaving the cafe, they returned to the hotel, where Nathan bought newspapers from San Antonio and Austin. Reaching their room, Nathan stretched out on the bed with the papers. Uneasy with the silence, King Fisher spoke.

"You're the only hombre I ever rode with that bought and read newspapers."

"It's a habit," Nathan said. "When you're stuck in town, there's nothing to do except drink and play poker. I've never got my tail in a crack, reading newspapers."

"If I had your luck," said Fisher, "I'd give up everything except poker."

"Here's something about Clay Allison," Nathan said. "On January seventh, he gunned down a gent name of Chunk Colbert, in Colfax County, New Mexico Territory."

"I've heard of him," said Fisher. "He's said to be chain

lightning with a Colt. He's got a horse ranch near Cimarron, almost on the Colorado line."*

Finding nothing else of interest in the papers, Nathan slept until the afternoon. When he awoke, King Fisher was gone, and it was near suppertime when he returned.

"I got restless," said Fisher, "and I've been out wandering about town. I reckon it's not too early for supper, if you're ready."

Nathan pulled on his boots, belted on his guns, donned his hat, and they returned to the cafe where they'd had breakfast.

"Let's go back to the Alamo for some more five-card stud," Fisher said. "I like your style and I'd like to watch you play."

Nathan said nothing, finding the praise a little embarrassing. Supper finished, they left the cafe, Nathan first. He was barely out the door when a slug ripped into the door frame just inches from his head. The shot had come from a vacant store building across the street. Colt in his hand, Nathan headed for it in a zigzag run, King Fisher right behind him. There were no more shots. On either side of the vacant building there was open space all the way to the alley, and Nathan took one side while Fisher took the other. The alley seemed deserted and the back door to the building stood open, hanging forlornly on a single hinge.

"Damn," said Fisher, "he could have ducked into any one of a dozen places down this alley. You got any idea who the varmint was?"

"Yes," Nathan replied. "This is the last of the bunch that was ridin' me down, when you saved my bacon."

"He's ain't got the sand to face you, then," said Fisher. "Do you know the varmit by sight?"

"Yes," Nathan replied, "and I don't aim to duck and dodge around while he stalks me. He's in this town somewhere, and I'm going after him."

"By God," said Fisher, "this is my kind of game. If you don't mind, I'll trail along, so's he don't plug you in the back."

"He's that kind," Nathan replied. "Come on."

They visited every hotel and rooming house Fisher could

---

*Clay Allison eventually fled Cimarron after killing a sheriff who came to arrest him.

...ink of, but found none that had rented a room to Jubal ...ells.

"Maybe he's usin' another name," Fisher suggested.

"Maybe he hasn't taken a room anywhere," said Nathan. He could be just prowling the streets, keeping out of sight, ...aiting for another chance."

"Then let's give him that chance," Fisher said. "We'll go ...ack to the Alamo Saloon and have a beer or two. Just ...nside the back door, there's a storeroom. We'll go in there ...ust long enough for you to take my hat and coat and for ...ne to take yours. By then it'll be dark enough for an hom- ...re across the street to mistake me for you. You'll ease out ...he back door of the Alamo and around to the front, keep- ...n' in the shadow of the overhang. After giving you time ...o get in position, I will step out the front door. When this bastard cuts down on me, you blast him to hell and gone."

"No," Nathan said. "I appreciate what you're offering to do, but I won't have you swapping your life for mine. With a lamp on each side of the door, how could he miss?"

"Hell, we don't know that he'll fall for it," said Fisher, "but I believe he will. There's nothin' to get excited about when somebody fires a shot, unless there's a dead body, and we shucked out from that cafe before anybody could call the law. Now, unless you've got a better plan, let's use mine. There's some risk for me, but a lot more for you, until you gun down this slippery coyote."

King Fisher was dead serious, because the element of danger excited him. Realizing it was something the man actually wanted to do, Nathan agreed. There was always a chance that Wells could attempt another ambush before they were able to carry out Fisher's plan, but that, too, was part of the risk. Fisher walked behind Nathan, and Nathan entered the Alamo Saloon first. After one beer, they made as if to exit by the back door, but instead, went into the storeroom. There, they swapped hats and coats.

"Just be damn sure you allow me enough time to get into position," said Nathan.

"I aim to," Fisher replied. "I won't deny you the plea- sure of saltin' down this coyote, if possible, but keep one thing in mind; with a sidewinder throwin' lead at me, it's plumb against my religion not to shoot back."

"I'm not selfish," said Nathan. "You're taking all the risk. If you can nail him before I do, then be my guest."

Nathan slipped out the back door of the saloon, and keeping well within the shadow of the roof's overhang, made his way along the building's outside wall, toward the front. He reached his position, feeling certain he hadn' been seen. A killer would have his eyes on the well-lighted front entrance, and therein lay King Fisher's risk. His Colt ready, Nathan peeked around the corner, his eyes on the front entrance. King Fisher stepped out, and seeming to drop something, bent over. At that very instant, two slugs slammed into the wall, chest-high. Nathan's Colt roared as he fired at the muzzle flashes, and adding to it was the thunder from King Fisher's weapon, as, on his knees, he returned fire. It was over as suddenly as it had begun, and men boiled out of the Alamo Saloon. The sheriff, Owen Perryman, came on the run, and the first man he saw was King Fisher.

"Damn it, I might have known, with all this shootin' goin' on, you'd somehow be in the middle of it. You got some explaining to do, Fisher."

"Maybe I'd better explain it, Sheriff," said Nathan. "I've had a bushwhacker stalking me, and King just stepped out of the saloon wearing my hat and coat. He drew fire from the other side of the street, and if you're needin' somebody to blame for all this, have a look over there."

The sheriff lighted the lantern he'd brought with him, and accompanied by a horde of men from the saloon, headed across the street. He returned almost immediately, followed by shouting men.

"Damn it," Perryman bawled, "hold it down." The shouting ceased and the sheriff spoke to Nathan. "He's dead as he'll ever be, with a pistol in his hand. From what I can see, there'll be no charges, if you're claiming self-defense."

"That's exactly what I'm claiming," said Nathan. "He'd already had one shot at me today, and my friend Fisher joined me in setting a trap for him."

"By God, you done a prime job," somebody said. "That hombre was drilled through his middle, three times."

Nathan and Fisher got away before anybody got around to questioning them, taking a roundabout way through the back entrance of the Cattleman's Hotel, just down the street.

"It's been a while since I've had any excitement," Fisher

said, when they had reached their room. "But you saw how it was. I kill some skunk that's tryin' to kill me, and the law's there, Johnny-on-the-spot, ready to plant me in the *juzgado*. By God, if it gets any more civilized around here, I'll have to move the Pendencia ranch to the Mex side of the river."

Nathan laughed. "I reckon this has ruined our Saturday night. We won't be able to go anywhere in town without having to answer questions I'd as soon leave unanswered."

"No matter," said Fisher. "When I can get shot at and live to talk about it and ride out sober with two hundred in poker winnings, I reckon it's time to go. There'll be other nights, other poker games, and we never even got to the women."

Eventually, having been seen with King Fisher, Nathan was accepted in San Antonio and Uvalde. Despite his winning far more than he lost, Nathan Stone was respected for his honest game. When he won he didn't gloat and when he lost he didn't whine. On a third visit to San Antonio, Nathan and Fisher arrived in the early afternoon.

"I'd better go by the bank and stash some of this money," Fisher said. "Then if I hit a losin' streak, I won't be tempted to try and recoup my losses."

They had dismounted when a shot rang out within the bank. The doors were flung open and four men came out on the run, guns blazing. A slug burned King Fisher's horse, and the animal reared. Lead kicked up dust at Nathan's feet, chunked into the hitching rail, and ripped into a water trough. Drawing his Colt, Nathan went to his knees, while King Fisher bellied-down behind the water trough, and the two of them cut down on the bank robbers. Three of the men fell, one of whom had the sack with the loot from the robbery. The fourth man reached his horse and rode for his life.

"Damn," said Nathan, wiping his sweaty face on the sleeve of his shirt, "a man can get ventilated in this town, just minding his own business."

"Almost never a dull moment," King Fisher said, "and the fun ain't over. Our amigo, Sheriff Perryman, will come gallopin' along just any time, now, and we'll have to explain all this to him. He'll likely try to arrest us as part of the gang."

But when Sheriff Perryman arrived, the bank personnel were there, lavish with their praise for Nathan and King Fisher. While a teller had been wounded, three of the bandits had been killed and all the money recovered. Almost grudgingly, Sheriff Perryman turned to Nathan and Fisher.

"Good piece of work. Now you hombres go on about your business."

Reynosa, Old Mexico. May 1, 1874

Nathan and Fisher reined up at a little adobe hut just across the Rio Grande. A rider stepped out of a nearby log barn. His enormous sombrero shaded his face. His shirt and trousers were of rough homespun, while his *chaqueta* and *chaparreras* were of leather. King Fisher nodded to Nathan and they dismounted.

"*Hola, mi amigo*," said Fisher.

"*Buenos Dias, señor*," the Mexican replied.

"Nathan," Fisher said, "this is Pancho Gomez. Pancho, this is my amigo, Nathan Stone. He will accompany us in the hunt for *caballos*."

"*Si*," Pancho said. "*Bienvenido*."

Nathan and Fisher followed Pancho into the adobe hut, and he led them to the small kitchen where there was a crude wooden table with a bench on either side. A Mexican woman nodded to them.

"Nathan, this is Maria," said Fisher, by way of introduction.

Following Pancho's lead, Nathan and Fisher took their seats at the table, while Maria brought each of them a heavy earthen mug.

"*Doloroso*," Pancho said. "No coffee."

"There's pulque and goat's milk," said Fisher. "I recommend the goat's milk. I reckon the pulque's about a hundred and forty proof."

"I'll pass on both," Nathan said.

They waited only a few minutes. At the sound of approaching horses, Pancho led them outside to greet the rest of the riders. They dismounted, all of them dressed much like Pancho. Some of them had cartwheel spurs with underslung chains that chinged with every step. They swept off their sombreros as King Fisher introduced them to Nathan.

"This is Juan Corona," said Fisher. "He thinks like a wild horse, and the critter next to him is Hidalgo Allende,

nd he eats like one. Then there's Pedro Calzada and Jar-
in Panduro. They drink pulque instead of water, and man-
ge to stay alive. God alone knows how."

The Mexicans, comfortable with Fisher's humor, laughed
proariously. They looked approvingly upon the two
oaded packhorses Fisher had brought, and Nathan began
o appreciate the Texan's relationship with his neighbors
cross the river.

"Whoa," said Fisher, "I almost forgot something." Going
to his horse, he removed a cloth sack from his saddlebag.
This he gave to Pancho. "Coffee beans for Maria," he said.

"Gracias," Pancho replied, starting for the adobe hut.

When Pancho returned, they mounted and rode south,
Pancho leading the way. As they rode deeper into the country, there was a series of breaks—rough terrain—shot full
of washes and gullies. On exposed ridgetops and dry slopes,
there was no sign of life except occasional clumps of bris-
tlecone pine. There was some cholla and prickly pear cactus. Finally they rode for more than a mile across a barren
alkalai plain. At the edge of it was a spring. The horses
dearly wanted to get to the water, but Pancho shook his
head.

"Alkalai water," said Fisher.

"I don't see how anything can live in this country," Nathan said. "No graze."

"There's graze and water in the mountains and the foothills
surrounding them," said Fisher. "That's where we're going.
We won't get much done today, except set up camp."

Pancho Gomez knew exactly where he was going, and
three hours before sundown, he led them to a *cienaga,* a
cool hollow overhung with willows. At the base of the slope
was a spring with a runoff, fed by a never-ending fall of
water from a rock crevice above.

"Good water," said Fisher. "In this land, when you find
a good spring, you stay with it, even if you have to ride
fifty miles at day's end, gettin' back to it."

It was a good camp, and the Mexican riders proved amia-
ble companions. Even Cotton Blossom joined them for supper, a thing he rarely did when strangers were present that
he hadn't gotten used to.

"It'll be a long day," Fisher said, as they finished their
breakfast coffee. "There's two or three canyons we can use,

any of 'em a good two-hour ride from here. How handy are you with a double-bitted ax?"

"I can use it when I have to," said Nathan, "but I've never had much of a liking for it."

Fisher and the Mexican riders laughed. "Neither has any of us," Fisher replied, "but it purely has a place when you're buildin' a catch pen. I brought three of the critters, so we can take turns. When we're done with you, Stone, you'll be an honest-to-God wrangler, a *cazador de caballada.*"

When they broke camp, nothing was left behind. Despite the friendliness of the Mexican riders, they were still in hostile territory. As they rode, King Fisher explained some of the problems they might encounter.

"Sometimes, catching the horses is the easy part. There are bands of thieves who will steal a horse from under you, if you'll hold still. As any of my amigos can tell you, one of their favorite tricks is to wait until a catch has been made and the horses gentled. Then they'll steal the herd, drive the horses across the border, and sell them."

"That sounds like the *Comancheros* that used to steal cattle from Goodnight and other trail drivers, selling the cows to the military," Nathan said.

"Good comparison," said Fisher. "There's always a flock of thieving buzzards ready to swoop down and take what better men have paid for with sweat and callused hands."

"Not this time," Nathan said.

The canyon, when they reached it, seemed ideal, for there was a spring midway, with a substantial runoff.

"More work for us," said King Fisher, "because we'll have to block both ends, but the good water will bring the herds to us."

"This may sound like a greenhorn question," Nathan said, "but how can you barricade both ends of the canyon without scaring the horses away? Hell, there ain't a horse alive that don't recognize a fence."

"Damn good question," Fisher replied. "I don't know what's the best way, but I can tell you how we do it. Wild horse herds always come to water at night or at dawn, so our work has to be done in between waterings, and the surroundings can't change drastically enough for the wild ones to notice. Contrary to what some folks think, a wise old mare is usually leading the herd, while the stallion rings up the rear. We can't close either end of the canyon more than maybe a third or less, and we do that gradually, over three or four days. Across the part we leave open, we dig post holes, carefully removing the dirt and concealing the holes with dead leaves or grass. Fence rails are made ready. When the herd is into the canyon, riders at both ends will get the posts in place and then rawhide the rails into position, four-high."

"Sounds simple enough," said Nathan. "The horses never challenge the fence?"

"Not often," Fisher replied. "That stallion I was telling you about jumped the fence once, and we added a fourth rail. We ain't been able to catch him again."

"No rain," said Pedro Calzada. "Many *caballos* come here."

"That bein' the case," Fisher said, "we may have a chance at the big black."

"You have to gentle the horses enough so they can be driven," said Nathan. "How long does that take?"

"It mostly depends on how many we catch," Fisher replied. "Could take as long as two weeks."

Nathan said no more. He remembered the days in New Orleans when Eulie Prater had gone into the corral with an unruly black horse and had made friends with the animal just by talking to it. He wanted to observe the method King Fisher and the Mexican riders used with these wild ones.

The sun was an hour high before King Fisher was ready to begin work on the fence. The portion of the canyon whose walls were high enough to restrain wild horses was less than three-quarters of a mile in length.

"We'll use dead wood for a third of the fence at each end," King Fisher said. "Horses are smart enough to know something's not right, if they can smell the sap of newly cut trees and limbs. A couple of windblown trees snaked into position is a good start."

At the end of the first day, one entrance to the canyon was one-third blocked with a barricade of dead logs and brush higher than a man's head. Nathan had to admit it didn't look unnatural enough to frighten a horse.

"We'll wait another day or two to dig the post holes for the rest of the fence," Fisher said, "giving them a chance to become used to the brush and log pile. Tomorrow, we'll

go to the other end of the canyon and barricade part o
that entrance. Then we'll have only to dig the post holes
cut the posts, and the rails."

The building of the second barricade raised as much
sweat and blisters as the first, and when it was finished,
they set about cutting the necessary posts and rails. The
heavy posts were ten feet long, and starting three feet from
the bottom, were notched four times, two feet apart, where
the rails would be secured with rawhide. There would be
three posts and eight ten-foot-long rails required to close
each end of the canyon. By noon of the third day, the posts
and rails were ready.

"Now comes the hard part," Fisher said, "and I only
brought one post-hole digger, so we'll take turns. Hot as it
is, we'll all do a little digging, so it won't be so hard on
any of us. I'll go first."

After breaking through a crust of *caliche,* there was hard
clay, and before the first post hole was deep enough, every
man was sweating. Dirt removed from the hole was put on
a four-foot square of canvas, and taken away, lest the incoming herd be suspicious.

"Now," said Fisher, when the holes were finally finished,
"we'll cover all the ground around and near the holes with
dead leaves. We want the ground to look as natural as we
can make it. We'll be right here until we're ready to drive
the herd across the river."

"We can't go into the canyon," Nathan said. "What
about water?"

Hidalgo Allende pointed to the canyon rim.

"The water that forms the spring in the canyon originates
on the rim," Fisher said. "We'll water our mounts and get
water for our own use up there. We must stay away from
the spring where the wild ones go. There'll be a full moon
tonight, and I think we'll just observe those who come to
water, giving them a chance to overcome any suspicions
they may have."

Shortly after moonrise they took a position on the canyon rim from which they could see the spring and both
their brush barricades. The moon rose higher, a silver globe
that mantled the rugged, broken land with a spectral glow.
They waited for what seemed hours, shifting their positions
occasionally to rest tired, cramped muscles. The first sound

of their coming was so slight it might have existed only in imagination. But no! There it was again. Then, appearing silver in the moonlight, they could see the trailwise old white mare nearing the partially brush-barricaded canyon mouth. For a long moment she stood there, keening the down-canyon breeze, like a wolf. Finally, when she half turned to the waiting herd, the sound that came from her throat wasn't quite a nicker. It was more a rumble. And then the others came. There were sorrels, bays, duns, chestnuts, browns, blacks, grays, and grullas. A solid black stallion brought up the rear, nipping at the flanks of the stragglers. The watching men hardly dared breathe as the horses—thirty or more—made their way to the water. The majestic stallion remained where he was, lifting his head toward the canyon rims, seeming to sense the presence of danger. Not until the rest of the herd had drunk their fill did he approach the water, and even as he drank, he raised his head occasionally, listening. The white mare started back the way she had come, most of the herd following. The few that lingered received a painful nip from the stallion. They left as quietly as they had come, fading into the distance. Only then did anyone speak.

"My God," said King Fisher, "did you ever see the like?"

"He reminds me of a black I once knew," Nathan said. "He ran like the wind and in a quarter-mile run, could outrun anything on four feet. I'd bet all I ever hope to own that this big black could do as well or better."

"Damn it," said King Fisher, "I've got to have him. If I could take him to the races at San Antone on July fourth, I could bust every tinhorn gambler in south Texas."

"*Diablo*," Jardin Panduro said. "*Caballo de muerte.*"*

"*Si,*" the other Mexican riders agreed.

"Maybe," Fisher said, "but I don't believe there's a horse alive that can't be gentled, if it's done right and you take enough time."

"You may not have that much time," said Nathan, "unless you aim to spend the rest of the summer here in this canyon. It'll be a hell of a ride back to your place, if you're fightin' that big black on a lead rope all the way."

"*Si, si,*" the Mexican riders agreed.

*Devil. Horse of death.

King Fisher said nothing. He got up and stomped back toward the distant canyon in which they had picketed their horses.

"No *diablo caballo,* no mucho *pesos,*" said Pancho Gomez.

"Whoa," Nathan said. "You only have to catch the horse. You do not gentle him. If we catch this *diablo caballo,* will our trap hold him?"

"Per'ap," said Pancho Gomez.

"Then let's get him," Nathan said. "I want to see what our Texas amigo can do with him, if it does take all summer."

CHAPTER 14

The following day, time dragged, for the riders had time on their hands, waiting for nightfall. King Fisher seemed preoccupied, and said little. Nathan suspected he had on his mind the elusive black stallion. It was frustrating enough, not having been able to catch the black, but once captured, suppose he proved impossible to tame? They had supper well before dark, doused the fire, and picketed their horses in a canyon a good distance away from the canyon where the wild horses came to drink.

"Nathan," said Fisher, "you'll stay with Juan Corona, Hidalgo Allende, and me, at the upper end of the canyon. Pancho, you'll take Pedro and Jardin, and cover the lower end. With any luck, the herd won't show until after moonrise. Wait until they begin to drink before you make your move. Get those posts in place pronto. Once they discover we've got both ends of the canyon covered, there'll be some confusion, and that's all the advantage we'll have. We'll have just a matter of seconds to place the posts and secure the rails."

The Mexican riders said nothing, nor did they need to, because they had done this before. Nathan kept his silence, believing he was still on the bad side of King Fisher for having been so outspoken the day before. At dusk, they all took their assigned places, far enough back in the brush that there was no chance of discovery. Then they could only wait for the arrival of the herd. The full moon rose, bathing the rugged landscape in silver, and still they waited. The moon had already begun its descent when there was a sound near the mouth of the canyon, a sound so slight they almost dismissed it as imaginary, a trick of the mind. Then, seeming almost ghostly, they could see the wise old white mare picking her way down the canyon. Reaching the partial barrier they had erected, she paused for what seemed an eternity. Would she enter? Finally she did, sounding her approval, which was somewhere between a grunt and a nicker. Behind her came the herd, followed by the black stallion, ever wary. Fisher didn't move until the mare had reached the spring and the stallion was well past the place where the fence would be raised.

"Come on," Fisher hissed, "let's get those posts in position."

Fisher and each of the two Mexican riders seized a post, and when misfortune struck, it was Fisher himself who was at fault. A rock rolled under his boot and he fell, dropping the heavy post. Almost immediately there was a warning nicker from the stallion. Nathan took up the post and drove it into one of the prepared holes. Fisher came on the run with one of the rails. Nathan took one end, and they rawhided it to two of the posts in the top position. Juan Corona and Hidalgo Allende quickly secured another rail, while Nathan and Fisher ran back for a third. They had all but two rails lashed in place when they heard the stallion nicker again, as the herd started back down-canyon.

"By God, we got 'em all!" said King Fisher gleefully.

Nobody else said anything, but Nathan caught the swift looks that passed between the two Mexican riders. They had been successful only because of the swiftness of the riders at the other end of the canyon, for when King Fisher had fallen, the wild horses had been spooked in the other direction. That alone had given them enough time to recover from Fisher's noisy tumble. The black stallion galloped up to the fence and reared on his hind legs as though to crush the barrier. He then turned and raced to the other end of the canyon.

"If there's a way out," Nathan said, "he'll find it."

"Then he'd better find it before daylight," said Fisher.

"That's when him and me will start gettin' acquainted. You got to show a horse you're not afraid of him."

But Fisher was in for an unpleasant surprise. When he crawled through the fence, the black stallion came after him, teeth bared. Fisher didn't have time for anything except to hit the ground and roll under the fence, and even then, the stallion caught the back of his shirt in those mighty teeth. The fabric ripped, allowing Fisher to escape, minus most of his shirt. His hat was on the other side of the fence, and he watched the black stallion pulverize it with those lethal hooves. Pancho Gomez shook his head and said what the rest of them were thinking.

"He never be your *companero,* señor. You kill him or he kill you, I think."

"I don't care a damn what you think," Fisher shouted. "Find another canyon and herd the rest of these broomtails into it, leaving this black devil where he is. By God, I can hold out as long as he can."

Nathan had his doubts. For starters, he wondered how the Mexican riders were going to drive the wild horses anywhere, granted they were able to separate them from the black stallion. While King Fisher stood near the fence brooding over the vicious stallion, Nathan spoke quietly to Pancho Gomez.

"The rest of those horses are as wild as the stallion. How do you aim to drive them anywhere?"

"The white mare, señor. She has not always been wild, for she wears a brand. Per'ap she not forget."

To Nathan's surprise, the Mexican riders managed to find a box canyon with water and graze. They built a fence so that the rails could be removed. Pancho then began to work with the white mare, and five days later, the wild horses—with the exception of the stallion—were driven to the new holding pen. The Mexican riders began working with the wild horses, leaving King Fisher alone with his challenge. While Nathan would have liked to remain with the *vaqueros,* he decided what Fisher was attempting to do would be far more interesting. Besides, he might have to drag the Texan from beneath the deadly hooves of the stallion. The big black hadn't been still since his capture. He stalked from one end of his canyon prison to the other, seeking a way out. Five days after his first attempt, Fisher tried again. The stallion was at the far end of the canyon, but when

Fisher climbed over the fence, the horse came after him at a fast gallop. Fisher stood his ground, determined to defy the horse, and almost too late, he stepped aside. The stallion wheeled and came after him again, teeth bared. Fisher lost his nerve, but this time, he didn't make it under the fence. The black stallion sunk his teeth into Fisher's backside. Nathan drew his Colt and fired twice over the horse's head. Only then did he let go of Fisher, allowing him to get under the fence. Fisher lay belly-down, gasping for breath. Finally he got to his hands and knees. Nathan managed not to laugh and said nothing. The burden of any conversation lay with King Fisher, and to Nathan's surprise, the Texan spoke.

"It looks like, by God, I'll have to get a saddle on the bastard and ride him down."

"That's no way to tame a horse," Nathan said. "The best you'd ever have is a horse that hates your guts."

"Then what would you do with him?"

"I'd take down that fence and set him free," said Nathan.

"Never in hell," Fisher said.

"One way or the other," said Nathan, "you're going to lose him. Look."

The stallion was trying to climb the canyon wall. He had dug in his hooves, inching his way painfully along, only to lose his footing and fall to the canyon floor. Undaunted, he struggled to his feet, blood glistening on his rump. Three more times the horse tried to creep up the impossibly steep wall, and three times he fell. It was more than Nathan Stone could stand. With his knife he slashed the rawhide securing the rails to the posts, and the barrier was down.

"Damn it," Fisher shouted, "that's my horse!"

"No," said Nathan, "he's not your horse, and he never will be. He'll go free or he'll die. Now you and me are going to get our horses and ride away from here. You have the horses you came for, if you can keep this devil horse from taking them away from you."

They rode out, bound for the canyon where the Mexican cowboys held the rest of the captured horses. Cotton Blossom loped ahead. Pancho Gomez watched them ride up.

"Diablo caballo?" the Mexican inquired.

"I turned him loose," Fisher said. "Now we got to get the rest of these broomtails out of here before he comes lookin' for 'em."

Pancho shrugged, rolling his eyes heavenward, as though seeking strength. He then turned away, taking the unwelcome news to his companions. King Fisher stood up in his stirrups. In their argument over the stallion, Nathan had forgotten about the animal sinking its teeth into Fisher. It would be a touchy subject, but he spoke.

"That horse bite needs some attention. It could become infected."

"De nada," Fisher said. "Nothin' but a bruise. I'll have Shaniqua see to it when we get back to the ranch."

Nathan said no more. Like Ben Thompson, the big Texan was neck-deep in pride, and obviously didn't want the Mexican riders to know of his ignominious—and painful—retreat from the wild stallion. They rode on to the distant holding pen where the *vaqueros* held the captured horses.

"Caballos, ready," Pancho Gomez said.

King Fisher nodded, and the drive began. There were twenty-eight, including the mare with the brand, and to Nathan, they looked as unruly as ever. But the Mexican riders had worked wonders with the white mare, and she took the trail readily. The others followed, and were kept bunched. They stopped occasionally to rest their horses, milling the wild ones, lest they break away.

"We'll make camp near the first spring," Fisher shouted.

It was the spring where they had camped that first night after entering Mexico, and after a day under the relentless sun, even the wild horses forgot everything except the cool water at hand. After resting the horses, every man again took to the saddle. Supper, which consisted of jerked beef, they ate as they rode, constantly circling the captured horses.

"If that stallion shows up," Fisher said, "shoot the varmint. And don't wait till he's scattered the herd to hell and gone."

"The rest of you stay close to the herd," said Nathan. "Cotton Blossom and me will be a half mile out, riding a circle. If the stallion shows up, we'll try to spook him before he can reach the herd."

Fisher said nothing, but Nathan received grateful looks from the Mexican riders. They clearly didn't want to kill the stallion just to save King Fisher's captured herd, and Nathan shared their sentiment. It would be a long and tiring night, but another day of hard riding would take them to the Rio Grande. While Nathan said nothing to Fisher, he was weary of the mercenary aspects of wild horse hunting.

Sometime after midnight, Nathan reined up. Some distant sound had alerted him, but he thought it might be Cotton Blossom, for he hadn't seen the dog in a while. Then somewhere to the south of him, Cotton Blossom barked. The first was a warning bark, but as only a hound can, Cotton Blossom gave full voice to all that followed. Nathan kicked his horse into a gallop. Cotton Blossom hadn't liked the wild stallion, and Nathan suspected that if the two met, the hound would make a fuss similar to what he was now hearing. The barking continued, diminishing to a series of savage growls, as Cotton Blossom decided to get serious. Finally, lending reality to Nathan's suspicions, there was the angry squealing of a horse. As Nathan neared the scene, the squealing of the horse changed its tone. Now it seemed in pain. It was the nature of a wolf—or a dog—to hamstring a horse, elk, or deer, and if that happened, the animal so afflicted had to be shot.

"Cotton Blossom!" Nathan shouted. "Here!"

The commotion ceased for a moment, and then there was the unmistakable sound of retreat. Nathan sighed, for the stallion was still able to walk. Eventually a shadow separated itself from the brush. Cotton Blossom had arrived. But so had King Fisher, with his Winchester ready.

"Damn it," Fisher bawled, "while the dog had his attention, why didn't you shoot the varmint?"

"I didn't see the need for it," said Nathan mildly. "I reckon Cotton Blossom chewed on him some, and he backed off. Let's leave well enough alone."

Fisher said nothing, but mounted his horse and rode back to camp. The rest of the night was uninterrupted, and they moved out at first light, chewing on jerked beef as they rode. Nathan looked back occasionally, half expecting to see a thin plume of dust on their back trail.

"If that sneaking varmint trails us, I'll meet him with a Winchester," Fisher said.

Nathan said nothing, nor did the Mexican riders. They could only hope the stallion had given up and wouldn't follow. It was near sundown when they reached the Rio Grande and there they reined up, for the Mexican riders didn't wish to cross the river. King Fisher paid them in gold and allowed them to take some of the remaining supplies from the packhorses.

"Now," Fisher said, "it'll be up to the two of us to get these broomtails on across the river and into the corral."

It was no easy task, for the horses were still wild enough to balk at the very sight of a corral. Fisher finally managed to lead the white mare in, and the others very reluctantly followed. When the rails were in place, Fisher sagged against the fence and groaned.

"My God, of all the horse hunts we've ever done, this was the worst. I'm tempted to give up on horses and take to sticking up banks, if I wasn't such a big target."

Nathan laughed. "You'd have to get shot pretty low down to equal the pain from this horse hunt. I'd say you bottomed out."

"You won't never let me forget that, will you?"

"Probably not," said Nathan, "but at least I didn't tell your *Mejicano* riders."

They went on to the house and found Shaniqua had supper ready. It was the first decent meal they'd had since leaving the ranch. The Mexican cook fed Cotton Blossom in the kitchen, after which the hound curled up behind the stove.

"We'd better stand watch near the corral tonight," Nathan said. "I wouldn't be in the least surprised if that stallion don't come after his mares."

"He can try," said Fisher. "It's a five-rail fence, double-lashed with green rawhide. A bull buffalo couldn't break it down. I'm ready for a decent night's sleep."

"I can put Cotton Blossom outside," Nathan said.

"Hell, he's been without sleep as much as we have," said Fisher. "Leave him be."

The first rays of the rising sun were just painting the eastern sky when Nathan got up, got dressed, and made his way to the kitchen. Shaniqua always had the coffee ready, and she poured Nathan a cup. Cotton Blossom still drowsed behind the stove, and opened one eye for Nathan's benefit. Nathan put down his coffee cup and went to the kitchen window from which he could see the barn and the distant corral. Unbelieving, he rubbed his eyes and looked again. The corral was empty!

"God Almighty," he said aloud, "I don't believe it."

"Don't believe what?" King Fisher asked.

"The corral's empty."

King Fisher dropped his boots and sprang to the door in his sock feet. He paused on the porch, his eyes on the empty corral. He finally sat down on the steps, buried his face in his hands, and Nathan thought he was going to cry. Instead, he began cursing. Starting at the time of the flood, he cursed horses in general and wild stallions in particular, and when he ran dry, he started over.

"Here," Nathan said, dropping Fisher's boots on the step beside him, "we might as well go see how he did it."

Choosing one of the posts where the five fence rails had been secured with a double lashing of rawhide, the resourceful stallion had chewed through the iron-tough rawhide. As a result, the rails had fallen free, leaving a sufficient gap for the horses to escape.

"Damn him," Fisher shouted. "I should have shot the sneaking varmint when I had him behind a fence."

"No," said Nathan, "you shouldn't be relying on rawhide for a permanent corral fence. You made it easy for him. What do you aim to do now?"

"I'm riding to town for some nails. Spikes, maybe. Then I'll rebuild this damn corral six rails high. Then I'm goin' on another horse hunt, and then if that black varmint knows what's good for him, he'll stay shy of rifle range."

"I think I'll pass on the next hunt," said Nathan. "It's about time I was ridin' on."

"Ah, hell. I won't be goin' until the middle of July," Fisher said. "I'm considerably bent, but I ain't broke. Stick around for the horse races on July fourth. With your luck, I'd like to just lay my bets alongside yours. What's the most you ever won on a horse?"

"Ten thousand," Nathan said, "but I had to shoot my way out of town."

"By God, I wish I'd been with you. That kind of money's worth fightin' for. If I had your luck, I wouldn't lift nothin' heavier than a deck of cards."

"There are times," said Nathan, "when I wish I'd never seen a deck of cards. Take a man's money—even in an honest game—and you may have to shoot him to keep it. How many men do you kill before they begin to haunt you?"

"I can't figure you," Fisher said. "You got the golden touch with a pistol and with the cards, yet it bothers you to shoot them that's needful of it, and I get the feelin' you don't really like to gamble."

"Some questions are best left unanswered," said Nathan. "I reckon I'll stay for the race on July fourth. Maybe we'll both get lucky."

Uvalde, Texas. July 4, 1874
Uvalde, only a fraction of the size of nearby San Antonio, outdid itself in preparation for the Fourth of July festivities. Indeed, it seemed as though all of San Antonio had turned out for the celebration. Pits had been dug two days before, and several tons of beef and pork was being barbecued. Two wagonloads of watermelons were on hand, as well as a coopful of roosters for a planned *carrera del gallo.**

"I've never seen the like, for so small a town," said Nathan, as he and King Fisher rode in.

"You ain't seen nothin' yet," Fisher replied. "Every saloon, hotel, cafe, livery—even the whorehouses—throws money in the pot toward first-, second-, and third-place winners of the horse race. First prize has been as much as a thousand dollars. The fourth bein' on Saturday, the town will be roarin' all night tonight, all day tomorrow, and maybe most of tomorrow night. There'll be some high stakes poker games, too."

Cotton Blossom normally shied away from crowds, but the odor of roasting meat was tempting, and he followed his nose to the source. Nathan and King Fisher went to one of the saloons where bets were being taken on the Saturday afternoon horse race. There were fifteen horses entered.

"I don't like to bet on anybody's horse until I've seen it," Fisher said.

"I do," said Nathan. "They'll generally be one as good as the other, or they wouldn't be in the race. It's the long shot that pays."

There was a hand-printed poster on the saloon wall, near the bar. On it were names of the horses and the odds.

"Jumping Bean," Fisher said. "Dead last on the list, and that's likely how he'll finish."

"Maybe not," said Nathan. "With a name like that, he sounds like a cow horse. Look at those odds. Twenty-to-one!"

*Mexican rooster pull.

"Yeah," King Fisher said, "and there's likely a reason."

"Pardner," said Nathan to the man taking bets, "I'm layin' a hundred on Jumping Bean at twenty-to-one."

"Your money," the barkeep said, "but no payoff on second or third place."

"I'm aware of that," said Nathan. "Make it two hundred."

"Place me a bet just like it," Fisher said.

That drew some attention, wiping the grins off the faces of some, causing others to wonder if these two big spenders knew something others did not. After he and Nathan had left the saloon, King Fisher laughed.

"You could be a mite early with that," said Nathan. "My horses don't always win."

"Yeah," Fisher said, "but when they win, they do it big time. With those odds, a win would put four thousand dollars in my pocket. I could lay off horse huntin' for another year."

The race didn't begin until two o'clock. Nathan and Fisher took the time to load up on barbecue and watermelon. While Cotton Blossom didn't readily take to strangers, he was willing to make exceptions when they offered him food. Many of the diners were very young, and delighted in feeding the dog.

"After the race," said Fisher, "there'll be some serious poker games in the saloons."

"We may not be able to afford them," Nathan said, "if Jumping Bean lives up to what everybody seems to expect."

The horses were brought to the starting line almost an hour before the race was to begin, so that those placing bets could see the animals. Even though he already had his money on Jumping Bean, Nathan wanted to see the horse, and when he did, he wasn't disappointed. The horse was a bay, maybe fourteen hands, and even King Fisher was impressed.

"You was right about one thing," said the Texan. "He's a cow horse, born and bred, stocky, deep-muscled, and sturdy-legged. I like that deep chest, low withers, and powerful hindquarters. He's got a thick neck, while his head's broad and short. He'll hold his own in a quarter-mile run."*

*The breed was unnamed until 1941, when it officially became the quarter horse.

Suddenly there was a commotion where the barbecue was going on and a yelp from Cotton Blossom. When Nathan and Fisher reached the scene, Duro Ellison stood with his hand on the butt of his Colt, while Cotton Blossom inched closer, snarling.

"Cotton Blossom, no!" Nathan said.

Cotton Blossom ceased growling, but that wasn't enough for Duro. He forgot his Colt and turned on Nathan.

"Stone, your damn dog near took my leg off. What do you aim to do about it?"

"Nothing," said Nathan, "unless he attacked you without cause. Did he?"

"No," somebody shouted. "He kicked the dog. It wasn't botherin' him."

"In that case," Nathan said, "if the dog comes to any harm, Ellison, you'll answer to me. *Comprende?*"

Duro Ellison said nothing. Nathan and King Fisher returned to the scene of the horse race, as the animals were being lined up according to their numbers. Jumping Bean was in the tenth position.

"Some free advice, amigo," said Fisher. "Don't go turnin' your back on Duro Ellison. He's a bad apple, and his brothers, Paschal and Haynes, ain't no better. Any one of them would kill a dog—and likely anything else—just to see it die."

"Thanks," Nathan said. "I'll keep that in mind."

There was some confusion at the start of the race. Accidentally or intentionally, the horse in ninth position broke to the left, colliding with horses seven and eight. As some of the other entries paused, Jumping Bean surged ahead. The rider—Mexican or Indian—was only a boy, and he rode without a saddle. The other riders spurred and quirted their horses, trying to box Jumping Bean, but the sturdy little bay was too quick for them. His rider gave him his head, using neither spurs or quirt, and the horse quickly took the lead. First by a head, by a length, then two lengths. Clearly a winner, he crossed the finish line to the cheers of a few and the anguished groans of many.

"By God," King Fisher shouted, "you know how to pick 'em! Let's go collect our winnings."

Reaching the saloon, Nathan and Fisher were greeted by good-natured shouts of congratulation. But some of the heavy losers were contesting the victory of Jumping Bean, and one of them was Duro Ellison.

"Somethin' went wrong at the start of that race," Duro shouted, "an' I say it's got to be run again. Are we gonna let some Mex kid and his nag just ride away with a thousand dollars of our money?"

"Hell, no!" a dozen voices shouted. "Run the race again."

But all their shouting died away with the roar of a gun. King Fisher stood with his back to the wall, a Colt in each hand. Just loud enough for them all to hear, he spoke.

"Mexican, Indian, or Chinese, the kid won the race fair and square. He earned the money, and I aim to see that he gets it."

"You and who else?" somebody shouted.

"Me," said Nathan, taking his place beside Fisher.

"They're right," said one of the three judges, "and we're sticking to our decision. The winner had nothing to do with the fracas at the start of the race. If there's anybody of a mind to make trouble, we'll call in Sheriff Ward."

"I'm already here," the lawman said. "The race is over and the decision of the judges is final. If there's trouble, them that's the cause of it gets thirty days free room and board in the *juzgado*. Now break it up."

The protesters left the saloon, and while there was no more talk, Duro Ellison cast a murderous look at Nathan and Fisher.

"Come on," Fisher said. "There'll be one hell of a poker game goin' on at the Plains Saloon. We got a stake, and with your luck, maybe we can double it."

"Or lose it," said Nathan.

Fisher had been right. There were no less than three poker games in progress, with a line of men waiting their turn. Not of a mind to wait, Nathan and Fisher went on to the Eagle Saloon. There they sat in on a game, only to be interrupted an hour later by Sheriff Ward.

"Stone," said the lawman, "you'd better come along. Your dog's near dead."

Without a word, Nathan slid back his chair, and King Fisher started to follow.

"No, King," Nathan said.

CHAPTER 15

Sheriff Ward led Nathan to a big poplar tree near the area where the barbecue pits were. Beneath the tree lay Cotton Blossom, and at a distance, people had gathered. Nathan saw none of them. Cotton Blossom's lean body was wracked with convulsions.

"Some varmint poisoned him," Sheriff Ward said. "Coyote poison, I reckon."

Nathan said nothing, kneeling beside the stricken dog, and Sheriff Ward left them there. His eyes glazed with pain and the knowledge of approaching death, Cotton Blossom tried to drag himself to Nathan, but his hindquarters seemed paralyzed. Nathan knelt and placed his hand on the dog's head and Cotton Blossom closed his eyes. They didn't open again. Tears blinded Nathan's eyes, and when he finally got to his feet, a sympathetic woman he didn't know brought him a blanket. He nodded his thanks and spread it over Cotton Blossom. He then turned and walked toward the crowd that had gathered, and when he spoke, his voice was cold and his pale blue eyes colder.

"I want the two-legged snake that poisoned my dog."

Nobody said anything. Duro Ellison was there, and he met Nathan's hard eyes with no expression in his own. Finally Sheriff Ward spoke.

"I reckon nobody seen what happened. There's nothin' we can do."

"There's something *I* can do," Nathan said. "I aim to find out who's responsible, and that skunk—male or female—is going to die. Slow. Now somebody fed him poisoned meat, and some of you saw it. Who was the last to feed him?"

"Mister," shouted a boy of maybe twelve, "it was . . ."

His mother clapped a hand over his mouth, but he broke away. "It was him!"

The boy had pointed directly at Duro Ellison, and those

near him scrambled to get as far from him as they could. Sheriff Ward had his Colt drawn, and it was he who spoke.

"Stone, I won't have a shooting over a dog. Yours or anybody else's."

"Sheriff," said Nathan. "I'm going to kill him with my bare hands. There'll be no gunplay unless somebody tries to stop me. Now all of you back off."

Duro Ellison outweighed Nathan by thirty pounds or more, none of it fat. Looking at Nathan, he licked his lips in anticipation. King fisher had joined the crowd and had taken a position near Duro's brothers, Paschal and Haynes. They were armed, but had said or done nothing. Obviously they believed Duro could defend himself. Of the same mind as King Fisher, Sheriff Ward moved nearer to Paschal and Haynes. He had known the Ellisons all his life, and nobody fought one without fighting all three.

"Fists, then," Sheriff Ward said. "I'll plug the first hombre that pulls a gun."

It seemed directed as much to Paschal and Haynes Ellison as anybody else, and when the fight began, Duro Ellison started it. He rushed Nathan, who stepped aside and tripped him. He went belly-down, and somebody laughed. Duro got to his hands and knees and then to his feet, wiping dirt from his ruddy face on the sleeve of his shirt. He went after Nathan again, seeking a bear hug. This time, Nathan didn't step aside. Bringing a right from his knees, he missed Duro's chin and smashed his nose. While Duro didn't go down, he tottered, shaking his head like a wounded bull. Wary, he came after Nathan again, but changed his tactic. Nathan again stepped aside, but anticipating the move, Duro threw himself sideways, and the two of them went down in a tangle, Duro on top.

"Bust his head, Duro," Paschal shouted.

It was exactly what Duro had in mind. He was astraddle of Nathan, slamming his head against the hard ground. Nathan could feel the gravel cutting into the back of his head, and Duro's big hands around his throat were cutting off his wind. But Duro Ellison had one thing working against him. Nathan Stone was in a killing mood, and his fury lent him the strength he needed. With a mighty heave, he humped Ellison off, reversing their positions. Gritting his teeth, Nathan slammed Duro's head unmercifully against the ground, all the while choking the life out of him. Nathan Stone saw nothing but the lean, tortured body of Cotton Blossom during the final minutes of his life.

"That's enough, Stone! That's enough!"

Slowly Nathan's eyes cleared as the fury subsided. It had taken Sheriff Ward and three other men to drag him off Duro Ellison, and even then they were too late. Paschal and Haynes Ellison had their hands on the butts of their pistols, but Sheriff Ward covered them with his Colt.

"I ain't sayin' the finish was what we expected," Sheriff Ward was saying, "but it was a fair fight. Stone didn't do nothin' to Duro that Duro wouldn't of done to him. Does any of you dispute that?"

"No!" a multitude of voices shouted. The Ellisons—individually or as a trio—weren't popular, bullying others when they could get away with it.

"By God, we dispute that," Paschal Ellison snarled. "You can't hide behind the law forever, Stone. You're a dead man."

"When you're ready," said Nathan, through clenched teeth.

"That's enough," Sheriff Ward snapped. "You Ellisons take Duro and do with him what you will, and then I want you out of town. Move, damn it."

They removed the dead Duro, casting murderous looks at Nathan. When they had gone, Nathan spoke.

"Sheriff, I need the loan of a spade."

"I got one in the wagon," a man said, "and you're welcome to it."

Nathan followed him to his wagon, took the spade, and nodded his thanks. He then went to the old poplar where the blanket-wrapped Cotton Blossom lay. People watched him in sympathetic silence as he dug a grave. Finished, he tucked the blanket around the cold, stiffening body and laid it to rest. He filled the grave, mounding the dirt. In silence, he went to the man who had lent him the spade.

"Mucho gracias, amigo," he said.

Only then did King Fisher step forward. "Come on, Nathan, let's ride to the ranch."

"It's well past time I was ridin' on, King. I'm obliged for your hospitality, and I'll see you when I ride this way again. Adios."

He turned away, and King Fisher knew better than to follow. Nathan had brought the packhorse, leaving it and the grulla at the livery. He went there, paid his bill, saddled the grulla, loaded the packhorse, and rode north. But for the time Cotton Blossom had been shot and laid up in Colorado, the hound had been with Nathan for eight years, since that long ago day in Virginia, when he had headed west in search of the renegades who had murdered his family. Now he rode alone, his sorrow all but blinding him to the danger that lay ahead. A covey of birds swooped down toward a thicket and just as quickly flew away. He reined up and dismounted, still out of gun range.

"You in the thicket," he said. "You have one chance to come out and stand on your hind legs like men, or I'm coming after you with a Winchester."

"Come on, then, damn you. The Ellisons are ready."

Taking his Winchester from the boot, Nathan circled around behind the stand of scrub oak, where it was less dense. There he bellied down, the Winchester in the crook of his arms, and began a slow advance. There was no avoiding the rattle of dry oak leaves, and it was what Nathan was counting on. He must make enough noise to draw fire, to play on the nerves of the pair who awaited him, because he didn't know where they were. His danger was great, and his first shot must count, for when he returned fire, he became a prime target for the second gunman. The first shot, when it came, burned a fiery path across his left arm, above the elbow, while the second clipped an oak limb just above his head. To his relief, the shots had come from ahead of him, and he returned the fire. There was a grunt, followed by a shout.

"Paschal, I'm hit."

It was enough to rattle Paschal, and in his haste, his accuracy suffered. Two slugs kicked up leaves just inches ahead of Nathan, and he fired twice. There were no more shots, but he waited, lest one or both were playing possum, waiting for him to try and advance. Growing impatient, he got to his knees, and drawing no fire, stood up. The Ellisons had died with their guns in their hands, each of them having been hit once.

"Good luck with the buzzards and coyotes," Nathan said aloud. Mounting the grulla, he took the lead rope of the packhorse and rode north. Reaching San Antonio, he left his horses at a livery and took a room at a hotel. How many times had he avoided the towns depending on Cotton

Blossom to warn him of danger approaching their lonely camp? Now he was alone, and this first lonely night, he didn't *want* to be alone. After supper, he went to a saloon and did a thing he had never done before. He bought a bottle of Kentucky bourbon and returned to his hotel room. He leaned a ladder-back chair under the doorknob, and removing only his hat, gun belt, and boots, stretched out on the bed. Finally, he downed half the whiskey, coughing and wheezing until his eyes watered. If he slept at all, he would need help.

Nathan awoke with a pounding head to find the sun streaming in through the window. The events of the day before all seemed like a bad dream, but they quickly became reality. How many times had he awakened to find Cotton Blossom beside him on some lonely trail or lying beside the bed? Swallowing a lump in his throat, he sat up and took another pull from the whiskey bottle. Slowly he got to his feet, went to the dresser, and opened one of the drawers. Into it he dropped the rest of the bottle of whiskey and closed the drawer.

"Never again," he said aloud. His left arm hurt, and he realized he had forgotten the lead that had creased him. Stripping off the shirt, he studied the angry red gash in which the blood had dried. He took a clean bandanna from his pocket. Going to the dresser, he took the whiskey from the drawer and used most of it to cleanse the wound, and the rest of it to soak the bandanna. Using his right hand and his teeth, he managed to bind the wound. He then put on his shirt, tugged on his boots, belted on his guns, and donned his hat. He needed hot, black coffee, and not until he had downed three cups of it did he even consider food. He then had breakfast and began to feel better. Having no business in San Antonio, he paid his livery bill, saddled the grulla, loaded the packhorse, and rode north. Briefly he considered returning to El Paso, but changed his mind. He had gunned down the son of the town's richest man, and that would take some time to blow over, if it ever did. Recalling what the ranger, Bodie West, had said, he set out for Austin.

Austin, Texas. July 6, 1874
"I'm glad you came by," said Bodie, when Nathan entered the small office. "Sit down."

Nathan sat, and from a desk drawer, the young ranger took a sealed brown envelope. He handed it to Nathan. His name had been written on it in pencil, and with hands not quite steady, he broke the seal. Within the envelope was a square of leather, folded in the middle. He opened it to reveal the famed star-in-a-circle silver shield of the Texas Rangers. There was nothing else.

"I was told that Captain Jennings sealed that for you the day before he died," Bodie said. "The shield has a three on the back because he was the third man to join the rangers when they were organized in 1835. He had no family. It was his life."

"My God," said Nathan, "I can't believe it. I'll guard it with my life. But ... is it legal for me to have it?"

"It is," West said. "I made sure of that. Headquarters knows what you did for the captain, and after wearing that shield for thirty-nine years, it was his privilege to do with it as he wished, and he wanted you to have it."

"I really don't know what to say," said Nathan, "except thanks. I consider it an honor to have known such a man."

There seemed little more to be said, and Nathan prepared to leave. He had his hand on the doorknob when Bodie West spoke.

"One thing more, Stone. When you're in Texas and you need help, don't hesitate to call on the rangers. Tell them you knew Captain Jennings. They'll remember."

Nathan rode north, his mind on the enormity of what he had just experienced. Having no particular destination in mind, he decided to ride to Fort Worth, to renew his friendship with Captain Ferguson. Reaching Waco, he quietly took a room there for the night. He wanted no repeat of his last time there, when he had been forced to kill a bushwhacker. The beard he had grown as a means of hiding his identity had begun to bother him, and he shaved it off. He would take his chances on being recognized.

Fort Worth, Texas. July 9, 1874
"I'm sorry I had to be the bearer of bad news," Captain Ferguson said. "I'm afraid the post surgeon had something to do with Captain Jennings's death. He felt it was his duty to tell the captain that he would never walk again, that there was no cure for the paralysis that had resulted from his being shot."

"So Captain Jennings had no other way out," said Nathan. "He willed himself to die."

"That's what the doctor thinks," Ferguson said, "but he had to be told."

"I agree," said Nathan. "There are worse things than dying. Like lying on your back, unable to get up."

"It's good that you came this way," Ferguson said. "A friend of yours is here. Knock on the door of cabin five, officers' quarters."

Nathan knocked on the door, and when it was opened, found himself facing Byron Silver. With a grin, he seized Nathan's hand.

"Quick," said Nathan, "let me in and close the door. Every time I get near you, I got hombres throwing lead at me."

"Well, hell," Silver said, "I tried to get you to come to work in Washington. You'll still have hombres throwing lead at you, but the pay's better. Where's Cotton Blossom?"

Nathan told his story and Silver shook his head.

"I reckon life's hell on the frontier for just about everybody," said Silver. "It came as a shock. Captain Jennings cashing in. I'd have taken the time to come here, if I'd known he was that bad off. A damn shame, him dying with neither of us here."

"We didn't know just how hard that hit him, being laid up and unable to move," said Nathan. "I reckon he took what seemed to him the best way out. I tracked down Clint Barkley, the varmint that ambushed him."

"He was buried with military honors," Silver said. "By the way, I owe you one. I got off the train in Dodge the same day you scattered those wagonloads of Winchesters all over Kansas, Colorado, New Mexico, and Texas. Those gunrunners left Saint Louis sooner than we expected."

"Sorry I spoiled your fun," said Nathan, "but when that third wagon broke up, I saw the guns, and they wouldn't let me go. They aimed to kill me, and I decided not to hang around. It kind of took their minds off me, when the wagons blew."

Silver laughed. "I daresay it did. Sheriff Harrington and me had just finished supper. He told me about some of the folks who have been gunning for you."

"There have been a few misunderstandings," Nathan said.

"I'm on three weeks' leave," said Silver. "Why don't you spend a few days here and let the dust settle?"

"I believe I'd like that," Nathan said.

*   *   *

Nathan remained at Fort Worth for most of the three weeks that Silver was there. The day before Silver was to leave for Washington, he spoke to Nathan about something that had been on his mind.

"Amigo, Sheriff Harrington in Dodge suggested something I believe you ought to consider. The AT and SF—the Atchison, Topeka and Santa Fe—is having a continuing battle with train robbers. They're wanting to hire a man to take charge of railroad security, and Sheriff Harrington told them about you."

"I know," Nathan said. "He mentioned it while I was there."

"I believe you should consider it," said Silver. "Each time there's a payroll, you would make the run from Kansas City to Pueblo, Colorado. You would receive room and board and five hundred dollars a month. By the time law and order comes to the frontier, you'll be a rich man, amigo."

"I don't need the money," Nathan replied, "and frankly, I don't care a damn about becoming a rich man. I don't know what I want."

"Then maybe we should talk about something you *don't* want," said Silver. "Does the name Bart Hankins mean anything to you?"

"Not particularly," Nathan replied. "Should it?"

"That will be your decision," said Silver. "What I am about to tell you is in strict confidence and off the record. *Comprende?*"

"*Si,*" Nathan replied.

"In 1867, in a little Missouri town, Hankins was shot to death during an aborted bank robbery by the James and Dalton gangs. The shot that killed Hankins spooked the robbers and they left the bank empty-handed. One of the gang was later captured and has sworn that none of the bandits killed Hankins. The Hankins family called in the Pinkertons, and it seems that, after checking army records, Hankins and six other men deserted."

"I reckon that's how you learned what you're telling me," said Nathan.

"Exactly," Silver said, "but that's by no means all of it. While the Pinkertons have been unable to account for all these six men, they have learned that at least one of them was gunned down in Denver. The law called the shooting justified, and nobody's contesting that. However, the Pinkertons are claiming there's a pattern, that the man who shot Bart Hankins may have killed his six companions. You, my friend, are a prime suspect, and the recent editorials in the Kansas City *Liberty-Tribune* about the Pinkertons tracking you down so the Limbaugh woman could fill you full of lead haven't helped. You embarrassed hell out of the Pinkertons, and they'd like nothing better than nailing you on a legitimate murder charge. They aim to present your head on a platter to the Hankins family, if they can."

"And you think they can."

"I don't know," said Silver, "but evidently *they* think they can."

"Assuming they can," Nathan said, "what does that have to do with me hiring on with the AT and SF Railroad?"

"If you're working security for the Atchison, Topeka and Santa Fe," said Silver, "the railroad will take a dim view of the Pinkertons harassing you. You'll have the railroad on your side, and it can be made to appear the Pinkertons are after you because of all those embarrassing newspaper stories. We don't know that they aren't, do we?"

"No," Nathan said, "but I don't want others stomping my snakes, and that includes the railroads."

"Damn it," said Silver, "shove that pride back in your pocket. You learned what a five-thousand-dollar reward—unjustified—can do. If the Pinkertons can lay what even *appears* to be a legitimate charge on you, the Hankins family is prepared to offer a ten-thousand-dollar reward for you, dead or alive. Are you prepared for that?"

"I reckon not," Nathan admitted, "but why should the railroad stand up for me? I'm not the only hombre in the territory that's quick with a gun."

"No," said Silver, "but your record of success with the Kansas-Pacific stands mighty tall. There's nobody else around who can measure up to that."

"Sometime back," Nathan said, "I interrupted a holdup involving an AT and SF train, and the guards were Pinkerton men. Has there been a falling out?"

Silver laughed. "You could say that. During the very next holdup, a Pinkerton man got nervous and shot a railroad brakeman. The thieves got away with a payroll, and that convinced the AT and SF the Pinkertons weren't worth a damn as railroad detectives. That, and the train crew reminded the railroad brass that you alone, with a Winchester, had prevented a robbery and saved the payroll."

Nathan laughed. "I felt a little sorry for the Pinkertons. They had told the railroad men the thieves wouldn't dynamite the baggage car, but when I arrived, there wasn't a hell of a lot of it left. I never saw anything in the papers about a Pinkerton man shooting a railroad brakeman, or of the Pinkertons being dismissed as railroad security."

"The AT and SF hushed it up," said Silver. "It would have hurt the railroad's credibility and served no good purpose. However, if the Pinkertons are hell-bent on nailing you with a murder charge, the AT and SF might change their minds. That brakeman died, and while the railroad took care of his family, railroad lawyers could prepare one hell of a negligence suit. The Pinkertons could have a day in court they'll never forget, and in the process, forget all about Nathan Stone."

"Silver, if I'm ever on trial for my life, guilty or innocent, I want you to plead my case. Why should I limit myself to an occasional bushwhacker on some lonely trail, when I can be shot at two or three days a week, all the way from Missouri to Colorado?"

"By God," said Silver, "you've got the straight of it. If I wasn't already in solid with the Federals, I'd root you out and take the job myself."

"Do me one more favor," Nathan said. "If the Pinkertons come up with charges that might put that ten-thousand-dollar bounty on my head, get word to me."

"I'll do that," said Silver. "I'll even go a step farther. I'll wire Foster Hagerman, of the AT and SF, in Dodge. He'll go after the Pinkertons with a fistful of legal thunderbolts."

"Damn it, Silver, I'd prefer that the whole world not know about this investigation. Don't be telling Hagerman anything, unless you have to."

"He already knows the story, and he's quite familiar with the manner in which the Pinkertons tried to set you up for an ambush. You have friends, Nathan. Swallow some of that pride and don't wait until you've been gut-shot to allow some of them to help you."

The time spent at Fort Worth with Byron Silver had done wonders for Nathan. While he still missed Cotton

Blossom and always would, he had accepted the fact the
faithful dog was gone. Nathan rode west to Fort Griffin
and north from there, avoiding Indian Territory entirely.
The first thing he learned, after reaching Fort Worth, was
that there had been a major battle in the Texas panhandle
between buffalo hunters and plains Indians. Twenty-eight
men, with only an adobe ruins for cover, had driven away
seven hundred Cheyenne, Kiowa, and Comanche warriors,
led by the young Comanche chief, Quanah Parker.*

The buffalo had been virtually cleaned out in west Texas,
further infuriating the plains Indians. The ride from Fort
Griffin to the Cimarron was more than two hundred miles,
and Nathan spent two nights on the trail, depending on his
horses to warn him of danger. He breathed easier when he
had crossed the Cimarron into Kansas Territory.

Dodge City, Kansas. July 29, 1874

"Good to see you again," Sheriff Harrington said. "You
just missed a friend of yours when you were here the last
time."

"I spent some time with him at Fort Worth, and he convinced me I should accept that railroad security position
with the AT and SF. I'm supposed to meet Foster Hagerman here."

"My God, will he ever be glad to see you," said Harrington. "Three damn robberies in July, and three lost military
payrolls. Where's your dog?"

"Dead," Nathan replied. He again told the story, finding
it less painful as he repeated it. Harrington was properly
sympathetic.

"You should meet Hagerman before you do anything
else," said Harrington. "He'll be able to get you a monthly
rate at the livery, and he keeps a few rooms reserved at
the Dodge House. It's by far the best hotel in town."

The AT and SF offices were located in one end of the
railroad terminal, and Nathan had no trouble finding Foster Hagerman.

"Come in, come in," Hagerman invited. "I've been expecting you."

"Silver and the damned telegraph," said Nathan.

Hagerman laughed. "Mr. Silver understands our di-

*The second Battle of Adobe Walls, June 27, 1874.

nma. I've delayed a payroll in Fort Leavenworth for
out as long as I can. Are you prepared to take a train
Kansas City tonight and ride the baggage car back
morrow?"

"I reckon," said Nathan. "I'll need a hotel room for my
elongings and a livery for my mount and my packhorse."

"Here," Hagerman said, passing Nathan several sheets
paper embossed with the AT and SF logo. "One of these
ou'll present to the livery, the other to the desk clerk at
e Dodge House. You have two hours before train time.
ake your meals at Delmonico's. You have a tab there."

Nathan rode to the livery, presented his authorization,
nd left his horses. At his request, his saddle and packsad-
le were stored in a tack room. From there he went to
e Dodge House, received his key, and found his room.
Dropping his saddlebags in a corner, he changed his mind
nd took them with him. Including the four thousand he
ad won on the horse race in Uvalde, he had almost six
housand dollars in the saddlebags, too much to leave in a
otel room. He went to the Dodge City bank and deposited
ll but five hundred dollars. With that, what he had on
eposit in the Kansas City bank, and the five hundred from
he railroad each month, he might never have to gamble
gain. He hadn't thought of Eulie Prater in a long time,
ut he did now. She had hated having him in the saloon
to gamble, and when he had shot his way out of one in
San Antonio, she had saved his life. Leaving the bank, he
started for Delmonico's arriving just in time to meet Sheriff Harrington.

"You were right," Nathan said. "First class all the way.
Join me for supper?"

"Don't mind if I do," said the sheriff. "When do you
start?"

"In less than two hours," Nathan replied. "I'm taking
the next train to Kansas City and riding west in the morning, with a payroll."

"Be careful," said Harrington. "I think these robberies
can all be laid to the same pack of outlaws. They manage
to get close enough to dynamite the express car."

"You've just given me an idea," Nathan said. "I need to
talk to Hagerman one more time before I go."

"He'll still be there," said Harrington. "He goes early
and stays late."

After supper, Nathan left Sheriff Harrington at Delmoico's and returned to the depot where Hagerman's offiwas located. He knocked on the door and was bid enter.

"Just one thing more I need," Nathan said. "When th
payroll train heads west in the morning, I want you to b
sure there's a caboose. In that caboose, I want a case o
dynamite with sufficient caps and fuse."

"But the payroll will be in the express coach."

"Which is where it should be," said Nathan, "and that
where the thieves will expect you to have a guard. Can yo
limit the train to four cars, the fourth being the caboose?

"Yes," Hagerman said. "The brakeman will be ridin;
with you."

"Good," said Nathan. "Will he have the sand to do wha
I tell him to do, under fire?"

"He'll side you, up to and including gunfire, if need be
He's Enos Pilpaw, brother to a brakeman who was killed
during a robbery last month."

"Be sure there's a sending instrument aboard," Nathan
said. "I'll telegraph you if we need help repairing damaged track."

CHAPTER 16

Kansas City, Kansas. July 31, 1874
Arriving in Kansas City, Nathan was assigned a cot in a
room directly behind the railroad dispatcher's office. There
he lay awake far into the night, unable to sleep for the
continuous clang of locomotive bells and the shriek of whistles. Eventually he slept until he was awakened at six
o'clock by the dispatcher on duty.

"Train time is eight o'clock," the dispatcher said. "Plenty
of time for breakfast."

Nathan left his Winchester with the dispatcher and had
breakfast in a cafe near the railroad depot. When he returned to the dispatcher's office, the big clock on the wall
said seven forty-five.

"That's your train on track two," said the dispatcher. "Engine three thirty-eight. Good luck."

"Thanks," Nathan replied. Taking his Winchester, he walked to the train. The door to the express car was open, and he stopped there. He had no trouble getting the attention of the expressman because he was expected.

"God, am I glad to see you," the railroad man said. "I'm Art Raines. I'm glad to have you ridin' with me."

"Sorry," said Nathan, "but I won't be riding with you. They'll expect that. I'm Nathan Stone, and I'll be in the caboose. I aim to see to it they don't get to you."

Nathan went on to the caboose, climbed the metal steps, and opened the door. He was greeted by a young man who couldn't have been more than twenty-two. He grinned and offered his hand.

"I'm Enos Pilpaw," he said.

"I'm Nathan Stone. I asked for some dynamite; is it aboard?"

"It's here, with caps and fuse."

"That cupola up there," said Nathan. "Does it open to the roof of the caboose?"

"It does," Enos said, "but it's glassed in. You can see in any direction with it closed."

"That's good," said Nathan, "but I'm going to need to reach the roof, and I don't aim to step out that door and climb the ladder."

The caboose lurched as the locomotive took up the slack, and there were three blasts from the whistle. A trainman slid the express car's door shut and locked it. Slowly the train began to move.

"It's time to fuse and cap the dynamite," said Nathan. He dragged the wooden box out from under one of the bench seats and found the lid had been removed. Removing the coil of fuse, he found the end and with his knife, began cutting what he hoped were forty-five-second lengths. He then fused and capped two dozen sticks of the explosive, and from his shirt pocket he took an oilskin pouch of matches.

"I may need your help, Enos," he said. "If I need this dynamite, I want you to light the fuses one at a time and pass me the sticks until I stop you. *Comprende?*"

"Yes, sir," said Enos.

"I'm going to climb up there on that high bench so that

I can see out," Nathan said. "Do the outlaws usually stop the train by ripping up some of the track?"

"They always have when I've been on this run," said Enos. "They usually come at us from behind the train. They'll leave one man to cover me, and then move on to the express car. There's always a man within rifle range on each side of the engine, keepin' the engineer and fireman covered."

"Allowing them to dynamite the express car," Nathan said.

"Yes, sir. The Pinkertons always rode inside the express car, with the payroll."

"This time," said Nathan, "I aim to stop them before they reach the express car. Does this train stop anywhere between here and Dodge?"

"There's a water stop at Wichita," Enos said. "Most of the robberies have taken place between Wichita and Dodge."

A pattern that was likely to continue, Nathan thought, but he couldn't count on that.

"I have a Winchester," said Enos helpfully, "and I generally hit what I'm shootin' at."

"Keep it loaded and handy," Nathan said. "If they get past the welcome I have planned for them, I'll need all the help I can get."

Reaching the outskirts of Kansas City, the locomotive picked up speed. For once, the flat, seemingly endless Kansas plain seemed a blessing.

"Forty miles an hour," said Enos. "Who would ever have thought a man would travel this fast? We'll be in Wichita in a little over two hours."

They were an hour out of Kansas City when the outlaws struck. The train had crossed a bridge that spanned a creek, when the train slowed, slamming the caboose hard into the coupling of the car ahead. Willows lined the creek, which they had just crossed, and it was from this cover the dozen mounted men emerged. Two of them split off, well out of rifle range, one to each side of the train. Their guns would cover the fireman and engineer.

"Enos," said Nathan, "get two sticks of dynamite ready and prepare to light the fuses when I give the word."

"They're ready," Enos said.

On the riders came. Nathan waited until they were perilusly close before opening the cupola hatch. "Dynamite, Enos," he said.

Nathan held the explosive a few seconds until most of the fuse was consumed. He then flung the stick as high and as hard as he could. Enos handed him the second stick and he repeated the procedure. The first stick of dynamite detonated in the air above the mounted men, followed seconds later by the second explosion. Horses screamed and reared as Nathan climbed to the roof of the caboose with his Winchester. Five of the outlaws lay on the ground, while the remaining five seemed dazed. Three horses were down and the others had galloped away, riderless. The five outlaws had gotten their wits about them and had begun firing. Slugs shattered glass in the back door of the caboose, but Enos had cut loose with his Winchester. Nathan bellied down on the roof of the caboose as lead cut the air just inches above his head. One of the attackers was hit, and in rapid succession, two more. The remaining pair turned and ran back the way they had come. Lead struck the cupola, throwing splinters in Nathan's face. The two outlaws who had ridden ahead to cover the fireman and engineer were firing at Nathan. He got to his knees and then to his feet, and over the tops of the railroad cars, ran toward the outlaws, a Colt in each hand. One man was hit, and slumping over in his saddle, kicked his horse into a gallop. His companion, finding himself facing two blazing Colts, galloped away to the north. Nathan continued along the tops of the cars until he reached the tender.

"It's over, gents," he told the fireman and engineer. "Time to see how much damage they've done to the track."

"My God," said the fireman, "you drove that bunch away, by yourself?"

"I had help," Nathan replied. "The young man in the caboose can shoot. Four of these varmints escaped. Eight of them won't be goin' anywhere."

"We'll have a look at the track," the engineer said. "If they didn't damage the rails or ties, we can maybe patch up the track and go on."

Nathan went with them. If there was a lengthy delay, he must telegraph Hagerman in Dodge City. Starting at a coupling joint, the outlaws had taken an ax to a dozen crossties, chopping away enough of the wood to withdraw the spikes that secured the rail. The rail had then been

separated at the coupling joint, leaving enough of a gap t[
have derailed the locomotive.

"You gents have almighty sharp eyes," Nathan said
"How did you spot this in time to stop the train?"

"I couldn't have done it without the help of the sun,"
said the engineer. "When you're keepin' your eyes on the
rails, they're like two streaks of light. When one rail has
been twisted out of line, it's like a section of the light's
gone out. I'm Collins, and my fireman is Handy. Will you
be ridin' shotgun with us on other runs?"

"For as long as you need me, I reckon," Nathan said.
"Can you repair this damage, or should I telegraph Dodge
or Wichita for a work crew?"

"Those ties can't be used," said Handy. "If you telegraph
Wichita, they can be here in maybe an hour. Tell them
they'll need to replace a dozen damaged ties. When you
wire the dispatcher at Dodge, have him sidetrack the eastbound from Pueblo, giving us the main line. We'll be reaching Dodge at least two hours behind schedule."

Nathan met Enos at the express coach.

"We'd better tell Art he ain't gonna lose this one," said
Enos. He unlocked the door and slid it open.

"What in hell happened?" Art asked. "It sounded like
they blew up the caboose."

"They didn't blow up anything, this time," said Enos. "It
was them that got blown up. It was this hombre we got
ridin' with us that used the dynamite. Eight of the varmints
are dead, and one of them that got away took some lead
with him."

"I need the telegraph instrument and lineman's spurs,"
Nathan said. "I'm telegraphing Wichita to send a repair
crew and Dodge City to sidetrack the eastbound."

The outlaws had become so bold, they no longer bothered cutting the telegraph line, and for that, Nathan was
thankful. He climbed a pole, and establishing contact with
Dodge, sent Foster Hagerman's message first. He asked for
an acknowledgment, and waited until he received it. He
then telegraphed Kansas City, asking that a repair crew be
dispatched from Wichita. He listened until he heard the
order being sent to Wichita, and waited for the response.
When it came, he disconnected his instrument and returned
to the train.

"Nothing to do now, but wait," said Collins, the engieer. "Lucky we took on wood and water at Wichita. At east we can keep up steam."

Nathan and Enos walked back to the scene of devastaion. Nathan didn't recognize any of the dead men.

"I wish we could have gotten them without killing the hree horses," Enos said.

"So do I," said Nathan. "Unless the next gang is all new ands, this trick won't work again."

"You think this same gang has been responsible for all the holdups?"

"I suspect they have," Nathan said. "It's been my experience with train robbers that as long as they're successful, they won't change their habits. Only because we made some changes in the railroad's defense did we beat them this time. From now on, we'll have to be ready for anything."

The work train—consisting of a locomotive, tender, and flat car—arrived an hour and a half after Nathan had telegraphed Kansas City. It cost them another hour while the crew replaced the mutilated ties and spiked the rail back in place.

"Pardner," said Nathan to the engineer of the work train, "there's eight dead men back yonder behind our caboose. When you're ready to return to Wichita, load that bunch on your flat car. Tell the sheriff or marshal they're two-thirds of the pack of coyotes who have been stealing payrolls from the railroad. Some of them may be wanted by the law for other things."

"I don't know you," said the engineer. "By what right are you giving me orders?"

"This is a request," Nathan said mildly. "If it has to be an order, we can telegraph Foster Hagerman, the division boss, in Dodge. Will that be necessary?"

"I reckon not. Who am I to say is responsible for these dead bodies?"

"Compliments of Nathan Stone. Anybody questioning my authority is welcome to telegraph Mr. Hagerman, in Dodge."

Nathan joined Enos in the caboose, and with a triumphant blast of the whistle, three thirty-eight picked up steam, high-balling westward.

"Makes a man feel better," Enos said, "rollin' in without our express car bein' blowed all to hell and another payroll gone."

With three blasts of her whistle, three thirty-eight approached Dodge. The westbound waited on a siding, the engine chuff-chuff-chuffing as it kept up steam. She lurched ahead as three thirty-eight cleared the main line and rolled into the depot two hours and forty-five minutes late. To Nathan's surprise, a crowd was waiting. Among them was Foster Hagerman, and he stepped forward to take Nathan's hand.

"I just had a telegram from Kansas City," Hagerman said. "The marshal at Wichita has identified three of the robbers. They were wanted by the law in Missouri. Damn fine piece of work, Stone. Take the next three days off. I'll talk to you again on Wednesday."

But Nathan was besieged by the curious, one of them Eli Kirby, editor of the town's weekly newspaper, the *Dodge City Bulletin*.

"Mr. Stone," Kirby said, "you not only thwarted a train robbery, you accounted for eight of the robbers. What do you have to say that I can print?"

"That we saved the payroll and accounted for eight of the outlaws," said Nathan.

"But how?" Kirby persisted. "I want the details. Our readers will want to know how you did it."

"So will other train robbers," said Nathan.

With that, he walked away, but he saw Kirby going after three thirty-eight's fireman and engineer. He wished he had cautioned Hagerman against allowing the trainmen to talk about the robbery. For sure, the next band of train robbers wouldn't ride in bunched for a greeting with a lighted stick of dynamite.

"Supper's on me," Sheriff Harrington said, as Nathan passed the jail. "Delmonico's?"

"Yes," said Nathan, "but give me a couple of hours. I feel like I've been throwed and stomped."

Returning to his room at the Dodge House, Nathan let himself in and locked the door behind him. He threw his hat on the bed, unbuckled his gun belt, and tugged off his boots. He then peeled off his shirt, trousers, and socks, and pouring water into a basin, proceeded to give himself as much of a bath as was possible. Using a large towel provided by the hotel, he dried himself and stretched out on the bed. Awakening refreshed, he got up, took clean clothes and socks from his saddlebag, and got dressed. Reaching Delmonico's he found Sheriff Harrington already there, drinking coffee and reading a copy of the Kansas City *Liberty-Tribune*. Nathan hooked a chair with his foot and sat down.

"You're becoming a celebrity," said Harrington, looking at him over the top of the newspaper.

"Not by choice," Nathan replied. "Damn it, this is all I need. There'll be gun throwers taking the train just to get a shot at me. I can hold my own with the outlaws. It's all the young fools who haven't started to shave, looking for a fast reputation, that bother me."

"I'll help you all I can," said Harrington. "Any of them that show up here, I'll take away their guns, put 'em on a fast train, and send 'em home."

Nathan laughed. "I'm obliged, Sheriff."

Dodge City, Kansas. August 5, 1874

Knocking on Foster Hagerman's door, Nathan was bid enter. Hagerman nodded toward a chair, and Nathan sat down. The railroad man shuffled through some papers on his desk until he found the one he wanted. Finally he spoke.

"Saturday, you'll be taking the train to Pueblo. Monday morning, you'll take the eastbound for Kansas City. There'll be no passengers, with stops only for fuel and water. On board will be a shipment of more than fifty thousand dollars in raw silver. Need I say any more?"

"My God, no!" Nathan replied. "That's enough to draw every outlaw from the Trinity to the Yellowstone. But why are we taking this shipment? Most of the silver mines are near Denver. Why risk hauling that much silver a hundred miles, when the Kansas-Pacific has a terminal in Denver, with a line straight through to Kansas City?"

"Ah, the Kansas-Pacific has its share of holdups, too. The mines have taken to alternating their shipments, hoping to confuse the robbers. They managed to get their last shipment through on the Kansas-Pacific, but they aren't willing to gamble on a second one. They believe they stand a better chance, wagoning the silver to Pueblo under heavy guard and having us take it on to Kansas City."

"It strikes me thieves wouldn't have to be too bright to unravel a system like that," Nathan said. "They must have *some* idea as to the time schedule, when a shipment's ready to be sent east."

"You may be proven right," said Hagerman. "All we

know is that it's worked so far, and until it fails, I suppose we'll continue."

"How far is Pueblo from Kansas City?" Nathan asked.

"A little more than six hundred miles," Hagerman replied. "Including water and fuel stops, about sixteen hours. If there are no delays, you should reach Kansas City about ten o'clock Monday night. You can lay over until Wednesday and take three thirty-eight back here on Wednesday morning."

Nathan returned to the Dodge House. It was by far the best frontier hotel he had seen. Thanks to the railroad, there were almost always current copies of the St. Louis and Kansas City newspapers. Nathan bought a *St. Louis Globe-Democrat* and a *Kansas City Liberty-Tribune*. He read the Kansas City paper first, for it always seemed to have news of what had happened in Texas. There had been a shooting in Comanche, Texas, involving twenty-one-year-old John Wesley Hardin. After an argument in a saloon, Hardin had been involved in a shootout with Comanche County Deputy Sheriff Charles Webb. Assisted by his two companions, Jim Taylor and Bill Dixon, Hardin had killed Webb and had escaped with his companions. But in retribution, Tom Dixon, along with Hardin's brothers Joe and Bud were caught and lynched. In a separate incident in Comanche, Wild Bill Longley had killed a man. Longley had been caught and jailed, but had bought his way out. Turning to the St. Louis paper, Nathan found a piece involving the Younger gang. Following a train robbery, John and Jim Younger had been involved in a shootout with the Pinkertons near Monegaw Springs, Missouri. John had killed a Pinkerton man and had in turn been shot dead. Wounded, Jim Younger had escaped. Nathan put the papers aside. In between runs for the railroad, there was little to do except eat and sleep. Unless, of course, he started gambling again. But he wasn't hurting for money, and he resisted the urge to go back into the saloons.

Pueblo, Colorado. August 8, 1874

Nathan reached Pueblo early Saturday afternoon. Adjoining the railroad terminal was a bunkhouse for railroad men who had to lay over, and Nathan was assigned a bunk for the two nights he would be in Pueblo. The silver shipment was already there, he learned. There was a vault in the dispatcher's office, and besides the dispatcher, two armed guards were on duty around the clock. Having eaten breakfast before daylight, Nathan was hungry, and he didn't have to go far. There was a little cafe—The Starlight—near the terminal, and it seemed a gathering place for railroad men. Somebody called Nathan's name and he spotted the grinning crew of old three thirty-eight. There was Dub Collins, the engineer, Amos Handy, the fireman, Enos Pilpaw, the brakeman, and Art Raines from the express car.

"Drag up a chair," said Collins. "We ain't got a thing to do until Monday mornin' but eat and talk."

"I reckon you gents are taking three thirty-eight back to Kansas City, then," Nathan said. "I'll be leaving at six o'clock Monday morning, myself."

"Then you'll be ridin' with us," Enos Pilpaw said. "That makes me feel a sight better."

"Me, too," said Art Raines. "We been told not to talk about that run, but I reckon you know all about it."

"I know," Nathan said, "and I'm glad you gents will be in charge of the train."

A waitress behind the counter had her back to Nathan, and he caught his breath, for her build and the flowing, curly black hair reminded him of Molly Tremayne. He kept his eyes on her until she turned around, and she had Molly's dark eyes and sensuous lips. His heart skipped a beat, and the look on his face must have given him away, because his four companions laughed.

"That's Melanie Gavin," Enos said. "She and her Ma, Elsa, own this place. Mike Gavin was killed in a railroad accident, and Elsa used the money from the railroad to open a cafe. All the railroad men eat here, and the place never closes."

"She's a beautiful woman," said Nathan, "and she reminds me of someone I used to know in Saint Louis."

"You should of lured her into double harness," Art said. "I just wish Melanie had took to a railroad man, instead of the snake-eyed varmint that's sparkin' her."

"And who would that be?" Nathan asked.

"Clell Shanklin," said Art. "He owns Shanklin Freight Lines, hauling from here to Denver and from Denver back. His wagons brought in this shipment from the mines that's down at the dispatcher's office now."

"So he knows about these shipments before they leave Pueblo," Nathan said.

"He'd have to," said Amos Handy. "What are you thinking?"

"I'm wondering just how trustworthy Shanklin is," Nathan said.

"We can't answer that," said Dub Collins. "All we know is that none of us like him."

"Damn," Amos said. "Speak of the devil."

The man who entered the cafe looked like anything but a teamster. His black boots were polished to a shine, accenting his black trousers and black frock coat. His fancy white shirt had lace at the cuffs, his broad, black string tie was long and flowing, and topping it all was a pearl gray Stetson. The left armpit of the coat bulged just enough to suggest a shoulder holster. He looked as phony as a pair of loaded dice, and Nathan immediately decided he didn't like Clell Shanklin, either. Shanklin quickly gave them reason a-plenty for their dislike. Although the cafe was almost full, Shanklin seized Melanie, bent the girl over backward, and showered her with kisses. She broke loose, her face flaming, and obviously had to restrain herself. Nathan was wishing mightily that she had floored the insensitive Shanklin, but she didn't, and Shanklin laughed.

"God," said Enos, "I wish her ma would set her straight, and send that greasy coyote back to the wagon yard."

"Aw, hell," Art said, "she's a grown woman, likely twenty-five years old. Some gals never rise above greasy coyotes. Run one off, and she'll snag the next one."

Nathan left the cafe with his four companions, separating when the railroad men decided to visit some saloons. Nathan returned to the railroad bunkhouse, and despite the noise, managed to sleep. When he awoke, it was late, and some of the other bunks already had snoring occupants. As quietly as he could, he tugged on his boots, donned his hat, and buckled on his gun belt. Recalling that the Starlight Cafe never closed, he went there for supper. Except for a burly male cook and Melanie Gavin, the place was deserted. Nathan took a stool at the counter, and Melanie came to take his order.

"Cook me a steak all the way through," Nathan said, "with onions and potatoes on the side, and plenty of coffee."

"Gotcha," said the cook.

"I haven't seen you in here before," Melanie said.

"I was here for dinner," said Nathan, "but you were busy."

She stood there, her face scarlet, her eyes not meeting his. Nathan took pity on her and changed the subject.

"I'm Nathan Stone, and I'm with the railroad. I'd never been in here until today."

"You look more like a cowboy than a railroad man," she said. "You must be one of the guards for that silver ..."

Her voice trailed off as she realized what she was saying. Abruptly she turned away, filled a cup, and brought Nathan his coffee.

"Yes," Nathan said, "I'm with railroad security. I was of a mind to have some words with Clell Shanklin. I'm told he spends a lot of time here."

"That's none of your business," she said shortly. "He has an office here in town."

"I don't reckon I need to talk to him now," said Nathan. "I've learned what I needed to know."

Nathan said no more. When his meal was ready, he ate, paid his bill, and left. He then crossed the street as though returning to the railroad bunkhouse, but took refuge in the shadow of some boxcars on a railroad siding. Not more than a few minutes after he had left the cafe, Melanie slipped out the door. She stood there awhile, as though undecided, and then set off up the street toward the lights of town. Keeping to the shadows, Nathan followed. When she reached the wagon yard, he waited until she had climbed the steps and crossed the dock. Nathan reached the door in time to hear Shanklin's response to whatever the girl had told him.

"Damn you," Shanklin shouted, "what did you tell that railroad detective?"

"Nothing," Melanie cried. "He asked about you, and I ..."

There was the sound of a blow, a cry of pain, and the thump of a body hitting the floor. Nathan had heard enough. He stepped through the door and found Melanie on her knees, blood trickling from the corners of her mouth. Shanklin stood over her, his lean face a mask of fury.

"Get up and get out of here," Nathan told the girl.

Shanklin turned on Nathan, his hand darting beneath his coat, but it wasn't nearly as quick as Nathan's fist. It caught Shanklin on the point of his chin, snapped his head back, and lifted his feet off the floor. He slammed into a wall, bringing down a mess of harness and gear that had been hanging on pegs. He groaned once and lay still. Nathan turned to find Melanie standing there, wide-eyed and trembling.

"Damn it," said Nathan, "I told you to get out of here. Come on."

He took her arm and she didn't resist. He said nothing more until they were on the street, making their way toward the cafe, two blocks away.

"Do you want to return to the cafe, or do you want to go home?"

"To the cafe," she said. "I don't want Ma . . . ."

"You don't want her to know he hit you," Nathan finished.

"Through the back door," she said, when they were almost to the cafe.

He led her there, and from somewhere she produced a key, unlocking the door.

"Now get inside," said Nathan, "and stay away from that freight office."

"Come in," she said. "Please. I want to talk to you."

Not knowing what he might be in for, Nathan stepped inside and she locked the door.

CHAPTER 17

Nathan sat on a stool while Melanie bathed her face in cold water. Up front, in the cafe, there were voices and a rattle of dishes. Finally, the girl turned to Nathan and spoke.

"There's a bench by the door, where we can't be seen or heard from the front."

"Now," said Nathan, when they were seated, "what do you want to talk about?"

"Why are you after Clell?" she asked.

"I'm not after him," said Nathan. "Yet. He's told you things he should have kept in confidence, and I'm wondering who else he's told."

"What do you mean?"

"You know damn well what I mean. Why do you think raw silver is being freighted all the way from Denver to be shipped to Kansas City? One word to a band of thieves and all this security would be for nothing."

"And you're thinking Clell Shanklin might sell that information."

"I'm thinking that he could, and you're not all that sure that he won't, so you went to warn him, didn't you?"

"No!"

"Then why did you go?" Nathan demanded.

"I ... that's ... that's none of your business."

"I think it is my business," said Nathan. "Obviously, he thought you must have told me something. Or does he just slap you around to amuse himself?"

"Just go," she said tearfully. "Please go."

Nathan got up and turned the knob of the door, releasing the latch. Before leaving, he spoke quietly.

"You wanted to talk, and I think you need to talk. You can reach me by telegram at the AT and SF terminal, in Dodge City, Kansas."

She said nothing, and he stepped out, closing the door behind him. He looked around before making his way to the street. It was late, and seeing nobody, he crossed the street to the dispatcher's office. There was no light and the door was locked. He knocked once, drawing an immediate response.

"Who are you and what do you want?"

"Nathan Stone, security with the AT and SF. Just wanted to be sure there's nothing out of kilter."

"We appreciate your concern," said the guard, "but we have everything in order."

Nathan went on to the bunkhouse, vaguely uneasy. Melanie Gavin knew more than she was telling. Otherwise, why would Shanklin have reacted so violently when he learned Nathan had been questioning the girl? Nathan believed Clell Shanklin was already involved or about to become involved in some scheme that would jeopardize the silver shipment, but he had only his suspicions. To Nathan's surprise, late as it was, the railroad bunkhouse was virtually empty. Three thirty-eight's crew was there, however, and they were awake.

"Man, you should have been with us," Enos said. "Clell Shanklin come in the saloon with a bruise on his chin that was a real beaut. He was as riled as a stomped-on rattler."

"Damn," said Nathan, "I always miss out on the good stuff. Speaking of Shanklin, how long has he been hauling shipments from the mines to Pueblo?"

"We don't always make this run," Dub Collins said, "but far as we know, this could be Shanklin's first run. Last time we took a mine shipment to Kansas City, Shanklin wasn't doin' the hauling. He took the contract away from somebody else on a low bid, I hear."

"He's got a freight office here," said Enos, "so he's been around a while. The coyote's been sparkin' Miss Melanie for as long as I can remember."

"There ain't much hope for the rest of us," Art said, "when a slippery varmint like Shanklin can trap a pretty one like Melanie and keep her on his string. How in tarnation does he do that?"

Nathan found himself wondering the same thing, wondering if Melanie Gavin clung to Clell Shanklin to conceal a past she dared not have revealed. Clearly she feared the man, and had barely tolerated his embarrassing show of affection in the Starlight Cafe. Convinced there was nothing he could do to counter Shanklin's possible sellout to outlaws, Nathan reached a decision.

"Dub," Nathan said, "tomorrow and tomorrow night, how many westbounds will there be, coming from Kansas City?"

"Unless there's been changes," said Collins, "two. One pulls out of Kansas City at six in the morning, and the other at two o'clock tomorrow afternoon."

"Is there a schedule for these mine shipments? Do they always go out on Monday?"

"They have so far," Collins said. "They arrive on Saturday and are loaded on the first train out, on Monday. Why?"

"Because we're going to change that schedule, this time," said Nathan. "I'm going to telegraph Foster Hagerman in Dodge, and we're rolling out of here at six o'clock in the morning."

"Hell," Amos Handy said, "it's near midnight. The dispatcher's office is locked up tight, and them guards has got orders. That door stays locked until seven o'clock in the morning, and then nobody goes in but the dispatcher. You can't send a telegram, and even if you could, tomorrow bein' Sunday, Hagerman likely won't be in the office."

"Art," said Nathan, "the last time I rode with you gents, there was a telegraph sending instrument in the express car. Is it still there?"

"Yes," Raines said, "and the lineman's spurs, too."

"I'll be needing them," Nathan said. "Dub, do you have any idea who would be Foster Hagerman's boss?"

"Hell, I dunno," Collins said, "unless it's Pierce Malone, president of the railroad."

"He'll do," said Nathan. "I want those two westbounds sidetracked tomorrow. The six o'clock departure at Dodge and the two o'clock departure at Wichita."

"God," Collins said in awe, "can you *do* that?"

"We're about to find out," said Nathan. "The safety of that silver shipment may well depend on it. I want nothing said to *anybody* until I have heard from Kansas City. It'll take a telegram from Pierce Malone or Foster Hagerman to release that silver shipment, and I want not a word of this to get past the dispatcher's office."

"Do you want the telegraph key and the lineman's spurs now?" Art asked.

"Yes," said Nathan, "and I'd appreciate you keeping watch while I'm up the pole."

"Is there anything the rest of us can do?" Dub Collins asked.

"Not right now," said Nathan. "You'll need to get up-steam in the morning and be ready to roll when the dispatcher gets word to release that silver shipment. For now, all I can do is hope there's a dispatcher on duty in Kansas City who's got the sand to wake up the president of the AT and SF in the middle of the night."

Kansas City, Missouri. August 9, 1874
The sleepy dispatcher awakened to the chattering of the telegraph key, and he couldn't believe his ears. He knew of nothing more urgent than the routine departure of the six o'clock westbound. He had remained in the office because he had to be there at four, when the trainmen ar-

rived. He doubted there was a railroad dispatcher anywhere who was on the line past midnight, and he hurriedly lighted a lamp. The instrument was signaling the same message over and over, requesting permission to send. Hurriedly he copied the message. It was addressed to Pierce Malone, and it read:

Secured shipment leaving Pueblo at six Sunday morning highballing stop. Sidetrack first westbound at Dodge and second westbound at Wichita stop. Confirm.

The message was signed "Nathan Stone."

Quickly the dispatcher acknowledged, adding that response would not be immediate. He sighed, for it became his unpleasant duty to awaken Pierce Malone, president of the AT and SF railroad at one o'clock on Sunday morning.

A disgruntled butler answered the door with the expected response.

"Mr. Malone has retired for the night. He will be in the office Monday morning."

"This can't wait until Monday morning," said the dispatcher. "He must answer a telegram tonight. It's most urgent."

Malone eventually appeared, and in anything but a good mood.

"Just who *is* Nathan Stone," the railroad president demanded, "and *where* in hell is he? The dispatcher's office in Pueblo should be closed."

"He's tied directly into the line, sir," the dispatcher said, "and he knows the code as well as I do. I'm sorry to have awakened you, but if he's bringing a train east . . ."

"Damn it, Higgins, you did the right thing," Malone growled. "Wire Stone, tell him to get the hell off that pole and go to the dispatcher's office. I'll be in touch with him there within the hour. Then wire the dispatcher in Pueblo and tell him to let Stone in. Sign my name. Now get going."

"He's taking long enough," said Art Raines. "Suppose he doesn't answer?"

"He will," said Nathan, from his perch on the telegraph pole.

Within seconds, the instrument clicked out a request to send, and Nathan responded. With some relief, he listened to the response and acknowledged it. He then disconnected his patch and walked his way to the ground.

"That was mighty short," Art Raines said.

"That was the dispatcher in Kansas City," said Nathan. "He's contacting the dispatcher here, telling him to let me in. Malone will be in touch with me as soon as he can get to the dispatcher's office. Go on back to the bunkhouse and all of you get what sleep you can. We'll be rolling out of here at six, highballing."

By the time Nathan reached the dispatcher's office, a lamp had been lighted and one of the armed men stood outside the door. He demanded identification.

"I'm Nathan Stone."

The dispatcher sat before the telegraph key, rubbing his eyes. The two guards eyed Nathan doubtfully. Nathan said nothing, and it was the dispatcher who finally spoke.

"Mr. Malone's goin' to be mad as hell. This better be important."

"It is," Nathan said, "and I'm taking full responsibility. When Malone responds, step aside. I'll send my own message."

When Malone's message came, it was a question, blunt and to the point:

What is the purpose of your action?

Nathan's response was equally blunt:

Thieves know of Monday security shipment stop. Release shipment for six this morning highball stop. Sidetrack first westbound at Dodge and second at Wichita.

"Take over," Nathan told the dispatcher. "The next message should be for you."

When the key again began to chatter, the dispatcher took down the message. Nathan read it as it came over the wire:

Pueblo dispatcher release Monday security shipment stop. Authorize three thirty-eight departure at six this morning. Both westbounds sidetracked per Nathan Stone request.

It was signed, "Pierce Malone, President AT & SF."

"My God, mister," said the dispatcher, "you got some authority. Nothing like this ever happened before. I just hope three thirty-eight's crew ain't out in the saloons. They won't be expectin' this."

"They're in the bunkhouse," Nathan replied, "and they already know. I want the three of you to remain here until train time, and whatever happens, you are to tell nobody of this change in schedule. *Comprende?*"

They nodded and Nathan made his way back to the

bunkhouse. Not surprisingly, the trainmen were still awake, curious.

"Are we cleared?" Collins asked.

"We're cleared all the way to Kansas City," said Nathan, "by order of Pierce Malone himself. The first westbound will wait for us on the siding at Dodge, and the second will take the siding at Wichita."

"It'll take some time to build up steam," Amos Handy said. "We'll have to be up at four o'clock, so why don't we just get up now? We can go over to the Starlight and have us some breakfast."

"Go ahead," said Nathan. "Just don't say a word about this change in schedule. Not to anybody. If there's any questions, you've all been making the rounds of the saloons, and have worked up an appetite."

They dressed and left, leaving Nathan to stretch out on his bunk for the little time he had left for sleeping. When he awoke, Enos Pilpaw and Art Raines had returned.

"It's a few minutes past four," Enos said. "Dub and Amos are checking in with the dispatcher. Then they'll fire up old three thirty-eight and begin buildin' steam."

"While they're doing that," said Nathan, "I'm going for some breakfast and hot coffee. Who did you see at the Starlight Cafe?"

"Just the cook and Elsa Gavin," Enos said. "She never asked us any questions."

Nathan entered the cafe, and Elsa Gavin took his order. She was maybe twenty years older than Melanie, and while time had robbed her of some of her beauty, much remained. Nathan wondered where Melanie was, if she was with Clell Shanklin, and what Shanklin had in mind regarding the silver. While shipping it a day early might take thieves by surprise, such a tactic wouldn't work a second time. Try as he might, Nathan couldn't rid himself of the suspicion that Clell Shanklin was a potential thief, or at best, would sell information to others, regarding silver shipments. It was a situation he intended to discuss with Foster Hagerman at the earliest opportunity. By the time he left the cafe, Nathan could hear the chuff-chuff-chuff of the locomotive, as it built a head of steam. Art Raines and Enos Pilpaw sat on their bunks, waiting, when Nathan reached the bunkhouse.

"Amos will have up enough steam to leave at five o'clock," said Enos.

"No," Nathan said, "we'll stay with the schedule Pierce Malone accepted. We can't get past Dodge City before the first westbound takes the siding there, unless you want to risk meeting it head-on."

"You're right," Enos agreed. "You're a better railroad man than I am."

At five-thirty, Nathan, Enos, and Art left the bunkhouse and started for the train. At that point, Dub Collins put the locomotive in reverse and began backing toward the depot.

"They're ready to load the express car," said Art.

This time, there was the locomotive, the tender, the express car, and the caboose. Dub eased back until the express car was even with the dock, outside the dispatcher's office. The silver was in heavy canvas bags, and after being brought to the dock, was then moved quickly into the express car. Art entered the car and Enos locked the sliding door. Nathan and Enos mounted the metal steps of the caboose as the train began to move. Dub Collins let go with the whistle, two short blasts and a lengthy one, trailing off into silence.

"Damn!" Clell Shanklin growled, sitting up in his hotel bed, flinging the covers aside.

"It's only a train," said Melanie Gavin, trying to cover herself.

"Only a train, hell," Shanklin snarled. "By God, they're movin' the silver that wasn't supposed to go until tomorrow."

"You don't know that," said Melanie.

"What else could it be?" Shanklin roared. "It's that damn Nathan Stone's doing. And you, by God. You talked to him, made him suspicious."

"I didn't," she cried. "I want nothing to do with your schemes to steal from the railroad, and I'd be ashamed to have anyone know what I know about you."

He laughed, an evil sound, and she shuddered.

"Five years ago, when you was just nineteen, you didn't care what I done, long as I come up with money to get you to California," he said. "Changed your mind, have you?"

"When I was nineteen, I was a damn little fool," she said bitterly. "I let you take me, use me, ruin me. I wouldn't go to California with you, or anywhere else, for all the money in the world. Ma knew what you were, and she hated you. She hates you now, and if I got what I deserve, she'd disown me. Don't tell me any more of your sneaking, lowdown plans to take what doesn't belong to you. I didn't tell that railroad man anything, but if he asks me again, I might just spill my guts."

"Damn you," Shanklin snarled. He ripped her gown off and began beating her, driving his fists into her belly, slamming his knees into her thighs, and slapping her face. Finally he kicked her out of the bed and she fell facedown on the floor. She lay there weeping, and he got up, seized her by the hair and rolled her over to face him.

"I hate you!" she cried, and spat in his face.

He drove his fist into her face, slamming her head against the floor. Through clenched teeth he spoke. "You talk about me—to anybody—and by God, I'll kill you."

The train roared through eastern Colorado, and from the caboose, Nathan kept watch. He believed, once they left Colorado, there was little chance of a robbery. Thieves, alerted by Shanklin, likely wouldn't ride a hundred and fifty miles to rob a train, and that's what it would take to get them out of Colorado. Two hours out of Pueblo, they made their first water stop.

"We're in Kansas," said Enos, "for whatever it's worth."

"It's worth a lot," Nathan said. "This being an unscheduled run, I don't expect trouble from here on. How far are we from Dodge?"

"Little over a hundred miles," said Enos. "We're highballing, and that means we're up to near fifty miles an hour. If nothin' goes wrong, we'll be in Kansas City by six o'clock tonight. Twelve hours. That's a damn good run."

"Why cut back to forty miles an hour on other runs?" Nathan asked.

"Too dangerous," said Enos. "On cloudy or rainy days and at night, visibility is poor. We have to travel slowly enough to stop if there's somethin' on the track, if there's a rail loose or a bridge out. Highballing can be a risk, even in the daytime."

"Dodge is about halfway," Nathan said, "so there's a chance we'll get there ahead of the westbound from Kansas City."

"Yes," said Enos. "We could get there as much as an hour ahead of the westbound."

"Then we'll have to take the siding and wait for them to pass."

"No, we have priority and they have their orders," Enos said. "We'll take on water and fuel there, and we'll wait on the main line for the westbound to take the siding."

Three thirty-eight reached Dodge City a few minutes before noon, and the westbound had not arrived, for the siding was empty. There evidently had been some communication between Pierce Malone and Foster Hagerman, because Hagerman was there when Nathan and Enos swung down from the caboose.

"You're an hour ahead of the westbound," said Hagerman. "There's hot coffee in the dispatcher's office. Let's talk."

Nathan told Hagerman the little he knew and what he only suspected, concluding with the possibility that Clell Shanklin might jeopardize future shipments.

"I have no proof," Nathan said. "I had nothing more than a gut feeling to justify the changing of your schedule for this shipment. We might have waited until tomorrow and had it all come off without a hitch, but it didn't feel right to me."

"This is why we hired you," said Hagerman, "and when your suspicions call for some changes in schedule, don't be afraid to make those changes. Incidentally, I got a telegram from Pierce Malone this morning, commending you for your strategy in bringing in this shipment a day early, with an eleventh-hour change in schedule."

"When will there be another shipment from the mines?"

"Not until sometime in September," said Hagerman. "They ship once a month."

"I believe I should spend a few days in Pueblo," Nathan said, "and either confirm or drop these suspicions regarding Shanklin."

"I agree," said Hagerman. "Come up with some conclusive proof against Shanklin, and we can appeal to the mine owners to get rid of him, contract or no contract. Layover in Kansas City tonight, and take the six o'clock westbound back to Dodge in the morning. By the way, Malone canceled the two o'clock westbound for today, so when this oncoming train takes the siding, you'll have a clear track all the way to Kansas City."

By the time Nathan returned to the caboose, he could hear the distant wail of locomotive whistle. With a clanging of its bell, the westbound slowed to a crawl, allowing the brakeman to swing down and open the switch. While Nathan had talked with Hagerman, three thirty-eight had taken on wood and water and was ready to resume the journey. The train picked up speed, freeing the mainline for the westbound to leave on schedule.

"That's what I call smooth," Enos said, as they rolled into the Kansas City railroad yards. "The railroad ought to slip these mine shipments in at odd times, so that nobody knows which train they'll be on."

"You're gettin' ahead of me," said Nathan. "That's one change I aim to suggest, so I'd appreciate you keeping that possibility under your hat."

Adjacent to the bunkhouse, the Kansas City terminal included bathing facilities, and Nathan enjoyed a hot bath. By the time Nathan had changed clothes, the dispatcher was looking for him.

"So you're the gent that sent me to wake up the president of the railroad at one o'clock this morning. God, I thought heads would roll, startin' with mine. You, my friend, must lead a charmed life. Mr. Malone sent word for you to join him for supper tonight. I've written down the address."

"Thanks," Nathan said, taking the written message. The train had reached the terminal a few minutes before six o'clock, and it was now almost seven. Nathan hired a hack, and giving the driver the address, sat back to enjoy the ride. Pierce Malone's home was everything Nathan had expected, and more. A two-story white house with green shutters, it sat on a hill a few miles south of town. Telling the butler his name, he was shown in to the parlor. He remained standing, for the furniture looked fragile and expensive. When Malone entered the room, Nathan turned to face him.

"I'm Pierce Malone," he said, extending his hand.

Nathan took it. "I'm Nathan Stone."

"Come on in to the dining room," said Malone. "Supper will be served shortly. The coffee's ready now."

Malone asked only enough questions to get Nathan

started, and then he listened. He was told essentially what
Nathan had already told Foster Hagerman. When Nathan
had said about all he intended to, Malone drank the rest
of his coffee and spoke.

"I think I must commend Mr. Hagerman on his judgment. There's not another man in the employ of this railroad who would have taken it upon himself to make the
moves you made last night and this morning. I only recently
learned of the episode involving the dynamite and the saving of a military payroll that might otherwise have been
lost to train robbers."

Uneasy with all the praise, Nathan was saved by the arrival of the food.

"Enough talk," said Malone. "I suppose you're hungry."

"I am," Nathan said. "I had breakfast at four this morning, and nothing since."

It was a sumptuous meal, and Nathan enjoyed it. He
used the time to observe Pierce Malone, just as Malone
was observing him. The railroad man looked to be in his
fifties, and his hair was graying. His eyes were a piercing
blue, and Nathan liked the way those eyes maintained contact with his own while Malone was speaking. Unlike most
men, never once did Malone's eyes stray to the brace of
Colts on Nathan's hips. When they had finished eating and
were enjoying final cups of coffee, Malone spoke.

"There are times, Stone, when I feel those of us who are
forever driving the rails westward are miscalculating our
influence. We believe the coming of the rails parallels the
advance of civilization, when that rarely is the case. I am
referring to the lawlessness that prevails on the western
frontier. The railroads, rather than having a civilizing influence, are creating a series of boom towns allowing criminals
to rise to greater heights than ever."

"Like the James and Younger gangs," Nathan said. "Instead of robbing a bank and getting only a few hundred
dollars, they can hold up a train and escape with
thousands."

"Precisely," said Malone. "I suppose law and order will
come, but not in my lifetime or yours."

"We have law on the frontier, now," Nathan said, "but
it's law in its rawest form. It's the law of the gun. Men like
Wild Bill Hickok have stood for the law, only to have the
good people turn on them and drive them away, to face

their enemies they've accumulated. Hickok will likely die in some frontier town, shot in the back, with nobody to avenge his death.''

"And you, Nathan Stone?"

"Likely the same fate as Hickok," said Nathan. "I'm riding for the brand, Mr. Malone, and in looking out for the interests of the AT and SF, I'm on the legal side of the fence. On the frontier, a man's enemies have no respect for the law, in whatever form it appears. I could be wearing the shield of a Texas Ranger, but I refuse to hide behind a badge. There are men who would gun me down just to prove they're faster with a gun, and the time may come when you'll curse me. The time may come when I'll have to shoot some fool kid to save my own life, when I have a price on my head, when the good people and the big newspapers are drumming up a legal lynch mob. Then—if not sooner—I'll be leaving you, Mr. Malone, for your railroad won't need the bad name.''

"By God," Malone said, aghast at the grim picture Nathan had painted, "a man does what he must. As long as you're loyal to the AT and SF, I'll side you till hell freezes.''

Nathan laughed. "I believe you, Mr. Malone, and I'm obliged.''

"I mean every word," said Malone. "Thank you for this visit. I'll have someone take you back to the terminal in the buckboard.''

The butler who had greeted Nathan at the door drove him back to the railroad terminal, and they exchanged not a word until Nathan thanked him. For a long time, Nathan lay awake pondering the railroad man's words. Might there *be* a future for him with the railroad, despite his deadly reputation with a gun? The uncertainty crept away, only to sink its teeth into him anew three days later, when Pierce Malone died in his sleep. . . .

Dodge City, Kansas. August 11, 1874
Nathan stepped down from the train on Tuesday, a few minutes past noon. He went immediately to Foster Hagerman's office.

"You'll still want to spend some time in Pueblo," Hagerman said, "but I think there's been some changes in the situation there. A visitor arrived on the train a while ago, and won't talk to anybody but you. I sent her on to the Dodge House."

When Nathan walked into the hotel, Melanie Gavin came to meet him. He almost didn't recognize her, for she wore a hat with a heavy veil.

"Come on to my room," he said, "unless you fear for your reputation."

"There's nothing you can do that could worsen my reputation," she said bitterly. "If I wasn't such a coward, I'd kill myself."

CHAPTER 18

Nathan unlocked the door to his room, allowing Melanie to enter first. He then locked the door behind them. Nathan sat on the bed, leaving her the chair, but she didn't sit.

"Now," said Nathan, "you talk and I'll listen."

"First I have something to show you," she said. She removed the hat and veil, revealing a massive bruise that spread from her mouth and chin to her right cheek.

"My God," Nathan said.

"That's just the beginning," she said. "There's more." Unbuttoning her dress, she let it fall to the floor. She wore nothing beneath it. There were black-and-blue bruises from her knees to her shoulders.

"I should have killed the bastard when I had the chance," said Nathan. "I suppose he had a reason for that?"

"Yes," she said. "He believed it was something I told you that caused you to change the schedule on that shipment from the mines. He threatened to kill me."

"Why didn't you go to the law?"

"Then he *would* have killed me. I had no proof that he'd done anything, although I knew he was planning to."

"Have you been to a doctor?"

"No," she said. "I was ashamed to go. I only wanted to get away from him."

"So you came to me. What am I supposed to do with you?"

"Nothing," she said, refusing to look at him. "I . . . I was hoping I might . . . stay with you until . . ."

"But you have no proof, nothing that can be used against Shanklin," Nathan said.

"No," she said, "but I can tell you what he's said he's going to do, the names of the men he's been talking to. . . ."

"I'll want to hear all of that," said Nathan. "While we don't have any real evidence, I want to know what he's planning to do. Now why don't you get dressed and we'll go to Delmonico's for some food."

"I'm ashamed to be seen, with my face looking like . . . this," she said. "Maybe later . . . tomorrow . . ."

The more Nathan looked at her, the more she reminded him of Molly Tremayne. She sat on the bed beside him, and the next thing he knew, she had her arms around him, weeping as though her heart would break. Finally the tears subsided, and when her eyes looked into his, Nathan felt chills creeping up his spine.

"Please," she said. "I'm not hungry. Perhaps after dark, when nobody can see me so well. All I want is someone to care, someone who won't hurt me. I'm so tired . . . I haven't slept in days. Could I . . . stay here for just . . . a while?"

The way she tilted her head, the way her dark eyes met his, she reminded Nathan all the more of Molly Tremayne. He grew weak in the knees and his heart felt like it had risen to his throat. He had to swallow hard before he could speak.

"You stay here and sleep," he said. "I have some railroad business to attend to. When I return, we'll go to supper."

He helped her to her feet and turned back the covers for her. Gratefully she kicked off her shoes, got into the bed, and he smoothed the covers over her. He then stepped out the door, locked it behind him, and stood in the hall, breathing hard. He knew he must get his priorities in order, but how could he, when she reminded him so much of Molly? With his mind in a turmoil, he left the Dodge House, only to have a slug furrow the flesh along his left side. A second one narrowly missed his head. Drawing his Colt, he started across the street on the run, but there were no more shots. He could still smell powder smoke when he reached the alley, but there was no sign of the gunman. There were saloons and innumerable other places of business whose back doors opened into the alley, and a search would be fruitless. Nathan turned back toward the Dodge House and found several men had been drawn by the shooting. One of them was Sheriff Harrington, and he saw the blood on Nathan's shirt.

"Ambush, I reckon," said Harrington.

"Good try," Nathan replied. "I lost him in the alley."

"See the doc, and then come back by the office," said Harrington.

Nathan paid the doctor two dollars to swab out the wound with alcohol and apply a wide cloth bandage. He then went to Harrington's office. Harrington nodded to a chair and Nathan sat down. From his desk drawer, the sheriff took a sheet of paper. This he passed to Nathan. It was a telegram, addressed to "Sheriff, Dodge City," and it read:

Melanie Gavin missing stop. My daughter stop. Respond if whereabouts known stop.

It was signed "Elsa Gavin, of Pueblo, Colorado."

"Should I answer this?"

"No," said Nathan. "I can't tell you anything at this point, except that the girl fears for her life, and I believe she has reason to. She's been involved with a man who has a contract with the mines for the hauling of silver to the railroad. I have reason to believe this varmint is a thief himself, or is selling information to outlaws. I'm telling you this in confidence, only because the girl, Melanie Gavin, is here, asking for help."

"I'll sit on it, then," Harrington said, "but there's something about this that doesn't ring true. If Elsa Gavin is so concerned about her daughter—if they're that close—why did the girl turn to you, instead of her mother? Is there no law in that town?"

"The law there's just like the law anywhere else," said Nathan. "They don't care a damn about your suspicions. They want proof. I don't know to what extent Elsa Gavin is involved, or if she's involved at all. I do know there's been considerable conflict between mother and daughter over a no-account varmint name of Clell Shanklin."

"Shanklin bein' the questionable hombre who has the hauling contract with the mines, I reckon," Harrington said.

"Yes," said Nathan. "I've told you enough; you know as much as I do. Until I'm sure where Elsa Gavin stands, I'm telling her nothing. Shanklin could be behind this telegram you received."

"My God, you believe the girl's mother would betray her to a man who's trying to kill her?"

"I don't know," Nathan said, "but I'm not going to risk it. This Shanklin is slick as a greased pig, and I wouldn't put it past him, playing both ends against the middle. Suppose he's been using both the mother *and* the daughter? He might then turn one against the other, if it suited his purpose."

"I see what you mean," said Harrington. "Do you think that ambush a while ago had anything to do with the situation in Pueblo?"

"I don't see how," Nathan said. "Since I left, there's been only one train from there, and that's today's, the one on which Melanie arrived. I reckon I've managed to accumulate enough people who want to see me dead, that they're everywhere."

From the sheriff's office, Nathan returned to the railroad terminal and Foster Hagerman's office. Nathan took a chair, and Hagerman said nothing, waiting for Nathan to speak.

"You know about the telegram that came from Pueblo this morning, I reckon," Nathan said. "Supposedly from Elsa Gavin to Sheriff Harrington."

"Supposedly?" said Hagerman, raising his eyebrows.

"You heard me right," Nathan said. "The girl's afraid for her life, and I can't imagine Elsa Gavin not being aware of that. Can you?"

"This whole thing may be deeper than we thought, then," said Hagerman. "My God, how can a woman betray her own daughter to a man who's trying to kill her?"

"We don't know that's the case," Nathan said, "but it's starting to look that way. I'll be talking to Melanie tonight, after she's rested, and maybe we can nail down some truth from all our suspicions."

"There's blood on your shirt," said Hagerman. "Did that have anything to do with the gunfire I heard a while ago?"

"It did," Nathan said. "A bushwhacker, and he got away."

"You're about to uncover something in Colorado," said Hagerman. "Perhaps I should hire some men to help you."

"No," Nathan said. "That would only give them more targets. I work better alone."

"We have a few days before there's another military payroll, and there won't be another mine shipment until next month," said Hagerman. "When you're ready to spend a few days in Pueblo, let me know."

"It's going to take some time, getting information out of Melanie Gavin," Nathan said, "and when I go, I'll want to leave her here."

"If you need a room for her, the railroad will pay for it," said Hagerman.

"We can manage," Nathan replied. "I promised her protection, and I can't guarantee that, with her in a room alone, can I?"

"Hardly," said Hagerman with a straight face. He saved his grin until Nathan was out the door.

Nathan returned to the Dodge House, and while he tried to be quiet, the sound of the key in the lock awakened Melanie Gavin. She sat up, rubbing her eyes, and he thought the bruise on her face wasn't quite as severe. He debated with himself as to whether he should tell her of the telegram Sheriff Harrington had received, and finally decided that he should. Perhaps her reaction might tell him something about her relationship with Elsa Gavin. He locked the door and sat down on the bed beside her.

"The sheriff received a telegram this morning," Nathan said. "Your mother's name was signed to it. She wants to know where you are."

"Oh, God," she cried, "don't let him tell her!"

"He hasn't answered the telegram," said Nathan. "I asked him not to, at least until I had talked to you. Why don't you want your mother knowing where you are?"

"Because she'll tell *him*. Why do you think I left without telling her?"

"I don't understand you," Nathan said. "Somehow, I got the impression your mother hated Clell Shanklin and was opposed to you being involved with him."

"She did, for a while," said Melanie bitterly, "but things have changed. She accused him of ruining me, but then she became less and less critical, and just within the past few days, I found out ... about them...."

"Shanklin threw you down for your mother?"

"No," she cried, "he's been using us both. We've always operated the cafe in shifts. Both of us are never there at the same time. When I'd be there, he'd spend his time with her, and when she'd be there, he'd spend his time with me."

"My God," said Nathan, "I never heard of such. Do you think your mother is part of Shanklin's schemes?"

"I don't know," she said miserably, "just as I don't know if she would help him find me. I do know that she'll take his word over mine, because she's called me a liar when I've tried to tell her what he was doing to us."

"I reckon it's best that they don't know where you are, then," said Nathan. "I aim to go back to Pueblo for a few days, and see what I can learn."

"You're going to leave me?"

"I must, if I'm ever going to get to the bottom of this," Nathan said, "but you won't be alone. I'll introduce you to Sheriff Harrington, and he'll keep an eye on you. Anyway, I won't be going until you're feeling better. Now I want you to think of what you know about Clell Shanklin, anything that might be helpful to me in building a case against him."

"Back when he was . . . still talking to me about his plans, he spoke of Chapa Gonzolos. He is a Spaniard and an outlaw from Santa Fe. It is he and his band of robbers who would stop the train and take the silver. In a wagon they would take it into New Mexico, where it would be hidden until they could dispose of it. Clell wouldn't take part in the robbery, leaving him in a position to pass along information to the thieves about other shipments. I think he had already sent them word when the last shipment was going out, and when you took it a day early, it spoiled their plans. That's when he beat me, and threatened to kill me, when he heard the locomotive whistle on Sunday morning."

"Can you think of anything else?" Nathan asked.

"Once when I was at the freight office, men were unloading cases of dynamite from one of the wagons. When I asked him what the dynamite was for, he only laughed."

"It'll be dark in a few minutes," said Nathan. "Are you feeling well enough to go out for supper?"

"I suppose I'll have to. I haven't eaten since the night before I left Pueblo."

She threw back the covers and sat up, and again Nathan saw the ugly bruises that all but covered her body. He

...nded her the wrinkled dress that still lay on the floor,
...d it brought to mind a question.

"Didn't you bring any clothes with you?"

"Only what I was wearing," she said. "I bought the hat
...nd the veil at a secondhand shop after I left the hotel."

"Hotel?"

"Where I . . . stayed . . . with him . . . when he wanted
...e. . . ."

She kept her head down, her eyes not meeting his, and
... was just as well. Clenching his fists, his eyes went cold
...ith fury, as he thought of her with Clell Shanklin. Fighting
...o gain control of himself, he closed his eyes, for again he
...as seeing Molly Tremayne. His face was expressionless
...when she again looked at him. She got into her shoes, and
...tanding up, pulled the dress over her head.

"Would you button it for me?" she asked. "My arms are
...o sore . . ."

He fumbled with the buttons until she laughed at his
...lumsiness, causing him to fumble all the more, for she
...even laughed as he remembered Molly laughing. . . .

"Don't wear the hat and the veil," he said. "It would
...only make you seem all the more obvious."

Reaching Delmonico's, Nathan found Sheriff Harrington
was there. It seemed as good a time as any to introduce
Melanie Gavin. He spoke to the girl quietly before they
entered the cafe.

"We're going to join Sheriff Harrington. He's a good man,
and he's been a friend to me. I want you to meet him."

"No," she said. "Not now."

"Now," Nathan said, taking her arm.

Harrington slid back his chair and stood as they approached his table.

"Sheriff Harrington," said Nathan, "this is Melanie
Gavin. May we join you?"

"Please do," Harrington said. "Pleased to meet you,
Melanie."

For a while, Melanie said nothing, her eyes on the table.
Gradually, however, Nathan and the sheriff gained her interest, recalling humorous events involving themselves and
others. By the time their supper was served, she was laughing, and when the meal ended, she seemed genuinely sorry
to part with the friendly sheriff.

"You survived that," Nathan said. "Now we're going t the mercantile and buy you some clothes."

"I have no money."

"You're in luck," said Nathan, "because I do."

She was reluctant at first, but her eyes sparkled as sh tried on various dresses, and Nathan found himself enjoyin; her all the more. She finally settled on three dresses, a pai of shoes, and a bonnet.

"You should have some of these," Nathan said, steerin; her toward a big display of women's underclothes. "Or dc you always go jaybird naked under a dress?"

"Only when I leave town in a hurry," she said.

They returned to the Dodge House, Nathan apprehensive. Were his feelings for this girl genuine, or was he infatuated with her because in so many ways, she reminded him of Molly Tremayne? She hung her new dresses in the closet, admiring them as she did so. The new underclothes she placed in a dresser drawer. She then kicked off her shoes, unbuttoned the dress she wore, and stepped out of it. Uncertainly, Nathan watched her get into bed. Finally, he sat down beside her, and when she spoke, he was unprepared for her bitter words.

"You don't want me, do you? Well, I don't blame you. I'm used goods."

Nathan flung the cover off her and drew her to him, kissing her long and hard. When he let her go, he was breathing hard, and it was a moment before he could speak. When he did, it was his turn to shock her.

"Damn it, Melanie Gavin, I *do* want you. I've wanted you ever since that first time I saw you, in the cafe in Pueblo. Will you marry me?"

For a long moment she said nothing, and even in the poor light from the lamp, he could see the tears on her cheeks. But when she finally spoke, her voice was steady.

"No, I won't. It's too late to make an honest woman out of me, and I won't let you do something you'd regret later. Take me if you want me. It's the least I can do for a man who's been kind to me. Believe me, I have some feeling for you, and I'm thankful for it. I never believed I could care for a man again, after ... him. . . ."

It was a dilemma such as Nathan had never faced. Molly Tremayne had been the first woman in his life, and he had taken her without hesitation, only to lose her. Now this woman who reminded him so much of Molly had refused his proposal, leaving him angry and guilt-ridden. Feeling damned if he did and damned if he didn't, Nathan drew off his boots, unbuckled his gun belt, stepped out of his trousers, and removed his shirt. He then blew out the lamp and got into bed. . . .

When Nathan awoke, the sun was streaming in through the window. Melanie sat with her knees drawn up under her chin, her eyes on him.

"How do you feel?" she asked, her eyes twinkling.

"Not nearly as guilty as I expected," he said.

"Five years ago, I might have said that."

"Why don't you put those five years behind you?" said Nathan. "I don't care about your past or what you were. All I can see is what you are now."

"And what is that?"

"The most beautiful woman I've ever seen in my life," Nathan said, meaning it.

"Beauty is only skin deep," she said. "Perhaps you haven't looked deep enough."

"I made up my mind about you last night," said Nathan, "and nothing you can say or do will changed the way I feel."

"I don't believe you," she said. "I don't believe there's a man alive who will buy the cow when he's getting the milk for free."

"Then there's still something about men you don't know," said Nathan. "When a man knows what he wants, he's willing to pay the price. He wants to own it honestly, and to possess it any other way goes against the grain."

"Even if it's already been owned by scum like Clell Shanklin?"

"Even then," Nathan said, struggling to contain his temper.

She leaned over him, her eyes meeting his. "You're right, Nathan Stone. I don't know you. I've never known anyone like you. Give me some time. Then, if you still want me . . . then perhaps . . . I'll believe."

"I can wait," he said, "as long as I don't have to listen to you relive the last five years. Can you put that behind you and leave it there?"

"With your help, I can," she replied.

With that admission, all that had been missing the night before fell into place. Nathan no longer attempted to drive memories of Molly Tremayne from his mind. He didn't know where Molly ended and Melanie began, and he didn't care.

Nathan spent a week with Melanie before again meeting with Foster Hagerman. There was immediate bad news, as Hagerman told Nathan of the unexpected death of the AT and SF president, Pierce Malone.

"I think it's time for me to return to Pueblo," Nathan said.

"Stay as long as you believe necessary," said Hagerman.

Nathan made known his feelings for Melanie Gavin, arranging for Foster Hagerman and Sheriff Harrington to see to the woman's welfare while he was away. He left sufficient money with Melanie for her needs, and took a noon train to Pueblo.

Pueblo, Colorado. August 19, 1874
Reaching Pueblo, Nathan went immediately to the Starlight Cafe, only to find it closed, an OUT OF BUSINESS sign posted on the front door. He then checked into a hotel, hoping to attract less attention than he might by staying at the terminal bunkhouse. Nathan had no idea where Elsa Gavin lived, and he set about finding her. He began with the railroad dispatcher, Elbert Grimes.

"Got no idea," Grimes said. "You might try the county courthouse."

The suggestion proved valid, but when Nathan found the house, it was locked, and as best he could tell, vacant. As a last resort, he went to Shanklin's freight yard. Finally, when it seemed nobody was around, he climbed the steps to the dock, only to come face-to-face with a man leaving the office.

"I'm looking for a gent named Shanklin," Nathan said.

"He ain't here," the man said. "What can I do for you?"

"Nothing," said Nathan. "I'll try another time. When will he be returning?"

"He never bothers tellin' anybody and I ain't sure it's any of your business."

Nathan left, unsure as to his next move. Finally he returned to the county courthouse and inquired about freight lines. He was given the names of three, including Clell Shanklin's. He called on Moore's Freight first, finding the owner, Carlyle

Moore, was out of town. Calling on Colbert Lines, he found Taylor Colbert available but uncooperative.

"I got nothin' to say about Shanklin," Colbert said. "Now you go about your business and I'll go about mine."

Finally, not having any other leads, Nathan called on Sheriff Red Brodie, introducing himself and revealing his position with AT and SF.

"I really need to talk to Clell Shanklin," Nathan said, "since he has a hauling contract with the mines up near Denver."

"I reckon he's in Denver," Brodie said. "The whole town's been talking about him, but his freightin' business had nothin' to do with it. He's been sparkin' the Gavin gal since she was nineteen, and everybody reckoned they'd end up tyin' the knot. Well, a little more'n a week ago, the gal just plumb disappeared. Day before yesterday, old Shanklin just ups and marries Elsa, the gal's mother. She closed that cafe pronto, and her and Shanklin lit out for Denver. I reckon nobody will be seein' him for a while."

"Thanks, Sheriff," said Nathan. He went to the railroad dispatcher's office and sent a telegram to Foster Hagerman, at Dodge City:

Send names of mines and persons responsible for silver shipments stop. Riding to Denver.

He signed his name and waited for a response. Within minutes, he had the names of four mines and their superintendents. He then went to a livery and rented a horse and saddle.

"How far to Denver?" he asked the liveryman.

"Hunnert and fifty mile."

Nathan rode out. The silver mines, as he recalled, were all south of Denver. He really had no idea what he might learn, but he was accomplishing nothing in Pueblo. If nothing else, he might be told of what might be expected in future shipments. He recalled that some shipments left from Denver, on the Kansas-Pacific, which was far more convenient. The hauling of some shipments to Pueblo was for the purpose of confusing train robbers, which accomplished nothing if Shanklin was in cahoots with them. Nathan wondered if the contract involving shipments from Denver was also owned by Shanklin. That was one thing he hoped to learn by visiting the mines in question. He rode into Colorado Springs before sundown and took a room there for the night. At first light he was on the trail.

Many of the mines nearest Denver still produced gold, al-though they were playing out. The silver was being taken from four principal lodes, and they weren't that widely sep-arated. Nathan hoped he might gather all four superinten-dents and question them at the same time, rather than meeting them one at a time.

Denver, Colorado. August 24, 1874

Nathan rode to each of the four mines, identified himself, and arranged to meet with all four mine superintendents at the largest of the mines, the Silver Slipper. There was a miner's shack at the Silver Slipper, and Nathan was given a bunk for the night. Following breakfast, he met with su-perintendents representing the four mines. There was Bammister of the Silver Slipper, Knowles of the Five Star, Ledbetter of the Half Moon, and Chapman of the Faro.

"Gents," said Nathan, "I'm here on behalf of the AT and SF. We're concerned about getting your shipments to Kansas City. We avoided a robbery last time by a last-minute change of schedule, sending your shipment a day early. I'd like to know, for our sake and yours, how and when the next shipment will be going."

"October fifth," Bammister said, "by the Kansas-Pacific."

"Who has your hauling contract from the mines to the railroad?" Nathan asked.

"Shanklin," Bammister replied. "Same as the shipments on the AT and SF."

"Suppose I tell you that we suspect Shanklin of selling you out to thieves?"

"I'd want to see some proof," said Knowles. "He turned in a low bid for the job."

"I don't have any proof," Nathan said, "but with your help, I believe I can get some."

"Depends on what we got to do," said Ledbetter.

"You'll go ahead with your shipment from Denver as planned," Nathan said, "but with some changes. Shanklin will deliver that shipment. Those bags will be loaded with sand and sealed. The real shipment, about which Shanklin will know nothing, will go to Kansas City on the AT and SF. I'll bring a wagon and some line riders from Pueblo on October first and your shipment will go out on schedule."

"So we send a bogus shipment and a genuine shipment,"

Chapman said, "and you're telling us that the real one will go through, while the bogus one is stolen."

"That's what I'm telling you," said Nathan. "Send your genuine shipment from Denver, and you'll lose it. Can you afford the risk?"

"Hell, no," Bammister said. "I know you ain't rode all the way up here without good reason. If Shanklin's sellin' us out, we need to know. I say we go with Stone's plan."

"Damn right," the others agreed in one voice. "Go with the AT and SF."

CHAPTER 19

Hays, Kansas. August 25, 1874
"Damn it, Elsa, I know what I'm doing," Clell Shanklin said irritably. "Gonzolos and his boys was mad as hell when that last shipment slipped through a day early. Now I got to redeem myself, and this Kansas-Pacific shipment should do it."

"This time, you can't blame it on Melanie," Elsa snapped. "I can't believe she's gone."

"I told you what she had to say when I broke up with her," Shanklin lied. "She knows it's you and me, and she's gone off to sulk. She wants nothing more to do with you. Why do you reckon you've had no answer to your telegrams?"

"I suppose I'm getting what I deserve," said Elsa. "Ten days ago, I had a business of my own, a life of my own, and a daughter. Now all I have are the clothes on my back, a room in a grubby plains hotel, and a husband who's a damned thief."

Shanklin laughed. "Elsa, Elsa, you took me for better or worse, and you knew what the 'worse' was, goin' in. I'm a thief, but by God, I tried all the other ways, and you know what I got? A few mules, some secondhand wagons, and a never-ending drudgery of hauling other men's silver and gold. I aim to end up rich or dead."

"And I have an idea which it's going to be," said Elsa.

"How much longer do we have to squat here, waiting for this mangy coyote of a Mexican outlaw?"

"Chapa will be here when he gets here," Shanklin said, "and if you're smart, you'll be a mite more cautious how you speak of him when he's around. Chapa doesn't appreciate disloyalty, and whatever you think of our plans, you'll do well to keep your mouth shut."

When Chapa Gonzolos arrived, he stared at Elsa for a long moment, his expressionless black eyes roaming over her. He was every bit the Spaniard, with flat-crowned black hat, polished black boots, and black frock coat. His trousers were dark, and instead of a belt, there was a crimson sash around his middle. His shirt was white, with frills, and he had a rawhide thong around his neck. Down his back, Indian-fashion, hung a formidable Bowie knife. While he had no visible weapon, there was an ominous bulge beneath his coat, under each armpit. He spoke in clipped, precise English, lapsing into Spanish only when his venomous temper got the best of him. Few men who had fallen victim to his rapid-fire Spanish had lived to talk about it. Following his initial rude stare, he turned his attention to Shanklin, ignoring Elsa.

"Ah, Señor Shanklin, the *mulo* hombre whose trains run on silent tracks and whose silver is so fine the eye cannot see."

"Damn it, Chapa," Shanklin said, "that wasn't my fault. The information was good when I gave it to you. The railroad changed the schedule at the last minute."

"You will see that it does not happen a second time," said Gonzolos. He didn't speak of the consequences, nor did he need to. Clell Shanklin understood. He swallowed hard and spoke.

"The next shipment goes out October fifth, on the Kansas-Pacific," Shanklin said, "and you should stop the train a hundred miles west of here, just after it leaves Colorado. You will need two wagons. You will be four hundred and twenty-five miles east of Santa Fe."

"Seventeen days," said Gonzolos. "Time enough for the law to follow."

"The nearest town will be Hays, where we are right now," Shanklin replied. "Six men only. One to drive each agon, the other four as guards. The rest of your men will ollow the wagons, prepared for the *emboscada*."

Gonzolos nodded, and without another word, stepped ut the door.

"God," said Elsa, "he gives me the creeps. He reminds ne of an undertaker."

Shanklin laughed. "Under certain circumstances, that's vhat he is."

"And you're going to double-cross him," Elsa said.

"In a manner of speaking," said Shanklin, "but not noney-wisc. We'll be riding to Santa Fe for our share of the money, and as far as Chapa knows, I'll return to Pueblo and continue hauling for the mines. That's to prevent *him* from double-crossing me. He expects me to be there, feeding him information on future mine shipments. But all I need is one good stake, and we'll be on our way to California."

"I've heard that before," Elsa said. "Melanie threw that in my face five years ago."

"She lost the faith," said Shanklin. "She could have been where you are right now."

Elsa laughed. "Lucky me."

Dodge City, Kansas. August 28, 1874
"When I leave Pueblo October first," Nathan said, "I will need at least half a dozen armed men to guard the shipment on the return trip, and one teamster to drive the second wagon. I aim for us to reach the mines Sunday. We'll load and immediately begin the drive south. We should be in Pueblo October seventh."

"Then we'll get the shipment on the six o'clock eastbound the next morning," said Foster Hagerman. "I'll arrange to have the men and the wagons ready when you reach the terminal in Pueblo."

Nathan had gone immediately to Hagerman's office upon returning to Dodge. He now was faced with the unpleasant duty of telling Melanie Gavin her mother had married Clell Shanklin. It was early afternoon, and he found Melanie reading copies of the various newspapers. She was pleased to see him and he was pleased with her welcome.

"What did you learn?" she asked.

"Nothing good," he said. He went ahead and told her

about Elsa Gavin and Shanklin, of their going to Denver, of the closing of the Starlight Cafe.

"It's a shock," she said. "I don't know whether to laugh or to cry."

"Maybe you should laugh," he said. "Before this is over, reckon your mother will be crying enough for both of you."

"I'm sorry for her," said Melanie, "but there's nothing can do." She got to her feet and lifted the dress neck-high. "Look, the bruises are gone."

"So they are," he said, "and so is the one on your face. Have you been eating while I was away?"

"Oh, yes. I've been having breakfast with Sheriff Harrington, and Mr. Hagerman from the railroad took me to supper. They have been very, very kind."

"Well, Hagerman's out of luck tonight," said Nathan, "because I'm taking you out to supper. I've missed the food at Delmonico's."

The last rays of the setting sun spread crimson fingers across the western sky as they left the Dodge House. The sudden thunder of gunfire seemed unusually loud in the quiet of the evening, and a slug slammed into the door frame just inches from Nathan's head. But the bushwhacker didn't get a chance for a second shot. Nathan drew, and his return fire was a continuous sound, like the rolling of a drum. He ran toward the narrow passage between two buildings, and when he reached the rear of the structures, the wounded gunman was stumbling down the alley.

"That's far enough," Nathan shouted. "You're covered. Drop your gun."

But the bushwhacker turned and fired again. The slug kicked up dirt at Nathan's feet, and before the man could fire again, Nathan fired once. The gunman stumbled back against the wall of a store building and slid slowly to the ground.

"Nathan," Melanie cried, running toward him, "are you all right?"

"Yes," said Nathan.

He was reloading his Colt when Sheriff Harrington and half a dozen other men came down the alley.

"Again?" Harrington asked.

"Again," said Nathan, "but I don't know if it's the same man. I reckon I'll have to pay the Dodge House for a new door frame."

"Might as well see who he is, if we can," Sheriff Harringon said, kneeling beside the dead man. Removing a thin wallet from a hip pocket, he opened it and whistled.

"Who is he?" Nathan asked.

"Curt Limbaugh," said Harrington.

"Oh, God," Nathan groaned, "do I have to shoot the whole family?"

"Damned if it don't look like it," said Harrington. "Momma and Daddy may be next."

Nathan and Melanie went on to Delmonico's for supper, and there Nathan told her of his ongoing conflict with the Limbaughs.

"But how did he know where to find you?" Melanie asked.

"As long as I'm with the railroad, I can't escape the newspapers," said Nathan. "Every time I manage to out- smart some train robbers, it's news. Every time I have to shoot some damn fool who's trying to kill me. I'm forever proving how fast I am with a gun, adding more names to a growing list of potential killers who want a reputation at my expense."

"My God," she cried, "when will it all end?"

"When I face a man who's faster than I am," said Na- than. "Then he'll take up the burden I'm carrying now."

"Why can't you just go away, where nobody knows you? Must you work for the railroads?"

"It's a problem whether I'm working for the railroad or not," Nathan said. "It's just a little easier to find me, with the newspapers writing about me."

Dodge City, Kansas. September 4, 1874

"Monday morning," said Hagerman, "there'll be another military payroll coming from Kansas City. I'll want you on that train. You knocked out two-thirds of that gang the last time they struck, but they've had time to recruit some more men."

"I've been meaning to ask you," Nathan said, "why these varmints always know when there's a military payroll on board. Why can't you reschedule a shipment, like we did from the mines, sending it on a different train on short notice?"

"There are several reasons," said Hagerman. "The first, of course, is because of the way the military does things. They always pay between the first and the tenth of the

month, come hell or high water. In the case of the payroll
we handle, they always come out of Fort Leavenworth, and
they always arrive the day before they're to be shipped.
The other reason—to answer your question—is that any
band of outlaws with an eye toward stealing a payroll need
only have a man watching the fort. When the payroll and
its escort move out, it means one of the next day's westbounds will have the shipment aboard. The outlaws will
stop every train until they get the one they want."

"So there's no better way than just defending the train
carrying the payroll."

"That's it," said Hagerman. "This last bunch had a fond-
ness for dynamiting the express coach. It worked, because
nobody thought of attacking them like you did. Now, we
don't know how they'll come at us, so you'll have to be
prepared for anything. I can send some armed men with
you, if you wish."

"No," Nathan said, "but there is one thing you can do.
Let three thirty-eight and her crew make that run."

"They're not scheduled for it," said Hagerman, "but if
they're willing, I can make the change."

Kansas City, Missouri. September 6, 1874

Nathan arrived on Sunday afternoon, and went immediately to the terminal's huge call-board. The crew he had
requested—Dub Collins, engineer, Amos Handy, fireman,
Art Raines, baggageman, and Enos Pilpaw, brakeman—had
been assigned the early-morning run which would carry the
military payroll to Dodge. Nathan left his Winchester at
the dispatcher's office and found a cafe. After supper, he
bought copies of the *St. Louis Globe-Democrat* and the
Kansas City Liberty-Tribune. These he took back to the
terminal bunkhouse. Removing his boots and gun belt, he
stretched out on a bunk and read the newspapers without
finding anything of particular interest. Shortly after nine
o'clock, Enos Pilpaw and Art Raines arrived. Thirty minutes later, Dub Collins and Amos Handy came in.

"I hope I didn't spoil anybody's plans," Nathan said.

"When you work for the railroad," said Dub, "you don't
make a lot of plans. We was told you asked for us on this
run, and we took that as a compliment."

"I asked for you gents," Nathan said, "because I know
I can count on you not to fall into the jitters if the train

obbers come after us. Last time, we pretty well cured them
f dynamiting the express car, so I reckon we can look for
omething different if they come after us this time. Dub, I
vant you and Amos to arm yourselves with Winchesters.
Enos, that goes for you, too. Art, you're the exception,
because you'll be locked in."

"No matter," Art said. "I've cut some rifle holes in each
side of the express car, so I can use a rifle, too, if they
come within range."

"Trouble is," Nathan said, "if they come after us this
time, we don't know what they might do. Dub, you and
Amos keep close watch on the track ahead. They could
dynamite the track and derail the train. If they rip a rail
loose, like they've been doing, then we can count on them
attacking the train in some manner. Our defense will depend on how they attack us."

"If they rip a rail loose and try to rush us," said Dub,
"I can always reverse the train and leave them smelling
our smoke."

"You could," Nathan said, "but don't do it at the risk
of getting yourself shot."

By five o'clock the next morning, three thirty-eight had
steam up. Art Raines, Enos Pilpaw, and Nathan finished
breakfast at a quarter to six and boarded the train. Nathan
was again riding the caboose. They took on wood and water
at Wichita, and by the time they reached Newton, Nathan
was beginning to wonder if the outlaws had given up. But
half an hour west of Newton, the train began to slow. Nathan raised the cupola of the caboose, and for a moment,
saw nothing. He then heard shooting from the locomotive
cab, and saw the outlaws approaching the train from two
directions. They reined up and with rifles, began pouring
fire into both sides of the engine. The fire from the cab
ceased, and Nathan hoped it was because the trainmen had
taken cover. Nathan climbed out on top of the caboose and
began firing, but the outlaws were still out of range. Nathan
counted fourteen riders. Suddenly, six of them galloped
closer, and lead zipped all around Nathan like angry bees.
He was forced back inside the caboose, as slugs tore into
the cupola. Enos had the caboose's back door open and
was leaning over the side rail, firing at the outlaws creeping
alongside the train. Outlaw fire struck his Winchester, tear-

ing it from his hands and driving him back inside th
caboose.

"Four of 'em are covering the engine," said Enos, "an
the others are working their way back to us, using the trai
for cover. Their fire cost me my rifle."

"Take mine," Nathan said. "I'm going to get out on th
top of this train and go after the varmints who are comin
after us. Get just far enough up to see out this cupola an
lay down enough fire so those mounted coyotes near th
engine can't pick me off the roof."

Nathan reached the roof, but the moment he leaned ove
the edge, three of the outlaws began firing. He could hea
Enos firing from the roof of the caboose, and while the
outlaws beyond the engine posed no threat, those creeping
alongside the train were in a far better position than he.
There was a tender, a boxcar, the express coach, and the
caboose. In a matter of minutes, those using the train for
cover would rush Enos. But suddenly the train lurched
backward and began to move! Dub Collins was alive and
well. Rapidly the train gained speed, exposing the ten outlaws who had been using it for cover. Nathan stood atop
the swaying train, a Colt in each hand. Enos continued
firing from the top of the caboose, and at least one of the
railroad men was firing from the engine's cab. Ten of the
outlaws were down, dead or wounded. The four mounted
men galloped after the train, only to be met by fire from
Enos atop the caboose and from the engine's cab. After
one was shot out of the saddle, the others reined up. Dub
slowed the train as they neared the outskirts of Newton.
Nathan continued along the tops of the cars until he
reached the rear of the tender.

"Good work, amigos," he shouted. "Anybody hurt?"

"We're still in one piece," said Amos. "We had to back
off when things got too hot."

"Glad you did," Nathan said. "That was fast thinking,
Dub. If you hadn't backed away from them, they'd have
had us in a few more minutes."

"There's a rail out," said Dub. "You want to telegraph
Dodge and tell them we're rid of the outlaws and needin'
a work train?"

"Yes," Nathan said, "and I think we'll stay here at Newton for a while. Not all those varmints we gunned down
are dead."

Newton had no depot as such, but there was a telegra-
her's shack, and Nathan used the instrument to contact
agerman at Dodge. He requested the work train come
om Dodge rather than Kansas City or Wichita without
ving a reason. He doubted there would be any more trou-
le from the train robbers, but he wanted the damaged
ack repaired before the train bearing the payroll contin-
ed on its way.

"Figure three hours for the work train to get here," said
)ub, "and an hour to repair the track, and that makes us
our hours late."

"Hell," Amos said, "you can't have everything. We saved
he payroll."

"A big part of the credit goes to you gents in the cab
nd Enos in the caboose," said Nathan, "and I aim to see
hat the railroad knows it."

They waited two and a half hours before they saw the
dirty gray of smoke against the blue of the western sky.
There was a blast of the work train's whistle, and Dub
replied with an equal blast of three thirty-eight's whistle.
Nathan and Enos returned to the train's caboose and it
lurched into motion. When they reached the site of the
attempted robbery, none of the fallen outlaws were there.

"I don't believe it," Enos said. "I know I shot two of
them."

"We hurt them," said Nathan, "and they didn't want us
to know how bad. They toted away their dead along with
the wounded."

By the time three thirty-eight was within sight of the
twisted rail, the work train had arrived and men were hard
at work. A little more than an hour later, three thirty-eight
was steaming toward Dodge City, on the tail of the returning work train.

Dodge City, Kansas. September 7, 1874
"Another good piece of work," Hagerman said, when Nathan reported to him.

"I couldn't have done it without Dub Collins and his
crew," said Nathan. "The outlaws tore up the track and
then rushed us. Dub allowed most of them to dismount and
begin working their way along, using the train for cover.
Then he backed up, exposing them to our fire. We killed

or wounded eleven of the fourteen. They carried away t̶ dead so we'd not know how badly we hurt them."

"Another fight or two like that," Hagerman said, "a̶ it'll be damned hard for them to keep adding men to ̶ place those who have been killed or quit."

Nathan returned to the Dodge House. There was litt̶ else to do until the next shipment.

"I have almost a month until time for the next shipme̶ from the silver mines," said Nathan. "Is there anything ̶ particular you'd like to do?"

"No," Melanie said. "I'm just enjoying the peace an̶ quiet, without being cussed and slapped around. It's so nic̶ to be able to get up in the morning without being afrai̶ of the day ahead."

"Then we'll just lay low here in Dodge," said Nathan.

Denver, Colorado. October 4, 1874
Ten miles south of the Silver Slipper, where they woul̶ load the shipment, Nathan reined up his teams. He gath̶ ered the riders around him.

"Gents," he said. "I need the loan of a horse. Nobod̶ is to know of this shipment, and I need to ride ahead an̶ be sure it's safe for us to continue with the wagons."

"Take my horse," said Crump.

Nathan rode on toward the mines. Shanklin's wagons should have been there and taken the bogus shipment the day before, but Nathan had to be sure. Reaching the mine, he found Bammister in the office.

"We handled it the way you told us to," the mine superintendent said. "The genuine shipment is ready to be loaded."

Nathan returned to the wagons and the waiting riders. Returning Crump's horse, he mounted the wagon box and led out. Loading the wagons required less than half an hour. Nathan signed a receipt for the shipment and the caravan headed south, toward Pueblo.

Hays, Kansas. October 5, 1874
"Tomorrow," said Clell Shanklin, "we'll ride south. By then, Gonzolos and his bunch should have the shipment and be well on their way to New Mexico Territory."

"I don't see why we couldn't have gone on to Santa Fe and met them there," Elsa said. "I don't relish the idea of riding four hundred miles with a thieving Spaniard and his greasy gang of train robbers."

"That's just too damn bad," said Shanklin. "I don't relish the idea of having them take those wagons somewhere else, leaving me settin' on my hunkers in Santa Fe. We'll catch up and trail them as far as it takes, to get our cut."

"I suppose it hasn't crossed your mind," Elsa said, "but there's other ways to take it all for themselves. They could just kill us."

"They could," Shanklin agreed, "but I'm worth more to them alive than dead."

"When you're dealing with thieves and killers," said Elsa, "that can change."

Far to the south, near the Cimarron River, Chapa Gonzolos and his riders were having their share of trouble. While they had stopped the Kansas-Pacific eastbound and had taken what they had every reason to believe was a fortune in silver, they now gathered around a disabled wagon and cursed their luck. The wagon had seldom been greased, and the rear axle had snapped where the left rear wheel joined. Gonzolos had taken an ax from one of the wagons, and he pointed the handle of it at four of his dozen comrades.

"Take the ax and find a tree of the proper size," he ordered.

"But there are no trees," said one of the men, observing the flat Kansas plain.

"Then ride until there is one," Gonzolos roared.

It was already late afternoon, and the four rode west, along the Cimarron.

The sun was low on the western horizon when the four men returned to the wagon. Behind his horse, on a rope, one of the outlaws dragged a length of cedar. Gonzolos gave it a critical look. It would have to do. But there was another problem. There was no jack in either of the wagons.

"Gather large, flat stones," Gonzolos ordered. "We will have to lift the wagon and lay them underneath it, while the axle is replaced."

Several of the men were attempting to create a new axle from the cedar log, and doing a poor job of it, for all they had was the one ax. The others were gathering stones, many of which could not be used because they weren't flat enough. Finally Gonzolos judged they had enough stones.

"Come," said the outlaw leader, "let us raise the wagon. Bring the log."

But try as they might, using the would-be axle as a pry pole, they were unable to life the heavy wagon.

"It must be unloaded," Gonzolos said, to the groans of his companions.

Wearily, they set about unloading the heavy canvas bags, passing them from one man to another. They dropped one of the bags and a seam broke.

"Madre de Dios," one of the outlaws shouted, "sand!"

Gonzolos grabbed the ax and slashed every bag within reach, furious beyond words as sand spilled from each of them. He stalked to the second wagon, slammed down the tailgate, and began slashing bags. There was more sand. The outlaws stared at it, cursing.

"We have no further need of the wagons," Gonzolos said venomously. "Señor Shanklin will soon be coming for what is due him. I think we will wait here beside the river and see that he gets it."

Pueblo, Colorado. October 8, 1874

The two wagons reached the terminal without incident, and the shipment was loaded directly into the baggage car that would be coupled onto the next morning's eastbound. The dispatcher's office would remain open all night, Nathan was told, and guards would be near the car at all times. Nathan and his hired driver returned the rented wagons and the teams to the wagon yard, and Nathan returned to the terminal. He would remain there until it was time to board the eastbound the next morning.

Western Kansas, on the Cimarron. October 8, 1874

To the north of the Gonzolos camp, there came the distant moan of a locomotive whistle, as the eastbound steamed across the Kansas plains on its way to Kansas City. On board was Nathan Stone and a treasure in silver. As the whistle faded away to silence, Clell Shanklin and Elsa had sighted the wagons on the bank of the Cimarron.

"Come on," Shanklin shouted, kicking his horse into a gallop.

The outlaws watched in silence as Shanklin and Elsa forded the river. Shanklin swung down from his saddle and froze, for the ground was littered with mutilated canvas bags, all spilling out sand. Two of the outlaws seized Shanklin's arms. Gonzolos withdrew the deadly Bowie and approached the struggling, screaming Shanklin. One of the outlaws caught Elsa's horse, and she watched in horror as Gonzolos went to work on Shanklin.

"Do not harm the woman," Gonzolos said. "We will have use for her tonight."

Elsa put her hands over her ears, but she could still hear the terrified screams of Clell Shanklin. . . .

CHAPTER 20

Dodge City, Kansas. October 26, 1874

In Foster Hagerman's office to discuss the next silver shipment from Pueblo, Nathan was surprised when the railroad man handed him a letter of commendation from the mine owners. He—along with the AT and SF Railroad—had been praised for securing shipments from train robbers, and assured of continued business.

"That was sheer genius," Hagerman said, "sandbagging those outlaws with a shipment on the Kansas-Pacific, while taking the real shipment from Pueblo. The mines have learned a valuable lesson. They're buying their own wagons and hiring their own guards. The next shipment will leave Pueblo November ninth."

"I hated doing that to the Kansas-Pacific," said Nathan, "but there was no other way to prove to the mining people that Shanklin was selling them out."

"No harm was done," Hagerman said. "The Kansas-Pacific has been told what we did and our reason for it. They were in no way liable for a stolen shipment."

Nathan hadn't spoken to Sheriff Harrington recently, so he stopped by the office and found Harrington needing to talk to him.

"I just returned from Fort Dodge," said Harrington. "The commanding officer wanted me to talk to a Lieutenant McCoy, who just returned from a patrol to the south of here, along the Cimarron. McCoy and his men saw buz-

zards circling somewhere to the west of them and decided
to investigate. They found what was left of a man and a
woman and two abandoned wagons. The wagons had been
loaded with bags filled with sand. Some of the bags had
been cut open, and all of them bore the names of Colorado
silver mines. Since you're working with the railroad, I reckoned this might mean something to you."

"It does," Nathan said, "and since it's no longer a secret,
I'll tell you what happened."

He then told Harrington the strange story, starting with
his becoming suspicious of Clell Shanklin and ending with
the two shipments on separate railroads.

"So you think Shanklin and Elsa—Melanie's mother—
rode south to claim what they believed was a share of stolen silver?"

"I don't just think it," Nathan said, "I know it. The finish
of it fits the little we know of what became of Shanklin
and Elsa after they left Pueblo. They evidently traveled
east—probably to Hays—and from there, rode south. They
got everything that was coming to them. In spades."

Nathan saw no reason for keeping the grim news from
Melanie, and when he told her, the tears flowed briefly.

"I just feel sorry for her," said Melanie.

Santa Fe, New Mexico. October 28, 1874

Chapa Gonzolos had gathered his men to divulge plans for
their next robbery. Following his disastrous alliance with
Clell Shanklin, the outlaw had devised another approach
to stealing the silver.

"Saul and Kalpana," said Gonzolos, "you will ride north
and remain within sight of the mines. Then it matters not
who hauls the silver. When the wagons leave, you will ride
back and bring us the word. Somewhere north of the river,
before they reach Pueblo and the safety of the railroad, we
will attack. We will seize the wagons, drive them west of
the town, and then south to Santa Fe."

"The wagons are slow," said one of the outlaws, "and
so near the town, there will be a sheriff and posse quickly.
I like the train better. There are not so many hombres to
kill us."

"Estupido," Gonzolos said. "It takes but two men to

drive the wagons. The rest of us fall behind and set up the *emboscada*."*

"*Si,*" said Kalpana, "but they do not always use the railroad from Pueblo. Last time they do not."

"They do it to make fools of us," Gonzolos snapped. "From this time on, the wagons come south."

Saul and Kalpana mounted their horses and rode north to observe the mines and to wait for the wagons.

November seventh—the day before the silver from the mines was to leave Pueblo on the eastbound—Nathan met with Foster Hagerman just before boarding the train west.

"I understand the mines have hired a dozen armed men to escort the silver from the mines to Pueblo. The outlaws have always tried to rob the trains. Are you expecting them to try something different?"

"Wouldn't you?" Nathan asked. "We've outsmarted them twice, and once the silver reaches the terminal, they have no way of knowing which train it'll be on. From the little Melanie's been able to tell me, these outlaws are led by Chapa Gonzolos, and they hole up somewhere to the south, probably in New Mexico."

"Whatever happens," said Hagerman, "the silver's not our responsibility until it gets to the dispatcher's office and is locked safely away."

The locomotive whistle blew and Nathan climbed aboard the caboose.

Pueblo, Colorado. November 9, 1874

When Nathan reported to the dispatcher's office, he received grim news.

"There is no silver," he was told. "Yesterday, just north of the Arkansas River, outlaws killed everybody except one of the guards, and took the wagons. The man who got away rode in, shot up bad. He died last night."

"Has a posse gone after the outlaws?" Nathan asked.

"Sheriff Brodie and a dozen men rode out late yesterday. They ain't come back."

"I suppose you've contacted Hagerman in Dodge," Nathan said.

"I have," said the dispatcher. "You're to telegraph him."

*Ambush.

Nathan sat down at the instrument and tapped out a brief message to Hagerman:

Stone in Pueblo.

Almost immediately the instrument began to chatter a response, and Nathan wrote out the message.

Meet with sheriff and wire details.

Nathan went to Sheriff Red Brodie's office, joining an anxious deputy. The sun had just dipped below the horizon and scarlet spears streaked the western sky when the weary cavalcade wound its way in from the south. The sheriff and three men led horses bearing the bodies of the rest of the posse. Nine men were roped, belly-down, to their saddles. The four who had escaped had not done so unscathed, for bloody bandages were wrapped about their arms and legs. They dismounted, leaning wearily on their saddles. A crowd had gathered behind them, silent except for the women and children who wept for the dead. Sheriff Brodie stumbled toward the office, making it as far as the steps before his wounded leg gave out. He sat on the steps wiping his face with a bloody bandanna. Somebody went for the doctor, and he—a thin little man with a mustache—took charge.

"You men who are hurt, into the sheriff's office. That includes you, Sheriff."

Sheriff Brodie got up and went inside, the others following. A man from the local newspaper was trying to talk to a weeping woman who only wept all the harder. Nathan took the man by the front of his shirt and lifted him up on his toes.

"These people are in no mood to talk," Nathan said. "Take your pencil and get the hell away from here."

Many people had gathered around the door to the sheriff's office, trying to see inside. Other men, without being told, were releasing the roped-down dead, lifting them off their weary horses. Nathan helped remove one of the dead men who had been shot five times. In the back. It had been a slaughter of the most brutal kind, and Nathan gritted his teeth in frustration and anger. The doctor came to the door and Nathan got his attention.

"I'm Nathan Stone, and I'd like to speak to Sheriff Brodie as soon as he's able. I aim to round up that bunch of back-shootin' coyotes, and I need his advice."

"I'll talk to him," the doctor said. He returned in a moment, and nodded.

Nathan entered the office. Brodie sat in his office chair, his trousers down around his ankles. His right thigh was heavily bandaged. He looked up as Nathan leaned over the desk.

"Tell me what you can," said Nathan. "That bunch has to be stopped."

"They ambushed us," Brodie said. "The worst damn kind of ambush. There's at least a dozen of the varmints, and they split up. One bunch dropped back, and when we rode into them that was ahead of us, the others fell in behind, and they just shot hell out of us. I should have laid back and forced them to ride on, but it was near dark, and we thought we could take them. My God, there was a dozen of us. We got away in the dark, them of us that survived, but we was afoot. We hid out all night, and it took us most of today to catch up our horses and gather up our dead."

"I'll be going after them," said Nathan. "I represent the railroad, but there's more at stake here than stealing. I won't see nine good men die in vain."

Without another word he left the office. The doctor who had been listening shook his head, and Sheriff Brodie said nothing. Nathan went to the nearest livery and rented a horse and saddle. At a mercantile, he bought a bedroll, saddlebags, and provisions for a week. He then returned to the terminal, to the dispatcher's office, and sent a telegram to Foster Hagerman, at Dodge. It was blunt and to the point:

Posse wiped out stop. Going after outlaws.

He didn't wait for an answer because he knew what the answer would be. The railroad bore no responsibility for the stolen silver. But sight of the dead men—brutally shot in the back over riches not their own—had ignited a spark in Nathan. He recalled Captain Sage Jennings, shot in the back by a cowardly bushwhacker. But most of all, he could see in his mind's eye the evil El Gato, who had, with his band of killers, destroyed a part of Nathan Stone's life in the wilds of Indian Territory. Although it seemed so long ago, it all came back. He slipped his Winchester into the boot and swung into the saddle. Already it was dark, and while he couldn't take the trail until first light, he kicked the bay horse into a gallop, riding south. Reaching a creek, he dismounted. From his saddlebag he took some strips of jerked beef for his supper. His only edge, if he had one, was that the last thing the outlaws would expect would be pursuit by one man.

Dodge City, Kansas. November 10, 1874

"Why did he go after them alone?" Melanie asked, as she again read Nathan's few words to Foster Hagerman.

"I don't really know," said Hagerman. "I sent him a telegram asking him to give it up, but he expected that, for he had already gone. The silver was taken before it was ever in our hands, so we couldn't be responsible for that."

Melanie returned to the Dodge House, there to wait and worry.

Chapa Gonzolos and his men had driven the teams unmercifully, and by sundown of the day following the ambush, they had crossed the Rio Grande into New Mexico.

"It was as you say," Kalpana laughed. "We watch for the wagons and they come south to us for the taking."

Gonzolos said nothing, but he was pleased, for he had regained the confidence of his followers. No more would they pursue the trains. They would take the silver as it came from the mines, before it reached the railroad.

Nathan rose at first light, saddled the bay, and rode south, breakfasting on more of the jerked beef. He watched for barren ground, found the wagon tracks, and on top of them, tracks of many horses. He had no trouble identifying the scene of the ambush, for there was dried blood on dead leaves and grass, and bits of torn, bloody clothing. He rode on, knowing he must be careful. Just because they had gunned down one posse didn't mean there wouldn't be another. Once he had determined the direction they were traveling, Nathan rode a mile west and again rode south, paralleling their trail. When he reached the bank of the Rio Grande, he followed the river south until he found where the wagons had crossed. They had been traveling southwest, but after crossing the river, they followed the west bank. From a railroad map in Hagerman's office, he recalled that Santa Fe was practically on the banks of the Rio Grande. As a precaution, Nathan crossed the river, and keeping well away from the east bank, began following it south. It would allow him to keep on their trail without the possibility of riding up on them or stumbling into an ambush. There had been no recent rain, and the next day after reaching the Rio Grande, Nathan saw a thin plume of dust ahead. He eased the bay down to a walk. The sun was two hours high, and he reined up and dismounted. He rested the horse for a while and then led the animal down a low bank to water. Tonight, he would reach the outlaw camp.

Chapa Gonzolos and his men had begun to feel safe, and with Santa Fe near, they were in a jovial mood. Just before dark, one of them had shot an antelope, and they were broiling huge slabs of meat over an enormous fire. While every man had a weapon handy, they had not felt the need to post sentries. Suddenly, Gonzolos dropped his hunk of meat in the fire and snatched his Winchester.

"What is?" a companion asked.

"Silencio," Gonzolos snapped. "I hear something."

But there was no sound except the crackling of the fire, and they laughed as Gonzolos attempted to rescue his meat from the ashes.

Taking his Winchester, Nathan left the bay at least a mile north of the outlaw camp. There was no wind to betray him and the moon had yet to rise. The land was hilly, thick with cedar, and the starlight didn't penetrate the shadows. There were few dead leaves, and needles from pine and cedar made no noise under his boots. Once, as he neared the outlaw camp, Nathan stepped on a dead limb and it snapped. He froze as the outlaws became silent and watchful, moving ahead as they resumed their conversation and laughter. They were in a clearing, and he could see the firelight dancing off the canvas of the stolen wagons. Loss of this particular silver shipment didn't bother him nearly as much as the possibility of the outlaws escaping to steal and kill again. Strangely enough, he thought of the times Captain Sage Jennings had urged him to join the rangers, and wondered if there wasn't more of the lawman in him than he realized. But for that, what kind of damn fool would go after a dozen deadly outlaws who had virtually wiped out a sheriff's posse?

As near the camp as he dared go, Nathan paused. Now that he had caught up to the outlaws, what was he going to do? As he had learned in General Lee's army, one man with a rifle could raise hell within a larger force, with hit-and-run tactics. It was the simplest kind of warfare, where a sniper hurt the enemy as much as possible, and then escaped to launch a new attack. In daylight they might ride him down, but they would never find him in the dark. With that in mind, he raised his Winchester and firing rapidly, shot three of the outlaws. He rolled away as they fired at his muzzle flashes, and like a cat, was on his feet. He slipped among the cedars, keeping to the shadows, making his way back toward his horse. He loosed the reins, mounted, and rode several miles back up the river, until he could no longer hear any sound of pursuit. He had no idea how near they were to Santa Fe, and he suspected the town was large enough that the outlaws could lose themselves if they chose.

As Nathan had hoped, the outlaws soon gave up any thought of pursuit, for a gunman could pick them off one at a time in the dark. Gonzolos had put out the fire, lest the lone gunman circle around and attack from another direction.

"Sangre de Cristo," Kalpana said, "he is *El Diablo.* He shoot three time, in the dark, and three *companeros* die."

"El Diablo or not, he don't get away with this," said Gonzolos, seething with rage. "He leave tracks, we follow. *Por Dios,* come the dawn, we leave the wagons here. We find and kill this *bastardo* if we never do anything else. I, Chapa Gonzolos, have spoken."

Nathan was in the saddle at first light, prepared to stalk the outlaws, but to his dismay, they began stalking him. He could see puffs of dust at regular intervals, as they advanced. He retreated. There were several outcroppings of rock where he could have taken a stand, but with several of them keeping him pinned down, the others could circle around and get him from behind. He had to keep moving, lest they surround him, but his dust was as visible as was their own. Already, their skirmish line had taken on the shape of a large horseshoe, with its open end moving to engulf him. The sun was growing hot, and already the bay was sweating. They would stalk him until his horse gave out, and then ride him down. He had but one chance, and that was to break through their line to the south and outride them. He returned the Winchester to its boot and kicked the bay into a fast gallop. As long as they couldn't actually see him, he had a chance, but only if he broke through the line that was advancing to surround him. Two of the approaching riders discovered what he had in mind and converged on him, shooting. Returning their fire, he watched one man pitch from the saddle, but before he broke free, the other man fired and he felt the lead rip into his side. Hearing the shooting, the rest of the riders had circled and were on his trail. Another slug struck him in the back, high up. His bay was heaving and could not continue. Ahead, stretching across the Rio Grande, was a ridge of stone, over which a cascade of water fell. There was an upthrust of stone on the east bank, head-high. Nathan reined up the heaving bay and all but fell from the saddle. He stumbled into the rocks just above the falls, realizing that he had left his Winchester in the saddle boot. But he had his Colts with enough shells to last him until he bled to death. Already the outlaws had begun to fire, and lead spat against the rocks. It would be a matter of minutes until some of the outlaws crossed the river and cut down on him from the west bank. In desperation, he began searching for a way out and discovered a narrow, treacherous path down the rocky slope alongside the waterfall. Holstering his Colts, he started down. The outlaws intensified their fire; and a slug burned a fiery path just above Nathan's left ear. Off balance, he fell into the roiling water at the foot of the falls.

"Por Dios," Gonzolos shouted, "ride in and be sure he is dead."

Several of the outlaws dismounted and made their way to the precipitous bank from which Nathan had fallen. There was no sign of a body in the water below, and after a while, even Gonzolos was convinced the man they had sought was dead.

"Back to the wagons," Gonzolos ordered.

Before sundown, the wagons rumbled along the rutted Santa Fe Trail and reached the outskirts of the town of Santa Fe. There the caravan turned eastward, and five miles into the barren land that was northeastern New Mexico, they reached a sprawling ranch that had come into existence more than a hundred years previous, by Spanish grant. In an arch above the gate hung a long wooden slab. In Spanish, burned into the wood in large letters, were the words CASA DE EL AGUILA.*

One man dismounted and opened the gate, allowing the two wagons to pass through. They were taken beyond and

*House Of The Eagle.

around the ranch house, to a barn. Chapa Gonzolos and his riders dismounted before the house he had inherited from his father, and Gonzolos laughed triumphantly. Again, as had been his father before him, he was a respected citizen of Santa Fe, and the owner of a Spanish grant older than the town itself.

From the slug that had grazed his head, Nathan had blacked out, coming to his senses only when he was under the cold water. There was a narrow shelf of rock behind the fall, and after several failed tries, Nathan dragged himself up on it. So near to the fall was he that spray from it was flung in his face, but he was concealed from the men who had tried to kill him. While he couldn't understand their words, he could hear their voices on the bank above him. There was little he could do but wait until they presumed him dead and rode away.

He could feel the blood oozing out of his wounds, and if he did nothing else, he had to stop the bleeding. Besides being alive, there was one thing for which he could be thankful. There were exit wounds, telling him that neither slug had struck bone, for such a ricochet was almost always fatal. The spray in his face had a refreshing effect and kept him conscious most of the time. While he was fearful of sliding off the narrow shelf, it seemed impossible for him to keep his eyes open, and he slipped into unconsciousness for he knew not how long. He listened, and hearing nothing but the sound of the falling water, decided he must make his move. The constant spray had not allowed the blood to clot. He slid off the rock shelf and was in water neck-deep.

Fighting his way through the fall, he found it was late in the afternoon, the sun not more than an hour high. He waded to the shallows, and stood there listening. Somewhere, it seemed he could hear a horse cropping grass. The riverbank was high and he waded farther downstream. There, to his surprise, his saddled bay was grazing. The horse had been heaving with exhaustion, which accounted for the outlaws not having taken it. Nathan took handfuls of mud, and squeezing the water out of it, applied it to his wounds. His skull ached like seven kinds of hell from the graze, and a faint stream of blood still trailed down his jaw. Despite having been soaked to the hide most of the day, his face felt hot. It was the beginning of a fever that would rob him of his consciousness as it wore on.

Slowly, slipping and falling, he climbed the riverbank and headed for his grazing horse. The effort brought fresh blood flowing from his wounds. He knew not how far he was from Santa Fe. It would be his only source of aid, for he was three days south of Pueblo. Three times he tried before he was able to drag himself into the saddle. He kicked the bay into a lope, following the river south. The horse slowed to a walk, and Nathan allowed it to continue, for he wasn't sure how long he could remain conscious. A faster gait might jolt him out of the saddle, and he was in no condition to stop and rest the horse. He awoke to a cool night wind and darkness, aware that the fever was taking him. He never saw the light in a distant window or knew when the horse halted. He fell from the saddle and lay with unseeing eyes turned to the purple sky, with its silent, twinkling stars. . . .

Santa Fe, New Mexico. November 15, 1874

It was late, and but a single lamp burned in the window of Loretto Academy of Our Lady of Light. Assistant Pastor Thomas Hayes had been reading, and he paused, listening. There were hoofbeats, and when they ceased, Father Hayes went to the window and drew the curtain aside. At first, in the starlight, he could see only the riderless horse, but as his eyes grew accustomed to the darkness, he could see the body of a man on the ground. He hurried down the hall and knocked on the door of Father Augustine Truchard, the pastor.

"Yes," came a sleepy voice, "what is it?"

"There is a man—a horseman—lying in the yard, Father Truchard, and he appears to be hurt."

"Very well," said Father Truchard. "Allow me time to dress. Perhaps you should awaken Mother Magdalen."

"I am awake," Mother Magdalen said, when Father Hayes knocked on her door.

"There is a man lying in the yard," said Father Hayes, "and he appears to be hurt. Father Truchard and I are going to bring him inside. Perhaps you should prepare to receive him."

"Very well," Mother Magdalen replied. "Bring him into the room that adjoins your study. I will be there."

The priests carried the unconscious Nathan into the academy foyer and then into the room Mother Magdalen had

suggested. Already she had clean sheet spread over a
couch, and Sister Francisca had come to assist her. A medicine chest had been opened and Mother Magdalen was removing items she would need. She spoke quietly to
Father Truchard.

"If you will leave him with us, we will do what we can."

The priests went out, closing the door behind them.

"I will unsaddle and care for his horse," said Father
Hayes. "The animal is exhausted."

Father Truchard went into the study of Father Hayes
and sat down. He had seen gun-shot wounds before, and
the stranger had been shot twice. It would be a long night.

Nathan suffered a raging fever for a day and a night.
Mother Magdalen, Sister Lucia, Sister Rosana, and Sister
Francisca took turns looking after him. After the fever broke,
he slept for another day before regaining consciousness.

"Where am I?" he asked, when he finally could speak.

"In Santa Fe," said Mother Magdalen, "at the Loretto
Academy of Our Lady of Light. You have been here three
days and two nights."

"My name is Nathan Stone, and I . . ."

"You are still very weak," Mother Magdalen said. "Rest,
and I will have one of the sisters bring you some supper."

Nathan was fed soup until he could take solid food. He
learned, only after he had regained consciousness that the
doctor who tended him was there for the third time. Nobody questioned him, and his gun belt with its twin Colts
hung on the head of his bed. There in a corner was his
Winchester and saddlebags. His fifth day there, he had
begun to feel guilty, and he spoke to Mother Magdalen.

"Ma'am, I'm obliged for all you've done. I owe all of
you my life, and . . ."

"You owe us nothing," said Mother Magdalen. "We
have done no more than our duty, for what we have done
unto the least of His, we have done unto Him."

None of them would talk to him about what he considered his obligation. Besides Mother Magdalen, there was
Sister Rosana who played the organ, and Sisters Francisca
and Lucia, who were teachers. Only occasionally did he see
Father Augustine Truchard, or his assistant, Father Thomas
Hayes. Eventually, it was Father Hayes who began spending
some time with Nathan, inquiring about his travels, about the

frontier, and it was from Father Hayes that he learned much about Santa Fe, the building of the Loretto Academy of Our Lady of Light, and of the adjoining Loretto Chapel.

"When you are strong enough," Father Hayes said, "I will show you around. There is a newly built Loretto Chapel, just finished last year. It's the first Gothic structure west of the Mississippi."

This was Nathan Stone's first time in a church since he had been a child, led there by his mother's hand, and it stirred some long-forgotten feeling within him.

"Thank you," said Nathan. "I'll look forward to it."

"Perhaps tomorrow, then," Father Hayes replied.

CHAPTER 21

"I hope you are a patient man," said Father Hayes, as he joined Nathan for breakfast, "because it is difficult to tell you any of our history, without telling you all of it."

"Then tell me all of it," Nathan said.

"In September 1852, the Sisters of Loretto arrived," said Father Hayes. "They came to the Southwest by covered wagon and paddle steamer. Their journey had begun in May 1851 in Kentucky aboard a steamer named *The Lady Franklin,* which took them up the Mississippi to Saint Louis. From there to Independence, they took the *Kansas,* but on the way, their superior, Mother Matilda, took the cholera and died shortly after their arrival in Independence. Two other sisters who had been stricken, recovered."

Father Hayes refilled his own and Nathan's coffee cup. Then he continued.

"There were months of struggles and fears. Wagon axles and wheels broke, and under a terrible sun, there were days on barren prairies littered with animal and human bones. What was left of the group—Sisters Magdalen, Catherine, Hilaria, and Roberta—finally arrived in Santa Fe, and at the request of Bishop Lamy, Sister Magdalen was appointed superior of the group. She was a woman of faith and resolution, and the situation she and her sisters faced was a difficult one. The country was still raw and unsettled, and they had no comfortable convent waiting for them on arrival. They lived at first in a little, one-room adobe house, and the little town of Santa Fe was made up mostly of Indians and Mexicans at that time. But it soon became quite evident that, if the sisters were to fulfill the intentions of Bishop Lamy who had brought them to Santa Fe to teach the people, they must have a convent and a school. Mexican carpenters built the school, and when it was completed, it was called Loretto Academy of Our Lady of Light. Plans were made next for a beautiful chapel. It was designed by the same architect, Mr. Mouly, who designed the cathedral in Santa Fe. Bishop Lamy being from France, he wanted the sisters to have a chapel similar to his beloved Sainte Chapelle in Paris. It would be strictly Gothic."

"I still haven't had a good look at any of it from the outside," said Nathan. "I reckon I was pretty well used up when I got here."

"You'll be more appreciative of Loretto Chapel," Father Hayes said, "so I'm taking you there first. It was built by French and Italian masons, and it is twenty-five by seventy-five feet, with a height of eighty-five feet. It is larger than most of the mission chapels in this area. Mother Magdalen has recorded in the annals that the erection of the chapel was placed under the patronage of Saint Joseph, 'in whose honor we communicated every Wednesday that he might assist us.' The chapel work progressed with some financial worries and a maximum of faith on the part of the sisters. It was not until the chapel was nearly finished that they realized a dreadful mistake had been made. The chapel itself was wonderful and the choir loft was wonderful, too, but there was no connecting link between the two. There was no stairway and, because the loft is exceptionally high, there was no room for a stairway as ordinary stairways go. Mother Magdalen called in many carpenters to try and build a stairway. Each, in turn, measured and thought and then shook his head sadly saying 'it can't be done, Mother.' It seemed as though there were only two alternatives: to use a ladder to get to the choir—which seemed impractical in any case—or to tear the whole thing down and rebuild it differently."

"But they didn't tear it down," said Nathan.

"No," Father Hayes replied, "but you're getting ahead

of me. To destroy so beautiful a structure would have been heartbreaking. But the Sisters of Loretto are so devoted to Saint Joseph, they made a novena to him for a suitable solution to the problem."

"A novena?"

"A Roman Catholic nine-days' devotion," said Father Hayes. "On the last day of the novena, a gray-haired man came up to the convent with a donkey and a tool chest. Approaching Mother Magdalen, he asked if he might try to help the sisters by building a stairway. Mother Magdalen gladly gave her consent and he set to work. His few tools consisted of a hammer, a saw, and a T-square. It took him six to eight months to complete the work. When Mother Magdalen went to pay him, he had vanished. She went to the local lumber yard to pay for the wood, at least, but they knew nothing of it there. There is no record stating that the job was ever paid for. Now that you have heard the story, would you like to see those stairs?"

"I would," said Nathan.

They entered the chapel, and Father Hayes said not a word. Nathan swallowed a lump in his throat as he beheld the masterpiece of beauty and wonder the old man had left the sisters. It was a winding stairway that made two complete three-hundred-and-sixty-degree turns. But there was no supporting pole up the center as most circular stairways have.

"I've never seen anything so amazing in my life," said Nathan.

"Neither have I," Father Hayes said. "I've studied it almost daily. It hangs there with no support, with its entire weight on the base. Some architects have said that by all laws of gravity, it should have crashed to the floor the minute anyone stepped on it."

"I can believe that," said Nathan. "What do *you* reckon is holding it up?"

"The same faith that built it," Father Hayes replied.

"I'm enough of a believing man that I'd have to agree with you," said Nathan.

"I have gone over it many times," Father Hayes said, "and it was put together without nails. There are only wooden pegs. Architects who have heard of these inexplicable stairs—those who have seen them—cannot understand how the stairway was constructed. Most of them agree on one thing, that they have never seen or heard of a circular wooden stairway with three-hundred-and-sixty-degree turns that did not have a supporting pole down the center. One of the men who has examined the stairway says that perhaps the most baffling thing about it is the perfection of the curves of the stringers. The wood is spliced along the sides of the stringers with nine splices on the outside and seven on the inside. Each piece is perfectly curved. How this was done by just one man with so few tools remains a mystery."

"What kind of wood was used?" Nathan asked.

"Another mystery," said Father Hayes. "Some have said it's fir of some sort, while others believe it is long leaf yellow pine. But it's been claimed by good authority that none of the wood used came from New Mexico. So where the old carpenter got that wood is a mystery."

"It's a supernatural thing," Nathan said.

"The church is always cautious about making statements concerning things of a supernatural nature," said Father Hayes. "Therefore, the sisters and priests of Santa Fe have, in the same spirit, refrained from saying anything definitive about the stairway. But Mother Magdalen and the sisters at Loretto Academy know that the stairway is Saint Joseph's answer to prayers. Some like to think that the carpenter was Saint Joseph, himself."

"Thank you for telling me the story," Nathan said.

"We never tire of telling it," said Father Hayes. "I hope it becomes to you, as it has to us, a testimony of faith."

Santa Fe, New Mexico. December 10, 1874

While Nathan appreciated what had been done for him by the sisters and the priests of Loretto Academy, he had grown restless. It was time to move on. He had made a silent vow to track down Chapa Gonzolos and his gang, and to this end, he spoke to Father Hayes.

"Señor Chapa Gonzolos is a most respected member of the community," Father Hayes said. "His ranch, Casa De El Aguila, belonged to his father before him. It is five miles east of town, and covers many hundreds of acres. Are you a friend of Señor Gonzolos?"

"No," said Nathan truthfully. "I've heard of him, and that he lives in these parts."

*   *   *

The sisters and priests of Loretto genuinely hated to see Nathan go, and he felt a real sense of loss as he saddled the bay. He had known better than to offer them money for their compassion and kindness, but from his saddlebag he had taken ten gold double eagles. On his way down the hall, he ducked quickly into the study. Opening the center drawer of Father Hayes's desk, he left the gold there and silently closed the drawer.

"*Adios, muy bueno companeros,*" he said, as he rode away.

"*Vaya con Dios,*" they responded.

Nathan followed the rutted Santa Fe Trail on into town. Finding a telegraph office, he addressed the telegram to Foster Hagerman, Dodge City, Kansas. His message was brief:

Alive in Santa Fe stop. Unfinished business stop. Tell Melanie will see her in time for Christmas.

He signed off with only his first name. From there he rode until he found a livery, and leaving his horse there, went in search of a hotel. In the lobby he bought a copy of the local newspaper, *The New Mexican.* In his room, he studied the paper, wondering if he might find something on Chapa Gonzolos. It complicated things, learning that Gonzolos was apparently a respected member of the community. He was reminded of the James and Younger gangs, who presented a respectable front while riding to distant towns where they robbed banks or held up trains. What he had learned about Gonzolos answered probably the most important question, which was whether or not he could turn to the law for help. Obviously he could not, because if he accused Gonzolos of being a thief and a killer, there was absolutely no proof. The man might be prominent enough to turn the law against Nathan, forcing him to ride out of New Mexico with a price on his head. He found himself with just one course of action. If Gonzolos was brought to justice, then it would have to be a one-man vendetta. Tomorrow at first light he would find the Gonzolos ranch and determine a means of reaching Chapa Gonzolos. While he wanted the entire gang, he would settle for Gonzolos, if that was the best he could do.

Nathan arose at first light, found a cafe, and after breakfast, sought a mercantile. It was still early, and the store had just opened. The storekeeper seemed surprised to have a customer so early, and came to meet Nathan.

"Pardner," Nathan said, "I'm needin' a few sticks of dynamite, some caps, and fuses."

"I ain't got much. It's mostly used for mining, and nearly all that's farther south."

He brought out a wooden case that was two-thirds empty. "Twelve sticks is all I got," he said. "Will that help?"

"I'll make do," said Nathan. "Put it in a burlap sack, if you have one."

Nathan tied the sack behind his saddle and rode south. Let the storekeeper and others who might have seen him think he had ridden toward the distant mines. Once he was well away from town, he circled around and rode eastward. He had no real plan as to what he would do, and the dynamite was an ace in the hole, should the Gonzolos ranch actually be an impregnable stronghold. He half expected to see grazing cattle, but there were none. He suspected he was nearing the ranch when he came upon a clearly defined wagon road leading in from the northwest. If there were sentries, they most certainly would be watching the road, so he rode north for what he estimated was three miles.

The land was becoming thick with cedar and fir, allowing Nathan to see without being seen. When he was at last able to see the ranch, he was astounded, for it sprawled for what seemed half a mile. There were two long wings stretching from north to south, with a connecting link in the middle, like a huge letter H. Around the house and outbuildings there was a stone wall of what might be unscalable proportions. The entrance was secured by an arched iron gate, and even from a distance, Nathan could see men moving about. He would have to wait for darkness, and even then would have to leave his horse a great distance away, in the cover of trees.

Rather than sit and wait, he rode northeast, with the intention of circling the place, for it might be more vulnerable from another direction. There was a back gate, and as best he could tell, identical to the one at the front, including two armed sentries. After riding all the way around, he found not a single weakness in the massive wall. The only means of access other than the gates would be over the wall, for jutting above it at irregular intervals were stone uprights, like spearheads. These he could rope from the ground and thus breach the wall.

While at Loretto Academy, he had lost track of the moon's cycles. The last thing he needed was a full moon, but if it appeared, he could only wait for it to set. He rode far enough into the hills north of Casa De El Aguila to cook himself a meal beside a spring. There, with his picketed horse grazing, he dozed until a cooling west wind awakened him. The sun was down, painting the western sky with plumes of crimson. Within minutes, the first stars winked from purple heavens, but Nathan resisted the temptation to begin his dangerous quest. Full moon or not, he decided to wait until after moonset, so he settled down, his head on his saddle.

The moon rose, half full, and Nathan waited until it had fully set. Once it had, even the stars didn't seem to penetrate the darkness. He rode until the cedars began to thin and he could see the massive stone walls ahead. Already he had capped the dynamite, attaching the estimated forty-five-second fuses. He divided the explosive, half of it in each end of the sack, so that he could drape it around his neck. He decided against taking his Winchester, for he had no sling, and would need both hands to hoist himself over the wall. Carefully he picketed his horse so that the animal could not be seen, and far enough away so that if it nickered, it wouldn't reveal his presence. Taking his lariat, he crept through the darkness toward the wall. It loomed black and forbidding, like something from a fairy tale, and he readied his loop. His first throw missed, but the second caught and held. The outer wall proved to be smooth, virtually impossible for him to gain any purchase with his feet, throwing all his weight on his arms and shoulders. There was intense pain in his side and in his upper back, where he had been wounded, but he continued to struggle up the rope. Finally, exhausted and drenched with sweat, he sat on the wall, fighting to regain his wind.

Believing that he might need the rope, he removed the loop from the stone upright and took one end of the rope in each hand. He then looped the middle of it over the stone upright and descended to the ground. He was then able to loose one end of the rope and free it from the wall. Coiling the lariat, he hung it over his left arm and made his way toward the house. Nearing it, he could hear shouts and laughter. He crept to a window and beheld a table laden with food and drink. Men drank directly from bottles, and there were women in varying stages of undress. Chapa Gonzolos was not among the revelers. Nathan crept on around the house. While he wished to account for the entire gang, it was his intention to get Gonzolos first. Oddly, except for the hall from which the merrymaking just seemed to get louder, there were no more lighted windows. Nathan moved on, pausing when he saw a flicker of light against a windowpane somewhere ahead of him. As he drew closer, it proved to be the dying flames of a fire. He had become aware of it only because of its faint reflection in the window glass, and try as he might, he could see nothing or nobody inside the darkened room. He was near the center hall that connected one side of the H to the other, and when he made his way past the window where the fire had been reflected, he could see a door, standing partially open. He had reached the point where he must enter the house, and the door moved on silent hinges. Nathan stepped inside, and a floorboard creaked. Suddenly, a voice spoke from the darkness.

"Ah, señor, the good doctor told me the academy had taken in a man with gunshot wounds. *Por Dios,* it had to be you. I have the *pistola* ready, for I have been expecting you. This time you will die."

Nathan dropped to the floor, firing at the muzzle flash, but Gonzolos was firing over the back of a couch, and Nathan's slugs went deep into the upholstery. He rolled up against the back of the couch, and to his surprise, the burly Gonzolos launched himself over the back of it, coming down hard. The blade of a knife ripped through the collar of Nathan's shirt, narrowly missing his throat. He seized both of Gonzolos's arms and tried to hump him off, but Gonzolos had a weight advantage. Beneath him, Nathan could feel the Colt he had dropped. With his left hand, he let go of Gonzolos and grabbed the Colt. Swinging it as hard as he could, he slammed it into Gonzolos's head. The big man went limp and Nathan humped him off. Seizing the knife, he was about to drive it into Gonzolos when there came a thump of boots. When the first man darkened the door, Nathan fired, driving him back into one of his comrades. Nathan used the few seconds he had gained to get the couch between him and the door, barely in time to avoid a rain of lead.

"Madre de Dios!" Gonzolos bawled, "stop . . ."

But his drunken followers did not stop, and Chapa Gonzolos died under their guns. Nathan's eyes had grown accustomed to the darkened room, and on hands and knees, he crept along the wall toward the shadowy outline of another door. Realizing it would lead him deeper into the house, he had little choice. There were shouts of rage as the renegades realized he had escaped, and when they discovered the dead Gonzolos, they broke into a maudlin frenzy. They fired through the door into the darkness into which Nathan had disappeared, their lead smashing into walls, shattering lamps and mirrors. Nathan made his way through the darkened house until he found a door. Stepping outside, he made his way back toward the front of the house. The outlaws had left their women when the shooting had started. Now Nathan stepped into the room, a Colt in each hand and Gonzolos's Bowie knife under his belt. Some of the women screamed, and Nathan responded by shooting out all three lamps. Burning oil set fire to the deep carpet and sweeping velvet drapes. There had been enough commotion, including screams of the women, to attract the attention of the renegades, and they came on the run. Nathan lighted a stick of dynamite and threw it among them. Before the echo of the first blast died, Nathan threw a second stick. Every man was down, and whether dead or wounded, Nathan didn't know. The fire had taken hold and promised to burn the place to the ground, and such a conflagration wouldn't go unnoticed. Nathan made his way to the gate, which was no longer secured. Reaching his horse, he mounted and rode north. Topping a rise, he turned and looked back. The entire house was afire, shooting sparks and orange flame heavenward. Certainly there would be an investigation, and Chapa Gonzolos would be mourned for the man he was believed to have been. Nathan had but one regret, which was that Gonzolos couldn't have been revealed for the thief and murderer he had been, and made to suffer the disgrace as the result of it. He rode all night, resting the bay, and by dawn, was seventy miles away.

Pueblo, Colorado. December 14, 1874
Arriving in Pueblo, Nathan went first to the sheriff's office. There he told Sheriff Brodie what had happened.

"I reckon if word ever gets out, I'll have a price on my head in New Mexico, but you see that the kin of those who died in that ambush know that the killers have paid."

"I'll do that," Brodie said, "and if you ever get in trouble as a result of it, you send me word. We'll bring enough people and raise enough hell till everybody west of the Mississippi knows the truth about Gonzolos and his gang."

"I'm obliged," said Nathan.

Dodge City, Kansas. December 16, 1874

"My God," Foster Hagerman said, "we thought you was a goner. I eventually got a full report from the dispatcher in Pueblo about the posse being ambushed. Then, when we got the word you had gone after the outlaws ... alone ..."

"It took me a while," said Nathan. He then told Hagerman the whole story, from the time he had first jumped the outlaws to the death of Chapa Gonzolos and the destruction of his empire.

"You should never have taken on a task like that, by yourself," Hagerman said. "The mine owners will bless you, the AT and SF will bless you, but it's a miracle you're alive."

"I reckon," said Nathan, "but that's my last official act for the AT and SF. I want to go somewhere with Melanie where there's no trains, no outlaws, no payrolls ..."

"I wish I didn't have to tell you this," Hagerman said, "but Melanie Gavin is gone. We last heard from you on November tenth, and December first, she left, believing you were dead. Said she was goin' to Columbus, Ohio, that she's got kin there."

Nathan said nothing. Hagerman paid him through the end of December, and took the time to stop by Sheriff Harrington's office.

"I'm sorry to see you go," Harrington said, "and sorry to see Melanie leave without giving it some time. I hope you'll go on to Columbus and track her down."

"No," said Nathan. "I reckon we'd just be prolonging her grieving. This time, I came out of it forked-end down. The next time I might not, and she'd be going through it all over again. I'm obliged to you for your kindness to her, and for standing by me. If you're ever needin' a friend, somebody to watch your back, get word to me."

"I'll do that," Harrington said, extending his hand, "and

you're ever needin' somebody to watch *your* back, remember you have a friend in Dodge."

Nathan checked out of the Dodge house and went to the livery for his packhorse and the grulla. Both animals had grown fat from livery feed. Nathan loaded the packhorse, saddled the grulla, mounted, and rode south. He was tired, his latest wounds still bothered him, and he wanted solitude. He rode by the bank and found that Melanie had taken only a hundred dollars of the money he had left her, which was probably her fare back to Ohio. Nathan still had the four thousand he had won in Uvalde, plus his earnings from the railroad, so he wasn't hurting for money. It had been more than two years since he had been to New Orleans, and he longed to go there, to spend some time with his friends, Barnabas and Bess McQueen. Despite his travels, the many places he had been, he always felt he was going home when he rode down the oak-lined lane to the McQueen place. It was there that Eulie Prater was buried, and late at night, when the wind was from the west, he could hear the mournful wail of steamboat whistles. He rode south, intending to spend a few days at Fort Worth, with Captain Ferguson. He avoided towns, spending his nights in lonely camps beneath the stars. Reaching Fort Griffin, he stopped in the sutler's store to replenish some of his dwindling supplies. Three men—apparently buffalo hunters—came in, and one of them looked at Nathan and spoke to his companions. Nathan appeared not to see them, but he was very much aware of their interest in him. He continued rounding up the things he needed, and only when the three came up behind him did he turn to face them.

"If you gents have something to say to me, then say it. It's not healthy, comin' up behind a man's back."

"We was just wonderin'," said one, "if it wasn't you that gunned down that kid in a saloon in El Paso a few months back. His daddy's done raised the ante on your head."

"And I reckon you're of a mind to try and collect it," Nathan said grimly.

"Like I said, we was just wonderin'. I ain't said we're doin' anything more."

Nathan said no more. The three left ahead of him, and when he went out, there was no sign of them. Having loaded his purchases on the packhorse, he was about to mount the grulla when a familiar voice spoke.

"Didn't seem right, gittin' the store all bloodied up. Now you just turn around and do whatever you're of a min to do."

Nathan didn't know if he was facing one man or three There didn't seem to be anyone else around, so there woul be no witnesses. Nathan threw himself under the grulla' belly, coming up on one knee with a Colt in each hand The man who had spoken to him in the store had his Col out, and Nathan shot him once, just above the belt buckle His two companions had their hands up as the third mar crumpled to the ground.

"Unless you're buying in," Nathan said, "vamoose."

Quickly they moved away. A soldier arrived to investigate the shooting, and several men left the store, apparently to see what was going on.

"He drew first," said Nathan.

"Any witnesses?" the lieutenant asked.

"His two friends," said Nathan. "I invited them to leave."

"I saw it through the window," said one of the men from the store. "The dead man already had his gun out before this gent made a move."

"I was about to ride out," said Nathan.

"Then go ahead," the lieutenant replied. "You have a witness. I'll file a report and have him sign it."

Nathan rode away, all the old bitterness creeping back, as he recalled that unfortunate day in El Paso. The bounty having been raised, what chance did he ever have of returning there? Would he ever see Myra, Jamie, and Ellie again? He rode on toward Fort Worth, more determined than ever to return to New Orleans, seeking the peace that seemed to be forever just beyond his reach. . . .

Fort Worth, Texas. December 23, 1874

There was a festive air about the fort when Nathan arrived, for it seemed the Indian problem was about to be resolved. Quanah Parker and his Comanche followers were the last desperate holdouts, and more soldiers were being sent west to reinforce the undermanned frontier outposts. Christmas had lost its meaning to Nathan, his only recollection of it being from his childhood, which now seemed so long ago and so far away.

"We're always glad to have you with us," said Captain

erguson. "Occasionally we get word from Fort Dodge
hen something unusual takes place. You've been making
ome big tracks with the railroad in those parts."

"If I'm goin' to be shot at, I might as well get paid for
," Nathan said.

Nathan remained at Fort Worth for a week. He was still
early five hundred miles from New Orleans, and he felt
he need to be on his way.

CHAPTER 22

Dallas, Texas. January 1, 1875

Having friends at Fort Worth, having access to the telegraph there, Nathan had spent little time in Dallas, a growing town just a short ride to the east. This day, however, a
new saloon had opened for business, and there were plac-
ards touting it as the biggest and most luxurious in Texas.
The name of it was simply Austin's, named after the man
who had bankrolled it. Nathan left his horses at a livery
and took a room at a hotel. He noted with interest that
the town had a daily newspaper, *The Dallas Daily Herald*.
It was late afternoon, but still a while before suppertime,
so he walked the two blocks to the saloon. It wouldn't cost
him anything for a look at the fancy new watering hole.
Already there was a five-handed poker game in progress
and trouble in the making. One of the gamblers, a man
with dark hair and a flowing mustache, was pounding on
the table with the butt of a Colt.

"New deck, barkeep."

"You ain't played but one hand," the barkeep protested,
"and it was a new deck when you started."

"Damn it, I'm John Henry Holliday, and I want a new
deck."

Suddenly, except for Holliday, the table was empty, as
men got out of the way. When the barkeep ducked down,
he came up with a sawed-off shotgun, but before he could
use it, Holliday's Colt was roaring. The shotgun was ripped
out of the barkeep's hands and was flung against the wall.

It came down hard on the stock and both barrels let g
with a blast that seemed to shake the building.

"Leave it where it is," Holliday said. "I don't think muc
of your fancy diggings." He holstered his Colt and stalke
out the door.

"He leads his temper on a short rope," said Nathan.

"Damn little rooster," the barkeep said contemptuousl

One of the former poker players laughed. "One of then
salty Rebs that'd like to start the war all over, and win i
all by hisself."

"That was Doc Holliday," another patron observed, "an
he's chain lightning with a pistol. I seen him draw agin tw
hombres in Fort Smith, an' they had the drop."

Nathan went to a cafe, had supper, and returned to hi
hotel. There he bought a newspaper and went to his room.
The more he saw of saloons, the less they appealed to him.

Anxious to be on his way, Nathan was up at first light.
After breakfast, he went to the livery for his horses. He
loaded the packhorse, saddled the grulla, and rode out.
Careful to avoid towns, he spent his nights beside a creek
or spring, depending on his picketed horses to warn him of
unwelcome company.

New Orleans. January 10, 1875

Nathan rode down familiar streets, passing the St. Charles
Hotel, where he had first met Byron Silver. It was Sunday
afternoon, and the moan of steamboat whistles brought
back memories. He rode down the lane toward the
McQueen place, oak leaves crunching beneath the hooves
of his horses. In all their travels, Cotton Blossom had most
loved to come here, and Nathan had a lump in his throat
and tears in his eyes. As he neared the house, McQueen's
hounds set up a clamor, and when they appeared, there
was six of them. Three of them were younger versions of
one of the females, and the lot of them seemed about to
eat Nathan alive until McQueen called them off.

"I'll go to the barn with you and help you unsaddle,"
said McQueen. "Where's Cotton Blossom?"

Briefly and painfully, Nathan told him.

"We'll miss him," McQueen said. "Later, when you've
rested and we've had supper, maybe I'll have a surprise
for you."

Bess McQueen had seen Nathan ride in, and by the time e and Barnabas reached the house, she had washed the our off her hands and made herself presentable. Without esitation, she threw her arms around him with a welcome e had come to appreciate and expect. Barnabas looked on nd laughed.

"Go take your places at the table," said Bess, "and I'll ring the coffee. Supper will be ready in just a few ninutes."

"I'm counting on that," Nathan said. "I've been eating ny own cooking ever since I left Dallas."

"Bring Cotton Blossom in," said Bess. "I'll feed him in he kitchen."

"He won't be comin' in, Bess," Barnabas said. He spared Nathan, repeating what he had been told of Cotton Blossom's fate.

"He was a fine one," said Bess. "Barnabas, have you told him . . ."

"After supper," Barnabas said. "He's likely starved, and I know I am."

Nathan told them of some of his months with the railroad, avoiding any mention of his brief relationship with Melanie Gavin. He concluded with his ill-fated pursuit of Chapa Gonzolos and his gang, of his recuperation at Loretto Academy in Santa Fe, and finally, of the destruction of Gonzolos and his empire.

"Nathan," said Bess, "there must be something you can do where you aren't always getting shot."

Nathan was spared answering that, when a horrendous dogfight began somewhere behind the house. Barnabas went out and broke it up, and when he returned, a hound trotted in ahead of him. Nathan dropped his coffee cup, for the dog was a younger version of the departed Cotton Blossom!

"I reckon you know who his pappy was," Barnabas said.

"My God," said Nathan, "another six months, and he'll be . . ."

"Cotton Blossom," Bess said.

Nathan got up, but when he approached the dog, it bared its teeth. Bess went to the kitchen, and without urging, Cotton Blossom's offspring followed. Behind the stove, Bess fed him.

"He's a strange one," Barnabas said. "There was four in

the litter, and you've seen the other three. Bess calls hi
Empty, because he never seems to get enough to eat. She
been feeding him inside, because the others gang up o
him at every opportunity."

"He's not afraid of them?"

"God, no," said Barnabas. "Just the opposite. He'll leav
his food to fight them. He goes off and hunts. Sometime
he'll be gone for three days. If you can make friends wit
him . . ."

"There'll never be another Cotton Blossom," Nathar
said. "It wouldn't be fair to this one, because I'd always b
comparing him."

"He'll measure up," said Barnabas. "Somehow, I think he'.
been waiting for you, even though he doesn't realize it."

"I feel the same way," Bess said. "He accepts us, bu
that's as far as he'll go. I think he's been waiting fo
something."

Nathan began trying to make friends with Empty, and
although the dog was no longer hostile, neither was he
friendly. For the lack of anything better to do, Nathan
began walking the fields and the bayous that surrounded
the McQueen place. On one such walk, he heard something. Drawing his Colt, he turned to find Empty looking
at him from the underbrush. The dog quickly was gone,
and Nathan didn't see him again the rest of the day. Eventually Nathan could count on seeing Empty at some point
during his daily walks, and he believed the dog was watching for him.

"You're getting to him," Barnabas said. "Just don't push
it. Let him think it's all his idea. He's a loner, like you. He
senses that in you, and one day he'll come to you."

Nathan had been at the McQueens' place for six weeks,
and was becoming weary of the inactivity. While he still
saw Empty on his daily outings, the dog hadn't attempted
to come any closer. The dramatic change came one afternoon when Nathan heard a noise in the brush. Expecting
it to be Empty, he remained where he was, only to be
confronted by three wild hogs. Barnabas had warned him
about the animals, and at the first hostile move, he would
shoot them. But when they broke toward him, squealing,
they came like greased lightning. He shot two of them and
the third escaped, but he was unaware of the fourth. It

arged him from behind, only to run headlong into Empty.
e dog fought like a demon, and Nathan dared not shoot,
t he kill Empty. The fight ended when the wild hog gave
) and vanished into the underbrush. Bleeding from a mass
cuts, Empty tried to rise but could not. Both his front
gs were mangled and bleeding. Nathan took a step for-
ard, and when the dog's eyes met his own, he knew
mpty wasn't going to bite him. He began with a hand on
e bloody head, ruffling the dog's ears. Then, as gently as
could, he lifted Empty and began the long walk back to
e McQueen house. He was forced to stop and rest often,
r the dog was heavier than he looked. The McQueens
aw him coming and waited for him on the porch.

"We met some wild hogs," Nathan said. "I shot two of
hem, and another was about to tear into me from behind.
Empty fought him, and I'm not sure the hog didn't win."

"I'll get some blankets, hot water, and medicine," said
Bess, "and you can doctor him here on the porch. Barnabas, you'd better find a box for him and put it behind the
tove. With him crippled, he can't stay outside. These other
varmints of his own kind will kill him while he can't de-
'end himself."

"I don't reckon they'd find it an easy task," Nathan said,
"but he does need to heal a mite before he jumps into
another fracas."

Using the medicines Bess provided, Nathan patched up
the dog as best he could. The wild hog's fangs had gone
deep into Empty's front legs, and after drenching them in
alcohol, Nathan applied healing salve and bandaged them.
Other wounds were treated in a similar manner, but without bandages. Barnabas came from the barn with a large
wooden box, and Bess lined it with blankets.

"Now, old son," Nathan said, "you're goin' to enjoy two
weeks of rest, whether you like it or not." He lifted Empty
into the box, and with Barnabas helping, they carried the
box into the kitchen and placed it behind the stove. One
side of the wooden box was lower than the others, and it
was there that Bess placed a pan of water and food. Empty
gulped down the food and chased it with most of the water.

"Nothing bothers his appetite," Barnabas observed.

"By the time he's up and about, Nathan, you'll have
yourself a dog," said Bess.

Every day for a week, Nathan changed the bandages on

Empty's front legs, until the wounds had healed. By the
the dog was restless.

"I'll take him out for a while," Nathan said. "I'm n
sure he's ready to engage in any battles, though."

"I think you'd better keep him inside for another day
two," said Barnabas. "Damn if I know what the rest
them have against him, but I reckon they'd kill him, if th
got the chance."

"I'm about to see what kind of control I have over him
Nathan said. "If I'm guessing wrong, be prepared to rescu
him and me from one hell of a dog fight."

The rest of the dogs watched in silence as Nathan an
Empty left the porch, but that didn't last long. There wa
a chorus of growls, but to Nathan's delight, Empty ignore
them. He followed Nathan, and the rest of the dog
dropped back. Empty still seemed a bit unsteady on hi
feet, and he didn't take any wild runs through the brush
He seemed to know what his limitations were, and whe
Nathan leaned against a windblown tree to rest, the do
lay down.

"Your daddy will be hard to replace," Nathan said, "bu
old son, I have the feeling you're about to give him a rur
for his money."

By the first of April, the grass had begun to green and
there were signs of an early spring. Empty began looking
more and more like the departed Cotton Blossom, and
after the incident with the wild hogs, the dog took to Nathan in a manner that, as Bess had predicted, seemed almost preordained. Nathan began saddling the grulla, and
with Empty trotting alongside, they roamed the fields and
woods. The dog learned quickly to remain with the horse
upon command, and there were silent commands. The
pointing of a finger would send him on ahead, or the way
they had come, scouting the back trail. With Colt and Winchester, Nathan fired from many positions, until Empty became comfortable with the weapons. The first week in April
a letter came, addressed to Nathan Stone, in care of Barnabas McQueen. There was no return address, and when Nathan opened it, there was a single paragraph:

*Need your help. Meet me in St. Louis at Pioneer Hotel,
April 15.*

It was signed simply "Silver." Nathan passed it to Barnabas, and Bess read it with him.

"Sounds serious," Barnabas said. "You'll have to take a steamboat to reach Saint Louis by the fifteenth."

"I reckon," said Nathan. "Can I impose on you to board my horses while I'm gone?"

"You don't even have to ask," Barnabas replied. "Is Empty going with you?"

"Yes," said Nathan. "I don't know what I'll be getting into, but I can't afford to leave him now. Do you have any idea what the schedule is to Saint Louis?"

"Unless there's been changes, there's boats on Tuesdays and Thursdays," Barnabas said. "The next one should be leaving the day after tomorrow, at seven in the morning."

"You'll be getting there well before the fifteenth," said Bess.

"I aim to," Nathan replied. "If I know Byron Silver, he's already there, and since he's expecting me to dance, I'm goin' to learn as much about the fiddlers as I can."

New Orleans. April 8, 1875

Barnabas drove Nathan and Empty into New Orleans, to the steamboat landing.

"Good luck," Barnabas said, offering his hand. "If you need us, we'll be here."

"I know you will," said Nathan, shaking his hand, "and I'm obliged."

Barnabas drove away. When the steamboat pulled into the landing, there was a blast from the whistle, and Empty jumped like he had been shot.

Nathan laughed. "You'd better get used to that, pardner. There'll be three days aboard this one, and Saint Louis will be full of them."

One of the ship's officers was greeting passengers as they went aboard, and as Nathan approached, he held up his hand.

"I'm not sure dogs are allowed aboard," he said. "In any case, he'll have to ride on a lower deck, with the freight."

"Freight, hell," said Nathan. "I paid for first-class passage, and where I go, he goes."

"By whose authority?"

Nathan took from his pocket the watch Byron Silver had presented to him. Opening the cover, he displayed the great seal of the United States under which was inscribed the office of the attorney general.

"Is that enough authority?" he asked.

"Yes, sir," the ship's officer said.

Nathan decided he would resolve the only other problem he could foresee during the time they would be aboard *The St. Louis*. He sought out the captain, Travis Guthrie.

"We'll be traveling with you to Saint Louis," said Nathan, "and when I take my meals, I want to have my dog fed. I'll pay extra, if need be."

"That won't be necessary," the captain said. "I'll speak to the cooks, and if you will go to the dining room half an hour early, both of you will be served."

Nathan proceeded to his assigned cabin, Empty at his heels. When the steamboat departed with a blast of its whistle, the dog didn't flinch.

St. Louis, Missouri. April 11, 1875

Nathan had been to St. Louis often enough to know his way around, and after three days aboard the steamboat, he felt like walking. With Empty beside him, they set out for the Pioneer Hotel, five blocks away. Reaching the hotel, Nathan approached the desk. The clerk looked at the register after Nathan had signed, and presented him with a key.

"The first room at the head of the stairs. Charges have been guaranteed for as long as you remain with us."

The hotel had three floors, and Nathan's room was twenty-one. He wondered if that had been intentional on Silver's part, since twenty-one was his code with the government. Nathan unlocked the door and found the room more elegant than anything he would have taken for himself. Instead of a single chair, there was a fancy couch, and beside the bed, a bell cord, which would summon a bell boy. The broad dresser had brass drawer pulls and a wide mirror, which wasn't cracked. That alone was a novelty on the frontier. The bed was larger than most, with a fancy maroon and gold spread. There were maroon drapes at the window and plush gold carpet on the floor. On the dresser was an elaborate menu for the restaurant downstairs.

"Fancy diggings for a wandering gun-thrower," Nathan said aloud. "The government don't cut any corners."

Come suppertime, Nathan took one look at the Pioneer's fancy dining room and went in search of one of the little

:afes in which Cotton Blossom had always been welcome.
He found one, and since it was still early, it wasn't crowded.

"Pardner," said Nathan, "me and my dog's hungry. He's
a payin' customer if he's welcome."

"He's welcome," the cook said. "He can't be any more
uncivilized than some of the two-legged varmints that drifts
in here."

After supper, Nathan and Empty returned to the Pioneer. Nathan removed his boots, hat, and gun belt and
stretched out on the bed. He had been tempted to inquire
at the desk about Silver, but changed his mind, for he had
no idea what kind of security was involved. Nathan was
dozing when Empty growled low in his throat. There was
a light knock on the door.

"Identify yourself," Nathan said.

"Twenty-one," came the reply.

Nathan unlocked the door, locking it immediately after
Byron Silver had entered. The two shook hands.

"How did you know I was at the McQueens' place?"
Nathan asked.

"It took me two telegrams to track you down," said Silver. "I wired Hagerman in Dodge, and learned you had
quit the railroad. After that, I played a hunch and telegraphed Captain Ferguson, at Fort Worth. By God, that
dog looks enough like old Cotton Blossom to be his son."

Nathan laughed. "That's exactly who he is. I have one
of McQueen's dogs to thank. He answers to Empty, and
he owes that to Bess McQueen."

"I reckon you're chomping at the bit to know why I
asked you here," said Silver,

"To some degree," Nathan said, "but I was more interested in why you specified April fifteenth."

"Because that's the day B.H. Bristow, U.S. Secretary of
the Treasury, will be here. I have told him about you, and
he insists on meeting you."

"I'll meet him," said Nathan, "but for what purpose? Is
he just being neighborly?"

"He has need of a man with your particular talents, and
I recommended you highly."

"Thanks," Nathan said dryly. "Who's going to be shooting at me besides those who already want me dead?"

"I'm not exactly sure," said Silver. "You'll have to talk

to Bristow. But I'm fair to middlin' sure you'll be allowed to shoot back."

"That's another question," Nathan said. "Why are you breaking trail for the treasury? From what I've heard, from what I've read, they have agents of their own."

"Of course they do," said Silver, "but this involves a conspiracy *within* the treasury, and Bristow isn't entirely sure who he can trust."

"I'm reminded of the Credit Mobilier scandal during President Grant's first term," said Nathan. "Is this something similar to the Union Pacific fraud?"*

"No," Silver replied. "This is more complex, and could involve several hundred people in Saint Louis, Chicago, and Milwaukee. You see, following the Civil War, the government was in need of money. Liquor taxes were raised, in some cases, to eight times the price of the liquor."

"My God," said Nathan, "that's an almighty expensive tax."

"I fully agree," Silver said, "but it's the law, and the distillers have been collecting the tax. The trouble is, the largest distillers—in Saint Louis, Chicago, and Milwaukee—haven't been turning this tax over to the government. Government officials high and low have been bribed in order for these distillers to keep the collected taxes for themselves. This has been going on for a while. It's become a public scandal, in fact, but it's politically hot. The whiskey ring is considered impregnable because of its strong political connections. One of the prime suspects is President Grant's secretary, O.E. Babcock."

"God Almighty," said Nathan, "this thing could destroy Grant."

"It could, and it might," Silver replied, "but Secretary of the Treasury Bristow intends to break the conspiracy, letting the chips fall where they may. And there, my friend is where you come in."

"Hell, Silver," Nathan said, "the war's been over nearly ten years. How much money is at stake?"

"More than three million dollars," said Silver.

"My God, where could that much money be hidden?"

"Renegade bankers may be concealing some of it," Silver

*During building of the Union Pacific Railroad, the U.S. was defrauded of $20 million.

said, "but there's a chance of hundreds of thousands of dollars being secreted in warehouses belonging to distilleries or their agents."

"So this U.S. Secretary of the Treasury aims to find all this money," said Nathan, "and he thinks I can help. How?"

"By joining the ranks of the whiskey ring," Silver said, "and there's more involved than just recovering the money. Bristow wants to collect sufficient evidence to destroy this organization. He believes he can do this only by assigning secret investigators outside the Treasury Department."

"So I'm to be one of those investigators," said Nathan. "I'm flattered, Silver, but by what right am I qualified?"

"You're quick with your wits, your guns, and your fists," Silver replied, "and there is absolutely no obvious connection between you and the Department of the Treasury. There is a possibility you may be called upon to rob one of the suspected banks."

"No, by God."

Silver laughed. "You would in no way be operating outside the law. Several banks are believed to have double sets of books, the second containing illegal deposits belonging to a number of distilleries implicated in this conspiracy."

"All that's going to get you is evidence of double-dealing by some bankers," Nathan said. "So a bank has a few hundred thousand that it can't account for legally. How do you aim to prove it's whiskey taxes owed the government?"

"Damn it, I don't have all the answers," said Silver. "I offered to help, at least with the situation here in Saint Louis, because I believed you were quick-witted enough, smooth enough, and tough enough to pull it off. I've given you some idea as to what Bristow has in mind, without knowing his reasons. Do this. Wait until you talk to Bristow, and then if he can't answer your questions to your satisfaction, then just tell him it's no deal. I made him no promises beyond asking you here for a meeting. *Comprende?*"

"Yeah," said Nathan. "I'll wait and see what Bristow has to say."

St. Louis, Missouri. April 15, 1875

Despite himself, Nathan was impressed with B.H. Bristow. He had gray hair, gray eyes, and a firm handshake. He wasted no time in outlining what he had in mind.

"We already have undercover agents at work in Milwaukee and Chicago, Stone, and I am especially anxious to have you in charge of our investigation here in Saint Louis. I must say that I am impressed with what Mr. Silver has told me about you. However, it is up to you as to whether you wish to become involved in this operation. I trust that Silver has introduced you to the problem and possibly some of the means by which we're hoping to resolve it?"

"He has," Nathan replied, "and like I've told him, I'm flattered, but I'm not sure that I am qualified as an investigator. As I understand it, there are no rules. You'll be depending on me to come up with evidence against people involved in this whiskey ring, when I have no way of knowing what you consider evidence. Why don't you spell out what you're expecting me to do, and I'll consider it."

"Very well," Bristow said. "There are two distilleries here. One of them is operated by Woodard Slaughter and the other by Peavey Hohnmeyer. Both are involved in this tax fraud, and if we can get the goods on one of them, we can convict them both. It is Mr. Silver's belief that with our help, you can ingratiate yourself with one or both these men and work your way into their operations. From such a vantage point, you will then be in a position to secure the evidence we need."

"Or get myself shot graveyard dead," said Nathan.

"I won't deny that's a possibility," Bristow said, "because Slaughter and Hohnmeyer have surrounded themselves with gunmen. But rest assured you won't be alone. While Mr. Silver is unable to join you undercover, he and a force of agents will monitor your every move."

"If you get shot," said Silver, "then so will I."

Nathan laughed grimly. "That makes me feel some better."

"Then you'll work with us?" Bristow asked.

"Yes," said Nathan.

"Good," Bristow replied. "Now here's how we'll get you on the good side of Slaughter and Hohnmeyer...."

CHAPTER 23

Nathan listened as Bristow outlined his plan by which he believed Nathan might gain the confidence of the distillery moguls.

"Many people don't know this," Bristow said, "but Slaughter and Hohnmeyer actually are brothers-in-law. Their wives are younger women, and they are under the protection of armed men, twenty-four hours a day. These ladies are going to be abducted, Mr. Stone, and while no harm will come to them, Slaughter and Hohnmeyer won't be aware of that. I expect them to offer substantial rewards for the return of their wives. You, Mr. Stone, are going to rescue these ladies at the risk of your life. With the cooperation of the local authorities and a contrived newspaper story, you will be credited with the killing of the abductors. That should quickly get you into the good graces of our distillers."

"Just as quickly adding to my reputation as a fast gun," said Nathan, "increasing my chances of being gunned down by some varmint lookin' for a name at my expense."

"Not necessarily," Bristow replied. "Slaughter and Hohnmeyer have some of the best lawyers money can buy, and they'll leave no stone unturned to avoid any unfavorable publicity."

"I reckon that'll be a mite difficult, with a story in the newspaper," said Nathan.

"Men who can buy lawyers can buy newspapermen, too," Bristow said. "You'll just have to take my word for it that Slaughter and Hohnmeyer will keep the affair as quiet as they can."

"There's a reason for that," Silver added. "Let the word get out that they're being hit for reward money for the return of their women, and they'll be fair game for every thief and outlaw in Missouri."

"Exactly," said Bristow. "We'll see that they're allowed to hush this up. We'll depend on you, Mr. Stone, to pull off a convincing rescue. The abductors, of course, will be my agents, and they must die convincingly when you appear to shoot them. Mr. Silver will see that you are given blank cartridges for your pistols."

"*Pistol*," said Nathan. "I go nowhere, Mr. Bristow, with both my weapons loaded with blank cartridges. Not for you, not for Silver, not for the president."

Silver laughed. "One pistol loaded with blanks, Bristow. You'll just have to depend on Señor Stone to remember which Colt has live shells."

"Very well," said Bristow. "Do you have any more questions, Stone?"

"Yeah," Nathan said. "With all the secrecy, how am I supposed to know about any of this? How do you know Slaughter and Hohnmeyer won't turn to the Pinkertons?"

"Because they suspect we've had the Pinkertons after them," said Bristow. "They'll go to the law, because they believe they have friends. One of those friends will supposedly pass the word on to you. After we've allowed them to sweat for a few days, you will then rescue the ladies and impress Slaughter and Hohnmeyer. Don't accept the reward money they'll offer you, and don't seem anxious to hire out to them."

"Suppose they don't hire me?"

"It's a calculated risk," said Bristow, "but my men are going to make you look damn good before the abducted ladies. I'm counting on them to influence their husbands."

"I don't like traveling under false colors, of being a Judas," Nathan said.

"It's for the good of the country," said Silver.

"So the country can collect eight times the price of a bottle of whiskey," Nathan said. "You're just damn lucky I don't drink the stuff, unless I've been shot."

"If you're shot," said Bristow, "I'll see that you don't pay for the whiskey."

For a while after Bristow had departed, there was silence. Finally, Nathan spoke.

"This just seems like a flimsy, damn fool way of going after evidence, and I've agreed to go along with it only as a favor to you."

"Thanks," said Silver. "I consider that a tribute to our friendship. Frankly, I'm not all that concerned about the financial state of the country. I'm a little sorry for the president, because I don't think he's involved in this, and the only way to spare Grant is to root out the guilty varmints."

"I reckon you're right," Nathan replied. "With Grant's friends and kin, the man sure as hell don't need any enemies."

Nathan and Empty spent their days wandering along the back streets of St. Louis and at the landing, watching the steamboats arrive and depart. Only occasionally did Nathan and Silver meet. Not until two weeks following Nathan's meeting with Bristow did Silver come to Nathan with news that the proposed abduction had taken place.

"Annie Slaughter and Myrtle Hohnmeyer are being held in a deserted warehouse across the river, in East Saint Louis," Silver said. "Two of Bristow's men replaced the two gunmen hired by Slaughter and Hohnmeyer. The abduction has been reported, but just as Bristow expected, it's being kept quiet. So far, these big spenders are each offering a five-hundred-dollar reward."

"I reckon they're saving that whiskey tax for their old age," said Nathan. "When do I make this damn fool rescue?"

"Bristow says give it another week. We can't have it look too easy. I'll be backing your play and covering you."

East St. Louis, Illinois. June 2, 1875

"The warehouse door is locked," said Silver. "To make this look good, you'll have to bust out a window and gun down the two abductors."

"And what am I to do with these ladies, after I've rescued them?" Nathan asked.

"Mount them on the horses that belonged to their abductors," said Silver, "and take them to the sheriff's office. Sheriff Rainey has been sworn to secrecy, and he'll send for Slaughter and Hohnmeyer. When they arrive, you're on your own. Remember, the objective is to make them *want* to hire you to replace the gunmen who allowed Annie and Myrtle to be kidnapped. Just become the hard-nosed bastard you're capable of being."

Nathan's face twisted into a vicious scowl and he dropped his right hand to the butt of his Colt.

"Is that one loaded with blank cartridges?"

"No," said Nathan. "The other one."

Nathan approached the old warehouse alone, coming at

it from one end, where there were no windows. Already he knew where the four horses were picketed. Empty was well behind Nathan because he wasn't sure what was about to take place. Reaching a corner of the building, Nathan kept his back against the wall, advancing toward the window designated by Silver. There was glass on the ground, evidence that some of the panes had been broken. The sun had slipped beneath the western horizon and shadows were beginning to shroud the land. It was suppertime, and the first bold stars shot forth silver rays across the deep purple of the darkening sky. The remaining windowpanes were dirty, and at first Nathan could see nothing. But then a man laughed, and he saw them. The women sat on a wooden plank supported by two kegs. Their abductors stood a few paces away, revolvers in their hands, making a good show of it. Nathan kicked the window in, and when the men whirled to face him, he drew his Colt loaded with blanks and fired four times. The women looked on in horror as the two men fell, apparently shot dead. Nathan stepped through the empty window frame, the smoking Colt still in his hand. Annie Slaughter and Myrtle Hohnmeyer were young, and were expensively dressed. Nathan wouldn't have considered either of them beautiful, and after the initial shock, they didn't seem afraid of him.

"Hohnmeyer and Slaughter?" Nathan asked.

"I'm Myrtle Hohnmeyer, and this is Annie Slaughter," said one of the women. "Who are you?"

"An hombre hoping to collect a reward," Nathan said. "There's horses outside. Come on. We're going to the sheriff's office."

Unbarring the door, he led them to the picketed horses. Annie Slaughter protested.

"Sir, we're not dressed for riding. It would be . . . indecent."

"I reckon you can stand it just this once," said Nathan.

Both women were slight, and seizing Annie, Nathan sat her astraddle of a roan horse. Before Myrtle could launch a similar protest, he sat her down in the saddle of a dun. Both women tried vainly to get their skirts down. Annie tried unsuccessfully to dismount, and came off head first, her voluminous skirt over her head. Nathan got her on her feet and hoisted her back into the saddle. Her face flaming, she was about to say something, when Nathan shut her up.

"Damn it, Annie Slaughter, you're going to ride that horse, if I have to rope you belly-down across the saddle."

Annie said nothing more, and whatever Myrtle Hohnmeyer might have said, she had second thoughts and remained silent. By the time the trio crossed the river, it was dark enough that nobody noticed the "indecently" mounted riders with skirts above their knees. Nobody spoke a word until they reached the sheriff's office. Empty wisely remained in the shadows, while Nathan helped the women to dismount and escorted them into the sheriff's office. Rainey had been waiting for them, although he did a good job of acting surprised.

"Sheriff," Annie Slaughter said, "this . . . this ruffian manhandled us."

"Is that a fact?" the sheriff said. "I don't recall the last time a gent manhandled a woman and then brought her to the sheriff's office."

"Sorry," said Nathan, "but they weren't dressed for riding, and from where I found them, it was too far to walk. I manhandled them into their saddles and manhandled them to the ground when we got here."

"Gib," Sheriff Rainey said to a deputy, "fetch Slaughter and Hohnmeyer. These ladies has had their dignity bruised a mite, but they don't seem hurt. Far as the law's concerned, the case is closed."

Slaughter and Hohnmeyer arrived, and they looked like what they were. Both were in their fifties, gone to fat, and partially bald. They were dressed in expensive town clothes, and rather than going immediately to their wives, they turned to Sheriff Rainey.

"I had nothing to do with this," said the sheriff. "There's the hombre you want, and I don't even know his name."

"Nathan Stone," said Nathan. He kept his thumbs hooked in his belt and said no more.

"I'm Hohnmeyer," said one of the men, "and this is Slaughter. My office is nearest. We can talk there." He steered Myrtle toward the door, and Slaughter followed with Annie.

Sheriff Rainey grinned at Nathan. "Good luck," he said under his breath.

Empty drifted out of the shadows when Nathan left the sheriff's office. As Hohnmeyer had said, it wasn't far to his office. They waited for Nathan to enter, and Hohnmeyer shut the door. They wasted no time.

"I suppose you want to claim the reward," said Hohnmeyer. "I will write you a check and Slaughter will write you a check, each for five hundred dollars. You may cash them in the morning. Then you will leave town and you will say nothing of this incident."

"Keep your money," Nathan said contemptuously. "I reckon it'll mean more to you than it will to me. As for leaving town, I'll go when I'm damn good and ready, and I'm not ready."

Myrtle Hohnmeyer laughed. "Instead of running him out of town, you should hire him. He's better than any dozen of what you've had."

"Myrtle's right," said Annie. "He was magnificent. He shot two men before they could make a move."

"I have seen Mr. Stone somewhere before," said Slaughter, "and I believe it was on a Pinkerton wanted dodger. Do you deny it, Stone?"

"No," Nathan said. "It was all a misunderstanding."

Slaughter laughed. "It always is. If you're on the bad side of the Pinkertons, I could learn to like you, Stone."

"I couldn't do the same for you," said Nathan. "Not if you walked on water."

Slaughter and Hohnmeyer laughed, and Nathan relaxed. The more he reviled them, the more they were drawn to him. He said nothing.

"Stone," Hohnmeyer said, "we can use a man like you. What's your price?"

"I'm not for sale," said Nathan.

"Every man's for sale," Hohnmeyer insisted.

"Hohnmeyer," said Nathan, "if I don't like a man, I don't care a damn if he's made of solid gold."

"And you don't like me," Hohnmeyer said.

"No," said Nathan.

"What about me?" Slaughter asked.

"I figure both you buzzards roost on the same limb," said Nathan.

Annie and Myrtle laughed, and on impulse, Nathan turned to them.

"You ladies are fresh out of hired guns, and those you had didn't impress me. Are you hiring?"

"Perhaps," Myrtle said, "but we had two. Who's the other?"

"There is no other," said Nathan. "I work alone."

"Ah," Slaughter said, "the others were paid five hundred dollars a month. You will be paid no more."

"I am replacing two men," said Nathan, "and I will be paid for two men. A thousand dollars a month."

"Hell, no," Hohnmeyer roared.

"Hell, yes," Nathan shouted.

"We want him," Myrtle Hohnmeyer said. "Pay him what he's asking."

'The first month in advance," said Nathan.

"No," Slaughter said. "Damn it, we've only known you for an hour, and for all we know, you've a fugitive from the law."

"I reckon I'm as clean as you and Hohnmeyer," said Nathan. "I've proven myself. If that's not good enough, ladies, I'll be going."

"I have my own funds," Myrtle Hohnmeyer said. "I'll write you a check, first month in advance."

"I'll pay my share," said Annie Slaughter.

Their aggressiveness visibly angered Slaughter and Hohnmeyer, but that wasn't the end of it.

"After this," Myrtle said, turning on Hohnmeyer, "Annie and I will remain together for our own protection. I will be at her place. Now, Mr. Stone, if you will be so kind as to escort us there, we will be going."

They left without another word, Nathan following. The moon had risen, and suddenly Empty appeared from the shadow of the roof's overhang. Annie screamed.

"That's my dog," Nathan said. "He goes where I go. I'm returning to the sheriff's office for my horse, and we'll go from there. Do you ladies aim to walk, or shall I manhandle you back into your saddles?"

"You can manhandle me back into the saddle," said Myrtle. "I believe you're the kind of man who's seen a woman's knees before."

Annie laughed, and Nathan said nothing. He suspected this pair wasn't nearly as helpless as they wished to appear. When they reached Sheriff Rainey's office, the lawman had the door open, grinning as Nathan hoisted the two women into their saddles. By the time Nathan mounted, they both had their horses in a lope. He followed, reining up before what seemed an enormous house on a dead-end street.

"I'll see both of you inside," Nathan said, "and then I'll see to the horses. Is there a stable?"

"Behind the house," said Annie. From somewhere she produced a key and unlocked the front door. She lighted a lamp on a table in the hall.

"Lock the door behind me," Nathan said. "I'll knock when I return."

"There are lanterns in the stable," said Annie. "Do you have matches?"

"Yes," Nathan replied.

Nathan led the three horses around the house, and with the moon still up, he could see the shadowy hulk of the stable ahead. Empty was beside him. A lantern hung just inside the stable door, and he lighted it. The stable was large, befitting a man of Woodard Slaughter's obvious wealth. There were no horses in the stable, and Nathan wondered why. He unsaddled the trio, rubbed them down, and forked down some hay from the loft. Then, somehow dreading it, he had no choice except to return to the house. He knocked, and Annie let him in. Empty followed, right on Nathan's heels.

"Come on to the kitchen," Annie said. "There'll be coffee in a few minutes, and we're cooking supper. Or breakfast, I suppose. There'll be ham, eggs, and biscuits."

Nathan kicked a chair back against the wall and sat down. Empty sat beside him, eyes on the unfamiliar women.

"Why is he looking at us like that?" Myrtle asked.

"He doesn't know you," said Nathan, "and he doesn't trust you."

"And what about you?" Annie wondered.

"That's a pretty good standard for dog or man," said Nathan.

"If we hadn't spoken up for you," Myrtle said, "you'd have just walked out without any reward, wouldn't you?"

"Yes, ma'am," said Nathan. "I don't want money from a man who begrudges it, so I'm a mite choosy about who I work for."

"Yet you'd work for us," Annie said.

"Why not?" said Nathan. "Do you believe you should be held accountable for all that Slaughter has done or failed to do?"

"I believe the coffee is ready," Myrtle said.

Nathan's question went unanswered, and he said nothing

more. He accepted the coffee Myrtle poured for him, and
when the food was ready, moved his chair to the table.
Without being asked, Annie filled a bowl with ham and
placed it before Empty, and he waited until she turned
away before eating. The meal was eaten in silence. It was
Annie who spoke when they had finished.

"I'll show you to your room, Mr. Stone."

"I'd prefer that you call me Nathan."

"Nathan, then."

Nathan and Empty followed her down a hall that led to
another wing of the house. It had four rooms, and she led
Nathan to the second one on the right.

"Myrtle and me will be in the rooms across the hall."

"What about this one next to me?" Nathan asked.

"Nobody sleeps there," said Annie. "That's a storage room."

Nathan wondered where Woodard Slaughter slept, if he
occupied the room with Annie, but he said nothing. Somehow, he believed Slaughter had a room of his own, in some
other part of the house. At the first opportunity, he would
enter the room next to his, to learn what was stored there.

"I reckon I don't have to remind you and Myrtle to lock
your bedroom doors every night," he said.

"No," she said, "but when we were abducted, we weren't
taken from our beds."

"Then maybe I should be outside at night," Nathan said.
"I'm not sure it's proper, me being alone with two married ladies."

"That's our decision, not yours," said Annie. "We want
you inside. This key that I'll give you fits your doors and
ours. Feel free to enter our rooms at any time, if you feel
there is cause."

Nathan said nothing. It was an outrageous thing for a
married woman to say, and it told Nathan a lot about the
probable relationship these women had with their much
older husbands. But he was less concerned with that than
with the possibility that this same key might also unlock
the storage room. Taking the key she offered, he unlocked
the door to his room and stepped inside. Empty followed,
and he closed the door. He waited, listening to Annie's
receding footsteps. Easing the door open, he looked out
into the hall. At the far end, where they had entered, a
bracket lamp burned. Nathan tugged off his boots, stepped
out into the hall, and went to the door of the storage room.

Quickly he tried his key, but the lock held fast. He dropped
the key in his pocket and returned to his room, elated over
his discovery. Striking a match, he lighted the lamp on the
dresser. As he had approached the house, he had seen the
high gables, suggestive of an attic. Carefully he studied the
ceiling and then took the lamp into the closet. There was
no evidence of a trapdoor to the attic anywhere in the
ceiling. Any time he left his room, he must be careful, because he had no doubt that just as his key would unlock
the doors to the rooms occupied by Annie and Myrtle, their
keys would unlock the door to his room. He set the lamp
on the table beside the bed and sat down in the room's
only chair. Empty sat down on a throw rug, his eyes meeting Nathan's.

"Damn it, Empty, we stacked the deck and everything
looks good, but I got me a gut feeling that I could end up
with a busted flush. Are these women what they seem, or
have they seen through Bristow's plan, pulling me in to
keep an eye on me?"

Tossing his hat on the dresser, Nathan hung his gun belt
on the head of the bed. As he so often had done when
faced with uncertainty, he blew out the lamp and stretched
out on the bed, fully dressed. It was a long time before
he slept.

Nothing had been said to Nathan about when his day
would begin, and he was awake well before first light. He
waited awhile, until the first gray light of dawn swept away
the darkness. He then stepped into the hall, Empty following. He moved quietly, listening, and he soon was rewarded
with the sound of voices. Woodard Slaughter was angry.

"... know nothing about the man, except that he's quick
with a gun, and was once on a Pinkerton reward dodger.
Damn it, we're in no position to take in strangers. There's
too much at stake, and it's almost time ..."

"Give Myrtle and me credit for some sense," Annie
snapped, "and for God's sake, do lower your voice."

Slaughter did lower his voice, and Nathan heard nothing
more. He waited until there was no more conversation, so
they wouldn't know he had overheard anything. He then
made his way to the kitchen, wondering what Slaughter had
been about to say. Annie and Myrtle sat at the table drinking coffee. Nathan took a cup, poured coffee for himself,

and dragged out a chair at the end of the table. He drank his coffee and kept his silence. After what he had heard, he believed he had them on the defensive. After a prolonged and uneasy silence, Myrtle spoke.

"We have no plans for today. Just remain near."

"I'll be outside, near the stable," said Nathan.

The very last thing he wanted was to spend the day trapped in the house with these two strange, unpredictable women. After breakfast, he and Empty headed for the stable. He doubted he would learn anything at the stable, but he was more comfortable there than in the house. Finally he climbed into the loft and stretched out on the hay, leaving Empty on watch below. The day dragged on. The stable was back far enough for him to see beyond the house, and he saw nobody until Slaughter drove up in a buckboard, an hour before sundown. He entered the house, leaving the team hitched. Nathan waited a decent interval before going to the house. When he entered, he closed the door loudly enough for them to be aware of his presence. When he reached the kitchen, there was only Annie and Myrtle. Nathan took a seat at the table, his back to a wall. Nobody said anything until they heard the buckboard being driven away, and it was Annie who spoke.

"Mr. Slaughter has decided to take a room in town for a while."

"I'm not surprised," Nathan said. "Is that supposed to mean something to me?"

"He rarely confides in me," said Annie. "You'll have to ask him."

"Then I reckon he'll be even less likely to confide in me," Nathan said. "If he wants me to know what's on his mind, then he'll just have to stand up on his hind legs and tell me."

Myrtle Hohnmeyer laughed, smiling at Nathan as she poured herself another cup of coffee. Annie said nothing, her eyes on Myrtle, and Nathan didn't like the expression on her face. Supper came and went, and with nothing better to do, Nathan made his way down the hall to his room. Empty followed, not liking this house or the people inhabiting it. Nathan closed and locked the door to his room, wondering what good it would do, with these two strange women having keys. Empty lay down beneath the window, his eyes on the locked door. Nathan didn't bother lighting

the lamp. Again, he removed only his hat, his gun belt, and
his boots before lying down on the bed. Empty got up,
walked to the door, and stood there, as though waiting to
go out. Nathan got up and unlocked the door, but when
he opened it, the dog turned away and lay down beneath
the window. Uneasy, Nathan got up. He bunched the blankets so that in the darkness it might appear that he was
under them. Then, taking his pillow and one of his Colts,
he stretched out on the floor beside the bed. He lay awake
for a long time, unable to sleep. Finally he dozed, only to
awaken to a low growl from Empty. But there was only
the chirp of crickets and the distant bark of a dog. But
something—more sensed than heard—was bothering
Empty. Nathan moved farther from the bed, out of line
with the faint starlight that shone through the window. The
sound, when it came, was so faint that had Nathan been
asleep, he wouldn't have heard it. The key turned slowly,
and then there was only silence. An arm around Empty to
quiet him, Nathan waited. The door's hinges being well
oiled, it opened without a sound, its only warning a breath
of air. In the stillness, the shotgun blast sounded like a
cannon. The lethal charge tore into the bundle of blankets
on the bed, and from flat on his back on the floor, Nathan
fired three times. The door was slammed shut from the
force of the lead and Nathan remained where he was listening. Had the attack taken place in the open, the gunman
would be dead, but with the door for a partial shield, Nathan couldn't be sure.

"Nathan? Are you all right?"

"Yes," Nathan replied.

The door opened and Annie Slaughter stood there in a
nightgown, holding a lamp. In the hall behind her was Myrtle Hohnmeyer. Nathan got to his feet, keeping away from
the window. Empty growled.

"Dear God," said Annie, her eyes on the mutilated blankets and the splinters torn from the bed's wooden
headboard.

"I suppose neither of you saw anybody in the hall," Nathan said.

"No," said Annie.

"Then get back to your rooms and lock your doors,"
Nathan said. "We'll talk about this tomorrow."

CHAPTER 24

Rather than light the lamp, Nathan waited until dawn to examine the splintered door to his room. His three slugs had struck the thick edge of the door, where it met the frame and none of them had gone on through. That meant the gunman had escaped unharmed, and faint powder burns on the edge of the door was Nathan's only clue. He already knew what he was going to say when Annie and Myrtle questioned him about the shooting. When he reached the kitchen, he poured himself a cup of coffee and took a chair at the table. Both women looked at him as though they expected to see some change. When he said nothing, Annie spoke.

"Do you have any idea who shot at you last night?"

"I don't have a name," Nathan said, "but I know he's left-handed."

"How could you know that?" Myrtle asked.

"There are powder burns on the door's edge," said Nathan. "He stood to the right of the door as it opened. A man firing right-handed would have stood to the left of the door, and if the weapon had touched anything, it would have been the door frame. There are no powder burns on the door frame. Who do you know that's left-handed?"

"I don't know," Annie said. "I can't think of anybody, except . . ."

"Woodard Slaughter," Nathan finished.

"Why, that's ridiculous," said Annie. "Woodard doesn't even own a shotgun."

"Nobody said anything about a shotgun," Nathan replied.

"Nobody had to," said Annie. "I've fired one myself. So has Myrtle."

"But neither of you are left-handed," Nathan said.

"Are you going to the law?" Myrtle asked.

"The law's never been around when I was in need of it," said Nathan, "and I've always stomped my own snakes."

"If you believe someone's trying to kill you because of us," said Annie, "we won't try to keep you here. You can leave."

"I wouldn't think of it," Nathan said. "I'll finish what I started, with one difference. I won't be spending my nights in a bed. I may be in the house or I may be outside. Nobody is going to know for sure. Next time the varmint cuts down on me, there won't be a door between us."

At Peavey Hohnmeyer's residence, Hohnmeyer and Slaughter were seated at the table in the kitchen, sharing a bottle of bourbon.

"I tried, damn it," Slaughter growled, "but the bastard wasn't in the bed."

"You worry too much," said Hohnmeyer. "Hell, we're indebted to Stone for stirring up Annie and Myrtle. Otherwise, it might not have been so easy, gettin' the two of them to move out on us. A week from now, we'll be in Mexico, with a million in gold."

"I don't feel right, leavin' Annie," Slaughter said. "It don't bother you, leavin' Myrtle behind?"

"Don't go soft on me now, damn you," said Hohnmeyer. "We're goin' to be dead, remember? Besides, it wouldn't surprise me if Stone's taking turns sleeping with Annie and Myrtle. With half a million in gold, you can snare any woman in Mexico, and if you don't like the pickings there, you can import some."

They laughed. Hohnmeyer refilling their glasses from the almost empty bottle.

Nathan did exactly as he had promised, spending his nights in different places, always where he could observe the house. Depending on Empty to warn him of impending danger, he slept well. His third day at the Slaughter house, he rode to town and bought copies of the St. Louis and Kansas City newspapers. He unsaddled his horse, climbed into the loft, and settled down to read the papers. Normally he didn't read newspaper gossip, but there were the names Slaughter and Hohnmeyer in the headlines of an article. The writer seemed very much aware of trouble that had been brewing in the homes of the Slaughters and the Hohnmeyers, and as evidence of his knowledge, pointed out that Woodard Slaughter had moved in with Peavey Hohnmeyer, while Myrtle Hohnmeyer was dwelling with her sister, Annie Slaughter. There was speculation that the separations might become permanent, but not a word as to the cause. Certainly it was to the credit of B.H. Bristow that he had kept Nathan's name out of it. That wasn't surprising, but another part of the story was. It claimed that Slaughter had moved in with Hohnmeyer, while Annie had specifically stated that Slaughter had taken a room in town. Why were Slaughter and Hohnmeyer together, and why had they wanted it known? Nathan had his suspicions, and late that night when he might have been watching the Slaughter house, he saddled a horse and rode into town. The lobby of the Pioneer Hotel was deserted, except for a sleepy desk clerk, and Nathan made his way quietly up the stairs. He tapped softly on the door. Twice, then after a pause, the third time. The door was opened, and after he was inside, immediately closed.

"You're taking a chance coming here," Silver said. "Why did you?"

"Because I'm accomplishing nothing at the Slaughter house," said Nathan, "except for providing a target for some hombre with a shotgun. Did you read the story in today's Saint Louis paper about the breakup of the Slaughters and Hohnmeyers?"

"Yes," Silver said, "but we kept you out of it. Bristow said he would."

"That's not what concerns me," said Nathan. "Annie told me Slaughter was taking a room in town. The newspaper makes it a point of saying Slaughter moved into the Hohnmeyer house. There has to be a reason they're both together."

"Don't go waltzing all around this thing," Silver said. "I know you've got some kind of handle on it, or you wouldn't be here. Right now, I don't care a damn about proof, if you've got a good, solid hunch. What is it?"

"Annie and Myrtle have nothing to do with this conspiracy in which Slaughter and Hohnmeyer are involved, so I haven't gone looking for any evidence. You won't find the money at the house, either."

"Then where the hell *is* it?" Silver growled. "Bristow's already gone after questionable banks, and found nothing. We're virtually certain it's not at the distilleries. What about Hohnmeyer's house?"

"No," said Nathan. "I believe it's been sent, a little at a time, to some point where it can be taken out of the country. I figure Mexico or South America."

"Solid thinking," Silver said, "and if that's the case, Slaughter and Hohnmeyer have to fly the coop. But when, and how?"

"Tell Bristow to have men at every railroad terminal and every steamboat landing. Not to arrest Slaughter and Hohnmeyer, but to trail them. Somehow, they're going to try and escape, and it will only make sense if the money's somewhere waiting for them."

"You're right," said Silver. "I don't know *how* I know, but I do. Go on back to the Slaughter place and play out your hand. You'll know when to call on me again."

Slaughter and Hohnmeyer made their move three days after Nathan had met with Byron Silver. It was past midnight. Nathan and Empty sat on the porch. The wind was out of the west, and Nathan smelled smoke. He left the porch, getting away from the house and its surrounding trees, and to the west he could see an ever-growing pink cloud. Quickly he saddled his horse and with Empty running alongside, he rode toward town. The house, when he arrived, had fallen in. All the efforts of the horse-drawn fire wagons had been futile. Sheriff Rainey took off his hat, wiping his face with a bandanna.

"The Hohnmeyer place, I reckon," said Nathan.

"It is ... was ..." Sheriff Rainey said. "How did you know?"

"Just guessing," said Nathan. "Where's Slaughter and Hohnmeyer?"

"In the house, as far as I've been able to determine," Rainey said. "I've asked around, and found a saloon where Slaughter and Hohnmeyer were drinking. The barkeep says they were drunk and rowdy, and he made them leave. Somebody from the saloon was goin' their way, and he saw 'em to the front door. Nobody saw 'em after that."

"That was some hell of a fire, to just suddenly break out," Nathan said. "It's been hot as blazes all day, so you can forget about a fireplace, and I can't imagine a pair of drunks firing up a cookstove, can you?"

"No," said Rainey, "I can't. Soon as the ruins cool down some, I aim to look around. It'll be a grisly search, because if Slaughter and Hohnmeyer was in there, I'll have to find some remains before I can break the news to Annie and Myrtle."

"How *can* you identify a man after he's gone through something like that?"

"Hell, I don't know," Rainey said. "I've never had to do it before. I'm inclined to take the word of the gent who saw them from the saloon to the house. He said they was just purely owl-eyed by the time they got home."

"Good luck," said Nathan.

It was almost two o'clock in the morning when Nathan reached the Pioneer Hotel, and following the familiar knock, it was a while before Silver got to the door.

"Come in," Silver said. "I was about to get up in six more hours, anyway."

"You said I'd know, and you were right," said Nathan. "It's time."

Quickly he told Silver of the fire, and of the circumstances that pointed to the deaths of Slaughter and Hohnmeyer.

"There it is," Silver said. "Just as you predicted, and I passed it on to Bristow. We'll soon know if he took you seriously or not."

"The easy part's over," said Nathan. "Now I've got to ride back to Slaughter's home and talk my way out of Annie's and Myrtle's clutches."

Silver laughed. "If you're able to get loose, come on back to the Pioneer. I reckon we can justify staying here until we get some word from Bristow."

"But we need you more than ever, now that we're alone in the world," Annie begged.

"Yes," Myrtle said. "We now have two distilleries, and we know absolutely nothing about running them."

"Neither do I," said Nathan, "and I'm a slow learner."

Nathan was spared further agony by the arrival of Sheriff Rainey.

"Ladies," Rainey said, "I have been told to inform you that the United States Department of the Treasury has seized both distilleries and frozen both bank accounts."

"Damn them!" Annie cried. "For what reason?"

"They're Federals," said Rainey. "I'm not sure they need a reason, but that's between you and them."

"I'll save you a thousand dollars a month," Nathan said. "I'm resigning my position."

"Must you go?" Annie asked. "We could make it up to you in other ways."

"Many other ways," Myrtle added.

Nathan mounted up and rode back to town with Sheriff Rainey.

"A right handsome pair," said Rainey with a grin. "Too bad you didn't hang around and see what kind of trade they had in mind."

"I think I know," Nathan replied.

St. Louis, Missouri. June 27, 1875

B.H. Bristow returned to St. Louis specifically to thank Nathan Stone.

"It was just as you predicted, Stone," said Bristow. "They rode a hundred miles south of here before boarding a steamboat to New Orleans. I telegraphed our agents there, and they followed Slaughter and Hohnmeyer to a million dollars in gold. I'm sure there will be a reward. . . ."

"If there is," Nathan said, "send it to Annie Slaughter and Myrtle Hohnmeyer. While they're not widowed after all, I reckon Slaughter and Hohnmeyer will go to jail."

"We're going to do our best," said Bristow. "So far, we've arrested 176, and have recovered more than three million dollars in taxes."

St. Louis, Missouri. July 1, 1875

"Let me know if Grant goes after a third term," said Nathan, "and I'll stay as far away from the telegraph as I can get. You'll be on your own."

"Hell, he may not survive *this* term," Silver said. "The man has no friends. The best he can hope for is a better class of enemies."*

Nathan only wanted to leave St. Louis, and he and Empty departed on the first steamboat bound for New Orleans. The river was calm and the skies were blue, and they spent their daylight hours on the upper deck. Empty still was wary of strangers, and kept close to Nathan, but the trip south was uneventful. When the steamboat had docked in New Orleans, Nathan and Empty were the first ashore.

*President Grant's secretary, O.E. Babcock, was acquitted.

Nathan hired a hack to drive him to the McQueen place, and Empty trotted along behind.

"Bess had started to worry about you," McQueen said, as Nathan came into the house.

"And you didn't," said Bess.

Empty reared up on Bess and could almost look her in the eye.

"That dog has grown some since he left here," Barnabas said.

"He's still a little nervous when there's too many people around," said Nathan, "but he proved himself when I needed him. If he didn't inherit anything else, he's got his daddy's ears and his appetite."

"Supper will be ready in a few minutes," Bess said. "When we've eaten, tell us about your stay in Saint Louis."

"I've been out of touch with Texas," said Nathan. "Has there been any news from that direction since I've been gone?"

"Same old foolishness," Barnabas said. "The Horrell-Higgins feud flared up again. Pink Higgins done some shootin' in Lampasas County. There's been fights in Mason City and all over Mason County, in what they're callin' the Mason County War. Really, it's between the Anglos and Germans. There's been lots of cattle rustling, with each side blamin' the other. Scott Cooley, the gent that's doin' most of the hell-raising, used to be a Texas Ranger, and he's already killed two men."

"Gold has been discovered in the Black Hills, in Dakota Territory," said Bess.

"I'd forgotten about that," Barnabas said. "There's already been a party from here set out for the diggings. There's going to be some dead men, sure as hell. The government ceded that land to the Indians. Now that gold's been found, Washington has promised all manner of things, trying to regain control of Indian land."

"That's Sioux territory," said Nathan. "I reckon they've learned what the white man's word is worth."

"They have, for a fact," McQueen said. "Sheridan and his men tried to enforce the law by keeping whites off Indian land, but it was like trying to hold back a buffalo stampede. Miners have swarmed into the territory by the hundreds, defying the government as well as the Sioux. Now Washington's making things worse by hunting down

Indians who have killed trespassing miners. There are ru‐
mors that George Custer and the Seventh Cavalry will b‐
sent into the territory to control the Sioux."

"According to the newspaper," said Bess, "it was Custe‐
who first announced there was gold in the black hills."

"I've heard some pretty grim things about Custer anc
his method of dealing with the Indians," Nathan said.

"So have I," said Barnabas. "The Federals are going tc
regret the day they send Mr. Custer to Dakota Territory
to try and make peace with the Sioux."

"I've never been to the Dakotas," Nathan said. "Maybe
I'll go there and see what it's like in a gold-crazy boom
town."

"Nathan," said Bess, "someday . . ."

"I'm going to die," Nathan finished. "Bess, every man is
born with the seeds of death in him. The only unanswered
questions are the time and the place. If I stayed here long
enough, I'd be gunned down in New Orleans."

Barnabas laughed. "So you've become a wanderer,
avoiding that time and place."

"For as long as I can," Nathan replied. "There's some‐
thing—I call it a premonition—that bears on my mind, tell‐
ing me it's time to move on. It touched me today just
before the steamboat docked, and it's never been stronger
than it is right now."

"Have you ever resisted?" Bess asked.

"Once," said Nathan. "The day Eulie was shot and
killed."*

"You can't take the blame for that," Barnabas said. "She
was determined to stay here for that horse race. She
wouldn't have gone with you."

"No," said Nathan, "and that's all the comfort I've had.
That, and the possibility that she had played out her hand,
that she had come to the time and place."

"I still miss her," Bess said softly, "and I tend her
grave often."

"I'm obliged," said Nathan, swallowing a lump in his
throat. "Barnabas, I'm going to give up the packhorse. He's
yours. You can have the packsaddle, too. Most of my
money is in a Kansas City bank, and I aim to leave it there.
I'll be leaving them instructions that if they don't hear from

*The Dawn Of Fury (Book 1)

...e within two years, whatever is left in the account is to ...e paid to you and Bess."

"Nathan," Barnabas began, "we don't expect ..."

"I know you don't," said Nathan, "but I have no family. ...When I reach that appointed time and place, I want that ...money to go to someone who matters to me, and that's ...ou and Bess."

Bess hurried to the kitchen for more coffee, although ...heir cups were almost full. It was a moment before Barna-...as could speak.

"If that's the way you want it, Nathan. We're honored ...hat you feel that way. Bear in mind that you're always ...welcome here."

On July fifth, Nathan rode away from the McQueen place, Empty trotting on ahead. It seemed strange, not having the faithful packhorse on a lead rope, but Nathan could travel farther and faster. Reaching New Orleans, he found a saddlery and bought the largest pair of saddlebags available. He then went to the mercantile and bought enough provisions for a week on the trail. He and Empty could survive on jerked beef if necessary, but he refused to deny himself hot coffee. Being too large for the saddlebags, he secured the coffeepot in his bedroll and rode northwest, toward Shreveport. The money he carried was in double eagles, and except for a hundred dollars, was secured in his saddlebags. With what he had told the McQueens strong on his mind, he had decided to ride through Kansas City and make necessary arrangements with the bank. He spent his first night in the little town of Winfield, a few miles from Shreveport. Keeping to the small towns, he hoped to lessen the possibility that he might be recognized. The hotels and cafes were less pretentious, and less likely to turn up their noses at a dog. On the frontier, a man was lucky to own one good horse. Without the packhorse, Nathan believed he would attract less attention, and at the same time, avoid any suggestion of wealth. He had enough gun trouble already, without the possibility of thieves at every bend in the trail. The second day of travel took him across the Red River and into Indian Territory. There he spread his blankets beside a spring, and knowing the danger, didn't light a fire.

"Jerked beef tonight and in the morning, Empty, but

tomorrow, we should reach Fort Smith. Then we'll trea
ourselves to hot grub."

But that was before they encountered the tumblewee
wagon, with a pair of desperate killers bound for the gal
lows . . .

Indian Territory. July 8, 1875.

Empty had taken to running well ahead of Nathan, dropping back only if he came upon something unusual. The
sun was two hours high when the dog circled back and
Nathan reined up, listening. From the west there came the
unmistakable rattle of a wagon. Nathan rode to meet it,
sensing an urgency, for the teams were coming hard. The
man on the box had a star on his shirt, the reins in one
hand and a Winchester in the other. He reined up the heaving, lathered mules. Three teams was a little unusual, but
so was the wagon. The wagon box sat atop an iron cage, a
jail cell on wheels. Two men were behind the bars. The
man on the box had raised the Winchester, while Nathan
kept his thumbs hooked in his gun belt. He spoke.

"I'm on my way to Fort Smith, and I'm not looking for
trouble. I'm Nathan Stone."

"Mel Holt," said the man behind the badge. "Deputy
U.S. Marshal from Fort Smith. The varmints in back is
Blocker and Hines, a pair of killers on their way to a fair
trial before the hanging judge."

The men behind the bars laughed.

"I wore the badge out of Fort Smith for a while," Nathan
said. "Russ Lambert was a good friend. How is he?"

"He ain't," said Holt. "He was bushwhacked by these
bastards and the coyotes they run with. I just wish we had
the rest of 'em to hang along with these two."

"You were sent after them alone?"

"No," Holt said. "Me and Doak Graves volunteered.
Doak's behind me, on top of the wagon, wrapped in them
blankets. They got him, and they're after me. It's just a cat-
and-mouse thing, them figurin' I don't have a chance.
There's four more of 'em."

"Maybe we can even out the odds," said Nathan. "Rest
your teams and then go on. I reckon I'll keep an eye on
your back trail and skin me some coyotes in memory of
your pard, Doak Graves and my old amigo, Russ
Lambert."

"Bueno," Holt said.

Nathan rode back the way the wagon had come. Empty, aware that they were on a trail, ran on ahead. Eventually Nathan found what he was seeking. Leaving the grulla in a concealing thicket, he took cover in a cluster of rocks. The weakness of his position was that unless he cut down the outlaws almost immediately, they could flank him, laying down a deadly crossfire. Empty was still somewhere ahead, and he waited for the dog's return, a sign that danger approached. Lest an enemy follow, Empty circled back, never returning by a straight path. With a low growl to announce his presence, he came up behind Nathan.

"Stay, Empty," said Nathan, his arm around the dog.

Nathan cocked the Winchester, and when the outlaws appeared, they were riding in single file. Nathan waited as long as he dared, knowing that if he didn't gun down at least two men, he might become the hunted. He shot the lead rider out of the saddle, but just as he fired, the second man's horse reared. The slug from Nathan's Winchester struck the horse, and the outlaw kicked free of the saddle. A mounted comrade offered him a hand up, and the two escaped, riding double. The fourth outlaw was already well out of range. Nathan ran toward the thicket where he had left the grulla, knowing that his edge was gone. Shy a horse, the three could still pursue the wagon, creeping close under the cover of darkness. He judged they were still eighty miles south of Fort Smith, an impossible distance, with two prisoners, a wagon, and a trio of killers in pursuit. Catching up to the wagon, he rode alongside.

"I got one of them," he shouted, "but a horse reared into my second shot. With two of them on one horse, that'll slow 'em down."

"But not enough," said Holt. "They'll be coming after us."

"I'll be watching for them," Nathan said. "I look for them to lag behind until dark."

"That's what they done last night," said Holt. "That's when they plugged Doak, and I reckon they was waitin' for tonight to get me. I had no sleep last night, and no grub, but for some jerked beef."

"You can count on another night just like it," Nathan said. "We'll have to make ourselves damn scarce and do some effective shooting."

"Won't neither of you live to see daylight," one of the prisoners shouted.

"Get going," said Nathan, "but don't kill your teams. Rest them when you must, and water them when you can. I'll do my best to keep them at bay until we have to stop for the night. Then I reckon both of us will be almighty busy."

When they finally were forced to stop for the night, Holt reined up the teams along a creek that flowed through a valley. There was a gentle rise from either bank, leading to a treeline that was well beyond rifle range. The only cover was underbrush along the creek itself.

"There'll be a moon tonight," said Holt, "and they can't come at us down the slopes. They can come down the creek from either direction, but they'll have to be afoot. You take one end of the wagon, and I'll take the other."

"Damn it, we ain't et nothin' since you locked us in here," growled one of the men in the wagon.

"Shut up, Blocker," Holt said.

"We'll have one thing in our favor," said Nathan. "Empty, my dog, will warn us when they're getting close. I aim to stay out of that brush along the creek, and just belly-down with my Winchester. They can't make any moves toward the wagon until they've disposed of us."

"Maybe we'd better just belly-down beneath the wagon," Holt said. "There we'll be in shadow."

"There we'll be trapped," said Nathan. "Remember, there's one man without a horse, and I have a horse. If he can't get to the horse, he'll take a mule. I think, before they try to gun us down, they'll go after my horse or one of your mules. Then they'll stampede the others, leaving us afoot, with two prisoners in a useless wagon."

"By God, that makes sense," said Holt. "So we'll forget about the wagon for the time being, and wait for them to come after a horse or a mule."

"Yes," Nathan said. "What better way to flush us out than have one man stampede our animals? The other two, then, could gun us down. With that in mind, we may be able to get the varmint that comes after a horse or a mule, further reducing the odds. That could force the other two away for a spell, allowing us to position ourselves near the wagon."

"Stone, I like the way your mind works. Damned if I on't half believe we'll come out of this alive."

"Never drop your hand until you've drawn that last ard," said Nathan. "Now let's go stake out my horse and our mules."

CHAPTER 25

Nathan and Holt waited, their muscles cramping from inactivity, their patience growing thin. Moonset was still an hour away.

"Damn them," said Holt, "they're waiting for the moon to go down."

"Let them," Nathan replied. "If they come after a horse or mule, they'll still be out in the open, and the starlight will be enough."

The moon had been down only a few minutes when Empty growled once, low.

"Here they come," said Nathan. "I look for only one of them to try for a horse or a mule. I'll cut down on him, and unless I've figured everything wrong, the other two will fire at my muzzle flash. That'll be your target."

"*Bueno,*" Holt said, "but you're taking all the risk."

"Somebody has to open the ball," said Nathan, "and until they're forced to fire, you'll have nothing to shoot at. Just make that first shot good."

Nathan was positioned well away from his horse and the grazing mules, so that he was able to see anyone approaching the picketed animals. But the starlight was deceptive, and it was a while before he could actually be sure a questionable shadow was slowly but surely moving. The interloper was belly-down, with the patience of an Indian. When he had crept close enough, Nathan brushed Empty's head with his open hand and pointed to the creeping shadow. Empty sprang toward the outlaw, growling. The man scrambled to his feet and Nathan cut him down with a slug from the Winchester. Quickly, Nathan rolled away, as slugs ripped into the ground where he had been lying.

The shots had come from somewhere near the creek, an
Holt was already returning fire when Nathan got into th
fight. It all ended as suddenly as it had started. There wer
no more shots from the creek. Nathan and Holt cease
firing and waited. Empty made his way to the place fror
which the shots had come, barking once.

"That was a slick piece of work," said Holt. "What's h
tryin' to say?"

"They're dead or they've cleared out," Nathan said
"Let's have a look."

Holt had accounted for one of the outlaws, while the
other had apparently escaped. A mule had begun brayin
and several others joined in.

"They're gettin' spooked because of that dead hombre,"
said Nathan. "I'd better drag him away from them."

"Still one of them is on the loose," Holt said. "You
reckon he'll be fool enough to come after us again?"

"I doubt it," Nathan replied, "but if he does, I'll be ready
for him. Spread your roll and get what sleep you can.
Empty and me will keep watch the rest of the night."

Dawn broke with no sign of the escaped outlaw, and
Nathan soon had a fire going.

"God, I'd give a month's pay for some hot coffee,"
Holt said.

"We'll have some pronto," said Nathan, "and some
breakfast as well. If that varmint was spooked enough not
to come after us in the dark, I doubt he'll have enough
sand in his craw to make his play in daylight."

Fort Smith, Arkansas. July 11, 1875

"You saved my hide," Holt said, when they reached Fort
Smith. "If you'll come with me to the courthouse, I'll see
that you get credit, and there may be some reward money."

"I don't want the credit or the money," said Nathan.
"It's enough, just gettin' back at these varmints for cashing
in Russ Lambert."

Nathan took a room at Ma Dollar's boardinghouse,
where he had lived while he wore the badge of a deputy
U.S. marshal. Having had almost no sleep since encoun-
tering Mel Holt and the tumbleweed wagon, Nathan locked
his door and slept the rest of the day and the night. Arising,

he and Empty had breakfast in a nearby cafe. As they were leaving, Mel Holt came in.

"Except for the one who escaped," said Holt, "we wiped out the gang. The court has enough evidence to hang Blocker and Hines, the pair we brought in. With Russ and Doak gone, we're shy two good men. There's a badge waitin' for you, if you want it."

"I reckon not," Nathan said. "I'm bound for the Black Hills, in Dakota Territory. Why don't you hang up that badge and ride along?"

"No, thanks," said Holt. "I've heard about that gold strike. But that's Sioux country. Around here, all I got to bother me is bein' shot dead by renegades and outlaws who don't like the idea of bein' brought before the hanging judge and havin' their necks stretched."

Nathan didn't linger in Fort Smith, but rode north, bound for Kansas City. No sooner had he crossed into Missouri than he met a sheriff and a posse of nine men. They drew their guns and rode forward, circling Nathan.

"Who are you," the sheriff demanded, "and where are you bound?"

"I'm Nathan Stone. I just left Fort Smith, and I'm bound for Kansas City."

"Sheriff," said a member of the posse, "one of the bank robbers was ridin' a grulla, just like his."

Nathan didn't like the turn the conversation was taking. He appealed to the sheriff.

"Sheriff, I spent last night in Fort Smith, and I can prove it. There are other grullas, and I resent being linked to a bank robbery because of the horse I'm riding. Besides, if I was on the run from you and your posse, wouldn't you consider it a little strange that I'm meeting you, instead of riding away?"

"He's got a point, boys," the lawman said. "Stone, I'm Sheriff Drucker, from Joplin. Some varmints robbed the bank a while ago, and they lit out south. We lost their trail a ways back. One of the tellers thought he recognized Jesse James."

"I've seen nobody," Nathan said. "If they headed south, they're likely in Indian Territory by now."

"That's what we'd think," said Drucker, "except the James gang generally don't ride that far. Now I reckon we'll have to backtrack."

Nathan rode with them, some members of the posse eyeing him with suspicion. Finally they approached a creek, and there were so many tracks, it was impossible to determine if any had been made by horses ridden by the bank robbers or if they had all been made by horses ridden by the posse.

"This is likely where you lost them," said Nathan. "When you approached this creek, did you rein up and make sure the trail continued over and beyond the south bank?"

The men looked at one another in sheepish silence. Finally the sheriff spoke.

"I reckon we didn't. Suggs, you take four men and ride downstream. The rest of us will ride upstream. If you find where they left the creek, fire one shot."

They seemed to have forgotten about Nathan, and he rode on, careful to bypass Joplin and the scene of the bank robbery. He approached the little town of Nevada, Missouri, with some misgivings. It was here that Nathan had shot Bart Hankins, the first of seven men who had murdered his parents and his young sister in Virginia. The shooting of Hankins had taken place while the James and Younger gangs had been involved in an unsuccessful robbery attempt, and for a while, Hankins's death had been blamed on the bank robbers. But the Hankins family had concluded that Hankins's death was in no way related to the failed bank robbery, and the Pinkertons had been engaged to seek evidence linking Hankins's shooting to the deaths of the men who had accompanied Hankins back to Missouri. While Nathan didn't wish to kick any sleeping dogs, he wondered where the investigation stood, or if perhaps it had been dropped altogether. While he dared not ask any questions, there was one way he might get some answers. He reined up before the small office of the town's weekly newspaper, *The Nevada Sentinel.* A little wooden sign read: J. SAMUELS, ED. AND PROP.

"I'd like to buy some back issues," Nathan said.

"How far back?" Samuels inquired.

"At least three years," said Nathan.

"I don't have them for sale, back that far," Samuels said. "I only have for sale copies for the past six months. Beyond that, I have only file copies. You're welcome to look at those, if you wish."

"I'd be obliged," said Nathan.

"Have a seat at the table, then, and I'll bring them to

you. Since they're bound by the year, do you want to begin with this year, to date?''

"Yes," Nathan said. "I might not have to go back as far as three years." He sat down at the table, facing the window and the door.

"These are for 1875, through last Thursday," said Samuels. "I'll bring you the bound set for 1874 when you're finished with these."

The weekly consisted of four pages, the last two being mostly advertising. Nathan had gone through most of the bound set for 1874 before he found what he was seeking. Most of the front page had been devoted to Pinkerton findings that were related to the Hankins case. The Pinkertons, using military records, had learned the names of six men who had been known companions of Bart Hankins. At the time the newspaper had been printed, five of the men were known to be dead, all of them by shooting. The Pinkertons had declared there was a pattern, beginning with Hankins, and that the man who had killed Hankins had also killed five of his six companions. They had named Nathan Stone as the killer, based on the fact there was solid evidence he had killed at least two of Hankins's friends. All findings by the Pinkertons had been turned over to the Hankins family, and in the next issue of the paper there was a reward dodger. There was no photograph, no etching. In big, bold black print it said: *Nathan Stone. Wanted dead or alive, for the murder of Bart Hankins. Reward of ten thousand dollars will be paid by the Hankins family.*

Nathan read no further. If the Hankins family could afford such a reward, then there would be no limit to the number of dodgers they could print or the newspaper advertising they could afford to buy. He thanked Samuels for allowing him the use of the back issues and left the newspaper office. But he didn't get far. Suspicious eyes watched him from the other side of the street, and the man who fell in behind him wore a badge. Empty waited with the grulla, and the dog's low growl alerted Nathan to the stranger who followed. It would have been easy for Nathan to turn and fire, but he did not. He waited, and the lawman halted half a dozen yards away. When he spoke, it was less a question and more a statement of fact.

"You're Nathan Stone."

"Yes," Nathan said.

"Sheriff Roscoe Peeler. Lead your hoss down to the office."

Peeler made no move toward his weapon, and while Nathan had no idea what might lie ahead, he couldn't bring himself to gun down a lawman. While the Hankins family had only their suspicions, if he could escape only by killing a sheriff, he would unquestionably become a fugitive. The office was also the jail, and Peeler stepped back while Nathan looped the grulla's reins about the hitch rail.

"Stay, Empty," Nathan said. He mounted the steps, Peeler behind him.

"I reckon you'd better shuck them guns until I know where you stand," Peeler said.

Nathan unbuckled his gun belt and placed it on the desk. The door to the first cell stood open and a man lay on a bunk, snoring. Peeler grabbed a three-foot billy club and struck the bars.

"Damn it, Peck, get up and make yourself useful."

Peck sat up, rubbing his eyes.

"Light a shuck down to the bank," said Peeler, "and tell old Dan Hankins that Nathan Stone's here. If he aims to press charges, he's got to swear out a warrant. Today, damn it, not next week."

Peck stood up and shambled out, not in the least intimidated.

"For the time being," Peeler said, "I want you in that cell. If old Hankins has changed his mind about you, I'll turn you loose. If he ain't, then you'll be stayin' a spell."

Having little choice, Nathan entered the cell and sat down on the hard bunk. Peeler kicked the barred door shut and locked it. Peck returned in a few minutes, bearing the news Nathan had expected.

"He's filin' charges," said Peck. "He's goin' to the court-house right now."

"Sheriff," Nathan said. "I'd appreciate you bringin' in my saddle, saddlebags, and my Winchester. If you'll take my horse to the livery and see that my dog's fed, I'll pay."

"Peck," the sheriff said, "unsaddle the hoss, bringin' in the saddle, saddlebags, and the rifle. Then take the grulla to the livery."

Peck seemed about to refuse, but Sheriff Peeler's eyes were on him, and he thought better of it. He went out, shrugging his shoulders.

"Sheriff," Nathan said, "if it's not asking too much, what am I charged with?"

"Unless Hankins has changed his mind," said Peeler, "it'll be murder."

"I reckon he's got proof?"

"He thinks he has," Peeler said. "He hired half the Pinkertons in the country."

Before sundown, Nathan Stone had been charged with the murder of Bart Hankins, and the curious had gathered outside the jail.

"Go on home," Peeler shouted. "Damn it, this ain't no medicine show."

Nathan slept but little on the hard bunk, seeking a solution to this predicament which would put him on trial for his life for a shooting that had taken place more than ten years ago. He didn't doubt that the Pinkertons had linked him to the killing of those men who had accompanied Hankins that long-ago day in Virginia, and although those killings had been justified, accuse him of murdering Hankins. Beyond a doubt, Nathan Stone had friends who would stand by him till hell froze over. There were the McQueens in New Orleans, Captain Ferguson at Fort Worth, Sheriff Harrington in Dodge City, Foster Hagerman with the Atichison, Topeka and Santa Fe Railroad, Joel Netherton of the Kansas-Pacific, as well as the Texas Rangers. But not one of them could help him when he stood before the court and faced the damning evidence Daniel Hankins had accumulated. He was waiting for the lawman when Sheriff Peeler brought his breakfast.

"Sheriff, when am I going to trial?"

"July twenty-sixth," said Peeler. "Is there somebody you're needin' to telegraph or write to?"

"A telegram," Nathan said. "I'll pay if you'll send it for me."

"I'll bring you paper and a pencil," said Peeler.

He did so, and ignoring the breakfast, Nathan began to write. Addressing it to the attorney general's office in Washington, he made the message brief:

Twenty-one stop. Am in jail Nevada Missouri stop. Accused of murder.

He said no more, signing his name. He folded the paper and passed it to the sheriff, along with a gold eagle.

"Keep your money," said Peeler. "You're entitled to this. You expectin' an answer?"

"Maybe," Nathan said. "I'm not sure."

There was an answer, almost immediately. It read: *Twenty-one coming.* There was no signature. Despite his predicament, Nathan laughed at Sheriff Peeler's expression.

"Relax, Sheriff. We're not planning a jail break."

Nevada, Missouri. July 17, 1875

Silver rode in two hours before sundown, looking every bit the cowboy. His Levi's and denim shirt were faded almost white, his Texas boots were scuffed, and his Colt was thonged low on his right hip. Only his gray Stetson looked new. Sheriff Peeler got up from his desk, and Silver spoke.

"Silver's the name. I need some private conversation with Nathan Stone."

"You his lawyer?"

"I reckon you can call me that," Silver replied. "Lock me in the cell and take a walk."

Peeler looked a little offended, but complied. Silver said nothing until the sheriff had left the office and closed the door.

"I want you to tell me what you had against Hankins and those six *amigos* of his, and don't hold any of it back. The Pinkertons may not be worth a damn at guarding payrolls and mine shipments, but they know how to gather evidence."

Starting with his release from Libby Prison in Richmond, Nathan told his story, up to and including an eyewitness account of the murders committed by Hankins and his six companions.

"Old Malachi, the Negro, had lived with my family since before I was born," said Nathan, "and he remembered their names. I swore on my father's grave that I'd gun them down to the last man."*

"You had all the cause a man ever needed," Silver said, "but you also don't have any witnesses. I've checked the military records, and all these men were deserters from the Union army, but that won't help you. They're going to claim that you shot Bart Hankins in cold blood, that he was unarmed."

*The Dawn Of Fury (Book 1)

"That's a damn lie," said Nathan. "He had a sleeve gun, and I didn't make a move until he drew. His slug ripped into the top of his desk."

"The Pinkertons talked to the man who was sheriff at the time Hankins was shot, and he said there was no sign of a gun. However, he and everybody else believed Hankins had been shot during an attempted holdup, and he admits they might have missed something. I aim to do some investigating on my own. Meanwhile, put your mind to remembering that day, and to anything else that might sway a jury."

Time dragged, and Nathan saw Silver at least once a day, but Silver didn't always tell what he had learned, if anything. Instead, he urged Nathan to recall anything that might be helpful in his defense.

"How is Empty?" Nathan asked. "Is he being fed?"

"The sheriff's done a passable job of keeping him fed," said Silver, "and I've fed him a few times, myself. He's made friends with me, but he won't leave the jail. I reckon we'll have to bury him with you, if you get a hanging sentence."

"You really think that's possible, for a killing ten years old?"

"You're damned right it is," Silver said, "unless you can prove self-defense. There is no statute of limitations on murder."

"Bart Hankins and the two-legged skunks ridin' with him murdered my family," said Nathan, "and had it not been for me, they'd have gotten away with it."

"You were judge, jury, and executioner," Silver said, "and now you don't have a shred of evidence to justify your action. If you're hanged, that won't help your family."

"Damn it, Silver, those men were killers. How can I prove it?"

"I don't have the answer to that," said Silver. "There is no conclusive proof that you killed Hankins, but there is abundant proof that you killed his companions. The prosecution will try to prove that Hankins was part of that same vendetta that led to the deaths of his friends."

"Then what's going to be my defense?"

"There is no better defense than the truth," Silver said. "You will admit to the court that you shot Hankins, tell them your reason, and then plead self-defense."

"My God," said Nathan, "do you expect them to take my word?"

"Are you sure there was a sleeve gun, that Hankins pulled on you?"

"Damn it, Silver. I've been shot at enough until I know a .41-caliber derringer when I see one."

"Then someone took that gun," Silver said. "Someone in that bank, sometime after you killed Hankins, but before the sheriff came. I'm going to talk to everybody who was in there, everybody who could have taken that gun."

"Hell," said Nathan, "old man Hankins could have taken it. Might be easier than tellin' how his son ended up on the short end of a shootout."

"Maybe," Silver said, "but I doubt it. If the old man had any idea Bart had done what you're accusing him of doing, I doubt he'd be digging into this. This is a small town, and the Hankins name means something. It won't help when you brand Bart Hankins a killer who got what he deserved."

"Then tell old man Hankins that I'm going to name his son a cold-blooded killer," said Nathan. "That might cool his ambition for having me hung."

"And it might make him all the more determined," Silver said. "I'm not telling Daniel Hankins a damn thing. You'll need some surprises to throw in the faces of the jurors, and that means you keep your mouth shut until the trial."

"Hankins owns the only bank in town," said Nathan, "and I doubt there'll be a man on the jury that doesn't owe him money. You expect them to take my side, against Hankins?"

"No," Silver said. "We're going to ask for a change of venue, moving the trial to Kansas City."

"You can *do* that?"

"I can," said Silver, "for the very reason you just mentioned."

"You think Hankins won't oppose that?"

"I'm sure he will," Silver replied, "and I hope he does. That will be proof enough that he's expecting small-town bias in his own favor. Just keep quiet and let me see what I can uncover. I'll go to the court this morning and request a change of venue. Maybe I'll ask for a new court date, as well."

"Why?"

"I have my reasons," said Silver.

*   *   *

Silver was shown into Daniel Hankins's office, where he waited almost half an hour before the banker made his appearance. Hankins eased himself into his big leather chair and glared at Silver from behind a polished walnut desk. Silver shifted his Colt, crossed his legs, and glared back. Without a word, Hankins passed Silver a sheet of paper, and Silver quickly scanned it. He then asked Hankins a pointed question.

"Are these the names of everybody associated with this bank at the time your son was killed?"

"As nearly as I can recall," said Hankins stiffly.

"What about your wife? Do you have a daughter?"

"I have a wife *and* a daughter," Hankins said, "neither of whom work here, and they have *never* worked here."

"They've never been in here? Neither of them?"

"Of course they have!" Hankins roared. "What the hell *is* this? I resent being hounded in my own office by a ... a damned cow country counselor who wouldn't know a law book from a mess of horse droppings."

"One more thing," said Silver quietly, ignoring the insult, "who is Old Charlie?"

"Charlie Ekert," Hankins said sullenly. "He use to clean up, sweep floors, burn trash."

"He was here at the time your son was shot?"

"He was," said Hankins.

"Where is he now?"

"Living with his daughter, somewhere in Kansas City."

"I need an address."

"I don't have one," Hankins snarled.

"Then get one," said Silver. "I want it tomorrow."

"Damn it," Hankins bawled, "are you finished?"

"For now," said Silver. "I'll see you tomorrow."

When Silver arrived at the jail, Sheriff Peeler was waiting for him.

"You're gettin' on the bad side of Mr. Hankins," Peeler warned.

"I get on the bad side of a lot of people," said Silver. "The man leads his temper on a short fuse, and one day, it's going to get him in over his head."

"He's just got the word you aim to move the trial to Kansas City," the sheriff said, "and he says it ain't gonna happen. What's Kansas City got that we ain't got?"

"Some jurors that won't squat and jump when Daniel

Hankins hollers froggy," Silver replied, "and you can tell Hankins I said that."

"Anything you want Hankins told, tell him yourself," said the sheriff. "Are you here to talk to Stone?"

"I am," Silver said. "Lock me in and take a walk."

"Have you made any progress?" Nathan asked, when the sheriff had gone.

"Oh, yes," said Silver, and he laughed. "Mr. Daniel Hankins says I don't know a law book from a mess of horse droppings."

"Do you reckon you can convince him otherwise?"

"Ah reckon ah can," Silver said, in his finest Texas drawl. "Tomorrow, the court here will be receiving a telegram from the Missouri attorney general's office, in Jefferson City. We've been granted a change of venue. The trial will be held in Kansas City, on August thirty-first."

"Damn it," said Nathan, "that's five more weeks. Why are you stalling?"

"Intimidation," Silver said. "If you're fightin' Comanches, outlaws, or bankers that's too big for their britches, you do it on your ground, not theirs. Once you're in Kansas City, I can go before the judge and get you out on bail until the trial. Wouldn't you be a mite more comfortable at Eppie Bolivar's than in jail?"

"God, yes," said Nathan, "but I didn't know I could be released on bail, when the charge is murder."

"It depends on the court, on the judge," Silver said. "I have friends in places that Mr. Daniel Hankins can only dream about. You've sided me when I needed you, without asking for anything. Now you're going to fight, and you won't be alone."

"I'm obliged," said Nathan. "Who have you talked to at the bank?"

"Only Hankins," Silver replied, "but I'll get to the others. Some of them have moved away, but Hankins knows where they are. One of them—Charlie Ekert—is in Kansas City with his daughter. Would you believe I have telegrams from Foster Hagerman of the AT and SF, and from Joel Netherton of the Kansas-Pacific?"

"But how did they know . . ."

"I sent the entire story to the *Kansas City Liberty-Tribune*," said Silver. "That's just another reason for delaying the trial. The newspapers will pick up on your story, accusing

Bart Hankins and his bunch of murdering your family. That should lessen the impact of Daniel Hankins's charges of murder. Hagerman and Netherton are offering you the railroad's lawyers, if you need them. This is going to be some hell of a trial."

"I reckon I could appreciate it more," said Nathan, "if my neck wasn't at stake."

CHAPTER 26

Sheriff Roscoe Peeler had been sent for, and that irritated him as much or more than what he was likely to face when he arrived. He took a chair outside Daniel Hankins's door, prepared to wait until Hankins chose to see him, which could range from a few minutes to half an hour. He didn't like the look on Hankins's face when the banker finally opened the door and beckoned him in. Hankins didn't even wait for him to sit down.

"What the hell is this about a change of venue, of moving the trial to Kansas City? Am I suddenly without influence in this town?"

"The court believes you have too much influence in this town," Peeler said. "A change of venue is granted when the court believes a man can't get a fair trial because the jurors are prejudiced. Nobody's faulting you, but as the town banker, there ain't a man in thirty miles that ain't beholden to you in some way."

"Well, by God, I consider it an insult," said Hankins. "You sure there's nothin' can be done about it?"

"Try to block it," Peeler said, "and you'll come off lookin' like you're afraid to go to court where you can't influence the jurors."

"What do you know about Silver, this damn down-at-the-heels cowboy that's shown up to act as Stone's attorney?"

"I think he's a hell of a lot more than a down-at-the-heels cowboy. Was I you, I'd be on the trail of some damn good lawyers for the prosecution. I know he's made all the right moves to transfer Stone to Kansas City, and once there, he'll go before the judge to ask for bail."

"No, by God," Hankins shouted. "Not against a charge of murder."

"It's been granted before," said Peeler, "and I expect it will be this time. Now unless you have some further need of me, I have things to do."

Hankins just sat there gripping the arms of his chair in frustration, and Peeler took that as dismissal. He got up and stepped out the door, closing it behind him. Secretly, he was enjoying Hankins's frustration. For too long the old devil had used his position and influence to destroy anyone who stood in his way. Bart, the long-dead son, had been just like his father, and outside the family, few in Nevada had mourned his passing. Just for a moment, Sheriff Peeler had considered telling Hankins that Silver, the "down-at-the-heels" cowboy, had been summoned from Washington, from the attorney general's office. Now he was glad he had not; let Hankins learn *that* the hard way, the same way he learned everything else.

The trial was still four weeks away when Silver brought Nathan recent copies of the *Kansas City Liberty-Tribune*.

"I think you'll find the stories interesting," said Silver. "They've printed all Hankins's charges against you, but they've printed your charges against Bart Hankins and his renegade friends."

"Then I'll have no choice except to admit I shot Hankins and plead self-defense."

"Damn it, you have no other *sensible* choice," Silver said. "Old man Hankins has spent a king's ransom proving you shot Bart, and denying it would brand you a liar. Somebody in that bank heard the shots, and somebody took that sleeve gun. By the time this case comes to trial, I'll have some answers."

Nathan settled back to read the papers. To his surprise, there were quotes from Joel Netherton, of the Kansas-Pacific, Foster Hagerman of the AT and SF, Sheriff Harrington in Dodge City, and many of the trainmen with whom Nathan had ridden the rails as railroad security. There was evidence of Silver's work behind the scenes, for the newspaper had revealed the fact that Hankins and his six companions had deserted the Union army. Daniel Hankins had retained Kritzer and Dilworth, two of the state's most expensive attorneys, but there was no mention of Silver as Nathan's attorney.

Kansas City, Missouri. August 2, 1875

Having received authority from the court in Kansas City, it became Sheriff Peeler's responsibility to see that Nathan arrived there. Nathan and Peeler, accompanied by Silver, set out at dawn. Keeping a steady gait and resting their horses often, they reached Kansas City before sundown. Of necessity, Nathan was turned over to the sheriff, relieving Sheriff Peeler of his responsibility.

"Good luck, Stone," said Peeler. "I'll be here for the trial. I wouldn't miss it for six months' pay."

"Thanks, Sheriff," Nathan said. "I'm obliged to you for feeding my dog."

"Nathan," said Silver, when Sheriff Peeler had departed, "this is Sheriff Higdon. He'll have custody of you tonight. In the morning, we'll go before the judge and arrange bail."

Nathan nodded at Higdon, and the sheriff spoke.

"Silver, if he's being released on bail tomorrow, my taking custody tonight is just a formality. I'll leave you in charge of him tonight, if you'll guarantee his appearance in the morning."

"He'll be here," said Silver. "We're going to Eppie Bolivar's boardinghouse, where we aim to stay until the trial's over."

Nathan and Silver rode out, Empty following.

"I'm obliged for all this," Nathan said. "Eppie has a stable for the horses, and I can leave Empty with her."

"Tomorrow," said Silver, "after your bail has been arranged, I aim to talk to an old gent name of Charlie Ekert. He was a clean-up man at Hankins's bank, and he quit just a few days after Bart Hankins was shot."

"You think there's some connection?"

"I don't know," Silver said, "but I aim to find out. Just in case, I'm serving him with a subpoena as a witness for the defense. Whether or not he's of any use to us will depend on what I learn tomorrow."

Nathan hadn't seen Eppie Bolivar since the spring of 1872, but the old lady hadn't forgotten him. Her eyes lighted when she saw Empty, but he backed away.

"He's one of old Cotton Blossom's pups, Eppie," said

Nathan, "and if nothing else, he has his daddy's appetite. This is Byron Silver. Can you put us up for a month, until the court decides whether to hang me or not?"

"Dear Lord, Nathan," Eppie said, "don't joke about such a terrible thing. I've read all about it in the newspaper. What are you going to do?"

"He's going to lay low and keep his mouth shut," said Silver, "until I come up with a few answers to some troublesome questions. I'll have to ask you not to spread the word that we're here. The newspapers have been given all they're going to get until the day of the trial."

"I'll say nothing," Eppie assured him. "I have a nice big room in the back, with two beds. I rent to working folks who are gone during the day and mind their business when they're here."

Eppie won Empty's trust just as she had won Cotton Blossom's, by offering food and plenty of it. Nathan and Silver retired to their room early.

Silver rode out immediately after breakfast without promising when he would return. Nathan saddled the grulla, and leaving Empty still eating, headed for town. With nothing better to do, he rode to the bank where he had deposited ten thousand dollars, only to find it closed. There was a notice posted on the door, directing him to the law office of Beal Huffmeyer.

"The Pioneer Bank of Kansas City is insolvent," Huffmeyer said.

"Broke," said Nathan. "Damn it, I had money there."

"That's the correct term," Huffmeyer said. "Had."

"You're no help. Why is your name posted on the door?"

Huffmeyer laughed. "Someone has to tell the depositors they're broke."

"There's nothing you can do for the depositors?"

"I can sue the bank's owners," said Huffmeyer, "if somebody's willing to pay."

"What good would that do?"

"None," Huffmeyer replied. "If they had money, the bank wouldn't be insolvent. Anyway, we don't know where they are."

"Huffmeyer," said Nathan, "I'd gut-shoot you, except there's a bunch of little skunks somewhere that would be without a daddy."

Nathan mounted the grulla and rode slowly back to Eppie's. He wasn't broke, for in his saddlebags was four thousand dollars. If he went to court and was freed, he could then go on to Dakota Territory. Where there was a boom town there would be an abundance of saloons, and where there were saloons there would be gambling. As a means of making his living, he considered it only a cut or two above stealing, but it paid better than any other frontier trade. Thinking back, he recalled something Wild Bill Hickok had said:

"If a man's bound to gamble, somebody's got to take his money. It's just the decent thing to do, and I've always been a decent sort."

Reaching Eppie's boardinghouse, Nathan unsaddled the grulla. Rubbing the animal down with an old blanket, he stabled it and pitched down some hay. Silver's horse wasn't there, and Nathan wondered what Silver was doing. Asleep on the porch, Empty opened an eye as Nathan approached. It was almost suppertime when Silver returned, and he had not a word to say about the success or failure of his mission.

"Well," Nathan inquired, "did you serve the subpoena?"

"Yes," said Silver, "and don't ask me anything else."

Silver was silent throughout supper, but Nathan detected an excitement in him that seldom surfaced unless he had drawn the card he needed to win the hand.

Time dragged. Silver said little about the upcoming trial. Occasionally he had Nathan accompany him on trips to town, and although he often sent telegrams, he seldom got an answer. Nathan spent some time with Joel Netherton, at the Kansas-Pacific terminal, and once, when he visited the AT and SF offices to meet with Foster Hagerman, he encountered the four trainmen who ran three thirty-eight.

The last two weeks before the trial, not a word appeared in the newspapers. Finally, on the morning of August thirty-first, Silver briefed Nathan during breakfast.

"Remember, the prosecution will be laying it on thick. There may be a dozen or more Pinkertons who will testify. While they can't actually prove you shot Hankins, they'll be hell-bent on proving there was a vendetta—a conspiracy—that led you to kill Hankins and the six men who rode with him. If I must, I'm going to put you on the stand, and you're going to admit to going after Hankins and his renegades. You're going to tell the court what they did and why you went after them. Then I'm going to prove that Hankins fired first, and that you fired in self-defense.''

Nathan said nothing. If Silver failed, Nathan Stone was a gone beaver, but Nathan had no better defense than that which Silver had proposed. The courtroom was enormous, the most imposing Nathan had ever seen, and it was crowded. Many people spoke to Nathan, and he was surprised to find Sheriff Harrington there, from Dodge City. Nathan and Silver were seated at a table to the left of the bench, while at a similar table to the right sat Daniel Hankins and his attorneys.

"Everybody stand," said the bailiff.

From his chambers, the judge entered and took his seat.

"Court is now in session," the bailiff said, "Judge Holmes McClendon presiding. Case at hand is the State of Missouri versus Nathan Stone. The clerk will read the charges."

The charges were read at great length, to Nathan, each word sounding more damning than the last.

"Attorneys may make their opening statements," said Judge McClendon.

"The defense has no opening statement, Judge," Silver said.

There was a whispering between Kritzer and Dilworth, Hankins's lawyers. Finally, they consulted with Hankins himself.

"The court is waiting," said Judge McClendon. "Does the prosecution have an opening statement?"

Kritzer and Dilworth, Hankins's lawyers, approached the bench.

"Your honor," Kritzer said, "we request a short recess."

"Gentlemen," said Judge McClendon, "you have had ample time to prepare an opening statement. If you have none, then present your evidence. Request for recess denied."

"I will present an opening statement," Kritzer said. He then launched into an account of how Bart Hankins, unarmed, had been brutally murdered. He and Dilworth would present evidence through qualified testimony, and he closed by demanding a guilty verdict from the jury.

"Call your witnesses, then," said Judge McClendon.

Silver had called it close. There were no less than eleven

Pinkerton operatives, every one of whom had been involved in piecing together the lives and deaths of the men who had once ridden with Bart Hankins.

"Cross-examine," Kritzer said, following the first Pinkerton testimony.

"No cross-examination," said Silver.

And so it went. Following each Pinkerton testimony, Silver declined to cross-examine. By the time the last Pinkerton had testified, it was nearing three o'clock.

"Judge," Silver said, "because of the lateness of the hour, we request a recess until nine o'clock in the morning."

"Objection," Kritzer shouted.

"Overruled," said Judge McClendon. "Court stands adjourned."

"Based on all that Pinkerton testimony," Nathan said, "I might as well admit to shooting Hankins."

"That's what I've been trying to tell you," said Silver. "You *are* going to admit to the shooting. The key to this whole thing will be the proving of self-defense. I gave no opening statement, because it wasn't necessary. I've allowed Hankins's Pinkertons to bore the hell out of the jury, because tomorrow we're going to render all their testimony useless."

"With one witness?"

"One witness," said Silver. "I'm going to speak to Judge McClendon in the morning before court convenes."

Nathan and Silver reached the courthouse thirty minutes early. Silver was talking to Sheriff Harrington, and Nathan waited in the aisle, watching people file into the courtroom. Kritzer and Dilworth came in, followed by Daniel Hankins and a girl with blond hair, who looked to be maybe twenty-five. She had been in court with Hankins the day before. She paused, and when Nathan looked at her, she spat in his face.

"Murdering scum," she hissed.

But Nathan's quick eye had caught something, and he took Silver by the arm.

"What is it?" Silver asked.

"That girl with Hankins," said Nathan. "Who is she?"

"Hankins's daughter, I reckon," Silver said. "Why?"

"I have to talk to you," said Nathan. "Now."

"We'll take our seats before the bench," Silver said.

Until Judge McClendon entered the courtroom, Nathan spoke. Silver listened, and only then did he remember he hadn't spoken to the judge. When court had been called to order, the judge spoke.

"Is the defense ready?"

"Yes, your honor," Silver said. "We call as our first witness the young lady behind the prosecution's table, Miss Hankins."

"Objection," Kritzer and Dilworth shouted in a single voice.

"Overruled," said Judge McClendon. "What is your name, ma'am?"

"Katie Hankins," came the reply.

"Katie," said the judge, "please take the stand."

"But ... why ...?"

"Because the attorney for the defense wishes to question you," McClendon said. "Then perhaps all of us will know why."

Katie Hankins took the stand and took the oath.

"Miss Hankins," said Silver, "will you remove the locket you're wearing, so that I can have a look at it?"

"Objection," the Hankins's attorneys shouted.

"Mr. Silver," said Judge McClendon, "are you fishing, or is there some purpose behind this?"

"There is a purpose, your honor," Silver said.

"Objection overruled," said the judge. "Miss Hankins, remove the necklace."

It was a thin golden heart on a long chain. On its face was engraved a honeysuckle.

"Miss Hankins," Silver said, "when and where did you get this?"

"My brother Bart gave it to me, when he came back from the war."

Without another word, Silver turned to the table where Nathan sat.

"Nathan Stone, have you ever seen this before?"

"Yes," Nathan said, swallowing hard. "I had the honeysuckle engraved on it because it was my sister Rachel's favorite flower. I gave it to her on her thirteenth birthday, and she promised to wear it the rest of her life."

"Objection," Hankins's attorneys shouted, but they were drowned out by the uproar in the courtroom.

"Silence," Judge McClendon roared, "or I'll clear the courtroom."

"Objection," Kritzer said. "The engraving means nothing, and could have been done by anyone. The defense is grasping at straws and flaunting the dramatic. The purpose of this trial is to prove a man's guilt or innocence, and the charge is murder. Anything else is irrelevant to the case at hand."

"Mr. Silver," said Judge McClendon, "before I rule, exactly what are you attempting to prove, and how does it relate to the case at hand?"

"Your honor," Silver said, "the prosecution took all of yesterday attempting to prove that Nathan Stone shot Bart Hankins. We are prepared to admit that he did, and we're now about to demonstrate to the court *why* he did it."

"I'll overrule the objection," said Judge McClendon, "because frankly, I'm curious as to how the defense intends to prove innocence by admitting guilt."

"We're not admitting guilt, your honor," Silver said. "We are admitting that Nathan Stone shot Bart Hankins, but we are prepared to prove that Hankins was armed, that he fired first, and that Nathan Stone shot him in self-defense. First, however, to restore Mr. Stone's good name, we are going to prove that Bart Hankins was present the day Rachel Stone was ravished and murdered, and that he removed this necklace from her dead body. Take this locket, Judge, and my knife. Using the thinnest blade, see if that locket doesn't open. If it does, tell me what's inside."

Judge McClendon took the locket and the knife, but after several tries, was unable to open the locket.

"Sorry, Mr. Silver," said McClendon, "it's solid. It doesn't open."

"Sir," said Nathan, "it's the locket I gave Rachel. I can open it."

"Approach the bench," Judge McClendon said.

Nathan did, and McClendon handed him the knife and the locket. Quickly Nathan was able to separate the locket, and without a word, returned both the locket and the knife to the judge.

"There should be a name engraved inside," said Silver. "What is it?"

"Rachel," Judge McClendon said. "Do you want to pass it among the jury?"

"No," said Silver. "As the prosecution pointed out, Bart Hankins is not on trial here. However, Nathan Stone had all the reason a man ever needed for gunning down Hankins and his partners in crime. Now, as I promised, we are going to prove that not only was Bart Hankins armed, but that he drew first. Judge, in return for his testimony, I have promised this witness immunity from prosecution. Tell me if I am right. I've assured him he won't be charged for withholding evidence, for two reasons. First, at the time Hankins was shot, he was believed to have been killed during a failed bank robbery, so there was no investigation. Second, this happened more than ten years ago, and any possible statute of limitations has run out."

"You are correct on both counts," Judge McClendon said. He closed the locket and returned it to Katie Hankins. "You may step down, Miss Hankins."

But Katie Hankins didn't return to her seat. Instead, she walked to the table where Nathan sat, placing the locket before him. "I'm sorry," she said. "So very, very sorry."

"You may call your witness, Mr. Silver," said Judge McClendon.

"Charlie Ekert, please take the stand," Silver said.

Ekert, white-haired, was up in years, and he shuffled when he walked. Seating himself in the witness box, he took the oath, but kept his head down.

"Now, Charlie," Silver said, "you heard Judge McClendon. You've done no wrong, and you won't be faulted for telling the truth. Were you in the bank the day Bart Hankins was shot?"

"Yes," said Charlie.

"Where?"

"In that big office next to his," Charlie said. "He was takin' that big office for himself an' he had me in there gettin' it ready. Always pushin' me around, he was."

"Exactly what did you hear that day?" Silver asked.

"I first knowed somethin' was wrong," said Ekert, "when I heard this voice accusin' Hankins of killin' somebody in Virginia. Bart, he denied it, claimin' he didn't have a gun to defend himself. The other voice said 'I'll lay this Colt on the desk and give you more of a chance than you give my family.' There wasn't no more talking, an' the shootin' started."

"In what order were the shots?" Silver asked.

"I heard the derringer first," said Charlie, "and right on the heels of it, a bigger gun."

"A Colt, maybe?"

"Could of been," Ekert said.

"You heard Hankins say he wasn't armed, but he was, wasn't he?"

"Dang right he was," said Charlie. "One day he went out, leavin' his coat hangin' in his office. I checked it out an' found a double-barrel .41-caliber derringer."

"After the shooting stopped, Charlie, what did you do?" Silver asked.

Ekert licked his lips, swallowing hard, avoiding Silver's eyes. He spoke softly.

"The witness will speak up," said Judge McClendon. "We can't hear you."

"Louder, Charlie," Silver said. "You're not in trouble. We just want the truth."

"There was more shootin'," said Ekert, "but up near the front of the bank. While all hell was bustin' loose up there, I went into Bart Hankins's office an' found him dead. There wasn't no Colt on his desk, but he had the derringer in his hand."

"So you took the derringer," Silver said.

"Yeah," said Ekert, "I took it."

"Why?" Silver asked.

"I . . . I dunno," said Charlie.

"You quit your job at the bank soon afterward," Silver said. "Why?"

"I got to . . . thinkin' . . . I might be in trouble. If I'd of told, I'd of had to say that I took the derringer. So I just quit, thinkin' if I wasn't around, nobody would be able to ask me any questions."

"I have no more questions," said Silver. "Cross-examine?"

"The prosecution has no questions," Kritzer said sullenly.

"This court stands adjourned until such a time as the jury reaches a verdict," said Judge McClendon.

There were shouts from the jury box, and McClendon pounded his gavel for silence. When he finally got it, one of the jurors spoke.

"Your honor, we find Nathan Stone not guilty, and our

hats is off to him for a damn good piece of work. He give the varmint more of a chance than he deserved."

The courtroom went wild, and Judge McClendon gave up trying to restore order and retired to his chambers. A dozen men waited to shake Nathan's hand, including Sheriff Roscoe Peeler. Daniel Hankins was roundly cursing his attorneys.

"I've never seen such bungling," Hankins snarled. "You let Silver, a backwoods bumpkin, tromp hell out of you and disgrace me."

"Hankins," said Kritzer, "you'd best just crawl back to your small-town bank where your ignorance don't matter. Byron Silver is affiliated with the attorney general's office in Washington, and he can practice law before the U.S. Supreme Court."

Nathan and Silver finally broke loose and left the courthouse. It wasn't even noon, but in a festive mood, they found a fancy cafe and ordered steak.

"God," said Nathan, "no wonder the Federals swear by you. I've been in court a few times, but I've never seen anybody as slick as you."

Silver laughed. "I always stick to the truth. That was pretty shrewd on your part, recognizing that locket. That was enough to brand Bart Hankins for a skunk, as far as the jury was concerned, but with Charlie Ekert's testimony, old man Hankins won't dare open his mouth again. He's finished."

"All I wanted was a self-defense verdict," Nathan said. "I don't find any pleasure in destroying a man."

"It's no different than pulling a gun," said Silver. "Daniel Hankins, for all practical purposes, has been shot through the head. When you go after a man with a gun or with a judge and jury, finish him. If you don't, sooner or later he'll come after you, and next time, you may be holding a busted flush."

"Ah, hell, I know it," Nathan said, "but I feel sorry for the girl, Katie."

"After she spat in your face?"

"Even after that," said Nathan. "Thanks to her daddy, vindictive old buzzard that he is, she'll have the rest of her life to remember her brother for a renegade and a killer."

CHAPTER 27

"Too bad you can't take some time off and go with me to Dakota Territory," Nathan said. "It might be your last chance to see a boom town fired up by a gold strike."

"Sorry," said Silver, "but I had to get somebody to cover for me while I've been here in Kansas City. Now, every time he gets a hankerin' to go hunting or fishing, he'll call in all my debts."

Nathan had promised, before leaving Kansas City, to meet with Foster Hagerman of the AT and SF and Sheriff Harrington, from Dodge City. When he parted company with Silver, he rode on to the railroad terminal, believing he knew what his two friends had in mind. But Nathan was weary of riding the rails, and was prepared to reject any proposal to resume working security for the railroad. But that wasn't quite what his companions had in mind.

"Now that the Indian problem is about to be resolved," Hagerman said, "there are more and more settlers wishing to travel to north Texas and eastern New Mexico. There is no railroad any closer than Dodge City, and there's an increasing demand for men to guide emigrants from Dodge to points south. Pay would depend on the distance and the number of wagons. From Dodge to Fort Griffin, Texas, you could earn as much as three hundred dollars."

"I'm bound for the diggings in Dakota Territory," said Nathan. "There, it's possible I could earn three hundred dollars in one day. Or maybe an hour."

"It's also possible you could go broke keeping yourself in grub, and end up without a *peso*," Hagerman said. "It'll cost you more than ten dollars a day, just to eat, and in two more months, there'll be blizzards howling in from the Rockies. The strike in the Black Hills isn't even three months old, and there's not a hotel or boardinghouse any closer than Cheyenne."

"My God," said Nathan, "I've never seen you so fired up. Are you expecting *that* much business from emigrants?"

Harrington laughed. "He hasn't quite told you all of it. There's talk of a twice-a-week stage line from Dodge into Texas, and if it comes to pass, that will add considerably to the amount of mail the AT and SF is able to deliver. While there's not a whole lot in between, there's a hell of a lot of soldiers and civilians at Fort Griffin, while Fort Worth's not that far away. Just delivering government mail to those two outposts could buy Hagerman two or three new locomotives. Just looking at him, can't you tell he's hungry?"

"He does look a mite lank," Nathan said. "I reckon these emigrants will be buying the wagons, mules, and oxen in Dodge. Have you managed to get your hands on the wagon yard and the livery?"

"No," said Hagerman, "I'll have to be satisfied with emigrant fares to Dodge and if a stage line comes to pass, the increased mail delivery."

"Aside from Hagerman needing the money," Sheriff Harrington said, "you might want to take this on for a while, until they take some of the rough edges off that gold camp. If you went there in the spring—say next April— there might be some hotels and boardinghouses to shelter you from the blizzards."

"Better yet," said Hagerman, "you'd have the whole summer to strike it rich and get out of there before the blizzards come."

"Damn it," Nathan said, "you varmints just won't let a man have any peace. Suppose I agree to this pilgrim caravan; when do I start?"

"As soon as you can get back to Dodge," said Hagerman. "Your first run is to Fort Griffin, and there'll be three wagons."

"Hell," Nathan said, "I thought you were here because you were concerned that I might be strung up, when all you wanted was to get me back in harness, making money for you."

Harrington laughed. "He was concerned you might be strung up. Then he wouldn't have had anybody to lead those wagons to Fort Griffin."

They all laughed together, and then Hagerman got serious.

"I will be grateful if you'll help me get this off the ground. Washington assures me the problem with the plains ndians has been resolved. Quanah Parker and the last of the Comanches surrendered three months ago."*

"Then all I'll have to bother with are the outlaws from ndian Territory," said Nathan.

"They shouldn't be that much of a problem," Hagerman said. "Once a stage line has been established, there may be some valuable shipments, but emigrant wagons shouldn't be much of a temptation."

"It sounds safe enough," said Nathan, "but if there are no Indians and no outlaws, why do you need me?"

"Because I can't promise you there'll be no outlaws," Hagerman said, "and because we are dealing with Eastern-ers who fear for their lives."

"And you think one man's going to convince them they're safe," said Nathan.

"Not just *any* one man," Hagerman replied. "Nathan Stone. Even in the East, you have a reputation."

"You're nine feet tall, bite rattlers to watch them die, and so tough you wear out your britches from the inside," said Sheriff Harrington. "At the very sight of you, grown men cringe and the ladies swoon."

"By God," Nathan said, "I have enough problems with-out such foolishness as that bein' spread around. I'll have some damn fool testing me with a gun every day."

Hagerman laughed. "I haven't gone quite that far, but it will be a comfort to people who are new to the frontier, knowing there's a man of your experience guiding them."

"I'm to be a guide, then."

"Yes," Hagerman replied. "In case of outlaws, you would dispose of them, of course."

"Of course," said Nathan.

"I can count on you, then?"

"Until spring," Nathan said. "Then, despite expensive grub, blizzards, and a total lack of hotels, I'm riding to Dakota Territory."

"I've arranged a boxcar for your horse," said Hagerman. "We leave in one hour."

Dodge City, Kansas. September 2, 1875

Nathan again had a room at the Dodge House, courtesy of the AT and SF. Hagerman had arranged for him to meet

*Quanah Parker, last chief of the Comanches, surrendered on June 2, 1875.

the emigrants whom he would guide south. They were ab
to meet for supper in Delmonico's dining room. Taking
time to shine his boots and brush his hat, Nathan wore hi
usual garb. When he arrived, there was Foster Hagerman
and eleven emigrants. Hagerman performed the
introductions.

"Ladies and gentlemen, this is your guide, Nathan Stone
Starting at my left, this is Owen and Emma Kilgore. The
Reverend Kilgore is bound for Fort Griffin. Next, there's
Tally Dismukes and his sons, Gabe, Cyrus, Lon, and Ellis.
They're going to Fort Griffin. Finally, bound for Mobeetie,
there's the . . . ah . . . ladies, Mamie, Cora, Winnie, and
Eula."

Nathan nodded, saying nothing. The Kilgores sat there
stern and unsmiling, as though their faces might crack like
a looking glass and tinkle to the floor. On the other hand,
the Dismukes all wore overalls, brogan shoes, and wide
grins. Tally Dismukes looked about two-thirds drunk, with
the sons at varying stages in between. The four women
were all dressed in revealing clothes and looked as though
they might have recently departed one of the many
whorehouses in Kansas City or St. Louis.

"You will be leaving the wagon yard in the morning at
dawn," said Hagerman. "If you have questions, I'm sure
Mr. Stone will be glad to answer them."

"Yeah," said Gabe, who looked to be the youngest of
the Dismukes. "Is them guns fer show, or can you use 'em
for real?"

"I can use them when I have to," Nathan said coldly,
"but sometimes a good spanking or switching is all it
takes."

That struck the rest of the Dismukes as hilariously funny.
They slapped their thighs and stomped their feet, drawing
venomous looks from the Reverend Owen Kilgore. The
four questionable women cast covert glances at Nathan and
giggled among themselves.

"If there are no more questions," said Hagerman, "all of
you are free to prepare for an early start in the morning."

"Damn," Nathan said, when the unlikely bunch had departed, "where did you come up with *them*?"

Hagerman laughed. "The three groups are paying a hundred dollars each for your company from here to Texas. It
should be an interesting experience."

Nathan sighed. "I reckon before I get there, compared to this bunch, the Indians and outlaws won't seem so bad."

When Nathan arrived at the wagon yard, Empty shied away from the strangers. Much to Nathan's surprise, the wagons were to be drawn by mules, instead of oxen. Mules had to have grain, and Nathan quickly learned that none of his charges had provided any. The women were the most aggravating.

"Well, now," said Mamie, "that just don't make no sense at all. Back in Kentucky, the critters lived on grass."

"Ma'am," Nathan said angrily, "those mules won't pull that wagon from here to Texas without grain. Until there's a hundred pounds of grain in that wagon, I'm not taking it out of this wagon yard."

The Reverend Owen Kilgore just looked at Nathan, and he spoke next to the sober but hungover Dismukes clan.

"We can't afford no grain," Tally said, "less'n we cut back on our grub."

"Or the whiskey," said Nathan. "This damn wagon won't be going anywhere until you buy some grain for the mules."

Nathan tied the reins of the grulla to a hitch rail and sat down on the edge of a water trough. Empty sidled over and sat down beside him, his eyes on the strangers with the wagons. The Reverend Kilgore was the first to comply with Nathan's request, rearranging the contents of the wagon to make room for the sack of grain. The four women—to the horror of the Kilgores—hoisted their skirts and began removing money from their secret places, while the Dismukes clan looked on in open admiration. Finally, when the show was over, Tally Dismuke arranged for the necessary sack of grain.

"Prepare to move out," Nathan shouted. He rode out, Empty trotting beside him.

Nathan looked back, and the wagons had fallen in behind him, the Kilgore wagon in the lead. Nathan sighed. At least they seemed capable enough to handle their teams and the wagons. They covered what Nathan believed was fifteen miles, stopping occasionally to rest the teams. Despite the fact they were all traveling together, there were three separate camps, and Nathan felt welcome in none of them. They were near a creek, and Nathan had picketed the grulla well away from the mules. Starting a small fire, he made supper for himself and Empty. The others built larger fires, and Nathan was thankful the Indian threat had been resolved. After supper, he went near enough to the wagons for everybody to hear what he had to say.

"We'll be moving out at first light. Anybody of a mind to have breakfast, you'd best roll out early enough to be done with it."

The Kilgores put out their fire and turned in early, but there was no evidence any of the others intended to follow their example. The laughter and shouting at the Dismukes's fire grew louder. It hadn't taken long for the four females to make friends with the Dismukes, and Nathan hadn't even removed his hat. He was dozing when one of the women screamed. When Nathan reached the Dismukes's wagon, Ellis was straddling a virtually naked Mamie, who was flat on her back.

"Get off her and get up," Nathan said.

"No, by God," said Ellis. "She drinks my whiskey, she does what I say."

Nathan drew his Colt, fired once, and the lobe of Ellis's left ear disappeared in a spray of blood.

"The bastard shot me!" Ellis bawled, stumbling to his feet.

"The next time I shoot you," said Nathan, "you won't be getting up. Mamie, you get up, get back to your wagon, and stay there. Cora, Winnie, and Eula, go with her. Now."

The four hastened to obey, Mamie grabbing the rag that had been her dress, trying to cover herself. The five Dismukes stared sullenly at Nathan, Ellis holding a bandanna to his bleeding ear.

"Damn you," said Tally, "we ain't payin' you fer this kind of treatment."

"You're paying me to get you to Fort Griffin," Nathan said, "and while you're with me, you travel under my rules, not yours. The next one of you I find hunkered over one of those women, I'll kill you. This is all the warning you're going to get."

"Hell," said Cyrus, "they ain't nothin' but whores, an' they drunk our whiskey."

"I'm not interested in your opinions," Nathan said, "and it's all I can do to stand you varmints cold sober. I think we'll get along better without the whiskey."

Three quart bottles stood on the wagon's lowered tail-ate. Nathan drew his Colt, and with a roar that sounded like a single shot, shattered every bottle.

"Damn you," said Tally. "Damn you. Give us back our money. We ain't goin' nowhere with you."

"Oh, but you are," Nathan said. "I agreed to see you safely to Fort Griffin, and by God, I keep my promises. If I have to, I'll hogtie the whole damn lot of you, chunk you in the wagon, and drive it myself."

"It's aways, yet," Ellis snarled, "an' you got to sleep sometime. We'll git you."

"I'm a light sleeper," said Nathan, "and when you come after me, wear your burying clothes, because you'll be needing them."

With that, he backed out of the circle of light cast by the dying fire and returned to his blankets. Empty was there, and he was thankful for the faithful dog's presence. There was no way they could approach him without a warning from Empty. He removed his gun belt, but kept one of the Colts in his hand.

The second day out of Dodge, they crossed the Cimarron River, spending the night at the very edge of Indian Territory's panhandle. Another day would see them in north Texas. Three more days, Nathan thought, and they would reach Mobeetie, where he would be rid of the four women. That would solve half his problem, for the Kilgores had avoided him. Leaving Mobeetie, he estimated he would be maybe a hundred and fifty miles north of Fort Griffin. Two more weeks of Kilgore silence and Dismukes hate.

Mobeetie, Texas. September 8, 1875
Mobeetie had begun with a trading post catering to buffalo hunters, but the buffalo were gone. All that had saved Mobeetie from total obscurity was the establishment of Fort Elliott, one-half mile south of Sweetwater Creek and about a mile from Mobeetie.*

"I reckon this is Mobeetie," Nathan said. "Mamie, Cora, Winnie, and Eula, this is as far as you go."

Mobeetie consisted of a trading post, a saloon, and three slab-sided shanties. Of all the buildings, the saloon was the

---

*Fort Elliott was established on June 5, 1875, in present-day Wheeler County.

most impressive, and it was there that the four wome
reined up their teams.

"The rest of you are about a hundred and fifty mile
north of Fort Griffin. We'll be staying the night at For
Elliott, a mile or so from here."

Fort Elliott was a new outpost, and seemed to justify the
determination of the women who had relocated to Mobee
tie. The buildings were long, rambling structures, built in a
rectangle, in the center of which was the parade ground
Some buildings were frame and some were adobe. Offices
were at the front, with enlisted men's quarters on one side
and officers' quarters on the other. Dining rooms and kitch-
ens adjoined at the back, and behind the post, along the
creek, were tepees of Indians who were part of the outpost's personnel. While there was no stockade, there was a
sentry on duty before the fort's offices. Nathan rode ahead
of the wagons and reined up.

"I'm Nathan Stone," he said, "guiding some folks south
to Fort Griffin. We aim to stay the night somewhere along
the creek. I reckon I'll say howdy to your post commander
if he'll see me."

"Go on in to the orderly room and talk to Sergeant
Wills," said the soldier.

Sergeant Wills greeted Nathan, heard his request, and
knocked on the door of the post commander. He entered
and returned almost immediately.

"Captain Selman will see you," the sergeant said.

Nathan entered the office and the captain stepped around
the desk to take his hand. Briefly Nathan told him of the
eventual plan to establish a twice-a-week stage run between
Dodge City and Fort Griffin.

"God knows, we'll welcome it," Selman said. "As things
now stand, the best we can expect is a once-a-month supply
train from Fort Dodge. When do the stages begin?"

"I don't know," said Nathan, "but probably sometime
between now and spring. Right now, I'm working with the
railroad, filling in the gap by guiding people from Dodge
City into Texas. I just left four women at the saloon in
Mobeetie."

"Thanks," Selman said wryly. "Given a choice, I'd consider swapping that saloon for Quanah Parker and the
Comanches."

"I reckon," said Nathan. "Add women to the whiskey

nd gambling, and you have all the necessary elements to end a man straight to hell."

"Or to the guard house," Selman said. "We're at full strength, with close to five hundred men, and on any given Monday morning, there's maybe twenty percent of them in the stockade, charged with drunk and disorderly conduct."

"I can see where you'd likely stand a better chance with the Indians," said Nathan. "I just wanted to tell you why we're here, and to get permission to spend the night along the creek."

"Permission granted," Selman said. "You and your emigrants are welcome to take your meals at the enlisted men's mess this evening and in the morning."

"That's generous of you, Captain," said Nathan. "I accept, and I'll mention it to the others."

Nathan mounted and rode back to the wagons, where he was greeted in stony silence.

"We'll take the wagons over yonder beyond those buildings at the far side of the post, and make our camp along the creek. Captain Selman has invited us to take supper tonight and breakfast in the morning with the enlisted men. I aim to be there, and I expect all of you to be on your best behavior. If there's trouble involving any of you, I'll have the captain lock you in the stockade and leave you there until you moss over."

"We ain't eatin' with no blue bellies," said Gabe. "We're goin' back to Mobeetie, to the saloon. That is, unless you're of a mind to try an' stop us."

"I won't stop you," Nathan said, "but I am going to warn you. Don't get involved in anything so deep you can't get out. If you aim to rear up on your hind legs like a man, be prepared to take whatever comes with the territory."

The five of them glared at him defiantly, saying nothing. The Reverend and the Mrs. Kilgore kept their silence, regarding Nathan with as much distaste as the Dismukes clan. Nathan rode on to the creek, beyond the post. There he dismounted, unsaddled, and after the grulla had time to roll, he rubbed the animal down. From the sack he carried behind his saddle, he fed the horse a ration of grain and turned it loose to graze. Stretching out, head on his saddle, he rested. The Kilgores had followed, and made their camp well beyond his. Nathan watched approvingly as Kilgore unharnessed his team, allowed the mules to roll, and then

rubbed them down. On the frontier, a man who failed t
tend his horse or mule was a fool. The Dismukes didn
show, and Nathan decided they had made good their b
to visit the saloon in Mobeetie. He fully expected the l
of them to be roaring drunk when he saw them again. Na
than dozed until the bugler blew mess call. Empty followe
him to the enlisted men's mess hall, lagging behind. Natha
waited until the soldiers had all been served before ap
proaching one of the cooks on the serving line.

"Pardner," said Nathan, "I'm guiding some wagons t
Fort Griffin. Captain Selman was kind enough to invite m
to eat with you gents tonight and in the morning. This i
my dog. His name's Empty, and he purely lives up to it
Will you feed him, too?"

"If he can eat what Washington sends us, he's welcome,"
the cook replied. He quickly won Empty's confidence with
a tin plate of meat scraps.

Despite the military rations, Nathan enjoyed the meal.
The soldiers were friendly, and he saw nothing wrong with
telling them of the proposed stage run from Dodge City
south to Fort Griffin. He spent a pleasant hour there, before going back to his place beside the creek, where his
horse grazed. Several hundred yards away, cook fires were
going before the Indian tepees. The Kilgores had already
prepared their supper, and the fire had died down to coals.
Suddenly there was a clatter of hooves, and astride one of
the mules, Cyrus Dismukes rode in. Blood dripped from
his nose and mouth, his shirt had been torn off, and his
upper body was a mass of bleeding cuts. He fell off the
mule, gasping, and it was a moment before he could speak.

"Them soldiers ... jumped us. They ... done kilt Lon,
an' ... they're beatin' hell out'n ... the others ..."

Despite his vow not to become involved, Nathan couldn't
afford to ignore the fight, since it involved the soldiers. By
now, he knew the Dismukes well enough to doubt that such
a brawl had engulfed them through no fault of their own.
Such uncivilized conduct by the Dismukes might sour the
military on other emigrants, making them unwelcome at
the forts, and Nathan Stone along with them. Quickly he
saddled the grulla and set out for the saloon in Mobeetie.
He arrived in time to see Tally Dismukes emerge head-first
through a window in a shower of glass. From inside there
came the sound of bottles smashing, and a woman

screamed. Nathan hit the ground running, and when he entered the saloon, a bottle shattered inches from his head, showering him with glass. Lon Dismukes lay on his back in a pool of blood, his throat slashed. The two remaining Dismukes were behind an upended table, while a dozen soldiers were advancing, some of them with knives in their hands.

"That's enough," Nathan shouted. He drew his Colt and fired twice into the ceiling.

"Step aside," said a voice behind Nathan.

Six armed soldiers entered the saloon. Quickly they disarmed their knife-wielding companions and backed them up against the wall. One of the military policemen turned on Nathan, pointing with the muzzle of his rifle toward the bloody Dismukes.

"Mister, do you know those men?"

"I'm afraid I do," Nathan said. "They're on their way to Fort Griffin, and we stopped here for the night. I have no idea how this started. I came to break it up, because just this evening I met with Captain Selman, and I want no trouble with the military."

Before it went any further, a barkeep came forward. Pointing to one of the soldiers, he spoke.

"He cut the man on the floor after the hombre come after him with a broken bottle."

"You Dismukes heard the charge," said Nathan. "What do you have to say?"

"He cut Lon without no cause," Tally bawled. He pushed his way back into the saloon, limping, bleeding from numerous cuts.

"That's a damn lie," some of the soldiers shouted.

"They're right," the barkeep said. "The dead one wanted one of the women, but she was with one of the soldiers. They fought over her, and he lost."

"Will that satisfy you soldiers," Nathan asked, "if we call the killing justified?"

"Hell, no, we ain't callin' it justified," Tally Dismukes shouted. "We ain't leavin' here till we git the bastard that killed Lon."

"If that's the way you want it," said Nathan. "I'm not involved in this. I'll let these men from the post put you in the stockade and the post commander can decide what to do with you. I aim to tell him that this entire affair appears to have been your fault, and I'm washing my hands of the lot of you."

One of the soldiers had Tally covered with a rifle, while two others hustled Ellis and Gabe to their feet.

"Damn it," Tally cried, "we're civilians. You can't lock us up."

"Wrong, mister," said one of the soldiers. "There's no law here except martial law, and that's us. Move!"

"Soldier," said the barkeep, "there's another of the varmints. He run off."

"He's there beside the creek, where they all should have been," Nathan said.

"Stone, you Judas bastard, we'll git you fer this," Tally shouted.

The three Dismukes were marched back to Fort Elliott, leaving the wagon where it stood. Nathan unharnessed the remaining three mules and led them back to the creek to join the one Cyrus had ridden. He was hunkered on the creek bank, washing the blood from his face and upper body. He stood up as Nathan approached.

"Lon started the fight in which he was killed," Nathan said. "I tried to get the lot of you out of it by calling things even, but your daddy wouldn't have it. So all of you will be locked in the stockade until the post commander decides what to do with you."

"No," Cyrus cried, "don't let them keep us here."

"Your daddy made that decision," said Nathan.

Two of the soldiers came, and despite all his protests, Cyrus was taken to join the rest of the Dismukes. Less than an hour later, one of the soldiers came for Nathan.

"Captain Selman wants to talk to you in his office."

Nathan entered the post commander's office and found the captain behind his desk, his face grim.

"Stone, I realize this isn't your doing, but I'm going to ask your help in resolving it. Like I told you, I have trouble enough keeping the men who are garrisoned here from killing one another, without civilian help from elsewhere. I'm going to turn this bunch loose in the morning on two conditions. One, I want them out of here at first light, and if they return, they're subject to being shot. Two, I have prepared a letter to the post commander at Fort Griffin, which you are to deliver. He is being warned of this incident here, and I am suggesting that these men—the Dismukes—be barred from the post in general, and the sutler's store in particular. God forbid that they should get their hands on any more whiskey. Does my decision meet with your approval?"

"It does, sir," said Nathan. "I'll do my best to rid you of them, and to warn the post commander at Fort Griffin."

"Thank you," Captain Selman said, offering his hand. "Consider yourself welcome here any time."

Nathan took the officer's hand, anxious to reach Fort Griffin and rid himself of the troublesome Dismukes.

CHAPTER 28

Nathan wisely said nothing to the Dismukes about the letter he carried to the post commander at Fort Griffin. He would wait until he reached the fort before informing the troublesome clan they weren't welcome. After Captain Selman had them released from the guard house, Nathan allowed the surviving Dismukes time to bury Lon.

"Preacher," said Nathan, approaching the Reverend Kilgore, "you could say a few words over the Dismukes boy."

"I could," Kilgore replied, "but for one thing. I have been taught that when one can say nothing good, it's best to say nothing at all."

Nathan said no more, allowing the Dismukes to proceed with the burying in whatever manner they chose. After lowering the body into the grave, they stood around it for a few minutes before filling it and mounding the dirt. Finally they returned to their waiting wagon and clambered aboard, Tally taking the reins. Nathan led out, riding south. Thanks to the Dismukes, their departure was two hours late, and when they paused for the night, Nathan estimated they had traveled not more than ten miles. The third day after leaving Fort Elliott, Nathan's uneasy alliance with the Dismukes blew up.

"We ain't follerin' you no further," Tally Dismukes announced, as Nathan was about to move out. "Take the sky pilot and his woman an' go on without us."

"I might remind you," said Nathan coldly, "that you're no longer welcome at Fort Elliott, and I'm delivering a letter to the post commander at Fort Griffin, barring you from that post."

"I ain't surprised," Tally growled. "We owe you a powerful lot, Stone. Now, you just git goin', and we'll do as we damn please."

Nathan said no more. They were grown men, and despite his threats, he couldn't see it as his responsibility to force them to follow him to Fort Griffin, especially since they, as a result of Captain Selman's warning, would be barred from the post. He looked back once, and only the Kilgore wagon was following. The Dismukes hadn't even harnessed their teams to the wagon. It was evident they didn't want Nathan knowing what destination they had in mind, but having taken their measure, he thought he knew.

"Pa," said Ellis, "I ain't wantin' to be locked in that guard house no more. They ain't nothin' we can do fer Lon. Why can't we just go on to Fort Griffin?"

"You heard what Stone said," Tally snarled. "We're still a hunnert mile from the damn place, an' already we been barred. Besides, we ain't done with them blue bellies back yonder at Fort Elliott."

"But there must be near five hunnert soldiers," said Gabe. "We ain't got a chance."

Tally laughed. "Not in a fair fight, mebbe, but us Dismukes ain't bound to fight fair. We still got that case of dynamite in the wagon. We'll circle that soldier fort in the dark, an' with some short fuses, we'll blow the place to hell an' gone."

"I like it, Pa," Cyrus said. "That'll show 'em they can't push us Dismukes around."

"We owe that bunch at the Mobeetie saloon a thing or two," said Tally. "Maybe we'll mosey by there and empty their cash drawer."

Two hours before sundown, Nathan reined up, waiting for the Kilgore wagon to reach him. The Kilgores said nothing, and Nathan spoke.

"Next water we come to, we'll make camp. I'm riding back to Fort Elliott to warn the post that the Dismukes are likely returning. I'll rejoin you as soon as I can."

"But that's unfair to us," Kilgore complained. "You agreed to lead us to Fort Griffin, and that means without delay."

"Wrong," said Nathan. "I promised to guide you to Fort Griffin, but time involved is up to me. This is the frontier, and a man is guided by circumstances, not time. There is a chance that men will die unless I warn Captain Selman at Fort Elliott. It's not quite fifty miles, and I should be back here by dawn. Put out your fire before dark and keep to your wagon. I'll see you in the morning."

Nathan rode northeast, not wishing to catch up to the Dismukes. Empty ran on ahead, dropping back once. The wind was from the west, and Nathan could hear the rattle of the wagon. The Dismukes weren't wasting any time. Once certain that he was ahead of the distant wagon, Nathan resumed a northerly direction. He spared the Grulla, resting the horse often. The Dismukes, if they pushed their teams, wouldn't cover more than twenty miles before being forced to halt for the night and to feed the mules. Pacing himself, resting his horse often, Nathan would reach Fort Elliott well before midnight. Having had experience with the Dismukes, Captain Selman wasn't likely to take the threat lightly.

"Halt," the sentry ordered. "Who goes there?"

"Nathan Stone. I must talk to Captain Selman."

"He will have retired for the night," said the soldier. "Can't it wait until morning?"

"No," Nathan replied. "The Dismukes—those varmints that spent the night in your guard house—are headin' this way, and I reckon they have mischief on their minds."

"Sergeant of the guard," the sentry shouted. "Sergeant of the guard."

Nathan waited until Sergeant Wills arrived. He remembered Nathan, and after hearing of the possible return of the Dismukes, agreed to awaken Captain Selman.

"Sorry to awaken you, Captain," said Nathan, "but the Dismukes refused to continue on to Fort Griffin. They're evidently on their way here, and I have no idea what kind of arms they may have inside their wagon. You should double your guard, at least, and while I realize the saloon in Mobeetie isn't your responsibility, it's a source of whiskey, which I'm doubting the Dismukes will overlook. You should send some men there in the morning, and keep them there until you resolve this."

"I respect your observations and the warning," said Captain Selman. "Whatever they're planning to do, we'll be prepared. Will you stay the night?"

"No," Nathan said. "I left the Kilgores more than forty miles south of here, and I've promised to return there by dawn. I'll stay the night with you on my way back to Dodge."

"Do that," said Selman, "and I'll fill you in on what happens here."

Nathan rode southeast, wary lest he stumble on the Dismukes's sleeping camp. But he had nothing to fear, for Empty was always out there ahead of him. When Nathan estimated he had ridden thirty miles, he changed direction, riding due south. Nathan had no trouble finding the Kilgore wagon, for its canvas had been silvered by a descending moon. All the mules grazed peacefully. Nathan unsaddled the grulla, allowed the animal to roll, and then rubbed him down. He then picketed the horse near the mules and spread his blankets near the creek, to sleep for what remained of the night. Empty lay down beside him, and Nathan ruffled the dog's ears. He would always miss Cotton Blossom, but there was much comfort in knowing the valiant hound had left behind a son who was rapidly walking in his sire's footsteps.

The Kilgores arose at dawn. They spoke not to Nathan, nor he to them. He took the time to broil bacon for himself and Empty, and finished with that, he made himself a pot of strong coffee. The Kilgores were ready and waiting for him, but he finished his coffee before saddling the grulla. He wanted only to deliver the surly, silent Kilgores to Fort Griffin and be rid of them. Nathan led out, riding south, Empty running ahead. The Kilgore wagon followed, and Nathan stepped up the pace. They might reach Fort Griffin in another five days.

Fort Griffin, Texas. September 16, 1875

Nathan was readily shown into the office of Fort Griffin's post commander, where he was greeted cordially by Captain Webb.

"This telegram came to me from Captain Selman, at Fort Elliott. It didn't seem to require an answer. It's worded in such a way that I believe he intended for you to tell me what it's all about."

He handed Nathan the message, and it was brief. It said: *Disregard letter Nathan Stone bringing stop. Dismukes all dead.*

It had been signed by Captain Selman. Nathan began with the fight at the saloon in Mobeetie and concluded with his all-night ride to warn Selman the hell-raising Dismukes were apparently returning to Fort Elliott.

"I can see where the letter Selman sent by you is now unnecessary," Webb said. "I'd say we all owe you a vote of thanks. He for your timely warning, and me for you not having brought them to Fort Griffin."

"I got saddled with them in Dodge City," said Nathan. "They were bound for here, and Captain Selman had seen enough of them to know they were trouble, especially after they got their hands on some whiskey. One of the sons started the fight in which he was killed, but his kin wouldn't accept that. They must have returned to the fort with some fool idea of getting revenge."

"So you're working for the railroad, guiding emigrants south. For what purpose?"

"I don't have the foggiest notion, Captain, except that they want to come," said Nathan. "They're Easterners, and with the plains Indians under control, I don't understand why they need or want a guide. I had three wagons. I left one of them—along with four women—at the saloon in Mobeetie, and brought you the third one. All you're getting this trip is a sourpuss preacher and his wife."

Captain Webb sighed. "I wondered what—or who—would replace the Comanches, and I can't say the alternative looks much better."

Nathan spent only one night at Fort Griffin. He was determined to have some better understanding with Foster Hagerman before guiding any more emigrants south. While he was perfectly capable of keeping his charges in line, he felt like a schoolmarm. Spring was a hell of a long ways off. One more bunch of rotgut-drinking, hell-raising misfits like the Dismukes, and he'd drop the whole deal right back in Foster Hagerman's lap. Nathan rode until near sundown, pausing near a spring for the night. With Empty close by, he was safe enough, and he slept soundly.

Fort Elliott, Texas. September 20, 1875

"We're considerably in your debt," Captain Selman said. "Two nights after you warned us, the Dismukes showed up. They had a case of dynamite, with short fuses, and they came at us from four directions. If we hadn't been expecting them, ready for them, then God knows how much damage they might have done. They were like mad men, refusing to surrender, and we had to shoot them down."

There came a knock on Captain Selman's door, and given permission, a first lieutenant entered. He saluted. Captain Selman returned it, and the lieutenant spoke.

"Sir, it's Sergeant King again. He started a brawl over a woman last night, and one of the barkeeps in the Mobeetie saloon laid him out cold with a bung starter."

Captain Selman sighed. "He's alive, I suppose?" He sounded mildly disappointed.

"Yes, sir," the lieutenant replied, "but he may have a concussion. He's being examined at the dispensary now. What do you want done with him?"

"Fine him a month's pay and lock him in the guard house for ten days," Selman said.

The lieutenant saluted and departed. Captain Selman said nothing, and it was Nathan who finally spoke.

"I reckon the women I brought down from Dodge are causing their share of trouble."

"Yes," said Selman, "but we can hardly blame that on you. If men don't have women, they'll fight over something else. I've busted sergeants back to corporals and corporals back to privates, but there's so little difference in the pay, nobody gives a damn."

Nathan spent the night at Fort Elliott, and he and Empty ate with the enlisted men.

"Captain," said Nathan, as he prepared to leave, "thank you for your hospitality. We'll likely be seein' you again in a few days."

Nathan had just left Texas and entered Indian Territory. About to cross the North Canadian River, he reined up and dismounted. The grulla wanted water, but he restrained it until the animal had rested. It was then that he saw the buzzards circling a few miles up ahead. Something or somebody was dead, or soon about to be. Nathan mounted and rode on across the North Canadian, bound for the Cimarron. Well before he reached the river, Empty circled back to meet him, evidence enough that something was wrong. Nathan eased the grulla down to a walk, hooking his right thumb in his gun belt, near the butt of his Colt. He saw the dead horse first, and the animal still wore a saddle. The horse had been shot through the head. There was an agonized groan and Nathan followed it to a shallow arroyo. The man lay on his back, and he had been gut-shot, for blood soaked the shirt where it covered his belly. Above the left breast pocket of his shirt was pinned a lawman's badge. The holster on his right hip was empty. The lawman's hat was missing and his receding hair was gray. He looked to be in his fifties, and when Nathan knelt beside him with a canteen, the wounded man's eyes fluttered open.

"I'll do what I can for you, pardner," Nathan said.

"Ain't . . . much . . ." the man gritted. "I'm . . . gut-shot. . . ."

It was true. Without question he was a dead man, the only uncertainty being how long he might suffer before death mercifully took him.

"Best if you don't talk," Nathan said. "I'll get some blankets . . ."

"No . . . no . . . ," the wounded man gasped. "No . . . time. Need . . . to . . . talk . . ."

"Then tell me who you are and what happened," said Nathan. "Maybe I can catch up to the varmint that shot you."

"Franklin . . . Monroe . . . " the wounded man said. "Sheriff . . . of . . . Santa Fe. My brother . . ."

"What about your brother?"

"Virg . . . Virgil . . . shot me . . ."

"Why?" Nathan asked.

"He . . . robbed a bank . . . and I . . . came after . . . him. Ma . . . made me . . . promise I'd . . . take care of . . . him. Kid brother . . . wild. I . . . caught up . . . to him . . . got the drop. Swore he'd go back . . . with me . . . take his . . . punishment. Caught me . . . off guard . . . shot me . . ."

He coughed once, and blood came out. Nathan tried to give him more water, but he was unable to take it. He lay back, coughing, wheezing, until at last he became silent, for he had strangled on his own blood. Nathan removed his hat and stood there a moment. He had no tools, no means of burying the man, but he couldn't leave him to the coyotes and the relentless, circling buzzards. He took one of his blankets and covered the corpse. The shallow arroyo would have to do, and the only available cover was stones. Nathan started gathering them, as large as he could carry, and it took him a good three hours to cover the dead man to the extent the predators couldn't get at him. Only when he had finished did he realize he had failed to search the man's body, and he wasn't about to remove all the stones. He knew the man's name and the name of the brother who had done the killing, and that it had been the result of a bank robbery in Santa Fe. Killing a man over stolen money was bad enough, but it seemed especially heinous when that man was one's own brother. Nathan circled the area until he picked up the tracks of the killer's horse, and not surprisingly, they led north. It was entirely possible that Virgil Monroe was on his way to Dodge City. There, Nathan could tell his story to Sheriff Harrington, who might be able to arrest the killer and recover the stolen money. Nathan's sympathy was with the dead lawman, and if the murdering kid brother got the rope, it would be no more than he deserved.

Dodge City, Kansas. September 21, 1875

"I'll check the liveries first," Sheriff Harrington said, "and see if there have been any strangers in town today."

"I'll ride along with you," said Nathan. "After that bunch of immigrants I already took south, I'm in no hurry to get back to Hagerman for more."

They learned nothing at the first livery, but at the second, Sheriff Harrington found what he was looking for.

"Gent rode in here this mornin' on a pretty well used-up roan," the liveryman said. "I rubbed the hoss down and grained him."

"Did he leave anything here?" Harrington asked. "Saddlebags, bedroll . . ."

"Nothin' but his saddle," said the liveryman. "Took his saddlebags an' rifle with him."

"I reckon we'll try the hotels and boardin' houses," Harrington said, "but I doubt this gent will sign in under his own name."

"He might," said Nathan. "He had no way of knowing I'd learn of what he's done, and then ride into Dodge practically on his heels. Let's try the Dodge House first."

"I don't want no trouble here, Sheriff," the desk clerk said.

"Wiggins, if the hombre we're lookin' for is here, he

is trouble," Harrington replied. "Has anybody signed in this morning?"

"One," said Wiggins grudgingly. "We don't get many until the evenin' train . . ."

"Let me see that register," Harrington said.

The scrawled signature read "Franklin Monroe."

"The no-account varmint signed his dead brother's name," said Nathan. "Is he here?"

"No," Wiggins replied.

"I'll need a key to his room," said Harrington, "unless you're going to insist on seeing a search warrant."

"I suppose not," Wiggins said.

He produced a key, and when Nathan and Sheriff Harrington reached the room, the sheriff knocked on the door. There was no response from within, but Harrington stood to one side as he inserted the key. Slowly he turned the knob, and when the latch let go, he kicked the door open. The bed hadn't been disturbed. Lying across it was a Winchester and saddlebags. Swiftly Harrington unbuckled the flaps of the saddlebags. In one side there was a clean shirt, two pairs of socks, and an extra tin of shells. The other side yielded only a strip of paper, but printed on it were the words, *Bank of Santa Fe.*

"If a dying man's word means anything," Nathan said, "we're justified in tracking down this varmint."

"We've about eliminated everything except the saloons," said Harrington. "This gent, with money in his pockets, will be looking for a place to spend it. That usually leads to a poker table or a whorehouse, and at this time of day, I'd consider a poker table the most likely."

They tried the Long Branch and found no game in progress, but their luck improved when they reached the Oasis. A four-handed game was underway, and while Nathan knew few of the residents of Dodge, he detected a slight reaction from one of the men when he saw Harrington's badge. He sat with his back to the wall, and dropped his hand below the table. The move wasn't lost on the sheriff.

"Take your hand away from your gun," said Harrington, "and stand up, Monroe."

"I never seen you before in my life, and you ain't got nothin' on me."

Sensing trouble, his three companions slid back their

chairs and got out of the way. Monroe was left alone. Slowly he got to his feet.

"Now," Harrington said, "unbuckle your gun belt and let it fall to the floor."

"No," said Monroe. "You got nothin' on me."

"We have the words of a dying man," Harrington said, "and he accused you, Virgil Monroe, of shooting him."

"I ain't told you my name."

"You don't have to," said Harrington. "Your actions spoke for you. Now, unbuckle the gun belt and we'll mosey over to the jail. That coat you're wearing looks a mite heavy in places, and I'm wondering why."

Slowly Monroe unbuckled the gun belt and allowed it to fall to the floor. The sheriff had not drawn his gun, and Monroe moved just enough to place Harrington between himself and Nathan. Only Monroe's right arm moved, as he palmed the sleeve gun. Nathan saw it coming, but for just a crucial second, Sheriff Harrington was between him and Monroe. The derringer spoke once and Harrington stumbled, slumping to the floor. Nathan drew his Colt and shot Monroe just as the killer squeezed off the second shot from the derringer. The lead burned a raw furrow along Nathan's left arm, above the elbow. Monroe was slammed against the wall and the sleeve gun clattered to the floor. The barkeep and the three men who had been gambling with Monroe had gathered around. Nathan knelt beside the dying sheriff, leaning close to hear Harrington's last words.

"A man's . . . too old to . . . wear the badge when . . . he forgets . . . the . . . sleeve . . . guns. . . ."

Those were his final words. His eyes blurred and with a lump in his throat, Nathan got to his feet. The shots had drawn men from Delmonico's, across the street. One of the new arrivals was Foster Hagerman. He stared, unbelieving, at the dead man who had long been his friend. When he spoke, it was to Nathan.

"My God, what happened? Why?"

With some difficulty, Nathan explained. Others who had gathered around turned their hostile eyes on Nathan, and finally one of them said what the rest were thinking.

"Damn you, our sheriff was gunned down over somethin' you dragged in. Somethin' that wasn't no concern of his."

"He believed it was," said Nathan. "You'll find the man who shot him has all or most of the money stolen from the

Bank of Santa Fe. He's also guilty of having shot a lawman from Santa Fe, who was pursuing him."

"There'll have to be a sheriff appointed," Foster Hagerman said. "Brady, go fetch the acting mayor."

"A damn shame the sheriff had no deputy," said Nathan.

"I agree," Hagerman said, glaring at some of the men who had gathered around. "He'd been asking for one, but the town council's too damn cheap to pay a man. This comes at a bad time. Mayor Wright died last Sunday. The acting mayor is Rufus Langley, and he had to be drafted."

Nathan wasn't impressed with acting Mayor Langley. He arrived wearing the white apron of a storekeeper and the manner of a man who clearly wished he were somewhere else. Hatless, dressed in town clothes, he appeared to be in his fifties. He looked around, obviously uncertain as to what was expected of him.

"Rufus," said Hagerman, "since the town council saw fit not to hire a deputy, you're going to have to appoint a sheriff until an election can be held."

"What about you?" Langley suggested.

"Don't be a damn fool," said Hagerman. "I work for the railroad."

"So do I," Nathan added.

"Brady," said Langley, "go to the funeral parlor and have Creeker come for these dead men."

"The man who killed Sheriff Harrington should be searched," Nathan said. "He should be carrying all or most of the money stolen from the Bank of Santa Fe."

"All we got on that is your word," an onlooker said. "Search him yourself."

"Go ahead," Hagerman said. "You're more qualified than the rest of us."

"Only if you count the money and Mr. Langley takes charge of it on behalf of the town," said Nathan. "It should be returned to Santa Fe."

"Search the man," Langley said. "If he's a thief and the money is there, I'll see that it's returned to the bank from which it was stolen."

Nathan removed the bulky coat from the dead man, discovering the lining had been ripped and crudely resewn. He ripped the lining loose and shook out the bundles of bills, each packet bearing a Bank of Santa Fe identifying band. Nathan made no move toward the stolen money, allowing Langley to gather it up and place it on a table. Men crowded close.

"Stand back, all of you," Langley shouted. Removing his store apron, he used it to bundle up the packets of bills.

"I don't know that I'd trust him with all that," said Foster Hagerman quietly.

"I want nothing to do with it," Nathan said. "It *is* my fault Sheriff Harrington's dead. I brought him face-to-face with a thief and killer. It wasn't his responsibility to make that arrest."

"He didn't think of it as a responsibility," said Hagerman. "As a lawman, he saw it as a duty. The same duty that drove you into a near-fatal fight with Chapa Gonzolos and his band of outlaws. You *think* like a lawman. Someday, in some town on the frontier, you'll die with your boots on, going against impossible odds, for what you believe is right."

"If you're done fortune telling," Nathan said, "let's get out of here. I aim to go to the funeral parlor and put some money toward arrangements for Sheriff Harrington."

"The town will see to that," said Hagerman. "He was well thought of, and I doubt the hombre replacing him will fill his boots."

"I considered him one of my friends," Nathan said, "but I never knew his first name."

"Few people did," said Hagerman. "If your name was Percival, would you be usin' it?"

"No," Nathan said, "and I'd leave a will, begging them that done the burying not to chisel it into the stone."

"There'll be a stone," said Hagerman. "I'll see to that. Do you want to go ahead and get your room at the Dodge House, or do you want to go to my office and talk? There'll be time for the funeral later this afternoon, and if I'm not busy, I'll hole up somewhere and dread that."

"So will I," Nathan replied, "so let's talk. I want to tell you about the Dismukes."

"I've heard enough about them," said Hagerman. "Three days after you took the trail south, I learned they were wanted by the law in Missouri."

"They're out of reach of the law," Nathan said. "They let their hell-raising get ahead of their better judgment." He then told Hagerman what had become of the troublesome Dismukes clan.

"I don't know when there'll be another bunch going south," said Hagerman. "Maybe not until after Christmas."

"Then I can't promise you I'll hang around here until then," Nathan said. "I'll be where you can reach me, and I'll see it through until spring, but no longer."

Sheriff Harrington's funeral was well-attended, and it was evident the lawman would be missed. Empty howled mournfully while the grave was being filled, and Nathan led him away. It was a dreary, lonesome time, and the far away wail of the westbound's whistle added to the effect. Death had won another hand . . .

CHAPTER 29

The morning after Sheriff Harrington's funeral, Nathan had just ordered breakfast at Delmonico's when Foster Hagerman came in. Without waiting for an invitation, he hooked a chair with his boot and sat down at Nathan's table.

"Won't you join me?" Nathan asked.

"Thanks," said Hagerman. "I have a proposition for you, and I wanted to catch you in a good mood."

"I'm not in a good mood," Nathan replied.

"Then before your bad mood gets any worse," said Hagerman. "Since you're at loose ends for a while, I want you to take the sheriff's badge."

"No," Nathan said.

"Just temporarily, until we can find someone else. Do it for the town."

"Why should I?" said Nathan. "All this town's ever done for me is accuse me of getting its sheriff killed."

"Then, by God, do it for me," Hagerman said. "I've influenced the AT and SF to spend a bundle, touting the safety of the railroad and the railroad towns, inviting people to come west. If Dodge is allowed to backslide into a lawless cattle town, I'm going to come off looking like a damn fool."

"Hagerman," said Nathan, "you're *always* out on some

kind of limb. One day I aim to back off and see just how big a fool you can make of yourself. So much natural talent just shouldn't go to waste."

"Then you'll do it?"

"On a temporary basis," Nathan said. "Like I told you, I'm riding to Dakota Territory in the spring, even if you have to board up Dodge and shut down the railroad. Now where do I go to be sworn in?"

"Over to the mercantile," Hagerman said. "I told Langley you'd be there right after breakfast."

Only when Hagerman realized what he had said did he seem a trifle embarrassed, and he didn't miss the hard look in Nathan's eyes. Here was a man it didn't pay to take for granted, and Foster Hagerman knew he was near to stepping over the line.

"Your dog has been fed, sir," said the waiter who brought Nathan's breakfast.

"I'm obliged," Nathan said.

"Just coffee for me," said Hagerman.

Nothing more was said until Nathan had finished eating. Finally Hagerman put down his coffee cup and spoke.

"The AT and SF will continue to pay for your room and meals."

Nathan nodded, shoved back his chair, and stood up. He didn't like Rufus Langley, and he wanted to be sworn in and done with the man. He left the cafe and found Empty waiting for him. It was still early, and the mercantile was deserted. Langley seemed ill at ease, stumbling through the swearing in, even though he had the procedure written down. When he had finished, he dropped the sheriff's badge and the key to the office. Nathan said nothing, waiting.

"Do you ... ah ... understand your duties?" Langley asked.

"Probably better than you," said Nathan. "Have you done anything toward returning the money taken from the Bank of Santa Fe?"

"No," Langley said. "I took possession of it late yesterday, and it's not even eight o'clock in the morning."

"Get it," said Nathan. "I'll see that it's returned, along with a report on Virgil Monroe and of his killing of Santa Fe's Sheriff Monroe."

Langley had transferred the bundles of bills to an enormous sack, and he surrendered it without a word. Nathan couldn't help wondering if the sack contained all the money he had taken off Virgil Monroe's body. Pinning the sheriff's badge on his shirt, Nathan put the office key in his pocket, took the sack of stolen money, and left the store. Reaching the sheriff's office, he unlocked the door and let himself in. The place was familiar to Empty, and he followed. Nathan sat down at the scarred desk, and in a drawer, found paper and pencils. He set about composing a telegram to the Bank of Santa Fe. Finished, he took it and the stolen money to the depot. There he knocked on Foster Hagerman's door.

"It's open," Hagerman said.

"This," said Nathan, dropping the sack on the desk, "I want you to lock in your safe until I'm told what to do with it. Now here's the telegram I want sent to the Bank of Santa Fe."

Nathan left Hagerman's office and walked around town. They might as well get used to him wearing the badge. Time dragged, and at noon, Nathan went to Delmonico's to eat. He wasn't all that hungry; there just was nothing better to do. When he heard the distant whistle of the westbound, he went to the depot to watch the train come in. He recalled the many times Sheriff Harrington had done this very thing, and now he understood the old sheriff's reason. Two men got off the train, and Nathan sized them up immediately as gamblers. Another reason Sheriff Harrington had always met the train, for a good lawman made it his business to be aware of newcomers and their purpose for being in town. On the frontier, many a man's purpose for being in town was his having been run out of the last one. At a distance Nathan followed, watching the new arrivals head for the Long Branch Saloon. It was the most popular of all the saloons in Dodge, and generally the less troublesome, insofar as gamblers were concerned. Empty had quickly developed a dislike for the saloons, and like Cotton Blossom, remained outside when Nathan entered one. Some saloon gambling went beyond poker and faro, with cockfights, dogfights, bare-knuckle boxing, and knife fights. The many times Nathan had been in Dodge, he had avoided these "sporting" saloons, because he disliked the cruelty. Now, wearing a badge, he felt he ought to know what was going on there. Some saloons featuring bloody entertainment had lower or "cellar" rooms for that purpose. One such saloon was the Saratoga, and it was near ten o'clock when Nathan arrived. A few men loitered around the bar and there was a poker game in progress, but most of the commotion came from below.

"What's going on down there?" Nathan asked.

"Dogfight," said the barkeep.

Nathan descended the stairs, and nobody even noticed him. Every eye was on the circular pit in which a pair of bleeding dogs stalked each other. Men shouted and cursed in turn, depending on which of the desperate animals seemed to have an edge. As Nathan's eyes grew accustomed to the poor light, he could see that only one of the animals was a dog. The other was a prairie wolf, or nearly so, and the odds clearly favored the wolf. It was gaunt, had likely been starved for the event, and there was more at stake than who won or lost the deadly match. The dog, when it could no longer defend itself, would be ripped to shreds and eaten.

"This has gone far enough," Nathan said. "I'm calling on the owners of those animals to separate them."

"Don't be a damn fool," somebody shouted. "That wolf will tear a man apart. He'll be shot when this is done."

"It's done now," said Nathan. He drew his Colt and shot the wolf.

"Damn you!" a dozen men shouted.

But Nathan had his back to the wall and had not holstered his Colt. The hapless dog was mortally wounded and would soon bleed to death. Nathan fired again, putting the dog out of its misery.

"I aim to look in on you gents every night," Nathan said. "There'll be no more of this foolishness while I'm wearing the badge in Dodge."

"You won't be wearin' it much longer," said a voice, and a dozen others shouted their agreement.

Nathan said nothing. He backed up the stairs, his Colt steady in his hand. Somebody seized him from behind, and he flung the man over his head, into those who followed him up the stairs. He turned, barely in time to meet the barkeep coming up with a sawed-off shotgun.

"Don't!" Nathan warned.

Slowly the barkeep lowered the weapon, placing it on the bar. The poker game had broken up, and Nathan worked his way toward the door, his back to the wall.

Reaching the door, he paused long enough to issue a warning.

"As long as I wear this badge, there'll be no more fights-to-the-death. If it happens again, somebody's going to the *calabozo*. You, maybe."

"It ain't agin the law," the barkeep said sullenly.

"It is now," Nathan replied. "Spread the word."

The word was spread, and more rapidly than Nathan had expected. Foster Hagerman again joined Nathan for breakfast, and his mood was somewhere between embarrassment and aggravation.

"The town council's meetin' tonight, and they want you there."

"I'll be there," Nathan said. "It wouldn't have anything to do with what I said and did at the Saratoga last night, would it?"

"It would," said Hagerman. "Damn it, you're enforcing laws that don't even exist."

"They should," Nathan replied. "Hagerman, I've killed men that were needful of it, and I will again, but I won't see one animal pitted against another to the death. I didn't want this damn badge, but you insisted. Now you tell Rufus Langley and his gutless council I'll meet with them for just as long as it takes to drop this badge in their laps."

"Nobody's going to ask for your badge, Nathan," said Hagerman.

Nathan said nothing more, and Hagerman departed after finishing his coffee. While the day seemed to drag on forever, there were some gratifying moments. Every woman Nathan met smiled at him, and he believed that was a result of the stand he had taken the night before, in the Saratoga Saloon. One thing bothered him. He felt guilty, as though he had cast Sheriff Harrington in a bad light. Hadn't Harrington been confronted with the same cruel fights-to-the-death that Nathan had witnessed? Was that what it took to become a successful lawman, overlooking popular but shameful activities that violated one's sense of right and wrong? With some misgivings he left the Dodge House a few minutes before seven o'clock, bound for the town hall. He had no idea how many members were on the town council, and was surprised to find there were ten, including Foster Hagerman. Most of them—like Rufus Langley—

were merchants, and they only nodded. Hagerman stood up and cleared his throat.

"On behalf of the council, you are to be commended for your action last night. In all due respect to the late Sheriff Harrington, we failed to stand behind him with laws that he could enforce. We're typical of most towns on the frontier, yielding to the saloons, allowing them to dictate to the rest of us."

"You're all commending me for enforcing laws that don't exist," said Nathan, "because none of you have to face up to the responsibility. You never gave Sheriff Harrington a legal leg to stand on, because you were—and still are—intimidated by the saloon owners. I'm in a position where if I continue what I started last night, every damn saloon owner in town has a perfect right to hate my guts. These fights-to-the-death should be illegal. Are you going to side me, or not?"

"I am," Foster Hagerman said. "I'm making a motion that saloon fights of all kinds be outlawed. Do I hear a second?"

There was no second. Nine men hung their heads, while Hagerman grew furious. He finally spoke, posing a question to the silent council.

"Why? Damn it, when you have a sheriff willing to enforce the law, you won't let him do it. Why?"

"I'll tell you," said Max Rucker, owner of the livery. "We all got wives, Foster, and they see what happened last night as the start of a movement that will eventually close the saloons on Sunday and the whorehouses permanent. We can't do a little without doin' it all; and that'll be the death of us. Come spring, when the herds come up the trail from Texas, you want the saloons dark on Sundays and the whorehouses shut for good? If that happens, it's purely goin' to ruin business."

Hagerman looked helplessly at Nathan, and it was he who spoke.

"I have nothing against saloons being open all night and all day, every day. If a man wants to drink, that's his business. I favor whorehouses, because there's a need for them. The men and women who make them possible are there by their own choosing. But damn it, when two animals are trapped in a pit, being forced to fight for their lives, they have no choice. I can't reform the world, but I aim to stand up for the dumb brutes that can't speak for themselves. Those of you whose women have you haltered and muzzled, I hope you can bust loose long enough to tell them where I stand. I'm my own man, and if I have to enforce the law according to my conscience, then I'll do it."

"Unless somebody has more to say on the subject," Hagerman said, "I'm declaring this meeting adjourned."

Nobody said anything, and Nathan didn't linger. He stepped out the door, and with Empty trotting along beside him, returned to the Dodge House. The saloons wouldn't begin to roar for another two hours, and he intended to rest while he could. There came a knock on the door.

"Identify yourself," Nathan said.

"Hagerman," a voice replied.

Nathan unlocked the door, allowing Hagerman to enter. Without waiting to be asked, he took a chair, leaving Nathan the bed.

"You see how it is," said Hagerman.

"Yes," Nathan said, "but you didn't come here to say that."

"No," said Hagerman. "I came here to tell you that what you said was exactly right. I don't agree with the position they're taking, but I understand it. It all comes back to the old adage that when you give somebody an inch, he'll take a mile. I never saw it coming to all this when I asked you to take the badge, and if you give it up, there'll be no hard feelings on my part."

"I reckon I'll just ride this bronc for a while," Nathan said. "I aim to see that Dodge gets more law than it's accustomed to. When I'm gone, and it falls back into its old hell-raising habits, your town council will be roasted over a slow fire."

Hagerman laughed. "Then you don't aim to close the saloons on Sunday and board up the whorehouses."

"Not until the town council makes them illegal. As a lawman, I'll try and keep men from killing one another without cause, abusing women, or torturing animals. I reckon the wives of the town council will be disappointed, but it's unlikely they'll ever find a man who can enforce the Ten Commandments for fifty dollars a month."

The moment Kurt Graves stepped off the westbound, Nathan suspected trouble. On his right hip the newcomer carried a thonged-down Colt and slung over his shoulder was a saddlebag. He was dressed entirely in black, including his hat. A black leather vest was studded with silver conchas. His belt buckle was a silver wagon wheel. His eyes paused on Nathan's twin Colts, worked their way up to his sheriff's badge, and finally focused on his face. Nathan's eyes never faltered as he went to meet the stranger. He paused a dozen yards away.

"You have business here, I reckon," Nathan said.

"I do," said the stranger. "My own. None of yours."

"I make it mine," Nathan said, "when a hombre looks a mite gun-handy."

"You got a gun ordinance here?"

"No," said Nathan. "I depend on a man's common sense as far as he'll let me. If you pull that iron, you'd better have a damn good reason, or I'll take it away from you."

"I'm Kurt Graves, and I'm not wanted by the law. Nobody's ever took my gun, and nobody ever will. You'd best keep that in mind."

Graves turned away and Nathan watched him out of sight. He looked maybe twenty-one or -two, and being well under six feet, he didn't seem the brawling kind. More likely he relied on his gun, and Nathan wondered how long it would take the little rooster to get himself involved in a shootout. Nathan generally made the rounds of all the saloons before ten o'clock every night, and again shortly before two in the morning, when most of them closed. Reaching the Oasis, he wasn't surprised to find Kurt Graves involved in a poker game. There was some grumbling when Graves won two pots. Nathan wasn't sure that Graves wasn't slick-dealing, but if he was, the little varmint was good at it. Unless somebody called him, it was none of Nathan's business. He had stepped out the door, bound for the Long Branch, when there was a shot from within the Oasis. Nathan was through the saloon door in an instant. A man was slumped over the poker table, a gun in his hand. Graves stood with his back to the wall, his thumb hooked in his gun belt, above the butt of his Colt. Nathan kept his eyes on Graves as he spoke.

"Who drew first?"

"Tidwell did," one of the gamblers said, "and God, he didn't have a chance. He had his gun out, but he was shot dead."

"Graves," Nathan said, "I warned you about pulling that gun. You'd better have a damn good reason."

"Oh, I do, sir," said Graves, with exaggerated politeness. "He called me a cheat, and I never touched my gun until he drew his."

"Is he telling the truth?" Nathan asked.

"Yeah," said one of the gamblers.

"Do any of the rest of you accuse him of cheating?" Nathan persisted.

Nobody said anything. Several men cut their eyes at Kurt Graves, but nobody spoke to Nathan. There was nothing he could do except declare it a case of self-defense. Before he reached the door, he heard Kurt Graves laughing. After making the rounds of the rest of the saloons, Nathan returned to the Dodge House. There he and Empty would rest until time for the rounds at two o'clock in the morning.

When Nathan arrived at Delmonico's for breakfast, he found Foster Hagerman already there. It had become a ritual, Nathan and Sheriff Harrington meeting there. But now that Harrington was gone, Hagerman seemed to have taken his place, a change of which Nathan didn't totally approve. While he liked Hagerman, he had become the spokesman for a less-than-adequate town council. Now Nathan was never sure whether he was meeting Hagerman as a friend or as a go-between for the whining town council.

"Heard about the shooting last night," said Hagerman. "That sort of thing, if it should happen too often, will play hell with the town's image."

"Is that how you feel, or is it the opinion of your silent town council?"

"Mostly that of the council," Hagerman said. "This is the frontier, and you can't fault a man for defending himself. But there are men who enjoy killing, and they justify it by provoking others into a shootout. Kurt Graves may be that kind."

"He may be," said Nathan, "but I can't arrest him as long as it's an even break and there are witnesses. You don't enforce the law by violating it. What does the council think should be done?"

"Hell, they don't know," Hagerman said in exasperation. "They're leaving it all up to you."

"Tell them I'm obliged," said Nathan grimly.

They finished breakfast in silence, but Hagerman had unknowingly touched on the very thing Nathan had been considering. Suppose Kurt Graves continued to antagonize men and gun them down in the name of self-defense? Where would it end? While he was tempted to just order Graves out of town, he had no legal right to do so. Besides, if the gunman refused to leave, it would result in a Mexican standoff, branding Nathan Stone the biggest damn fool between the Trinity and the Yellowstone. There was always a chance that Graves wouldn't repeat his performance of the night before, and with that slight hope, Nathan made his way to the sheriff's office. But that very afternoon, at the Varities Saloon, Kurt Graves gunned down another man. Again there were witnesses and again the claim was self-defense.

"The man's a killer," said Hagerman. "He's legally murdered two men. What are we going to do?"

"You're going to shut up," Nathan said, "before you get the town in an uproar. I aim to make my move tonight. If it fails, plant me alongside Sheriff Harrington and feed my dog."

Kurt Graves seemed to be making the rounds of all the saloons. His third night in Dodge, he drifted into the Long Branch. A four-handed poker game was in progress, and at the sight of Graves, two men folded and moved hurriedly away from the table. The pair remaining were drummers.

"I'm settin' in," said Graves, hauling out a chair.

"Hell," one of the drummers said, "I don't like three-handed poker."

"Keep your seat," said Nathan, taking the chair across from Graves. "I'm buying in."

"I don't play poker with lawdogs," Graves said contemptuously. "Pin a badge on some *pelado,* and he thinks he's got an edge."

"Don't let the badge bother you, Graves," Nathan said. Removing the star, he dropped it into his shirt pocket. "Now, you either play poker or tuck your tail between your legs and get the hell out of here."

Sensing a showdown, men lined the walls, careful to stay out of the potential line of fire. It was a ticklish situation for Kurt Graves, and there were beads of sweat on his forehead. Finally he did exactly what Nathan had expected him to do. Keeping his right hand well away from his Colt,

e shoved his left hand into his pocket and brought out a
andful of double eagles. These he slapped on the table as
n act of defiance.

"Five dollar bet," said one of the drummers. "Table
takes."

Nathan dropped a double eagle on the table and each of
he drummers matched it. The first three hands, Nathan
drew impossible cards. He took his losses, and when it
came his turn to shuffle the deck, he slick-dealt Graves an
unbeatable hand: four aces and a king. It took a moment
for Graves to understand what had happened, and his face
paled, but his money was already in the pot. There were
gasps from the onlookers when they saw the cards. It was
the perfect setup for Nathan to accuse Graves of cheating,
but Nathan spoke not a word. Graves had begun sweating,
but all he could do was rake in the pot. He slid back his
chair and started to get up, only to have one of the drummers speak.

"It's customary to allow the losers a chance to recoup
their losses."

There were hostile faces all around Graves, and across
the table. Nathan Stone's cold blue eyes never wavered.
Graves hunched his chair back up to the table and play
resumed. It seemed Kurt Graves couldn't lose, even without Nathan's help, and he took the next two pots. After he
won a third pot, he had trouble controlling the trembling
of his hands. But Nathan decided it had gone far enough,
and slid back his chair. He spoke softly, but it had the
effect of an explosion.

"Graves, you've been cheating but your luck just ran
out. Draw."

"No," Graves shouted. "You been settin' me up."

"You're a liar, a cheat, and a coward," said Nathan.
"Draw, damn you."

"No," Graves shouted defiantly.

"When the train pulls out of here tomorrow," said Nathan, "you'd better be on it." He stood up, kicking his chair
back under the table.

Somebody laughed, and then everybody did, but it died
away in a gasp. Nathan turned and drew, barely in time.
Graves had drawn, but his slug ripped into the tabletop as
lead from Nathan's Colt slammed into his chest. Graves
fell into his chair, and it topped over backward. Nathan

reloaded his Colt and returned his badge to its position on his shirt. Only then did he speak.

"I'm claiming self-defense. Does anybody dispute that?"

"My God, no," a barkeep exclaimed. "The little side winder come within a whisker of drillin' you in the back."

"A couple of you haul him out of here to the under taker," Nathan said.

Nathan didn't wait to see if they did or didn't. It was time to make the rounds of the other saloons. The shooting had drawn men who hadn't seen the showdown, and the event was recounted by those who had witnessed it.

"God," said a man who had seen Nathan draw, "he's quick as greased lightning, but he's as much a killer as the little varmint he gunned down."

"Most of the town believes you did what had to be done," Foster Hagerman said, when he met Nathan at Delmonico's.

"And what does the rest of it believe?" Nathan asked. "That I'm just a killer with a badge?"

"Nobody's saying that," said Hagerman.

"They're thinking it," Nathan replied. "This is the kind of thing that will be picked up by the newspapers, and there'll be a whole new crop of fast guns looking for me."

"I must admit I haven't considered that side of it," said Hagerman. "I'll speak to the town council and get you out of the public eye as fast as I can."

The days dragged on, and there was no more gun trouble in Dodge. The first week in January 1876, the Dodge town council hired Ellison Cox, an ex-buffalo hunter, to replace Nathan as sheriff. Two days later, Foster Hagerman invited Nathan to his office.

"I suppose you're still planning to ride to Dakota Territory," Hagerman said.

"I am," said Nathan, "and the sooner the better."

"You're still a ways from spring," Hagerman said. "Will you ride south again before you leave for Dakota?"

"I reckon," said Nathan. "How far, and for what purpose?"

"To Fort Elliott. You're to bring back the wagon and the teams that belonged to the Dismukes. The government wants them."

"The government already *has* them," Nathan said. "Fort Elliott *is* the government."

"Fifth Army Headquarters wants them brought here, to Dodge," said Hagerman, "and as for their reasons, don't ask me. I wasn't told, and I'm not about to ask."

CHAPTER 30

Fort Elliott, Texas. January 24, 1876

"In the military, the wheels turn slowly," Captain Selman said. "The sorry episode with the Dismukes took place, I think, last September. I filed a report with Washington and inquired about the disposition of the confiscated wagon and teams. I had heard nothing until three days ago, when I received word the property was being returned to Dodge."

"You haven't searched the wagon, then," said Nathan.

"No," Selman replied, "not beyond discovering they were traveling with a full case of dynamite. We would never search seized civilian wagons unless we were more than a little sure their loads were contraband."

"I don't aim to waste any time getting the teams and wagon back to Dodge," said Nathan.

Nathan and Empty again took supper with the enlisted men, and afterward, for the lack of anything better to do, Nathan rode into Mobeetie, to the saloon. It was crowded, for a Monday night, most of the patrons being soldiers. The one exception was a well-dressed man in a derby hat. While he was dressed like an Easterner, a thonged-down Colt on his right hip belied that appearance. It was still early, and no games of chance were in progress. The women Nathan had brought from Dodge—Mamie, Cora, Winnie, and Eula—recognized Nathan and shouted a greeting. There were other women, one of whom was with the stranger in the derby hat. The barkeep nodded, recognizing Nathan.

"We don't get many civilians in here," the barkeep said, when he brought Nathan's mug of beer. "That's Bat Masterson in the Yankee hat."

"I've heard of him," Nathan said. "Buffalo hunter. Bι the buffalo are gone."

"That they are," said the barkeep, "and that's not wh he's here. That girl with him is Molly Brennan, and he' here to see her. I was hopin' he'd move on before th soldiers at Fort Elliott got off duty."

"I reckon you've had your share of trouble," Nathaɪ said. "Civilians and soldiers just don't mix well, do they?'

"Not in these parts, anyhow. One of the soldiers—Ser geant King—has been more of a nuisance than all the oth ers combined. He spends all his time—when he's not oɪ duty or in the guard house—with Molly Brennan. If hε shows up tonight, while Masterson's with her, God only knows what he'll do."

Nathan didn't know Sergeant King, but knew of him from Captain Selman. It was early, and since Nathan had nothing better to do, he remained at the bar, talking to the friendly barkeep. The troublesome Sergeant King arrived before Nathan had finished a second beer.

"Oh, God," the barkeep groaned, "he's here."

"You in the sissy hat," King bawled, "get up. You're with my woman."

"Soldier," the barkeep said, "this is a saloon, not a matrimony bureau."

But King had a pistol in his hand, and when he fired, the slug struck Masterson in the left arm. The ex-buffalo hunter rolled out of his chair, drawing his Colt, just as King fired a second time. King's slug caught Molly Brennan in the back, and she slumped across the table. From the floor, Masterson fired once, and King stumbled. Dropping the pistol, he caught the back of a chair, but he was dying. Taking the chair with him, he went down and didn't move.*

"My God," said the barkeep, "he's killed Molly."

Masterson got to his feet. His Colt still in his hand, he stood over the dead Sergeant King as though considering shooting the man a second time. Nathan and the barkeep were moving Molly to a couch, when one of the other girls arrived with a blanket. She spread it over the dead girl. Masterson returned his Colt to its holster, and only then did he speak.

*This is the only recorded instance where Bat Masterson actually killed a man.

"I'll ride to the fort and turn myself in, barkeep. I suppose there'll be an investigation and I'll be obliged if those of you who witnessed what happened will speak on my behalf."

"I saw it, Mr. Masterson," the barkeep said. "He shot you before you made a move."

"I saw it the same way," Nathan said, "and I'll go with you to the fort. I consider the commanding officer, Captain Selman, a friend of mine. My name is Nathan Stone."

"I've heard of you," said Masterson, "and I'll be obliged if you'll speak to the captain. I expect we'd better go before he gets word of this through someone else."

It was sound thinking. The echo of the gunfire had barely faded when most of the other soldiers were out the door. In conflicts involving soldiers and civilians, soldiers had been known to protect their own, at the expense of the civilians. Reaching the fort, Nathan had no trouble getting himself and Masterson in to see Captain Selman. Masterson removed his coat, revealing the bloody left sleeve of his shirt, while Nathan explained to the captain what Sergeant King had done. Captain Selman sighed, and it was a moment before he spoke.

"I've seen this coming, but there was nothing I could do. Naturally I'll have to file a report, but with the bartender and Stone as witnesses, it will be routine. Mr. Masterson, if you'll go to the dispensary, your wound will be attended to. You are welcome to stay the night and take breakfast with the enlisted men."

"Thank you, Captain," Masterson said.

"You're welcome to share my camp by the creek," Nathan said, when they had left Selman's office.

"I'm obliged," said Masterson. "I'll be riding on to Dodge in the morning, after Molly has been laid to rest."

"You're welcome to ride with me," Nathan said, "because that's where I'm going."

Nathan built a fire and made coffee, and during the course of the evening, found himself liking Bat Masterson. He was a good listener, and seemed to enjoy Nathan's account of his experiences with the nefarious Dismukes.

"Now," Nathan concluded, "I'm here to return the Dismukes's wagon and teams to Dodge, for reasons only the government knows."

*   *   *

At dawn, the chaplain from Fort Elliott conducting the ceremony, Molly Brennan was laid to rest. Nothing was said about the burial of Sergeant King, nor did Captain Selman have anything further to say to Bat Masterson. Before departing, Nathan took the time to speak to Captain Selman. He tied his grulla behind the wagon, mounted the box, and led out to the north. Masterson rode alongside, while Empty loped ahead. After they had crossed the North Canadian, Masterson galloped ahead. He then rode slowly back, and when he was again riding alongside the wagon, he had a question.

"Is this the way you rode in from Dodge?"

"It is," said Nathan. "Why?"

"You had seven riders trailing you."

"How do you know they were trailing me?"

"Because I didn't see their tracks until we crossed the North Canadian," said Masterson. "That's where they veered off. If they weren't trailing you, why didn't they continue south, the way they were headed?"

"I have no idea," Nathan said, "any more than I know why they'd be trailing me."

"Maybe they know something you don't," said Masterson. "Something about this Dismukes's wagon that makes it so valuable to the government."

"I've been thinking about that," Nathan said. "I learned the Dismukes were wanted by the law in Missouri, but I wasn't told why. There's a case of dynamite, capped and fused, here in the wagon."

"Maybe we can add that to something I learned at Fort Griffin and come up with an answer," said Masterson. "Last August, somewhere north of Sedalia, Missouri, a train was robbed. A military payroll, and a substantial one. While several of the thieves were killed, the payroll—in gold—was never recovered."

"I know what you're leadin' up to," Nathan said, "but I can't picture the Dismukes as bein' smart enough to pull that off."

"I can," said Masterson, "from what you told me about them going after Fort Elliott with dynamite. Outlaws like the James and Younger gangs usually fell a tree across a railroad track or rip out a rail, but how do you reckon this bunch stopped the train and took that payroll near Sedalia?"

"Dynamite?

"Dynamite," said Masterson, "but it went beyond anything sensible men would even consider. They dynamited the track, and without warning, literally blew up the express car. A railroad man died in the express car and two more were gunned down by the outlaws. It appears to have been the most brutal robbery of all time."

"While the Dismukes didn't have the brains to set it up, I'd have to admit the brutal nature of it might have appealed to them. What I find hard to believe is that they managed to get their hands on the gold and get out of Missouri."

"My friend," said Masterson, "I'd bet everything I own—which isn't much—that this wagon has a fortune beneath the wagon box. I'd say the government only suspects it, but the seven hombres that trailed you to the North Canadian are dead sure of it."

"Your idea fits the little we know of the facts," Nathan said, "and you've come about as far with me as you can afford to. The sensible thing for you to do is to ride on. This bunch—if they're still trailing me—won't bother you."

"Given a choice, a man seldom does the sensible thing," said Masterson. "If you were alone, they'd ride you down, flank you, and shoot you off the box. I have a .50-caliber Sharps buffalo gun in the boot, and I promise you, I can hit a moving target from as far away as I can see it. So I'll just ride along with you, unless you object."

"I'm pleased and honored to have you," Nathan said. "Your being here will buy us some time. They'll wait until we stop for the night, and come after us in the dark, but we have an edge."

"The dynamite?"

"That," said Nathan, "and Empty, my dog. He'll warn us when they're coming. We're outnumbered now, but you'd be surprised how a couple sticks of dynamite with short fuses can even the odds."

"How well I know," Masterson said. "I learned to use the stuff when my brother and me was clearing right-of-way for the AT and SF. Later, when we took to huntin' buffalo in west Texas, the dynamite we had left we took with us. One day the Comanches jumped us, and there must have been fifty to the four of us, and not a shred of cover. We all had our Sharps, but after the first volley,

they'd have ridden us down before we could have loaded
They knew it and we knew it, but they didn't know abou
the dynamite. There was still a few coals from our breakfas
fire, and we all grabbed us a stick of dynamite, waitin' fo
'em to attack. When they did, they split up and come at u
from two directions, so we split up, two of us facing eacl
group of attackers. Just as they were about to cut down or
us, we touched our fuses to coals of fire and flung our
dynamite."

"Bad medicine," Nathan said.

"Lord Almighty," said Masterson, "you wouldn't believe
our luck. We unhorsed about half of them, including their
medicine man, and all the horses ran like hell wouldn't
have it. First time I ever seen Comanches afoot, running
for their lives. My God, we guarded the rest of that dynamite like it was gold, and the Comanches never bothered
us again."

Nathan laughed, appreciating the scenario, and feeling
better about their precarious situation. Without bragging,
Bat Masterson had made it clear he could take care of
himself. The day wore on, and they saw nobody, but that
meant little. Their pursuers—if they were being pursued—
wouldn't risk being seen on the flat Kansas plain. They
would know the limitations of a wagon, and could easily
catch up under the cover of darkness.

"With a wagon, we're making good time," Nathan said.
"We're nearing a spring that's a good stopping place. I
reckon we'll cook us some grub, boil us some coffee, and
get the fire out before dark."

"But saving a coal or two for the dynamite," said
Masterson.

They finished supper well before dark, and leaving the
spring, Nathan climbed to the rim of the arroyo, where he
searched the plains to the south. He saw nothing, forcing
him to consider the possibility that his and Masterson's suspicions were groundless. But Nathan didn't believe that.
The stolen payroll hadn't been recovered, and what more
likely a hiding place than beneath the bed of the Dismukes's wagon?

"They won't show until it's good and dark," Masterson
said. "Do you aim to challenge them, or wait until they cut
loose with their guns?"

"In situations like this," said Nathan, "I generally let

them open the ball, and then fire at their muzzle flashes. But there's only two of us, seven of them, and a chance they won't all cut loose with their guns. For that reason, we're fortunate to have the dynamite. It's the only way we can be sure that none of them escape. I reckon we'd better move our bedrolls well away from the wagon, and in case they wait for moonrise, give them something to shoot at."

Their bedrolls were positioned beneath the arroyo's overhang, where they would be in shadow even after moonrise. Blankets were arranged so that they appeared to conceal sleeping men, and with the arroyo's rim directly above, the attackers would be forced to fire from the opposite rim.

"Now," said Nathan, scooping up some coals with a piece of bark, "we'll settle down on that opposite bank and wait for them to come looking for us. Bring four sticks of the dynamite from the wagon."

Empty followed them to their position, remaining only long enough to be sure that was where they intended to remain. He then quickly disappeared.

"He knows we're waiting for somebody," said Masterson.

"He does," Nathan said, "and he'll let us know they're coming long before they're even close."

Nathan broke up bits of bark, keeping their coals live. Not only might a sulfur match fail them at a critical moment, its flame could draw fire before they had a chance to light and throw the dynamite. The moon rose, and still there was no sign of the attackers or of Empty. There was no talk, for in the silence of the night, the slightest sound might carry for a great distance. When Empty returned, he growled once, deep in his throat. Nathan kept his eyes on the farthest rim of the arroyo. The men would have to be afoot, lest their horses betray their presence. When they came, they were belly-down, their movement almost imperceptible. Nathan shielded the glowing coals with his hat, lest the sparking of the lighted dynamite fuses draw attention. He and Masterson lighted their fuses at the same time, just as guns roared on the farthest rim. When the dynamite exploded, it seemed like an echo of the blazing guns. There was no more gunfire. Empty was gone, and Nathan did not make a move until the dog returned. Empty barked once.

"We can go over there now," Nathan said.

Nathan and Masterson rounded the upper end of the arroyo, above the spring, and when they reached the opposite bank, found six dead men. Their features were clear enough in the moonlight.

"We lost one of them," Masterson said. "He might have stayed with the horses."

"Maybe," said Nathan. "I'll back-trail them in the morning. When it comes to this, I don't like leaving loose ends. I reckon I'll have to search this bunch. There might be some evidence that will tie them in with the robbery. I don't recognize any of them. Do you?"

"No," Masterson said.

Nathan's search produced nothing except a few gold eagles and double eagles, along with pocket knives, plug tobacco, and several bags of Durham. Every man was armed, and all had died with their Colts in their hands.

"I'm tempted to pile them all in the wagon and deliver them to Dodge," said Nathan, "but we're still three days out. Even if we could stand the smell, half the buzzards in Kansas would be trailing us."

The rest of the night passed uneventfully, and after breakfast, Nathan back-trailed the six men involved in the ill-fated ambush. There had been seven riders, and the seventh man had remained with the horses. When it had become obvious the bushwhacking had gone sour, he had ridden away, taking the extra horses with him. Nathan rode back to the wagon where Masterson waited.

"They left one man with the horses," Nathan said, "and when he lit out, he took the extra horses with him,. He's ridin' east."

"He'll double back to Indian Territory or ride on to Wichita," said Masterson. "One man leadin' six horses wouldn't dare show up in Dodge."

Dodge City, Kansas. January 29, 1876

"I'm going to stable my horse and take a room at the Dodge House," Masterson said, "and then I'm going to Delmonico's for some town grub."

"I'll join you there," said Nathan, "after I rid myself of this wagon."

Quickly he told Hagerman of the attempted ambush, suggesting the possibility that the stolen military payroll might be concealed beneath the wagon box.

"My God," Hagerman said, "I can't afford that kind of

responsibility. I'll have to send some telegrams, get some answers . . ."

"The first thing you'd better do is get that wagon under lock and key or post some armed men," said Nathan. "Of those seven varmints trailing me, intending to take the wagon, one escaped. And there may be others."

"Would you . . ."

"No," Nathan said, "I wouldn't. I aim to have a good meal, a bath, and a good night's sleep. Tomorrow morning, I aim to ride north, to Dakota Territory."

Leaving his horse at the livery, Nathan went on to Delmonico's. He was hungry, and the bath would have to wait. Empty loped on ahead, for the cooks knew him. Masterson was already there, and Nathan took a chair across the table from him.

"A mite early for supper," Nathan said, "but come suppertime, we can eat again."

"Not me," said Masterson. "I'll be taking the train to Kansas City in the morning, and I'll be turning in early."

Muted by distance came the moan of the westbound's whistle, and by the time the waiter brought the steaks, the train rolled in to the depot with a clanging of its bell and a hiss of steam.

"I reckon I'll go on back to the Dodge House with you," said Nathan. "I don't dare go back to Hagerman's office. He'll be lookin' for somebody to take a scattergun and bed down beside that wagon until somebody relieves him of it."

When they reached the front door of the Dodge House, Empty growled.

"There's somebody waiting inside the door," Nathan said, drawing his Colt. "You, in there. Identify yourself."

"I'm Vivian Stafford," said a feminine voice, "and I want to speak to Nathan Stone."

"I'm Nathan Stone. Step outside."

She had red hair that curled to her shoulders, blue eyes, and a sprinkling of freckles. Her paisley dress had faded with age and many washings, while her battered carpetbag was almost flat.

"This is Bat Masterson, a friend of mine," said Nathan.

"Pleased, ma'am," Masterson said, tipping his hat. "Now, if you'll excuse me . . ."

He entered the Dodge House, closing the door behind him.

"Ma'am," said Nathan, "if you haven't eaten, we can go to Delmonico's. I've already had supper, but I can stand some more coffee. Then we'll talk."

"No," she said, "I . . ."

"I'm buying," Nathan said. "Come on."

Empty followed, uncertain as to why they were returning to the cafe so soon. He held back when they went inside. Suspecting the girl's reluctance might stem from a lack of money, Nathan ordered for her. The waiter brought their coffee, and she held the cup with both hands to still their trembling. Nathan didn't press her, and when food was brought, she seemed to forget all about him. Not until she had finished eating did she finally speak.

"Thank you. I suppose you think I've never had a decent meal in my life, and that's near the truth. I hadn't eaten in four days. I had just enough money for a ticket to Dodge City."

"You came here looking for me?"

"No," she said. "I'd never heard of you. I came west looking for my brother, and Mr. Hagerman at the depot said perhaps you could help me."

"That's generous of him," said Nathan, "but how can I help?"

"You're going to the new gold strike in Dakota Territory. I'm hoping my brother will be there."

"Ma'am . . ."

"Call me Vivian, please."

"Vivian," Nathan said, "none of this is making any sense. Why don't you start at the beginning and tell me everything? I don't mean to meddle in your business, but if you're going to involve me, then I want the straight of it."

"I'm from the Virginia side of Bristol," she said. "I was sixteen when Harley, my only brother, joined the confederacy. We had given him up for dead, when he finally returned in the summer of 1866. But he was changed, bitter, uncaring. He had been wounded, left for dead, and had been confined to a Yankee prison for months. He came home to find our father in poor health, Mother losing her sight, and us living off the little we were able to grow in the garden. He went west, seeking his fortune in the gold and silver mines, but we never saw him again. Father died in seventy-three and mother a year later."

"So you stayed with them until their deaths."

"Yes," she said. "There was nobody else. I have no one else except Harley."

"My God," said Nathan, "he's been gone ten years. He could be ..."

"Dead," she finished. "But I must know."

"Vivian, there are mines all over the frontier, from the silver mines of southern New Mexico Territory to the gold fields of Montana. You haven't been to any of them, so why the rush to get to the new diggings in Dakota Territory?"

"I must start somewhere," she said, "and you're going there."

"You left home after your mother died," said Nathan, "so it's taken you two years to work your way this far west."

"Yes," she said, "and I know what you're getting at, so I might as well tell you. The day I left Virginia, I had only the clothes on my back. I begged food when I could, went hungry when I had to, and I learned a hard lesson. A woman alone becomes a drudge or a whore, and you don't earn traveling money scrubbing floors."

She looked at Nathan as though she expected him to be shocked or outraged, but he said nothing. She continued.

"I know it's asking a lot, and I have no money, but I'm willing to pay in the only way that I ... I can, Mr. Stone."

"Call me Nathan," he said, "and I won't accept the kind of payment you're offering. I understand what you've had to do, and your reasons for it, and I don't condemn you. But when it comes to a woman, she has to want me and I have to want her. It's the kind of thing that can't be bought or sold."

For a long moment, unbelieving, she just looked at him. Then she buried her face in her hands. It was Nathan who finally broke the silence.

"Vivian, I didn't say I wouldn't help you."

"But I have no money," she said, as the tears began.

"I'm asking for none," said Nathan. "Suppose I take you to Dakota Territory, to the gold diggings, and you're unable to find your brother? You'll still be alone in likely one of the rawest towns on the frontier."

"Beyond that, I won't ask anything of you," she said.

"Tomorrow," said Nathan, "I'll have Hagerman send a few telegrams. The AT and SF is the carrier for most of the mines in Colorado, and it may be possible to reach

some of the superintendents of various mines. If your
brother came west with an eye toward the mines, the nearest ones would be in Colorado, and we might find some
word of him there."

"I don't understand you, Nathan Stone. You're spending
your time and your money to help me, and when I try to
pay in the only way I can, you don't want me. It makes
me feel old, ugly, and used."

"I'm not saying I don't want you," said Nathan. "I'm
saying I don't want you as payment for helping you find
your brother. If what you're offering me is only a means
of paying your debts, then I don't want it. Is that so hard
to understand?"

"Not when you put it that way. The war started when I
was barely sixteen, and I . . . I had no experience with men,
until I left Virginia. I don't know how to be a woman, to
. . . have a man want me for anything besides . . . that."

"I'll get you a room at the Dodge House," said Nathan.
"We may be here several days waiting for replies to
those telegrams."

"I appreciate your kindness, but I don't like being a burden. I could sleep on the floor of your room. I've slept on
the ground."

"So have I," Nathan said, "and it helps me appreciate a
bed when I can get one. I'll rent you a room, with your
own bed."

Nathan was awake well before first light, and shaved by
a coal oil lamp. He knocked on Vivian's door and received
a sleepy response. Waiting awhile, he knocked again, and
when she didn't answer, he tried the knob. The door
opened, and he found her sitting on the bed, stark naked,
her head in her hands. Thinking something was the matter
with her, he stepped inside, closing the door.

"Vivian, is anything wrong?"

"Oh, God, I was just so tired. I didn't realize it until I
lay down. I don't want to get up, but I know I must."

"Yes," Nathan said, "unless you don't want breakfast."

"You don't know just how much I want it. Yesterday
you bought me the first decent meal I'd had in months."

"Knock on my door when you're ready," said Nathan.

"Sit down," she said. "If you leave me alone, I might go
back to sleep."

CHAPTER 31

Foster Hagerman sent telegrams to the mine superintendents with whom the AT and SF had dealings, and only one response proved helpful. Nathan and Vivian were in the Dodge House drinking coffee when Hagerman brought the reply from the Silver Slipper, south of Denver. It read:

Harley Stafford shot and killed a miner stop. Served two years in territorial prison stop. Released February last year.

"Now we know he's probably not in Colorado," said Nathan.

"Where are the next nearest mines?"

"From Denver," Nathan said, "one direction's about equal to another. There are mines in Nevada, a few in southern Arizona and New Mexico territories, and a large number to the north, in Montana Territory."

"Then there's no way of knowing where he might have gone, where he is."

"No," said Nathan. "Probably the only reason there was a record of him in Colorado was because of the killing and a prison sentence. If I'd been in his boots, I'd have lit out for Montana."

"So that's probably where he is now."

"I doubt it," Nathan said. "While the diggings there were prime in sixty-four and sixty-five, that's been ten years. I reckon it'd be slim pickings, for a hombre new to the territory, with hopes of staking a claim. We've eliminated Colorado, and if he's interested in mining, what would be more promising than a new strike?"

"Which would take him to the Dakotas," she said excitedly.

"It looks more promising," said Nathan, "assuming that he's left Colorado. Tomorrow we'll ride out. That is, if you can ride. Can you?"

"Yes, but I . . ."

"Need a horse, a saddle, boots, and riding clothes," he finished.

"Yes," she said. "All I have to my name is that long dress, and I'd as soon straddle a horse naked as to ride in that."

"We'll get you some Levi's and flannel shirts," said Nathan, "and you'll need a heavy coat. When we reach the diggings, we'll be five hundred miles farther north."

They went to Rufus Langley's mercantile and bought everything Vivian needed except a horse and saddle. There were two pairs of Levi's, two flannel shirts, wool socks, boots with pointed toes and undershot heels, a hat, and a sheepskin-lined coat. Nathan bought copies of the Kansas City and St. Louis newspapers, suspecting there would be none in the Dakotas, far from the railroads. At the livery, Nathan bought a sĕcondhand saddle and a bay horse.

"My God," Vivian said, "you've spent almost two hundred dollars on me."

"Only for things you need," said Nathan.

They left Vivian's purchases at the Dodge House and went to Delmonico's for supper. Empty had begun to accept Vivian, and trotted alongside them. While they waited for their meal, they read the newspapers Nathan had bought.

"Well, I never would have believed it," Nathan said, as he read a story in the St. Louis paper. "Wild Bill Hickok's married."

"There are worse things that can happen to a man," said Vivian. "Do you know him?"

"Yes," said Nathan. "I know him well. According to this paper, he's in Saint Louis, and plans to take an expedition to Dakota Territory, to the gold fields."

"Perhaps you'll see him there," Vivian said. "It sounds like an exciting place."

"I've never been to a gold-crazy boomtown," said Nathan. "God knows who we'll find there. Tell me something about Harley, your brother."

"He was seventeen when he went to war, and when he came back, he didn't talk about it. He was moody, and he walked with a limp. He was wounded during one of the last big battles, before Lee's surrender. When he got home, for the little time he stayed, he almost never slept. He'd sit on the porch way into the night, playing the French harp. His favorite song was 'Barbara Allen,' and he played it over and over."

" 'Barbara Allen!' " Nathan cried. "Redheaded as a woodpecker and always blowin' on his harp. By God, Vivian, I *knew* him, but not by his name. He was in my company, but not in my platoon. Because of that old song, everybody called him 'Barb.' The Yanks purely gave us hell, and his platoon got it the day ahead of mine. We were told his platoon had been wiped out to the last man."

"But not Harley," said Vivian. "His wounds must have been terrible, but he wouldn't talk about them. A few days after he came home, I slipped away and found him bathing in the creek. His legs, from the knees down, were no more than skin stretched over the bone. There were scars all over him, with a large one on his back extending down to his left side."

"Saber wound," said Nathan. "God, I didn't have any wounds, compared to his."

"I'm so excited that you actually knew Harley," she said. "It makes me feel closer to him, just being with you."

"We should get back to the Dodge House," said Nathan. "We'll need to turn in early so we can get an early start in the morning."

"I'm ashamed of myself, being such a burden," she said. "I told you I could sleep on the floor in your room. . . ."

"Enjoy the bed while you can, because we'll be sleeping on the ground, probably from Hays to the Dakotas."

Empty growled once, just loud enough for Nathan to hear, and he was wide awake. His gun belt hung on the head of the bed, and quietly he drew one of the Colts. There was a soft knock on the door.

"Who is it?" Nathan asked.

"Vivian."

He got up, not lighting the lamp, for he wore only his socks. Opening the door just enough for her to enter, he locked it behind her.

"I'm cold," she said, "and I don't want to spend the night alone."

He said nothing, and he could hear the whisper of cloth as the dress slid to the floor. She came to him, trembling, and he held her tight. Their lips met once, twice, three times, and when he turned back to the bed, she didn't hesitate . . .

*   *   *

When Nathan awoke, the sun was streaming in through the window, and Empty sat by the door.

"My God," Nathan said, "it must be noon."

"We still didn't sleep much," said Vivian. "It took a while for me to get warm."

"It did, for a fact," Nathan said.

"I don't care how long it took," she replied, "because it was the first time for me."

"But you said . . ."

"My first time to do it because I wanted to," she said. "I'll never sell myself again, if I starve."

"Are you warm enough now?" he asked.

"Not really," she said. "Are you going to stir up the fire again?"

"I might as well. We'll still reach Hays before dark."

Hays City, Kansas. February 4, 1876

Vivian leaned forward, backward, and then from one side to the other. When they finally reached Hays—a distance of not quite fifty miles—the girl all but fell off the bay.

"Damn it," Nathan said, "you told me you could ride."

"I can . . . could," she said, "but it's been years. When Harley went to war, he took our only saddle horse. The Yankees took our mules."

"I'll get us a room for the night," said Nathan, "and then I'll rub you down with sulfur salve. At least you'll be able to sit down to eat, and by tomorrow you'll be able to ride again."

Nathan stretched her out, belly-down, across the bed. He then rubbed sulfur salve into all her saddle sores, while she groaned. But after being out of the saddle for a while, the salve soothed her sores enough so that she could sit down and enjoy supper. When it was time to turn in for the night, Nathan again applied sulfur salve.

"I'm not going to be good company tonight," she said.

"I'm not expecting you to be," said Nathan. "I've never seen so many saddle sores at one time, in the same place. Most folks get used to it, after a day or two, but before we ride out of here, I'll get two more tins of sulfur salve."

"I've never had anybody fuss over me like this," she said. "I was twenty-four before I was with men, and I can't imagine any of them caring enough to rub salve into my sore behind."

"They might have if you had been riddled with saddle sores," said Nathan, "because you wouldn't have been able to lie on your back."

She stiffened, and it took a moment for Nathan to realize what he had implied.

"I'm sorry, Vivian. I shouldn't have said that."

"Why not? It's true. A whore makes her living on her back."

"Damn it," Nathan shouted, "you said you were putting all that behind you. If I'm not thinking of you in that light, why must you think of yourself that way?"

"I don't know," she sobbed. "You've been decent to me since the day I met you, and I suppose I . . . I just don't feel deserving of it."

"Then you need to rid yourself of that feeling before you face your brother," Nathan said, "unless you're prepared to tell him all you've told me."

"Oh, God," she cried, "I could never do that. Harley has always been so fiercely and unwaveringly proud; if he didn't kill me, he'd disown me."

"Then Harley has some growing up to do," said Nathan. "My little sister was raped and murdered by renegades when she was just sixteen, while I was with the Confederacy. If she had managed to stay alive, I wouldn't care what she had done, she would still be my sister."

"When we find Harley—if we find him—I hope you'll stay with us for a while. He's in need of a friend, unless things have changed since I last saw him."

"I reckon I'll be around for a spell," Nathan said. "I haven't seen Bill Hickok in a long time. There was an unfortunate incident in 1871, when he shot and killed his own deputy, and as far as I know, he hasn't worn a lawman's star since. Bill's a hard drinker, and I get the feeling he may be nearing the end of the trail."

Despite the sulfur salve, Vivian was stiff and sore when it was time to mount up and leave Hays. Nathan helped her to mount, and she groaned as she settled into the saddle. He stopped often, presumably to rest the horses, but mostly to allow the girl to dismount and walk out some of her misery.

"God," she said, as they approached a swift-running creek, "if it wasn't February, I'd strip and jump in there."

"The wind's out of the northwest," said Nathan, "and by dark, it'll be downright cold. The next town will be North Platte, Nebraska, if my memory serves me right. It's maybe a hundred and seventy miles north. There we'll have us a bed for the night, and a chance to replenish our grub. If you do a lot of riding on the frontier, you have to develop a taste for beans, bacon, and coffee. There won't be much else, unless you take along a packhorse."

"Until my backside gets used to this saddle," she said, "everything else takes second place, including food."

Despite Vivian's difficulties, Nathan estimated that their first day out of Hays, they had covered seventy miles. They made their camp near a spring, on the lee side of a hill, out of reach of the chill night wind. They remained dressed except for their hats and boots, combining their blankets for extra warmth.

North Platte, Nebraska. February 8, 1876

North Platte was strictly a railroad town, owning its very existence and its survival to the Union Pacific. A westbound was departing as they rode into town.

"We'll find a livery and have the horses seen to," Nathan said. "No larger than North Platte is, we can walk to the hotel and the cafes."

"I'll be glad to walk," said Vivian, "if my legs still work. Let's find the hotel first. I may just forget all about eating."

But after resting, she changed her mind, as her misery had begun to subside. Reaching a cafe, Nathan arranged to have Empty fed. Being strangers in town, Nathan and Vivian drew some attention, most of it unwelcome. A man got up from a nearby table and approached. He was gray haired and wore town clothes, including a tie and boiled shirt.

"I'm Bradford Scott," he said, "editor of the *North Platte Journal,* and I never forget a face. Haven't I met you before?"

"No," said Nathan shortly.

"Ah," Scott said triumphantly, "now I remember. An etching in the *Kansas City Liberty-Tribune.* You're Nathan Stone, the gunfighter."

"I'm Nathan Stone," said Nathan coldly, "and I don't claim any titles."

"Ah, but you should," Scott said. "You're a legend on the frontier. Tell me something I can print. Anything."

"All newspapermen worry the hell out of folks who only want to be left alone," said Nathan. "Now, vamoose, damn it."

The rest of the patrons in the cafe had heard, and they all laughed. Except for one rider who had a Colt thonged to his right hip. He finished his coffee and left the cafe, but lingered outside, near the corner of the building. He waited until Nathan and Vivian left the cafe, and then issued his challenge.

"Nathan Stone, I'm callin' you out."

"Not until the lady returns to the cafe," said Nathan.

"No," Vivian cried, "no."

"Back to the cafe," said Nathan, his voice cold and brittle. "Now."

She obeyed, standing behind the door so that she could see through the glass pane.

Nathan's eyes never left those of his adversary, for they would warn him when the deadly moment arrived. Nathan judged him to be maybe nineteen. Maybe not even that.

"You're a fool, boy."

"I'm not a boy, damn you," the kid snarled. "I aim to beat you."

"When you're ready, then," Nathan said.

Nathan waited until the last possible second to draw, and his hand didn't move until the kid had cleared leather. Nathan fired once, and the kid stumbled backward. His Colt roared, the slug kicking up dust at his feet. For an agonized second, he seemed suspended, on his young face a look of surprise. Then he folded like an empty sack, his pistol still clutched in his hand. Swiftly Nathan ejected the spent shell from his Colt, reloading the empty chamber. In an instant, Vivian was by his side, weeping. Everybody, including the cook, spilled out of the cafe.

"Is there a sheriff in town?" Nathan asked.

"Otis Babcock," somebody said. "Here he comes now."

Babcock looked at the dead man and then at Nathan. Nathan said nothing, waiting.

"Who the hell started this?" Babcock demanded.

"The kid," they all responded in a single voice. "He drew first."

"Self-defense, then," said Babcock, turning on Nathan.

"Yes," Nathan said. "He pushed it."

"I reckon I can't contest that, but I want you out of here, just as quick as you're able to saddle up and ride. You're bad medicine."

"I'm also minding my own business and I have a room at the hotel," said Nathan. "I've broken no law, and I'll be here for the night. Now, if you have another hombre aiming to gain himself a reputation at my expense, you can talk some sense into him or measure him for a pine box."

With that, he took Vivian's arm and hustled her toward the hotel. Empty brought up the rear, knowing there had been trouble, not trusting these strangers. Most of those who had witnessed the gunfight were relating the details to those who had missed it. Scott, the newspaper editor, was in his glory. Nathan and Vivian reached the hotel, and when they were safely in their room, Nathan locked the door.

"My God," Vivian cried, "what did he have against you? What had you done to him?"

"Nothing," said Nathan. "He wanted to prove his gun was faster than mine."

"But he was only a boy."

"A boy with a gun," Nathan said.

"That wasn't the first time, was it?"

"No," said Nathan, "and it won't be the last. Not until I come up against the hombre whose gun *is* faster than mine."

"You're living in the very shadow of death."

"I reckon," he said, "but it's better than the alternative."

The wind had risen, and sleet rattled against the windowpanes. Nathan hadn't lighted the lamp, and he went to the window and looked out. Dirty gray clouds had moved in and the blackness of the night attested to the lack of moon and stars.

"There'll be snow before morning, Vivian. Unwelcome as I am in this town, I don't aim to ride out in a blizzard. Winter can be hell on the high plains, with the temperature dropping to forty below zero. We'll just have to make the best of it. Let's begin by getting to bed before it turns colder."

The storm struck with a vengeance during the night, and by morning, the snow and the cold had an icy grip on the high plains. The wind howled mournfully.

"God, it's cold in here," said Vivian. "My ears are like ice."

"Imagine what it's like outside," Nathan said.

"I don't want to think about it. Let's just stay here."

"We can't," said Nathan. "We have to eat, and Empty needs to go outside."

"So do I," she said, "but I'm not baring my behind in this kind of cold."

"There's the chamber pot," said Nathan. "That's the best you're likely to get, unless you aim to fight your way to the outhouse."

"I'll take the pot," she said, "and blizzard or not, I'm hungry. Besides, your poor dog is miserable. He wants out."

"Won't do him much good," said Nathan. "I look for the snow to be so deep, he can't hoist a leg."

The snow was deep, and it would be drifted much deeper at higher elevations. In the mountainous Dakota Territory, a horse wouldn't stand a chance. A path had been shoveled from the hotel to the outhouse and from the hotel to the cafe across the street. The wind swept in from the west, bringing with it more snow. The stove in the cafe roared, while a fire crackled in the fireplace. There was an enormous coffeepot, and one of the cooks made the rounds, refilling tin cups. One of the cooks who had fed Empty paused to speak to Nathan.

"Maybe I'm out of line, but there's some things you should know. The kid that forced the fight yesterday was Dobie Sutton. He's got two brothers, Dal and Dent, and there's their Ma, Subrina. They're the kind, if you cut one, they all bleed. They're hell on wheels, the lot of 'em. That's why Sheriff Babcock wanted you out of town. The rest of 'em will likely be after you."

"I'm obliged," said Nathan.

"God," Vivian said, "you only defended yourself. Can't the sheriff protect you from the others?"

"No," said Nathan, "and I don't expect him to. The law offers no protection, because these family clans are devilishly persistent, and they're all alike. Hurt one, and you have to fight the rest of them. You never know where the next bullet is coming from."

"If it wasn't for this damn blizzard, we could just ride on."

"Hell, it does me no good to ride on," Nathan said. "If there's settling to be done, I'd as soon settle it here. We'll wait out this storm right here in the hotel, and if this Sutton bunch wants my hide, they're welcome to try and take it. But I don't want you near me, out in the open. You'll cross to the cafe first, and I'll follow. When we're done, you'll go on across to the hotel, and I'll follow."

"I don't like it," she said. "Get me a gun and I'll stay with you."

"No," said Nathan. "I'm obliged to you for feeling that way, but I won't have them shoot you, trying to get to me."

When they were ready to leave the cafe, Nathan sent Vivian out first. She crossed to the hotel, and with Empty at his heels, Nathan followed. Visibility was poor, with the wind-whipped snow, and nothing happened. Nathan and Vivian took to the bed for warmth. They would take only breakfast and supper as long as they remained in North Platte. In the late afternoon there came a knock on their door. Nathan cocked one of his Colts and then issued a challenge.

"Who's there?"

"Otis Babcock. I want to talk to you."

"I can't see that we have anything to talk about," Nathan said. "I'm going nowhere until this storm blows itself out."

"I don't expect you to," said Babcock, "and that's not what I want to talk about. I'll wait in the lobby, so as not to disturb your missus."

"Damn it," Nathan said. "I'll have to go talk to him."

He got up, and with chattering teeth, got into his clothes. He stomped into his boots, strapped on his guns, and shrugged into his coat. Closing the door behind him, he made his way to the hotel lobby. A red-hot stove roared, and there Babcock waited. Nathan took a chair with his back to the wall, waiting for Babcock to speak. He did.

"I reckon you think I'm just an ornery old mossyhorn that likes to make it hard on folks, but that ain't the case. I got to live here, and it's a mite easier when there's nobody shootin' or bein' shot. In case you ain't found out, the Sutton kid you salted down is the youngest of three brothers. Dal and Dent is as bad or worse than Dobie was, while their Ma, old Subrina, is a ring-tailed wampus kitty. She carries a double barrel, sawed-off scattergun that'd drop a moose."

"I've heard most of that," said Nathan. "What are you leading up to?"

"For your own protection, until this storm blows over and you can leave town, I want to lock you up."

"I appreciate your concern, Sheriff, but I can protect myself. Put me behind bars, and I'd be fair game. Let me remind you that when I gunned down Dobie Sutton, he was about to shoot me. If you're so concerned with keeping the peace, I have a suggestion. Just lock up the Suttons until I'm gone."

"That's impossible," said Babcock.

"Then allow me to suggest something," Nathan said. "You go to the Suttons. Tell them I'm not going to be pushed around. If they come after me—one at a time or all at once—I'll defend myself. And I'll make you this promise, Sheriff. I'll not harm a one of them, unless I'm forced to. If they come shooting, I'll shoot back, and I don't miss."

Sheriff Babcock sighed. "That's your last word?"

"It is," said Nathan. "You keep that bunch away from me, and there'll be no trouble."

He turned away, and when he returned to his room, the door was standing open and Vivian was gone. He reached the lobby just as Babcock was about to leave.

"Damn you," Nathan shouted, seizing the sheriff by the shirtfront. "Vivian's gone. You lured me away so they could take her."

"I don't know what you're talkin' about," Babcock said. "If they took her, it wasn't my doing. Come on, I'll help you find her. With all this snow, there'll be tracks."

The sky was still overcast and gray, and the storm wasn't over, but the snow had dwindled to a few flurries. There were two sets of footprints leading from the back door of the hotel. Deep as the snow was, the abductors had brought horses, and their tracks were easily followed. Few had ventured out into the snow, and it soon became obvious the trail was leading away from town.

"By God," said Babcock, "there ain't nothin' up this way but the railroad depot."

"I reckon it has a stove," Nathan said. "All they need is a place to hole up just long enough to force me out into the open. Then they'll offer to swap Vivian for me."

"You don't have to agree to that," said Babcock. "If they harm the woman, they'll be breaking the law."

"Sheriff, before this day's done, you're goin' to learn tha some folks have no respect for the law. Get in the way and this bunch will shoot you as quick as they'll shoot me."

Almost immediately a Winchester cut loose and a slug sang over their heads. From the depot came a taunting voice.

"You're in bad company, Sheriff. This ain't your fight Get on back to town."

"You Suttons pay attention," Sheriff Babcock shouted "You have a woman in there who's done nothing to you Let her go, or I'm placing you all under arrest."

"Not by a jugful," the voice shouted. "We want the bas tard that gunned down Dobie, and when we get him, we turn his woman loose."

"Dobie was gunned down in a fair fight, a fight that he started," Sheriff Babcock shouted, "and I'll have no more shooting as a result of that. You're breaking the law."

"You got just five minutes to start that gun-throwe walkin' this way," the voice shouted in response. "You don't, then we'll strip this little gal an' do some interesting things with her."

"Subrina Sutton," Sheriff Babcock shouted, "are you i there?"

"I'm here," she replied.

"You and your sons are breaking the law," Babcoc shouted. "This is your last chance to back off and com out of it clean."

"You heard our terms," Subrina shouted back. "You send us that killer, and we'll turn the woman loose."

"I'll come," Nathan shouted, "but only if Dal and Den have the sand to face me. Dobie was a shorthorn, full o brag, but not a grain of sand in his craw. I'm guessing i runs in the family, that his two big brothers are all mouth Am I right?"

"Hell, no," a voice bawled. "Start walkin'. We'r comin'."

"My God," said Babcock, "you're not going to fac them both?"

"I am," Nathan said. "There's no other way."

CHAPTER 32

"Them's long odds," Babcock said. "Better if I side you."

"No," said Nathan, "I promised to face them alone. while their attention is on me, try to circle around and disarm the Sutton woman."

The Suttons had begun their walk, one on either side of the railroad.

"The one to your right is Dal," Sheriff Babcock said, "an' the other is Dent. Both of 'em is sidewinder mean."

Sheriff Babcock moved well away from the railroad, apparently to take refuge behind a crisscrossed stack of railroad ties. Nathan began his walk, knowing that when the moment came, he must somehow improve the odds. As Nathan had learned, the walk itself could be a gunman's undoing, for his mind—as well as his drawn gun—would be focused on his adversary as an upright target. Should that target suddenly change position, the other man's brain must register that change, redirecting the drawn gun. Not surprisingly, both the Suttons drew together, but at that precise second, Nathan Stone seemed to stumble. He went belly-down in the snow, Colt in his hand, and the Sutton fire cut the empty air above him. Nathan fired twice and both the Suttons were driven backward. They crumpled to the snow and lay there unmoving.

"Damn you," Subrina Sutton screamed, "you've killed my boys."

Then came the ominous bellow of a shotgun, followed by silence. Nathan was on his feet and running toward the depot. Up the track aways, he could see Sheriff Babcock headed in the same direction. That meant Vivian Stafford had been at the mercy of Subrina Sutton and a loaded shotgun. But suddenly the door opened and Vivian stepped out. She wore the paisley dress, and the entire front of it was soaked with blood. Her eyes were on Nathan for a terrified moment, and then she collapsed facedown in the snow.

"My God," Sheriff Babcock groaned, "the old woman shot her."

But Nathan rolled Vivian over and found her looking at him. Her lips moved, but it was a moment before she could speak.

"I killed her. Dear God, I didn't mean to, but . . ."

"You done what you had to, ma'am," said Sheriff Babcock. "I'd best go in there and see what they done to the railroad agent."

"I'm taking Vivian back to the hotel," Nathan said. "Can you walk?" he asked, helping her to her feet.

"Yes," she said. "They didn't hurt me. God, I want to get this dress off. Her blood's all over me."

"It scared the hell out of me," said Nathan, as they made their way back toward the hotel. "When I heard that shotgun blast, I just knew she'd killed you."

"She was going to," Vivian said, "but I fought her for the shotgun. She wouldn't let go, and the muzzle of it was at her throat, when . . ."

"Great God," said Nathan. "I'd like for us to ride out of here today, but there'll be more snow tonight."

"I'm beginning to see it your way," she said. "If the Suttons wanted you badly enough to kill me, they'd have followed us. The storm kept us here, and as terrible as all this has been, I feel like we've settled it."

"I wish I could agree with you," said Nathan, "but there may be more in this town as foolish and glory-hungry as Dobie Sutton was. I reckon I can count on that damn newspaper man to spread word of it far and wide. I can see the headlines now: *Nathan Stone, killer, guns down Nebraska family.*"

"You didn't kill them all," Vivian said. "I killed one of them."

"It won't matter," said Nathan. "I'll be blamed for it all."

Nathan was quickly proven correct. With the storm continuing, they went nowhere except the cafe, and there they were ignored. Their orders were taken and their food was served in silence. Even Empty encountered hostility, and Nathan bought food for the dog. The storm finally blew itself out, but they were unable to travel for another two days. On February 12 they rode out, crossing the North Platte River.

"After what we went through in that town," said Vivian,

"I'd as soon just avoid all the others. There's worse things than sleeping on the ground."

"I agree," Nathan said. "Besides, there may not *be* any other towns, until we get to Deadwood. I figure we'll be there in another four days, if there are no more blizzards."

Deadwood Gulch, Dakota Territory. February 17, 1876
The new camp—Deadwood Gulch—was a dead-end canyon. Located within it were three camps: Crook City, Elizabeth City, and Deadwood. The most prominent of the three camps was Deadwood, and it was at the head of the canyon, where the road ended.*

"God," said Vivian, "I've never seen anything like it."

There was a main street that snaked in and out among the tree stumps and open holes left by the early arrivals. Along the street wandered a drunken string of hastily constructed frame buildings, thrown up mostly with rough, still-green boards. The only refinement appeared to be the boardwalks. What passed for the main street was ankle-deep in dust, but that would change when the rains came. There would be ankle-deep mud. Nathan and Vivian avoided the street because it was crowded with shoving, shouting men, horses, mules, oxen, wagons, buckboards, and two-wheeled carts. Somewhere a gun thundered, and there was a second shot that sounded like an echo of the first. Among the array of buildings, two had poorly painted signs proclaiming them HOTELS.

"Might as well see what they have to offer," Nathan said.

"Ten dollars a day, fifty dollars a week," he was told. "Bathtub an' hot water is five dollars. Grub at the cafe."

"I reckon there's no use going to the other one," said Nathan. "Somewhere there must be a canyon with water and an overhanging rim. Let's look for it."

The canyon, when they found it, had sufficient grass for their horses. It was deep enough, with enough rim overhang, to provide shelter. A spring provided water.

"It's so peaceful," Vivian said, "it's hard to believe there's a mining camp so near."

"I reckon we'll find prices in the cafes right up there

*On April 28, 1876, the three camps combined, becoming the town of Deadwood.

with the hotels," said Nathan. "If we can afford a coffeepot, a frying pan, and some grub, we can cook our own meals."

"I don't want to become any more of a burden than I am already," Vivian said. "All you promised to do was get me here."

"My daddy taught me to always go just a little further than you promised, and when you hire on, do just a little more than you're paid to do," said Nathan. "Since I know your brother, I reckon I'll hang around until you find him. I want to see Wild Bill again, too, and he may still be in Saint Louis, setting up that expedition."

"I wish we had thought to ask about Harley at the hotel," Vivian said. "If he's here, he has to stay somewhere."

"Unless he's set up a camp like we have," said Nathan. "When we ride in for grub, I'll ask about him."

When they reached the outskirts of the rip-roaring gold camp, Empty refused to go any farther.

"Keep to the brush, pardner," Nathan said. "We'll look for you when we ride out."

The makeshift lobbies of the hotels were jammed with shouting, cursing men, recently arrived and seeking beds.

"We'll go on to the mercantile for our grub," said Nathan. "Maybe I can learn something there."

Nathan and Vivian wandered through the store, astounded at the boomtown prices. A coffeepot, an iron skillet, eating tools, tin cups, a side of bacon, a sack of coffee beans, and five pounds of cornmeal cost forty dollars. Nathan asked about Harley Stafford.

"Pardner, I'm looking for a friend of mine. He's a red-headed gent, may or may not be a miner, and he's handy with a gun. Blows a mouth harp, too."

"You're talkin' about Red," the storekeeper replied. "Just sayin' he's handy with a gun ain't doin' him justice. Mister, with Winchester or Colt, he's downhill with a tailwind. He ain't bad on the harp, neither."

"That's him," Nathan said. "Where can I find him?"

"Can't, till tomorrer. He rides shotgun for the Deadwood stage. Cheyenne to Deadwood and back to Cheyenne. They'll roll in tomorrer near four o'clock. Ain't no better shotgun than Red, and no better driver than Johnny Slaughter."*

*Johnny Slaughter was murdered in 1877, when masked men robbed his stagecoach.

"I was afraid of that," said Vivian, when they'd left the store. "He's taken the most dangerous job he could find."

"He's likely earning more than most of the miners," Nathan said.

"Yes, but at what risk? I'll have to talk some sense into him."

"You do," said Nathan, "and he's likely to put you on a fast train back to Virginia. A man makes his own way on the frontier, and the quickest damn way to lose him for good is to go after him with blinders and a lead rope."

"I suppose you're speaking from experience."

"I am," he replied. "I thought you were an exception, since you haven't asked me anything about myself."

"I didn't consider it any of my business," she said, "but Harley's my brother, my only living kin."

"He's also a man," said Nathan, "and I expect all the protection he needs, he carries on his hip, like I do."

"Damn it," she said, "that's a woman's lot, worrying over a man while he's alive and then grieving over him, when he finally gets himself killed?"

Nathan laughed. "That's it. When you get down to the bare bones of it, a man ain't worth a damn, present company included."

"Nathan Stone," she said, taking his arm and looking into his eyes, "I know better than that. I came to you in Dodge, broke, hungry, not knowing which way to turn, and you took me in. My own brother couldn't—and probably wouldn't—have been as kind and caring."

"Your own brother may shoot me in the back, when he learns I'm sleeping with his sister," said Nathan.

"He'd better not say one word, or I'll tell him you rescued me from a whorehouse. If I was your sister, wouldn't you rather I'd be with one man, instead of all the soldiers and cowboys in Kansas?"

"I reckon I would," Nathan said, "given that choice, but I don't aim to come between you and your brother. It's been ten years, and he may not be the same man I knew when we both wore the gray under General Lee."

Their camp under the canyon rim was peaceful. With Empty roaming around and the horses cropping grass nearby, Nathan felt secure enough. He lay awake, wondering what tomorrow would bring, wondering how Harley Stafford would receive his sister. There was something not quite right. Harley Stafford had come west, leaving his sister and his aging parents behind, allowing ten years to pass without attempting to contact them. Would a man so uncaring welcome a sister he had obviously forsaken?

The arrival of the stage was nothing less than spectacular. Obviously, it was the event of the week because it was the only link to the outside world. There was mail, newspapers not even a week old, and more women to liven up the saloons. Down the narrow, winding street came the rattling stage, rocking on its leather through braces. Slaughter, yelling and cracking his whip, seemed utterly fearless. Then, with jangling harness and the squeal of brake shoes burning on iron rims, he brought the team to a shuddering halt. Dust rose in a cloud, settling on the waiting throng, but nobody seemed to care. Slaughter stepped down from the box. Harley Stafford, though older, had changed but little. He slid the shotgun into a boot alongside the box and stepped down. Nathan looked at Vivian, and now that the time was at hand, she seemed afraid. He stepped forward and spoke.

"Stafford."

The redhead turned, his hand on the butt of his Colt. Seeing no danger, he relaxed.

"I'm Nathan Stone. Remember the days in Easy Company, under General Lee?"

"Yeah," he said. "The Yanks shot us all to hell and then took us prisoner. We heard your platoon had been wiped out."

"I heard the same about yours," said Nathan. "I picked up some lead, along with a few months in Libby prison."

"Glad you made it, Stone, and it's good to see you. I'm beat, and I got to get a few hours' sleep before the turn-around, back to Cheyenne."

"Before you go," Nathan said, "I have someone with me who you'll want to see."

"Harley," she said, "it ... it's me. Vivian."

"What, for God's sake, are you doing here? This is no place for a woman."

"I had nowhere else to go," she said. "You're all the family I have."

"Oh, damn," he groaned. "I have nothing. I sleep in a

unk in Slaughter's freight office between runs. What am I
pposed to do with you?"

"She's your sister, Stafford," Nathan said, "and she's
one through a lot, getting to you. Can't you at least pre-
nd you're glad to see her?"

"We got shot in the same war, Stone, but it ends there.
Don't preach to me."

"Harley Stafford," Vivian cried angrily, "you watch your
mouth. If it wasn't for him, I wouldn't be here."

"Then you're his woman," said Harley. "Go with him. I
have no place for you."

With that, he stomped off through the gathering crowd.
Miners who had heard the bitter exchange looked at one
another in anger and disgust. Nathan took Vivian's arm
and led her away, toward the horses. Her face was pale
and she seemed in shock. Nathan had to help her into the
saddle, and she spoke not a word until they reached their
secluded camp. Nathan unsaddled the horses, and dreading
the moment, turned back to Vivian. She came to him and
he held her tight, allowing the tears to flow. It was precisely
the situation he had feared, and faced with the reality of
it, he had no answers.

"What am I going to do?" Vivian cried. "He's all the
family I have."

"You're going to stay here until he gets used to you,"
said Nathan. "You're blood kin, and unless he's a lowdown,
skunk-striped coyote, he'll face up to that."

"But I don't want you having to stay here because of
me. Will you dig for gold?"

"I won't be staying because of you," Nathan said. "I told
you I want to see my friend Hickok again, and he'll likely
be a while getting here. I won't be digging for gold. There's
something I haven't told you. I'm a saloon gambler. While
I'm not exactly proud of it, I've made a living at it since I
came west. There must be thirty saloons in this place, and
I'll likely try my luck in some of them."

"I want to go with you."

"A saloon is no place for a woman, Vivian," said Nathan.
"On the frontier, it's a place where men raise hell, cuss,
fight, and kill one another. They'll do and say all the things
a woman shouldn't see or hear."

"Nathan, there's not a man in this camp who could do

or say anything I haven't seen or heard. I refuse to squa—
over yonder in that canyon by myself."

"You won't be by yourself," said Nathan. "Empty wil
stay with you. He purely hates saloons."

"Then he has better taste than either of us. I appreciate
his company, but if you're going to gamble in the saloons
I'm going with you. I'll wear my riding clothes and stuf*
my hair under my hat."

Since they were already in town, and Vivian had been
virtually ignored by Harley, it seemed as good a time as
any to see what Deadwood had to offer. They quickly
learned that for every store, there were three or four saloons. They were so numerous that some of them had numbers instead of names. Above the click of dice and the
clatter of poker chips there were the voices of dealers and
players. There was no order, and to this mecca of lawlessness had flocked prostitutes, pimps, gamblers, con men,
pickpockets, mountain men, ex buffalo hunters, and ne'er-
do-wells of every imaginable stripe.

"Hey, babe," a brawny miner shouted, reaching for Vivian, "which saloon are you in?"

"None of them," said Nathan. His right fist caught the
miner on the chin and flattened him out in the dusty street.

"That's what you can expect," Nathan said, "and it'll be
worse in the saloons. How am I goin' to keep my mind on
the cards, while I'm keeping men away from you?"

"I'll wear one of your shirts," she said. "It'll be large
enough to hide the upper part of me, and with my hair
stuffed under my hat, I can pass for a man."

It was possible, Nathan decided, for her face had been
tanned by wind and sun. When the Deadwood stage departed, Nathan and Vivian were there, but Harley Stafford
seemed not to see them. The first time Vivian changed her
appearance, she accompanied Nathan to Saloon Number
Ten, where he won three hundred dollars.

"That was fun," she said. "I like being a man."

"Don't get too used to it," said Nathan. "You could end
up sleeping by yourself."

When the Deadwood stage returned a week later, Nathan and Vivian weren't there to meet it. Let Harley
Stafford wonder what had become of his sister. Again Nathan had spent a successful afternoon in one of the saloons,

...d as he and Vivian were leaving, they encountered Har-
...y Stafford, about to enter.

"Damn it," Stafford said, "is this how you take care of
...y sister, dragging her into the saloons?"

"At least I've tried," said Nathan, "and that's a hell of
lot more than can be said of you."

Vivian said nothing. When they were well away from the
...aloon, Nathan spoke.

"You just gained a little ground, I think. Maybe it's not
... bad idea, having you go into the saloons with me. It'll
...ive old Harley something to think about, while he's ridin'
...hotgun from Deadwood to Cheyenne."

In the days to come, Deadwood's population continued
...o increase. New arrivals included a doctor, three lawyers,
...more gamblers, and scores of women. Spring came early,
...and by the first of April, grass had begun to green. The
incessant west wind had lost its bite, and there was rain
instead of snow. Nathan and Vivian seldom bothered meeting the Deadwood stage, but they were there the fateful
day it arrived with only Johnny Slaughter on the box. He
managed the reins awkwardly with his left hand, and the
right sleeve of his shirt was soaked with blood.

"Where's Red?" somebody shouted.

"In the coach," said Slaughter. "We've been robbed.
Four masked men, maybe thirty miles out. Red got one of
them, but he's hard hit. Somebody get the doc."

Vivian pushed through the crowd, trying to reach the
coach, and Nathan followed. He managed to get the door
open, and what they saw wasn't encouraging. Harley
Stafford lay on one of the seats on his back, and he had
been hit more than once. From a nasty wound in his left
thigh, blood still oozed, and the left side of his shirt was
bloody. Nathan wasn't able to find a pulse until he gave up
on the wrist and tried the large artery in the neck.

"He's alive," Nathan said, "but not by much."

"The doc's here," Slaughter shouted. "Let him through."

Vivian had been inside the coach. Nathan helped her
down and spoke to the doctor.

"Doctor, I'm Nathan Stone, and this is Vivian, his sister."

"I'm Doctor Wilkes," the doctor said, "and I have a
stretcher outside. Help me lift him out."

Nathan helped Wilkes remove Harley Stafford from the

coach, and when he was on the stretcher, Nathan took on
end of it, while Wilkes took the other. They had to wrassl
it up rickety stairs, for Wilkes's office was above a saloon
From somewhere came the discordant rinky-tink of a piano
From the saloon below, there was laughter, cursing, and
the clink of glasses.

"May I stay with him, Doctor?" Vivian asked.

"No," said Wilkes. "I don't know how badly he's hurt
and I want no distractions. In two hours I should know
whether or not he'll live. I'll talk to you then."

Nathan and Vivian left the office, meeting Johnny
Slaughter at the foot of the stairs. Miners crowded around,
awaiting some word. Anything that interrupted the regular-
ity of the stage concerned them.

"We might as well find us a comfortable place to wait,"
Nathan said.

"I feel just terrible," said Vivian. "I should have tried
harder to get him to accept me. Now he may die, hating
me."

"He doesn't hate you," Nathan said. "I reckon he came
west and hasn't done all that well, so he feels uncomfortable with you."

"I didn't come looking for him because I believed he
was successful, or for what I thought he could do for me.
He's my kin, my brother, and what's all I cared about. Why
couldn't he understand that?"

"Maybe he will," said Nathan. "He'll be laid up awhile,
I expect, and if he's the man I think he is, he'll see you in
a different light."

At the appointed time, Nathan and Vivian returned to
the doctor's office. Wilkes had a grim look that Nathan
didn't like, and he heard Vivian catch her breath.

"He's still alive," Wilkes said, "but I had to dig the lead
out of his side, and he's lost a lot of blood. The bone in
his thigh has been damaged to some extent. When it mends,
he will walk with a limp. I'll need to keep him here for the
next several days, until the threat of infection has passed."

"One of us can set with him, if need be," said Nathan.

"There'll be plenty of need for that, later," Wilkes said.
"He'll be laid up for a good six weeks. Miss Stafford,
Johnny Slaughter wants to talk to you. He's arranged for
a room at one of the hotels for your brother, when he's
able to be moved."

Nathan and Vivian found Slaughter at his freight office, is arm in a sling.

"It's not much of a hotel or much of a room," said laughter, "but it's the best the town has to offer. It's his or as long as he needs it."

"We're obliged," Nathan said.

Fighting infection, Harley Stafford slept almost continuously for three days, awakening only when the doses of audanum were lessened. At first, Wilkes allowed only Vivan to see him, and he refused to speak to her.

"He just lies there," the girl cried.

"Doctor," said Nathan, "I want to talk to him."

"Go ahead," Wilkes said, "but don't excite him. Should he thrash around, he could get that wound to bleeding again, and he can't afford to lose any more blood."

"I don't aim to fight with him," said Nathan. "If he fires up his temper, I'll leave."

"Good," Wilkes said.

When Nathan entered the room, Harley Stafford lay on his back, his eyes on the rough plank ceiling.

"Harley," said Nathan, "I want to talk to you."

"Well, I don't want to talk to you."

"You're afraid of something," Nathan said. "What is it?"

"Damn you, I'm not afraid of anything or anybody, and you know it. Leave me be."

"I won't leave you be," said Nathan, "and I'm glad you're not afraid, because I aim to lay some truth on you that only a brave man could swallow. You're ashamed, Harley, and you don't want to face up to it, but by God, you're going to. Not so much for your sake, but for the sake of your sister. You came back from the war bitter, mad as hell, and not caring a damn for anybody but Harley Stafford. Your parents were old, in their declining years, and the war had stripped them of everything they owned. You left them, Harley, to be cared for by a girl who had only a garden for food and the clothes on her back. You pushed them out of your life for ten long years, and now you're hiding your guilt behind a wall of don't care. But you *do* care, damn it, and it's tearing you apart."

"Get out of here, you bastard," he said venomously. "Get out."

"I'm going," said Nathan, "but I'll be back. If you're the

Harley Stafford I knew—the man who survived Cemeter
Ridge and Chancellorsville—you'll have the guts to stan
up to this."

Nathan stepped out, closing the door.

"What did he say?" Vivian asked.

"Very little," said Nathan. "He told me to get out. Bu
I said some things that needed sayin', and if he's half th
man he used to be, he'll come around. If he fails, then h
might as well die."

"Oh, God," Vivian cried, "don't say that."

"He speaks the truth," said Doctor Wilkes. "A man mus
have the will to live."

For three weeks, Vivian sat with Harley, while he said
little or nothing. Nathan spent his time in the saloons, winning more than he lost, returning to the canyon each evening to cook his supper and feed Empty. Finally, when
Nathan saw Vivian, she had a surprise for him.

"Harley wants to see you, Nathan."

Nathan went to the hotel, knocked on the door, and
when Harley spoke, entered. He no longer lay in the bed,
but sat on the edge of it. There was no hostility in him
when he spoke.

"I need to talk to you before I talk to Vivian. You nailed
my hide to the wall, forcing me to take responsibility for
my own sorry life. I have nothing, Stone. No dreams, no
hope, and now I have two bad legs. I'm afraid to promise
Vivian any kind of life, because I'm not sure I can earn
enough to keep myself alive. If I can count you as a
friend—and God knows, I need one—what should I do?
What *can* I do?"

"I rode the rails, working security for the AT and SF
Railroad," said Nathan, "and there is a chance you could
be hired for the position I had. You'd be working out of
Dodge City and earning more than you've ever made riding
shotgun. If I can get Foster Hagerman to consider you, will
you do it?"

"I'd jump at it," he said, "and thank God for the
opportunity."

CHAPTER 33

Johnny Slaughter's wound had healed to the extent that he had again begun making his weekly runs with the Deadwood stage. Nathan, after speaking to Slaughter, wrote out a lengthy telegram for Slaughter to send from Cheyenne. To be sent to Foster Hagerman, the message highly recommended Harley Stafford as security for the AT and SF. Nathan asked for an immediate reply, so that Slaughter might bring it with him on the return run.

"Oh, I hope he accepts Harley," said Vivian. "He's starting to hope, to believe he can be somebody. But I'll miss you, Nathan. You will come to see us, won't you?"

"You know I will," Nathan said, "but I'll have to take a room in the Dodge House."

"No," said Vivian. "Harley knows about us, and about all you've done for me. He's no longer the man he was when he left Virginia. You'll see."

Harley Stafford lived up to Vivian's faith in him. Quickly he and Nathan Stone became friends, reliving the terrible last days of the war, recalling comrades who had gone seeking glory but found only death. Then came the day, when the Deadwood stage rolled in, that Johnny Slaughter handed Nathan the response to his telegram. The message was brief:

Stafford accepted stop. Need him immediately.

It was signed, "Foster Hagerman." Nathan passed it to Harley, and Vivian read it over his shoulder. With tears in his eyes, Harley turned to Nathan. Words failing him, he offered his hand and Nathan took it.

"I'll have just about enough wages coming to pay Dr. Wilkes and buy a horse," Harley said.

"You don't owe Dr. Wilkes anything," said Nathan, "and you won't need a horse to get to Dodge. You're going to take the stage to Cheyenne. From there, you'll take the Union Pacific to Omaha. From Omaha to Kansas City,

you'll take a steamboat, and when you reach Kansas Ci
you'll board an AT and SF westbound to Dodge."

"It sounds wonderful," Vivian said, "but we could nev
afford it."

"Oh, but you can," said Nathan. "Deadwood's payir
your way. I've won a thousand dollars at the poker table
and five hundred of that goes to you. That'll be enough
get you to Dodge and to keep you fed along the way."

"Nathan," said Harley, "I can't let you do it. You'v
already done more than enough."

"Harley," Nathan replied, "I'm a Reb by birth and
western man by choice. I look out for my friends, fightin
for them if need be. If the time ever comes when my back
to the wall, I hope my friends will remember."

"That's a code a man can live with," said Harley, "an
I'm making it my own. Should you ever have your back to
the wall, and I'm alive, I'll be there alongside you."

On June 5, 1876, Harley and Vivian took the stage to
Cheyenne. Nathan sold the extra horse, but continued to
make his camp in the canyon. Deadwood was intolerable
especially at night, and there was the possibility that some
drunken miner might shoot Empty, just for the sport of it.
Each time the stage arrived, Nathan expected to see Bill
Hickok step down, and each time he was disappointed. Finally, in an Omaha newspaper, Nathan found a few lines
on Hickok's proposed expedition. Hickok was in St. Louis,
preparing to depart for Dakota Territory. Unless one dug
for gold, there was little to do except gamble, and that's
what Nathan chose to do. His favorite of all the saloons
was the Bella Union, and it was there that he encountered
Jack McCall.

McCall was about twenty-five, in runover boots and the
rough clothes of a miner. But he had no claim, and as far
as anyone knew, he never laid hand to pick or shovel. He
fancied himself a gambler, and although he lost more than
he won, he never seemed to lack for money. There were
rumors that McCall was responsible for a rash of robberies
in which miners, for the gold in their pokes, were knocked
in the head or shot. But there was no law in Deadwood,
and nothing was ever proven. The game was five-card stud,
and Nathan was a hundred dollars ahead. It was a four-
handed game when McCall showed up.

"If nobody objects," said McCall, "I'm buyin' in."

"If you got money, come on," said one of the men. "Five-dollar bets. It'll cost you twenty dollars a hand."

McCall laid down his twenty, which he promptly lost. He lost three pots in a row, and each time he lost, Nathan won.

"By God," McCall shouted, his eyes on Nathan, "somethin' ain't right."

Nathan slid back his chair before he spoke, and when he did, his voice was cold.

"Are you by any chance accusing me of cheating?"

"I . . . I ain't got no gun," said McCall.

"You won't need one," Nathan said. With his left hand he seized a fistful of McCall's shirtfront, dragging him halfway across the poker table. A hard-driving right slammed into McCall's chin, sending him over the back of his chair and onto the floor.

"McCall," said the barkeep, "get up an' get the hell out of here."

McCall, dazed, got to his feet and stumbled toward the door. He seemed irrational, and Nathan felt a little sorry for having hit him.

"Old Broken-Nose Jack ain't playin' with a full deck," said a miner next to Nathan. "We just kinda tolerate him, like locusts an' blizzards."

Deadwood, Dakota Territory. July 4, 1876

While Dakota Territory wasn't part of the Union, most of the miners were from the states. What might have been a rip-roaring July Fourth fizzled out with the arrival of the stage. It brought newspapers from Cheyenne, Omaha, and Kansas City, and the headlines were shocking:

*Custer and half his command wiped out by the Sioux.**

"My God," said a miner, "twenty-five hunnert Sioux, an' it wasn't all that far from here. The gover'ment's playin' hell protectin' us."

The Custer massacre had a sobering effect, but it didn't cool the gold fever, and Deadwood continued to grow. While the weekly stage brought a few men seeking wealth, many more came by expedition, much along the lines of what Hickok had in mind. Leaders of expeditions, for a fee, gathered men at St. Louis, Kansas City, and Omaha.

*Custer and 265 of his men died June 25, 1876, at the Little Big Horn.

From Omaha the expeditions traveled the Union Pacific to Cheyenne, and by horse, mule, or wagon to Deadwood. Wild Bill Hickok arrived in Deadwood on July twelfth, and the few men with him fell far short of what was expected. Hickok was accompanied by longtime friends California Joe and Colorado Charlie, all of them friends of the recently slain George A. Custer. In memory of their friend, the three men got roaring drunk, and it was four days before Nathan had a chance to speak to Hickok. They met in the Bella Union.

"I've been expecting you," Nathan said. "A piece in the newspaper said you were in Saint Louis raising an expedition."

"I fared poorly," said Hickok. "Others spent huge sums of money for advertisement in the newspapers, and I couldn't match that, so I just brought a few friends. We'll stake out our claims and take our chances. I've never seen such an almighty lot of saloons. Maybe I'll try my luck at the poker table."

Hickok frequented the lesser saloons, such as Shingle's Number Three, Mann's Number Ten, and the Senate. He still carried two revolvers, butts-forward. They were the latest Colt .38-caliber-cartridge six-shooters, with the triggers filed off and the hammers filed smooth. There were rumors that when Hickok arrived in Deadwood, he brought with him a whole case of cartridges. He spent the first few days sizing up the town and locating a gold claim. He never mentioned his marriage or his wife, and Nathan questioned the truth of what he had read in the newspaper.

Deadwood being a lawless town, it was controlled by the cardsharps, gamblers, and gunmen. With killers such as Jim Levy and Charlie Storms in town, Deadwood had all the makings of an outlaw empire. While Hickok did nothing to attract attention, Nathan heard talk that Hickok was about to become the marshal of Deadwood. The lawless element had not forgotten what Hickok had accomplished in Hays and Abilene. While Hickok had made no threatening moves, Nathan sensed the growing danger, and feared for Hickok's life. He continued to gamble, but lost more often than he won, causing Nathan to wonder. Hickok avoided any pattern, making the rounds of many saloons as though hoping to confuse any who might waylay him. Wild Bill Hickok had become a changed man, and there were times when he was so preoccupied, he didn't even speak to his closest friends. Nathan believed the old frontiersman had a premonition of his own death, and one day, Hickok confirmed it.

"Bill," said Nathan, "maybe this is none of my business, but I've been hearing talk that the powers behind this town believe you're here to bid for a marshal's job, to do here what you did in Hays and Abilene."

"My days as a lawman are done," Hickok said. "How often can a man fail, and still call himself a man? For all my reputation, I couldn't raise an expedition in Saint Louis, and as for my gold claim here, I'd have to pay somebody to take it off my hands. Hell, even the cards have gone sour. If it gets any worse, when I draw a good hand, I'll be accused of cheating."

Nathan laughed, but Hickok did not. When he spoke again, he was dead serious.

"I had the feeling when I rode in here—and that feeling has grown stronger—that I have ridden my last trail, made my last camp, turned my last card. My friend, I doubt I'll be leaving this gulch alive."

When Deadwood's livery opened for business, Nathan was its first customer. While it was more expensive, living in the boomtown, Nathan had earned enough at the poker table to afford it. Several boardinghouses had sprung up, their weekly and monthly rates more reasonable than the makeshift hotels, and Nathan took a room where Empty was welcome. Nathan had received a letter from Vivian Stafford, telling him that she and Harley had reached Dodge City. While Nathan was glad for them, he still missed the woman, and living in town amid the shouting, shooting, and hell-raising, he was less inclined to think of her.

It was Friday, the first day of August. Nathan and Hickok had just left the Bella Union, on their way to a cafe for supper. The westering sun was an hour high, in their eyes, and just for a second, Nathan caught its reflection in a moving object. He literally fell into Hickok, shoving him into the dusty street. The slug struck Nathan in the right side and he fell across Hickok. A second slug kicked up dust just inches from Hickok's head, but he had freed one of his Colts and was returning fire. Men came on the run two of them moving Nathan onto the boardwalk.

"One of you get the doc," Hickok shouted.

Dr. Wilkes came, pulled aside Nathan's bloody shirt, and shook his head.

"Bad?" Hickok asked.

"Bad enough," said Doctor Wilkes. "A couple of you bring him to my office, and be quick about it."

Dr. Wilkes dug out the lead, bandaged the wound, and sat up with Nathan most of the night. When Nathan's temperature rose, the doctor dosed him with whiskey. Hickok and Nathan's few friends were there early on Saturday morning.

"With luck, he'll make it," Dr. Wilkes said.

Shortly after noon, Wild Bill—wearing a Prince Albert frock coat—entered Nuttall and Mann's Number Ten Saloon. Charles Rich, Captain Massie, and Carl Mann already had a game in progress. There were no more than ten men in the saloon.

"Sit down, Bill," Mann urged.

"Only if Charlie will swap me the wall seat," said Hickok.

"Aw, hell," Rich scoffed, "sit down. Nobody's gonna back-shoot you."

Uneasily, Hickok sat down, but after only a few minutes, he stood up.

"Charlie," said Hickok, "change seats with me."

This time, all three men laughed him down, and again Hickok took his seat. Rich was on his right, Mann on his left, and Massie right in front of him. Hickok had a clear view of the front door, but he was conscious of the small door behind him. The night before, Bill had beaten Massie, but was soon losing heavily to him. Hickok spoke to Harry Young, the barkeep.

"Harry, bring me fifteen dollars' worth of pocket checks."

Young left the bar, brought the pocket checks, and placed them on the table beside Hickok. At that time, Jack McCall came in through the front door. In a game the night before, Hickok had cleaned out McCall, and feeling sorry for him, had given McCall enough money for a drink and his supper. McCall leaned on the bar, looking around. Wild Bill sat facing him, but was busy studying his cards. Quickly

McCall moved down the bar, lest Wild Bill look up. Reaching the end of the bar, McCall stopped, but a few paces behind the stool on which Hickok sat. Suddenly there was the roar of a pistol.

"Damn you, take that!" McCall shouted. In his right hand he held a smoking pistol. The time was just past three P.M.

Wild Bill's head had jerked forward from the force of the slug, and for just a few seconds, his body remained upright. It then relaxed and fell backward off the stool. From his lifeless fingers, his cards fanned out on the floor: the ace of spades, the ace of clubs, and two black eights. Those, and the jack of diamonds. The dead man's hand . . .*

For a few seconds, nobody understood what had taken place. There was a numbness in Captain Massie's left wrist, for he had caught the spent slug after it had killed Hickok. All eyes were on Hickok, and when his body fell back, they knew, for McCall was backing toward the rear door. The gun was in his hand, pointed toward Carl Mann.

"Come on, ye sons of bitches," McCall snarled.

Twice McCall pulled the trigger, and twice the weapon misfired.

McCall ran out the back door, mounting the first horse at hand. Because of the heat, the saddle cinch had been loosened, and McCall fell sprawling. Staggering to his feet, he ran down the street, but the town had been alerted.

"Hickok's been shot! Wild Bill is dead!"

McCall ran into a butcher shop, but prodded with the muzzle of a Sharps, he was persuaded to come out. He surrendered without a struggle. Saloon Number Ten's doors were locked, with only Hickok's friends and persons of authority being allowed to enter. A miner's court was hurriedly assembled and Jack McCall was tried. His defense was that he owed Hickok money from a gambling debt and feared for his life, and that Hickok had murdered his brother. There was no proof of either claim, but the court set him free, and McCall immediately left town.

On August 3, 1876, Wild Bill Hickok was laid to rest in a coffin covered with black cloth and mounted with silver. His Springfield rifle was placed at his right hand.

*Hickok's best hand would have been a full house. The odds against him were 693–1.

*   *   *

Dosed with laudanum, Nathan Stone slept until the evening of August third, well after Hickok had been buried. Colorado Charlie brought the news.

"They got him, then," said Nathan grimly.

"Yes," Charlie said. "McCall pulled the trigger, but he was paid to do it. There's word goin' around that he was paid two hundred dollars, but no word as to where the money came from. I could name a dozen men who could have put up ten times that much."

"All I want to know," said Nathan, "is the direction McCall took when he rode out."

"South, toward Cheyenne," Charlie said.

"Why the hell didn't some of you go after him?" Nathan demanded.

"We all wanted to be here for Bill's buryin'," said Charlie. "Besides, you heard Bill and his talk of dying. It was his time. Wasn't but one live shell in McCall's forty-five."*

Three weeks after having been shot, against the doctor's orders, Nathan Stone got out of bed, dressed, and strapped on his Colts. Saying nothing, he bought a few provisions at the mercantile, and with Empty running ahead, rode south.

Cheyenne, Wyoming. August 29, 1876

Nathan's first stop was the Union Pacific depot, where he described Jack McCall to the railroad agent.

"Sorry, pardner," the man said, "but it's been months since I've had a passenger goin' east. They're all comin' *from* there."

Nathan sat down on a baggage cart, pondering his next move. It was possible that his quarry had climbed aboard a boxcar and thus escaped, but there was no way of knowing. If McCall hadn't come to Cheyenne with plans for taking the Union Pacific east, where *had* he gone? Nathan returned to the depot, where he had seen a huge map on the wall.

"Pardner, I'd like to study your map."

"Go ahead," said the railroad man.

Nathan studied the map and quickly decided that if McCall hadn't taken the train east, that he must be somewhere within riding distance of Cheyenne. There was Lara-

*Tested, every remaining cartridge in McCall's pistol misfired.

mie City, a few miles east, and Denver, Colorado—now a
state—a hundred miles south. Recalling all he had heard
about Jack McCall, it seemed the man had constantly been
in trouble. Before going to Deadwood, he had been involved in cattle rustling in Nebraska. Now, having left
Deadwood, Nathan considered it unlikely that McCall had
any money, for he had fancied himself a gambling man. It
seemed a good possibility that McCall had already run
afoul of the law somewhere, and with that thought in mind,
Nathan went looking for the office of the United States
marshal. The marshal's name was Dave Landers, and Nathan was honest with him, regarding his search for McCall.

"Your search is over," said Landers. "I had a telegram
this morning, from Deputy U.S. Marshal Balcombe, in Laramie City. McCall has been arrested there, and is charged
with murder. Balcombe heard him bragging about shooting
Hickok, and he's going to stand trial."

"He's already been tried in Deadwood and found not
guilty," said Nathan.

"That trial was illegal," Landers said, "and any act by a
vigilance committee or court is not recognized by courts of
the United States. At the time of Hickok's murder, Deadwood was—and still is—an outlaw town. Every man in
Deadwood is there illegally. By treaty, in 1868, the Black
Hills were set aside as an Indian Reservation, within the
jurisdiction of the United States."

"That all sounds legal," said Nathan, "but where will
McCall be tried? Here?"

"No," Landers said. "We at first intended bringing him
here for a preliminary hearing before the United States
commissioner, and then await a request from the governor
of Dakota Territory. But we've decided to keep McCall in
Laramie City. There he is to be examined before Judge
Blair, with court-appointed attorneys for his defense."

"Damn it," said Nathan, "he'll weasel out of it
somehow."

"I doubt it," Landers replied. "He's already confessed to
Deputy U.S. Marshal Balcombe, and he's promised to re-
peat his confession to Judge Blair. McCall will be taken to
Yankton, Dakota Territory, for trial and sentencing. Now,
I have some advice for you. Go about your business and

leave McCall to the law. there's been enough vigilante justice.''*

"I only went after McCall because it seemed he wasn't going to pay for killing Hickok. Now that I know he's in the hands of the law, that he'll be tried in a real court, then I'll back off and let the law have him."

"*Bueno*," said Landers.

Nathan found a hotel willing to accept Empty, and took a room for the night. He had no regrets about leaving Deadwood, for he had left Wild Bill in a grave there. While he had won a few hundred dollars in the saloons, the only thing he looked back on with pride was having united Vivian Stafford with her long-lost brother, and the friendship he had established with Harley. The more he thought about it, the more inclined he was to ride to Dodge and see how Harley had adapted to railroading. But after supper, when he and Empty had returned to their hotel room, he had to admit to himself that what he *really* wanted was to see Vivian Stafford again. At first light, he rode south.

Denver, Colorado. September 1, 1876

Nathan hadn't been to Denver for a long time, and he took a hotel room, preparing to stay at least a day or two. There were newspapers from St. Louis, Kansas City, and Denver's own *Rocky Mountain News*. The town was still celebrating, for on August first, Colorado had become the 38th state. The stars and stripes flew above the temporary state capitol on Cherry Street. It seemed the town was bursting with civic pride, and even some of the lesser saloons had been fancied up for the occasion. Fireworks crackled at all hours of the day and night, sounding like distant gunshots. Empty was skittish, keeping to the bushes when he could. Nathan discovered a new saloon called the Casa Verde, a two-story affair that promised gambling twenty-four hours a day, seven days a week. It was secluded, surrounded by trees and shrubs, offering sanctuary for Empty while Nathan was inside. The downstairs had a bar, a kitchen, tables for dining, a few poker tables, and a roulette wheel. Nathan suspected the high-stakes gambling took place upstairs, and had it confirmed when one of the waiters met him in the foyer.

*McCall was indicted for murder at Yankton Court House on October 18, 1876.

"If you wish to dine or gamble for table stakes, sir, it's the first floor. The high-stakes tables are upstairs, and so are the pretty girls."

"I'll go upstairs," said Nathan.

He had long been familiar with the "Pretty Girl Saloons." The women wore nothing, or close to it, catering to high rollers, their purpose being to take a man's mind off how much and how often he lost. The upstairs could only be described as plush. There was deep carpet on the floor, dusty rose, to match the drapes. The chairs had upholstered seats and backs, the fabric an elegant gray. The long bar and the tables were mahogany. The "pretty girls" went from table to table, laughing as they avoided groping hands. They wore pink slippers, pink bows in their hair, and a short pink jacket that covered only their shoulders and their arms to the elbow. The rest was bare. Nathan vowed to keep his mind on his cards, and for a while, managed to do so. But all his good intentions went to hell on greased skids when he looked up and found a near-naked Melanie Gavin staring at him in openmouthed surprise.

"This is a hell of a long ways from Ohio," said Nathan.

"I got as far as Kansas City," she said, "and I just couldn't go through with it. There was no kin in Ohio except Mother's snooty old maid sister. Life with her would have been hell."

"I don't see you wearing wings and a halo now," said Nathan. "In fact, I don't see you wearing much of anything."

"I have money in the bank," she snapped. "Would you prefer that I hire myself out as a drudge, for two dollars a week?"

"I'd prefer that you didn't prance around naked in a saloon," said Nathan, "if I had any say in the matter."

"Since before I was old enough to know my behind from my big toe, I've always had somebody telling me what to do or what not to do. There was mother, then Clell Shanklin, and then eventually, you. I don't expect you to understand, but it's important to me that I have control of my life, that I do what I want to do. Even if it means prancing naked in a saloon."

"I never tried to tell you what to do," Nathan said, "and I don't aim to start now. I may not agree with what you're doing, but I respect your right to do it."

"Do you honestly mean that?"

"I mean it," said Nathan. "How late are you here?"

"I get off at midnight. I have a room in a boardinghouse, three blocks from here."

"I'll walk you there," Nathan said. "Until then, I'll try my luck at the tables."

Nathan saw her just briefly the rest of the evening. In a Pretty Girl Saloon, it was bad for business, having a girl seem partial toward one man, and it encouraged familiarity. Nathan paid close attention to his cards and those of the other gamblers because they were playing five-card stud. The bets were ten dollars, and when Nathan folded, he was ahead two hundred dollars. The rest of the gamblers hardly noticed him leaving, and he waited downstairs for Melanie. She came down the stairs wearing a stylish long dress, but before they could depart, the barkeep waved her over. She spoke to him briefly, joined Nathan, and they left.

"What was that all about?" Nathan asked. "He looked at me like he thought I was about to drag you off and have my way with you."

"Well, aren't you?"

"I reckon," said Nathan.

She laughed. "The barmen have been told to watch out for the girls. They question us if somebody meets us there. An occasional gambler will follow us outside and try to buy what he saw upstairs."

"As I see it," Nathan said, "that's one of the problems with these naked girl saloons. Men get the wrong impression. They reckon if a girl's willing to show it, she's willing to sell it."

"It's not that way," said Melanie. "It's a look-but-don't-touch game, and any man wanting more than that belongs in a whorehouse. We're a pleasant distraction, keeping a man's mind off how much he's lost at the table. Most of our gamblers are well-to-do and won't miss the money, but you'd be surprised at how tight some of them are."

Nathan spent two days in Denver. Despite Melanie's questionable means of earning her living, he still enjoyed being with her, and when he finally rode away, it was with a standing invitation to return. After the initial shock of finding her in a Pretty Girl Saloon, he actually felt better about her. He had to admit that, in going into the saloon instead of the home of a stuffy old aunt, she had likely made the better of the two choices.

Dodge City, Kansas. September 7, 1876

Nathan went first to the railroad depot and found Foster Hagerman in his office. "If you're looking for your old job," said Hagerman, "you're out of luck. By God, this Harley Stafford is somethin' else."

"That's why I sent him to you," Nathan replied. "I'm good, and he's better than me. Where am I likely to find him?"

"In Pueblo," said Hagerman. "Won't be back for a couple of days. But Vivian's at the Dodge House, and I reckon that's why you're here."

"Not entirely," Nathan said. "I just got a bellyful of Dakota Territory."

"Good," said Hagerman. "I know you'll want to meet our new sheriff. He's a young gent name of Wyatt Earp."

CHAPTER 34

"I missed you terribly," Vivian said, when Nathan reached the Dodge House. "I just can't begin to tell you how much this means to Harley, and he'll be as glad to see you as I am. How long are you going to be here?"

"I haven't decided," said Nathan. "After you and Harley left Deadwood, everything just went to hell. I guess you've heard about Wild Bill."

"Yes," she said, "and I'm sorry. I'm so thankful you helped Harley get out of there, and I'm just as thankful you got out. You're not going back, are you?"

"My God, no," said Nathan. "Not unless we have to fight the Sioux and the government drafts me."

They were in Vivian's room at the Dodge House, and Empty dozed beneath the only window. It was near suppertime.

"I'm going to take a room so I'll have a place to leave my saddlebags," Nathan said, "and then we'll have supper at Delmonico's."

"Leave them here," said Vivian. "You don't need a room. We stayed together before we went to Deadwood, and nothing's changed."

"Oh, but it has," Nathan said. "Harley's here. I won't feel right, and there may be others who won't approve."

"Damn the others," she said. "Harley spends all his time with one of the girls from the Long Branch. I told him what I went through before I found you here in Dodge, and I promise you, you're welcome to anything he has or ever hopes to have."

"And that includes you?"

"That includes me," she said.

"Even if I ride off to Texas and you don't see me again for a year?"

"Even then," she said. "I believe in life the way you helped Harley see it. He says you play the hand as it's dealt to you, and sometimes you win. It's when you do nothing, hoping your luck will change, that you lose it all."

Nathan remained in Dodge until Harley returned, and for the week after. While he had expected some changes in Harley Stafford, he was amazed at the degree to which the man had changed in so short a time. He had gained weight and barely limped at all. Hagerman, recalling how helpful it had been to Nathan, had insisted that Harley learn Morse code.

"With my messed-up legs, I never expected to climb a telegraph pole," Harley said, "but when I had to do it, I did."

"Sometimes Hagerman's a hard man to work for," said Nathan, "but he believes in paying a man who can put up with him."

"He's paying me more in a month than I sometimes earned in a year," Harley said.

Nathan continued his habit of reading the newspapers from Kansas City and St. Louis, and in mid-September, he found interesting stories in both papers. The James and Younger gangs, attempting to rob the bank in the little town of Northfield, Minnesota, had been met with a hail of lead. While Frank and Jesse had escaped, the Youngers hadn't been so fortunate. Bob Younger had been seriously wounded. He, his brothers James and Cole, and Charlie Pitts—a member of the James gang—had been captured.

Nathan, Harley, Vivian, and Foster Hagerman were at Delmonico's, having Sunday dinner, when Wyatt Earp, Dodge City's new lawman, came in.

"Mr. Earp," said Hagerman, "this is Nathan Stone, one of the best security men the AT and SF ever had."

Nathan responded to Earp's nod, and while the lawman's eyes lingered on Vivian, he ignored Harley. Without speaking a word, he moved on. Vivian looked uncomfortable, and Foster Hagerman had his eyes on his plate. Nathan judged Earp to be near thirty. Slender, wearing a dark suit, boiled shirt, and string tie, he looked impressive enough.

"Mr. Earp is a little self-conscious," said Hagerman, when Earp had gone. "The town council insists on calling him a policeman. They believe the term 'sheriff' or 'marshal' has us sounding like a frontier town, instead of the thriving city, which we obviously are."

Nathan laughed at Hagerman's humor, but Harley and Vivian did not. Hagerman excused himself, and when he had gone, Nathan spoke.

"I get the feeling neither of you are fond of Mr. Earp, the new policeman."

"He was here when we arrived in Dodge," said Harley, "and he's never said howdy, go to hell, nothin'. But he's always got his eye on Vivian. Makes me wonder what he's up to, when I'm in Pueblo or Kansas City."

"Harley," Vivian said, "he's never bothered me. Besides, he's bound to know Nathan and me are . . . more than just friends."

"That's why I'm hoping you'll stay awhile, Nathan," said Harley. "Earp looks like the kind who'll take the measure of things, and move on, if everything doesn't suit him."

"I'd planned to stay a week or two," Nathan said. "Then I aim to ride to south Texas. King Fisher, an amigo of mine, has a ranch near Uvalde, and I reckoned I'd spend Christmas with him."

"Then take Vivian with you," said Harley. "Mining in Colorado is booming, and for the next few months, I'll be riding the rails between Pueblo and Kansas City, away from Dodge more often than I'm here."

"Harley," Nathan said, "there are men on the frontier who just plain don't like me, and others hell-bent on proving they're faster with a gun than I am. Riding with me is to tempt fate. I reckon she's told you what happened in Nebraska, on our way to Deadwood."

"Yes," said Harley, "and that's why I'd not be afraid for her to ride anywhere with you. She's becoming a western woman, and I think the ride to Texas would help her along."

"I may be gone for six months," Nathan said.

"So may I," Harley replied. "Vivian, speak up."

"I'd like to go," said Vivian, "and you won't need the sulfur salve."

Nathan got Vivian a horse and saddle from the livery, and on September seventeenth, they rode south toward Fort Elliott, less than a day's ride. It was a carefree time, and with the dark days at Deadwood behind him, Nathan felt better than he had since leaving the McQueen place, in New Orleans. Empty was enjoying the open plains, bounding ahead. Once they were well away from Dodge, Vivian told Nathan what he had already suspected.

"Harley was right," she said. "I was getting the fidgits, with Mr. Earp looking at me as though he had plans I didn't know about, but I couldn't say anything. Harley at last has a chance to make something of himself, to be his own man, and I won't have him throw it all away because of me. Anyway, it was reason enough for me to ride south with you."

"Harley is a tolerant man," said Nathan. "I feel better, him being with the railroad. He has access to the telegraph, and he can always reach us through the ranger outpost at San Antonio."

"Your relationship with the rangers is impressive."

"One of the best friends I ever had was a ranger," Nathan said. "He was ambushed."

"What became of the man who killed him?"

"He ran like the yellow coyote he was," said Nathan, "but somebody tracked him to New Mexico Territory and gave him what he deserved."

Vivian said nothing. She thought she knew who that "somebody" had been.

Fort Elliott, Texas. September 17, 1876

Captain Selman welcomed Nathan warmly, insisting that he and Vivian take an available cabin for the night. They ate with the enlisted men, and the soldiers made such a fuss over Vivian that she became embarrassed. Empty renewed his friendship with the cooks, and was rewarded accordingly.

*   *   *

Nathan and Vivian rode out after breakfast, bound for Fort Griffin. When they came to the saloon at Mobeetie, Nathan counted more than a dozen horses at the hitch rail. Two bearded men stood beside their horses, watching Nathan and Vivian ride past. When they stopped to rest the horses, Nathan studied their back trail, but saw nothing.

"What do you see?" Vivian asked.

"Nothing," said Nathan, "but on the frontier, it's as important to know who's behind as it is to know who's ahead."

In the late afternoon, his vigilance was rewarded. Far away, against the blue Texas sky, he could see two faint plumes of dust.

"We're being followed," he said.

"Who would follow us, and why?"

"Likely some of those men at the saloon in Mobeetie. They'll wait for dark, then try to ambush us, taking our horses, saddles, and any valuables we have."

"What are we going to do?" she asked.

"You're going to ride on, leading my horse," said Nathan. "I'm going to take my Winchester and welcome these hombres. When I send Empty for you, ride on back with my horse."

Nathan took his Winchester and positioned himself behind some rocks, so that he could see the back trail. He kept Empty beside him, and waited. When the two riders were but a few yards distant, he challenged them.

"That's far enough. You're covered. Drop your guns."

"We ain't done nothin' to you," one of the riders said.

"You're not going to, either," Nathan replied. "Now drop those guns."

Silently, Nathan pointed in the direction Vivian had ridden, and Empty trotted away. The disgruntled pair dropped their revolvers, but each had a rifle in his saddle boot.

"Now dismount," Nathan commanded.

Slowly they swung down from their saddles.

"Now take off your boots," said Nathan.

"No, damn you," one of the men shouted.

"Then I'll gut-shoot you," said Nathan. "Your choice."

By the time they had removed their boots, Vivian had returned.

"Vivian," Nathan said, "take the reins of their horses and lead them away. Then take their pistols there on the ground and step back out of the way. Now, you varmints, shuck your shirts and drop your britches."

"You aim to strip us afore a woman?"

"This woman's seen skinned coyotes before," said Nathan. "Now move!"

Slowly they peeled down to the hide, until they wore only their socks and their hats.

"Now," Nathan said, "just trot back the way you came."

"You heartless bastard," one of them shouted, "it's fifty mile back to Mobeetie."

"Good," said Nathan. "You'll have plenty of time to consider the error of your ways, and don't try sneaking back. Next time, I'll shoot the both of you."

"That was a terrible thing to do," Vivian said. "Before they reach Mobeetie, the sun will have blistered everything but their heads and the soles of their feet."

"I'll turn their horses loose in the morning," said Nathan. "If they're lucky, their horses will catch up to them sometime tomorrow."

"Suppose their horses don't return to Mobeetie?"

Nathan laughed. "Then I know a pair of varmints with a long walk ahead of them. Put their pistols in their saddlebags. I'll tie their clothes to their saddle horns, and we'll be on our way."

They rode south, and an hour before sundown, big gray thunderheads rolled in from the west. The wind had a chill to it.

"We'd better look for a dry place to hole up for the night," said Nathan. "We're close to the Red, and where the banks are high, there'll be some overhang."

Finding shelter, Nathan gathered enough dry wood for their cook fire before the rain began. The storm passed during the night. After breakfast, before they rode south, Nathan turned loose the horses taken from the two bushwhackers the day before.

Fort Griffin, Texas. September 20, 1876

Nathan and Vivian had supper with Captain Webb, and the officer relayed some interesting news.

"The Horrell-Higgins feud is on again. I understand you have a stake in that."

"No more," Nathan said. "An outlaw friend of theirs ambushed a ranger friend of mine, but that's been settled."

"Don't count on it," said Captain Webb. "Most of the trouble is near Lampasas, and I hear the Horrells have set out to settle up with anybody they believe has slighted them."

Nathan said nothing, and after they had parted company with Captain Webb, Vivian spoke.

"Where is Lampasas?"

"A few minutes' ride south of Waco," Nathan replied. "We can miss it by a good fifty miles. I can't believe the Horrells would come after me, but nothing they've ever done has made sense, so we won't gamble on it. We'll stop in Austin and talk to the rangers."

Austin, Texas. September 24, 1876

"We had hoped the Horrell-Higgins fight had burned itself out," Ranger Bodie West said, "but then the Horrells came back from New Mexico Territory, and it started all over again. So far, nobody's been killed, but I look for it any time. Then I reckon we'll have to move in and show the whole blessed bunch the error of their ways."

"Captain Webb, at Fort Griffin, says they're settling old debts," said Nathan. "While I don't aim to go looking for them, I sure as hell won't run."

"If they come after you," the ranger said, "don't be bashful. If you're forced to shoot some of them, don't worry about bein' on the wrong side of the law."

"I won't be hanging around Lampasas," said Nathan. "Vivian and me are on our way to Uvalde, to spend some time with my amigo, King Fisher."

West laughed. "You won't have to go to Lampasas. King Fisher's gone and done what most sensible folks think was a damn fool thing. He's got himself a woman, and she's a sister to Martin Horrell. Fisher met her at a dance in Waco and persuaded her to go home with him. Martin rode to King's place at Uvalde, got nasty, and Fisher plumb tied a knot in his tail and sent him packing. The Higgins bunch making it hot for the Horrells is all that's kept the lid on between the Horrells and King Fisher."

"Why are the Higgins and Horrell families fighting?" Vivian asked.

"God only knows," said West. "My guess is that they all came from somewhere else, and brought the feud with them. From what I hear, some of the women on both sides want the fighting to stop, but the men won't hear of it."

Nathan and Vivian took a room at a hotel where Empty was welcome. Not until they were through with supper did Vivian say what was on her mind.

"You could get yourself shot in somebody else's fight."

"I could," said Nathan, "and as I've been guilty of saying, it takes a damn fool to do that."

"But we're still going to Uvalde."

"Yes," Nathan said. "Where my friends are concerned, I am a damn fool, but I reckon King can use another gun."

Uvalde was a two-day ride, and they would start at first light.

Uvalde, Texas. September 26, 1876

Nathan and Vivian took "King Fisher's road," and long before they reached the house, Empty broke the silence with a warning bark. Nathan and Vivian reined up, as King Fisher stepped out of the brush. He had a Winchester under his arm and a grin on his rugged face. He spoke.

"I swear, if I didn't believe in the resurrection before, I do now. That's the same dog you buried last time you was here."

"I buried his daddy," said Nathan. "This is Empty. The lady is Vivian Stafford, the sister of a friend of mine."

"Pardner, you got some trusting friends. Ma'am, you just say the word, I'll set this varmint back on the road to San Antone, and take you on to the house with me."

Recognizing his humor for what it was, Vivian laughed.

"We heard you already got a woman at the house," said Nathan. "That's why we're here. The word's out that her kin aims to hang you upside down over a slow fire, and I reckoned you could use an extra gun."

"I could use a company of U.S. Cavalry," Fisher said. "You know about this bunch of Horrells?"

"I do," said Nathan. "Do you think the woman's worth it?"

"If I didn't, I wouldn't have brought her home with me," Fisher said. "After you've seen to your horses, come on to the house and see for yourselves. I'll go on ahead and tell Molly you're coming."

Nathan unsaddled the horses, quickly rubbed them down,

and found stalls for them in the barn. Then he and Vivian started for the house.

"I like him," Vivian said. "He's very young."

"Not more than twenty-one or -two," said Nathan, "but he's a Texan, a man to ride the river with."*

When they reached the house, King Fisher let them in. Shaniqua remembered Nathan, for it had been she who had doctored his many wounds after King Fisher had rescued him from bloodthirsty vigilantes. The girl, Molly, greeted them shyly. She had long, dark hair and brown eyes, and Nathan judged her to be eighteen.

"It's a mite early for supper," said Fisher, "but Shaniqua always has coffee ready."

He led the way into the dining room, drawing out chairs for Vivian and Molly. When they were seated, Shaniqua brought the coffee. It was an awkward situation for Nathan and Vivian, for they had no idea what they could or should say to Molly Horrell. Certainly she was a beautiful girl, and it was obvious why King Fisher had been taken with her. Fisher had to say something to bridge the gap, and he did.

"Molly, these folks are friends of mine, and they know about your background, so you don't have to be afraid to talk."

"I'm not afraid to talk," said Molly. "Mostly, I'm ashamed to. Martin and most all the others—the men— think Horrell women should be satisfied to cook, scrub clothes, and patch up the men after they've been shot by the Higgins bunch. King offered me a chance to get away, and I took it. I'll shoot myself before I'll go back."

As time passed, Vivian and Molly quickly became friends, and through Vivian, Nathan began to appreciate Molly Horrell for what she was. The Horrell and Higgins factions continued sniping at one another, and it began to look as though the Horrells might have let Molly go. But trouble erupted on Christmas day that had nothing to do with the Horrells. Nathan, Vivian, King, and Molly drove to San Antonio for Christmas dinner at one of the fancy hotels. They were about to enter the hotel dining room, when a cowboy took Molly's arm and tried to lead her away. In a fury, Fisher drew his Colt and pumped three slugs into the man.

*John King Fisher was born in 1854, in Collin County, Texas.

"My God," said Nathan, "you didn't have to kill him."

"The hell I didn't," Fisher said. "He's one of those damn Horrell riders. I've seen him before."

"He's never worked for the Horrells," Molly cried.

The cowboy's name was William Dunovan, and his friends testified he had been drunk. There was no evidence he was, or had ever been, employed by the Horrells. King Fisher was taken to the courthouse, where he would be released on bond. While Nathan, Vivian, and Molly waited, Nathan spoke to one of the rangers from the outpost at San Antonio. The ranger knew of Nathan, and they spent a few minutes in friendly conversation.

"Ben Thompson killed a man this morning in Austin," the ranger said. "This is shaping up to be a bloody Christmas."

"I know Thompson," said Nathan. "What's going to happen to him?"

"He'll be tried," the ranger said. "Probably sometime next spring.*

The holiday had been spoiled, and when Fisher was allowed to leave, they all got into the buckboard and returned to the ranch. Fisher said nothing, and Molly sat beside him, pale and shaken. Reaching the ranch, Fisher left Nathan to unhitch the team and rub them down. Vivian remained with him, while Fisher and Molly went on to the house.

"Dear God, I can't believe he did that," Vivian said.

"Neither can I," said Nathan. "He's seeing Horrells everywhere."

When Nathan and Vivian reached the house, King Fisher was at the dining-room table with a bottle of whiskey, downing it from a shot glass. Molly was in the kitchen, looking more distressed than ever. Shaniqua seemed unconcerned, as she went about getting dinner. Molly ate virtually nothing, and King Fisher skipped the meal entirely, retiring to the living room with his bottle. Nathan and Vivian retreated to their room early, at a loss as to what to say or do.

"I feel sorry for Molly," Vivian said. "King seemed so nice. What happened to him?'

"I don't know," said Nathan. "All I know is, he's not the man I thought he was. I'm of a mind to move on. King's

---

*In May 1877, Ben Thompson was tried and acquitted.

my friend, and I'll side him till hell freezes, if he needs me, but I don't know what he needs or wants. Worse yet, I don't think he knows. Tomorrow, I think we'll all have to reach a decision."

When Nathan and Vivian arose the next morning, King Fisher sat at the table downing black coffee the way he had been drinking whiskey the day before. Shaniqua was preparing breakfast, and there was no sign of Molly. Fisher looked at Nathan through bleary eyes for a moment before he spoke.

"You and me need to talk."

Vivian left the room, and Fisher drank the rest of his coffee before he spoke.

"Pardner, me and Molly had us a talk last night. She wants us to just step out of the picture for a while. What happened ... that shooting ... in San Antone, helped her to see what lies ahead, if somethin' don't change. Personal, I can't see none of them Horrells bein' worth the lead it'd take to blow 'em all to perdition, but they're Molly's kin, and there's not a damn thing I can do about that. I'm thinking it's time for another wild horse hunt. Just me, Molly, and our *Mejicano* riders. After that, maybe we'll camp across the river for a spell, just keepin' an eye on things. Was it just me, I'd set here with a Winchester and blast the ears off any varmint that drifted within range, but this is for Molly. Do you think she's worth it?"

"She's worth more than all the other Horrells, with the Higgins pack thrown in," said Nathan. "The worst thing you can do—for your sake and Molly's—is to allow yourself to be dragged into this Horrell-Higgins fight. The Horrells will get over Molly leaving, but if you kill one of them, they'll hound you as long as there's one of them alive. Back off."

"Thanks, Nathan," Fisher said. "That's how I finally come to see it last night. It ain't easy, admittin' I'm dodging the Horrells, but I'll do it for Molly."

"Vivian and me were ready to ride on," said Nathan. "I think when I see you again, this Horrell-Higgins thing will had burned itself out."

Nathan and Vivian rode out after breakfast, leaving King Fisher and Molly content with their decision to take an extended journey into Old Mexico.

"I feel so much better about them," Vivian said. "Molly left home to escape the fighting and killing, and now he's taking her away from it for good."

"King Fisher's a prideful man," said Nathan. "It took nerve for him to overcome that, for Molly's sake. There's no shame in backing off from a fight you can't win."

San Antonio, Texas. January 15, 1877

Nathan and Vivian took a room for the night. It was still early, but far to the west, thunderheads were gathering. There would be a storm before morning. After supper, they had some time before dark.

"Since we'll be leaving early in the morning," Nathan said, "we ought to stop by the ranger station, in case there's been a telegram for us."

"I don't like telegrams," said Vivian. "They're almost always bad news."

They reached the ranger outpost just as Ranger Jack Hardeman was locking the door. He knew Nathan from past visits, and he had been a close friend of Captain Sage Jennings.

"This is a welcome surprise," Hardeman said. "I've been here alone all day, and I was about to ride to Fisher's place, looking for you. Just a while ago, a telegram came for you, and it's urgent."

The message had been written in Hardeman's scrawl, and it was brief. It had been sent by Foster Hagerman, and it read:

Harley wounded and condition critical stop. Hospital in Pueblo.

Vivian took the message with shaking hands, and her tears fell as she read the words.

"When can we go," she cried, "and how long will it take us?"

"There's no point in leaving before morning," said Nathan, "and it must be near seven hundred miles. Pushing the horses, we can make it in ten days."

"Oh, God," she cried, "he could be dead by then."

"He could," said Nathan, "but I'm counting on him to hold on until we get there. I'll need to know what happened, so I can go after the varmints responsible."

"I was hoping he could avoid this, by taking a job with the railroad."

"His is a lawman's job, Vivian," Nathan said. "All he lacks is the badge, and while it's a mite dangerous, he could do worse. I was shot and shot at, and I'm alive."

Nathan and Vivian left San Antonio at first light, riding northwest. Empty ranged far ahead. They rode until darkness caught up to them, eating jerked beef and drinking spring water. Each morning they arose before daylight, and each day became a repetition of those past. They seldom spoke, each of them aware that at any moment, the clock might be ticking away the last seconds of Harley Stafford's life.

Pueblo, Colorado. January 26, 1877
Reaching the ten-bed hospital, Nathan and Vivian were surprised to find Hagerman there. He looked as though he hadn't slept much. The question was in their eyes, and he didn't wait for them to speak.

"Harley's alive," he said, "but just barely. If the doctor will let you see him, maybe it will make a difference."

CHAPTER 35

"You can have five minutes with him," the doctor said. "He's very weak from loss of blood."

Nathan caught his breath when they entered the room. Harley Stafford lay with eyes closed, almost as white as the sheet that covered him. Vivian knelt beside the bed.

"Harley," she said softly. "Harley."

Slowly the eyelids moved, as though even that small effort was too great. Finally, when his eyes opened, it took a moment for him to respond. Nathan knelt beside Vivian, to be sure Harley could hear him.

"Pardner," said Nathan, "I'll be going after them. They'll pay."

"Tomorrow," Harley whispered. "Need . . . to . . . talk."

"I'll wait," said Nathan. "Rest, so you'll feel like talking."

Nathan stepped out into the hall, leaving Vivian alone with Harley. Foster Hagerman was there, and until Nathan could talk to Harley, Hagerman would do.

"Tell me what you know," Nathan said.

"I know any normal man would be dead," said Hagerman. "My god, he was hit five times. I think he's been hanging on until you got here. The bastards dynamited the track thirty miles east of here. Harley got three of them before they shot him. They got away with fifty thousand dollars in gold."

"Damn it," Nathan said. "I thought you had learned not to set a specific schedule for those shipments. How could they have known which train it was on?"

"I don't know," said Hagerman, "unless there's a Judas among us."

"When did it happen?"

"Twelve days ago," Hagerman said. "It happened early in the morning of the day I sent you the telegram."

"Has no attempt been made to trail the outlaws?"

"No," said Hagerman. "The engineer reversed the train, bringing Harley in. A report was filed with the sheriff here, but he was unable to raise a posse. The town hasn't forgotten what happened when a posse took the trail of the Chapa Gonzolos gang. I suppose the only positive thing is the fact it hasn't rained since the robbery. The outlaws had two wagons."

"They've also had time to reach Santa Fe," said Nathan.

"You're going after them?"

"Yes," Nathan said. "They're going to pay for what they did to Harley."

"The gold shipment . . ."

"Damn the gold shipment," said Nathan. "All I can promise you is that this particular bunch of coyotes won't be robbing any more trains."

To everybody's surprise, Harley Stafford was stronger the next morning. Despite all the doctor's cautioning, he insisted on talking to Nathan.

"I counted a dozen of them," Harley said. "I was ridin' the caboose, and I got out of there when they stopped the train. But they expected that, and some of 'em had dropped back. Time I hit the ground, they had me in a crossfire."

"Do you remember anything that might help me iden-tify them?"

"Not much," said Harley. "I didn't have much time. Those I saw, close up, seemed to be Spanish or Mexican. One of them—maybe the leader—was duded up all in black, with a red sash around his middle, and he rode the biggest mule I ever saw."

"Vivian will be here with you," Nathan said, "and I want you to devote all your time to getting back on your feet. I'll see you when I've settled with this bunch of coyotes."

"I'm obliged," said Harley. *"Vaya con Dios, amigo."*

While Vivian hated to see Nathan go, Harley's improved condition raised her spirits. Nathan rode out, Empty surging ahead. They followed the AT and SF tracks to the place the train had been stopped. The track had been repaired, while the old rails lay in a twisted tangle some distance away. Nathan had no trouble picking up the trail. It led southwest, and there were nine riders. There were two wagons, drawn by mules for faster travel, and Nathan suspected the eventual destination was Santa Fe. It brought back memories of those days when Nathan had trailed Chapa Gonzolos and his renegades to Santa Fe, only to find that Gonzolos was a respectable man, thought to have inherited wealth. Nathan believed he was two hundred miles from Santa Fe, and he rode at a slow gallop, resting his horse at regular intervals.

Santa Fe, New Mexico Territory. January 31, 1877

Reaching Santa Fe late in the day, Nathan found a hotel willing to accept Empty, and took a room for the night. The trail he had followed had become lost, when he had entered the frequently traveled streets of town. Even if the outlaws had another destination in mind, they would still have gone through Santa Fe in the hope of confusing any possible pursuers. At least one of the outlaws rode a horse with a bad shoe, for part of the calk was missing. Before wasting time in Santa Fe, Nathan would ride a half circle to the south, seeking a continuation of the trail. After supper he bought a newspaper. He and Empty then returned to their hotel room. Nathan then went through the newspaper, finding only one article of interest. On January twenty-second, in a clash with the Higgins clan, Merritt Horrell had been killed.

"That's the start of it, Empty," said Nathan. "Thank God King Fisher wasn't foolish enough to get caught up in that."

Nathan rode out after breakfast. When he was far enough from town, he swung south in a half circle. To his dismay, he immediately found the trail he had lost upon reaching Santa Fe. He verified it by seeking and finding the print of the shoe with the broken calk. He had been on the trail five days, and the outlaws had a twelve-day start. But where in tarnation were they going? He considered the possibility they were bound for the border, their eventual destination being Old Mexico, but he soon rejected that. Had they been going to Old Mexico, they should have traveled due south following the robbery. Instead, they had taken a southwesterly course, and after passing through Santa Fe, had continued in that direction. Nathan rode on, conscious of a change in the land. The second day after riding out of Santa Fe, he began to recognize the territory. When he had been on the manhunt that had brought him west, he had searched the mining camps of Nevada and Arizona. He now was riding among the stately ponderosa pines that grew so prolifically in the territory. He sensed that the trail he followed must soon come to an end, for he had left Pueblo ten days ago. He was in a land where winter seldom ventured, and despite the dryness of the soil, there were wild flowers. It was rough country for wagons, and he soon found the remains of a broken wagon wheel. The wheel that had replaced it had a wider tire, and left a distinctive track. It would be something to remember if he had to identify the wagon.

Eventually he heard a dog barking somewhere ahead. Since he had no idea where the outlaws were bound, he couldn't ignore the possibility that he had reached their stronghold. Cautiously, he rode on. To his surprise, when he topped a ridge, he could see a village. There were fields in which men toiled, and the peaceful scene reminded him of those long-ago days in Virginia, before the war. If the outlaws he sought were bound for this village, they didn't have to know Nathan Stone was trailing them. The trail continued toward the main street of the town. Nathan could see a mercantile, a livery, a one-story hotel, and what looked like a courthouse or town hall. There were other false-fronted buildings that proved to be saloons. Beside a

saloon—The Yucca—were two wagons with canvas up. Nathan dismounted, looping the grulla's reins about the hitch
rail. He then went around to the side of the saloons where
the wagons were. On one of them, the right rear wheel was
just a little different, the tire a little wider. One of the
wagons he had been following. He entered the saloon, finding the bar lined with hard-eyed men. It was enough to
arouse his suspicion, for working men didn't spend their
daytime hours in a saloon. He noticed immediately that
every man was armed, their Colts thonged down. Several
carried two guns, and they all eyed Nathan. He ordered a
beer, made his way to a table, and sat down. Attention
shifted away from him, when another man elbowed his way
through the swinging doors. He spoke to one of the men
at the bar, and he looked at Nathan, his hand near the butt
of his Colt. He spoke.

"Mister, you was seen payin' attention to them wagons
outside. I reckon you'd better tell us what your interest is."

Nathan stood up. "I used to be a bull whacker, and I
have an interest in wagons. Now you tell me why that concerns you."

"I reckon you ain't near as concerned with that wagon
as you are with its cargo, and if you know what that is,
then I know why you're here."

He was fast, but not fast enough. Nathan fired once, and
with the Colt steady in his hand, he edged his way toward
the swinging doors.

"Drop the gun, bucko," said a voice from the door.
"You're covered."

Nathan had no choice. He dropped the gun, and quickly
the man behind him seized his other weapon. Then they
all rushed him, kicking, gouging, slugging. He was struck
with a pistol barrel, dazing him, and was finally beaten to
the floor.

"Couple of you get him over to the jail," one of his
assailants said.

Nathan awakened with a pounding headache, lying on a
slab of a bunk. He sat up, aware of the bars surrounding
him. In the corridor stood a man with a star.

"I defended myself," said Nathan. "Why am I in jail?"

"Murder. I'm Sheriff Hondo, an' I'm just goin' by what

the boys told me. Got plenty witnesses. Tomorrow, Judge Ponder will decide what to do with you."

Nathan had no idea what had become of Empty. The dog was resourceful, and would survive, unless one of the gunmen shot him. Late in the afternoon, a dozen heavily armed men rode in from the west. They laughed and shouted, and when they dismounted, heavy canvas bags were removed from their horses. They looked for the world like a band of thieves returning with their plunder.

"Everybody to the saloon," one of them shouted. "Drinks are on us."

Every man within hearing—one of whom was Sheriff Hondo—headed for the saloon. It gave Nathan something to think about, and the more he thought about it, the less he looked forward to his appearance before Judge Ponder. Peaceful though it seemed, the place had all the earmarks of an outlaw town, up to and including the sheriff and the judge. Nathan had no supper, and for breakfast, he was brought a pot of beans, bacon, and a tin cup of coffee. Judge Ponder's courtroom was in the rear of the building that housed the jail. Most of the men who had jumped Nathan in the saloon were in the courtroom.

"Ever'body stand," said Sheriff Hondo.

Nathan remained seated, earning himself a sour look from Judge Ponder, as he took his place on the bench.

"Who is this man, and what is he charged with?" Judge Ponder demanded.

They hadn't even bothered asking his name, and Nathan said nothing, forcing Sheriff Hondo to pose the question.

"What's your name?" Sheriff Hondo growled.

"Nathan Stone."

"His name's Nathan Stone, your honor," said Sheriff Hondo. "He shot and killed Billings yesterday, in the saloon."

"You have witnesses?"

"All them gents in front of you," Sheriff Hondo said.

"Swear them in," said Judge Ponder.

"All you varmints is sworn in," Sheriff Hondo said. "Did all of you see Stone shoot Billings yesterday?"

"Yeah," they answered. "We seen it."

"Who was first to draw?" Sheriff Hondo asked.

"Stone," they all shouted.

"Now get on over to the saloon an' have yourselves a shot," said Hondo. "Put it on my tab."

"Do you have anything to say in your own defense?" Judge Ponder asked.

"I'm not guilty," said Nathan, "and I want a trial by jury. I'm a citizen of the United States of America."

"You're not in the United States," Judge Ponder said. "This is Arizona Territory, and we make our own laws. You have been proved guilty, and there ain't nothin' a jury can do to change that. I'm sentencin' you to five years at hard labor."

"Come on, bucko," said Sheriff Hondo. "You look like you got a strong back. You'll need it. We're buildin' a dam, and you get the honor of helpin' it along."

Nathan was taken outside. Sheriff Hondo pointed to a buckboard, and Nathan climbed up to the box. The sheriff mounted the box and took the reins. Nathan was amazed at the many fields under cultivation. Long before they reached it, he could hear the roar of the river.*

"Trouble with this damn country," said Hondo, "is there ain't enough water. We aim to divert water to irrigate the crops, opening an' closin' the gates, as needed."

Nathan said nothing, marveling at the man's nerve, speaking as though they were old friends. Yet he was obviously a willing accomplice to a system that robbed men of their freedom, using their labor to further its own ends. The site they had chosen for the dam was at a bend in the river, where the natural elevation of the land would readily result in a runoff, when the dam was ready. But work on the dam had obviously just begun. Man labored, digging holes for pillars that would become the backbone of the dam. Piles of logs lay ready, and Nathan could hear the sound of axes and saws at work. There was the crash of a fallen tree. Sheriff Hondo reined up, waiting until one of the guards reached the buckboard.

"Quivado," said Sheriff Hondo, "this is Mr. Stone. He's going to help us build the dam. Mr. Stone, the other guard is Sanchez, and you'll meet him in time. Now, if you'll step down, Quivado will take charge of you."

Nathan climbed down, not liking the looks of Quivado.

---

*The Gila River flows across southern Arizona, emptying into the Gulf of California.

He was Mexican, some Indian, and the blacksnake whip coiled about his arm looked all business. He had long hair, a flowing mustache, and a grim mouth that looked as though it had never smiled. In one big hand was a set of leg irons. He knelt down to lock them in place, while Sheriff Hondo kept his eyes on Nathan.

"We trust you," said Sheriff Hondo, "so we're leaving your hands free. Besides, you'll need them to swing an ax and pull a saw."

The sheriff drove away, and Quivado looked at Nathan in anticipation. He nodded in the direction of the laboring men, and Nathan headed that way, the cumbersome chains jingling with every step. The three men peeling the pine logs paused, leaning on their axes and wiping their sweaty faces on their dirty sleeves.

"Damn it," shouted Quivado, speaking for the first time, "git back to work. This ain't no church social. Stone, take an ax an' git to peelin' them logs."

Nathan took an ax and joined the trio of sweating men. Quivado sought shade, taking a seat with his back to a half-grown pine, a Winchester across his knees. Sanchez, Nathan guessed, would be with the laboring men who were felling trees. Nathan said nothing to his companions, waiting for a better time. Their eyes, when they occasionally met his, were dull with hopelessness. When the sun was noon high, Quivado called a halt. There was no food. There was a bucket of water, a gourd dipper, and they were allowed a few minutes of rest. Quivado was always within hearing distance, and he never took his eyes off them. The labor continued until sundown, when two wagons arrived. Four men in chains were marched out of the woods. Behind them, with a Winchester, was the other guard, Sanchez. The leg irons were removed, allowing the men to climb into the wagons. Nathan and his three companions were in one, while the four who had been felling trees were in the other. Quivado and Sanchez were mounted, riding on either side of the second wagon.

Nathan expected a bunkhouse, but nothing like the one to which they were taken. It was long, low, without a single window, and it appeared there were accommodations for at least a hundred men. It also appeared that when they were locked in for the night, nobody would be allowed to leave until the next morning. Large earthen jars took the place of an outhouse, and the place stank to high heaven. There were buckets of water with dippers, and tin washbasins for washing face and hands. More wagons were coming in from the fields, and Nathan counted forty more laborers. He followed his companions into the stinking bunkhouse, and for the first time, one of them spoke to him.

"You got maybe fifteen minutes to wash up, if you're of a mind to. We got to eat an' git back here 'fore dark."

The reason for that wasn't difficult to understand. There wasn't a lamp in the place, nor was there a fireplace or a stove. The bunks—in tiers of two—lined the walls. There was only a thin straw tick over a slab of wood. Supper was a lackluster affair, consisting of beans, bacon, corn bread, and coffee. The men were then marched back to the bunkhouse and the doors were locked. Nathan took a bunk near the three men with whom he had worked during the day.

"Tell me about this place," he said in a low voice.

"Ain't that much to tell. I'm Withers. The other two gents is Strong and Rutledge. We been here maybe six months. It don't pay to talk too much. Some of this bunch is Judas to the bone. They'll sell you out for an extra spoonful of beans."

"How long are you in for?" Nathan asked.

"Hell, ever'body gets five years," said Withers, "an' don't go thinkin' you'll be let out when you've done your time. If you live that long, they'll trump up some charge and give you another five years. Ain't but two ways of gettin' out of here, an' one's as bad as the other. You can leave in a pine box, or they'll send you to the territorial prison, in Yuma."

"Why the prison? Hell, this is all the prison I ever want to see."

"Judge Ponder's workin' a deal with somebody at Yuma. For enough money—I hear it's ten thousand dollars—a man can buy his way out of the territorial prison. He's turned loose, like he escaped, and then the prison announces he's been captured. Only it ain't him that goes back to Yuma. Judge Ponder delivers them some poor damn fool like you or me, and *he* goes to Yuma, with added time for escaping."

"While Ponder and some bastard at Yuma splits the money," said Nathan.

"You got it," Withers said, "an' that ain't all. This damn

town is nothing more than an outlaw stronghold. I hear tha Ponder collects from fifty to a hundred dollars a month, pe man, for guaranteed safety from the law. This bein' a terri tory, there ain't a damn thing anybody can do about it."

"What about the farming?"

"That's a front," said Withers, "should some outsider ge nosy, but even that brings in money. The fruit, vegetables, and melons is hauled to Tucson, as well as some of the mining camps."

"Withers," somebody growled, "shut the hell up. How's a man to sleep?"

Nathan sighed, shifting positions. It looked truly hopeless. Nobody knew where he was, and there was no means of getting word to anyone who could and would come to his aid. But he dared not give up. He would mind his business and bide his time, which was all he could do....

Pueblo, Colorado. February 1, 1877

Harley Stafford was on his feet, restless, and worried.

"There's nothing we can do, Harley," said Vivian. "We don't know where Nathan went, and even if you were able to ride, there's no trail. There's been five days of rain."

"I'll give it one more week," Harley said, "and then I'm goin' lookin' for him. He's in neck-deep and can't reach us, or he's dead. In either case, there's some gun work that needs doin'. I aim to see it done."

"Then I'm going with you," said Vivian. "It's bad enough if I've lost Nathan, without waiting for days, weeks, or months, not knowing what's happened to you."

"I can't argue with that," Harley said. "I know how you feel."

"What about your position with the railroad?"

"Hagerman understands. Hell, he'd better. Nathan went after that bunch of outlaws when I was so shot up I couldn't move. That's railroad business."

"You know better than that," said Vivian. "He's doing this for you, because you're his friend. He may have given his life for you."

"You think I don't realize that?" Harley cried. "I told him I'd be there, if he ever had need of me, and by God, I'm going, if I have to crawl on my hands and knees."

*　　*　　*

The days wore on, and the men labored under the Arizona sun without their shirts. Nathan's hands went from blisters to calluses, while his upper body, arms, neck, and face turned a deep bronze. Occasionally, while they were in the woods, he caught a glimpse of Empty. He had no idea what had become of his saddlebags, with all the money he had. He hadn't been searched after they had taken his Colts. Long ago, he had prepared for just such a time as this, by having a small leather pocket sewn into the upper of his left boot. In that pocket he had placed the silver shield given him by Texas Ranger Captain Jennings, and the silver watch given him by Byron Silver. Somehow they would help him, if he had some means of reaching them. But they were far away, and the fires of his hopes burned dim, as one weary day dragged into another. . . .

Empty lay in the shade of a fir, near enough to the laboring men to hear the sound of their axes and saws. Small game was plentiful enough, and he had managed to keep himself alive. At first, he hadn't understood why Nathan remained with these strange men, but he well understood the destructive ability of the Winchesters the guards possessed. Many times, Empty had trotted along the back trail, pausing to look back, but each time he had returned. Unwilling to leave Nathan, he waited. . . .

Nathan kept his silence, avoiding trouble with his captors, but one morning everything changed. When it was time to go to breakfast, Withers still lay on his bunk, unable to get up. He was still there when the wagons came to take the prisoners to their day of labor.

"Withers is sick," one of the men told Quivado.

"I got the cure for what ails him," said Quivado, uncoiling his whip.

When he drew back the whip, Nathan caught his arm. His right fist came up, smashing Quivado in the face. The burly guard stumbled against the wall, but Nathan was unable to pursue his advantage. Sanchez, the other guard, slammed the butt of his Winchester into the back of Nathan's head, and he fell facedown.

"The rest of you get out of here," said Quivado, wiping his bleeding nose, "and take Withers with you. I aim to teach this damn fool a lesson he ain't likely to forget."

The rest of the men trooped out, two of his comrades carrying Withers. Quivado then set to work with the deadly blacksnake whip. He cut Nathan's shirt to ribbons, lashing him unmercifully, ceasing only when his arm grew tired. He then mounted his horse and rode after the wagons.

For a long time, Nathan lay there, trying to accept the agony that was his. He could feel the blood running down his back. Something must be done. He struggled to his hands and knees, and was finally able to sit on the edge of one of the bunks. He removed what was left of his shirt. When he was able to stand, he took a wooden bucket that was almost full of water, and stumbled outside. He found a place where the soil was loose, having been trampled by the hooves of horses and mules. He poured the water over as wide an area as he could, until there was a patch of mud. He then eased himself to the ground and lay down, his tortured back in the cooling mud. It was an old remedy, and he didn't know if it would save him from infection, but he had nothing else. . . .

Sheriff Hondo took a chair and sat down. Judge Ponder wasted no time in getting to the point.

"The first week in April," said Ponder, "there's going to be another escape at Yuma. You will capture the prisoner and return him to the territorial prison, as usual, for which authorities there will pay you a hundred dollars."

"There an' back," Sheriff Hondo said, "that's five hundred miles. Ain't it time I was gettin' more money for my part in this racket?"

"Keep referring to it as a 'racket,' " said Judge Ponder, "and you'll cease to be part of it. You're being paid as the sheriff, for which you do virtually nothing. Don't push your luck."

"You're takin' an almighty lot for granted," Sheriff Hondo said bitterly. "Suppose I ride away from here an' don't bother comin' back?"

"Then I'll be forced to put a price on your head, and telegraph every lawman on the frontier," said Ponder. "That would be a real problem for you, I think. Nobody likes an outlaw sheriff."

"You scruffy, double-dealing old coyote," Hondo said bitterly.

When he had gone, slamming the door behind him, Judge Ponder laughed.

Nathan lay on his back, closing his eyes to the sun, and eventually the searing pain subsided. He got to his feet, careful not to break the poultice of dried mud, and made his way back into the bunkhouse. Quivado had left him to live or die on his own, and for that, Nathan was thankful. He stretched out, belly-down, on his bunk, wondering what had happened to Withers.

When the wagons had reached the dam site, Withers had been dragged out and forced to stand. Each time, he collapsed in a heap on the ground, unmoving, even when Quivado struck him with the murderous whip.

"Damn him," said Quivado, "leave him be. I'll see that he does twice as much work tomorrow."

But it was a promise Quivado would be unable to keep. Before the sun was noon high, Withers was dead. . . .

CHAPTER 36

At the end of the day, when the rest of the men returned to the bunkhouse, nobody bothered Nathan. Quivado came in, evidently to see if Nathan was alive, and then left. The rest of the prisoners said nothing, their eyes on Nathan's mud-plastered back.

"Where's Withers?" Nathan asked.

"In the ground," somebody said. "You took a beating for nothing."

"I reckon that's a matter of opinion," said Nathan.

Despite his beating, Nathan went to supper. He looked Quivado in the eye, and the man looked away. Nathan slept belly-down, but he was in no condition to labor in the hot Arizona sun without a shirt. His guards had reached the same conclusion, for when the prisoners were taken to breakfast the next morning, Sanchez tossed Nathan a faded denim shirt. It was too large, allowing for his lacerated back. The wet mud had aided in the clotting of blood, and the torn skin had begun to scab over. The muscles were sore, aching from the beating, but Nathan vowed Quivado wouldn't have the satisfaction of knowing.

Several times, Nathan saw Empty, and the dog didn't look hungry. Obviously, he was puzzled by Nathan's circumstances, but his loyalty wouldn't allow him to leave. But where was he to go? He had no home, unless he remembered those days in New Orleans. Days passed, and Nathan's back healed. Quivado still looked at him in a way that Nathan didn't like, as though Quivado had plans for Nathan Stone. It was enough to prevent most of Nathan's companions from so much as speaking to him, for they feared any friendliness toward him might result in punishment from Quivado. Strong and Rutledge, who labored beside Nathan each day, spoke to him cautiously when Quivado wasn't around. While he dared not speak to the others about such, Nathan's mind was constantly in a turmoil, considering and rejecting all possible means of escape. He was in leg irons all day, constantly under guard, and at night the bunkhouse was locked, with guards outside. He needed a horse and his guns, and any chance of his getting to either began to seem more and more unlikely. Armed and mounted, he would have to shoot his way out, against virtually impossible odds. Every outlaw in town—even those paying for sanctuary—would kill him if they could, for his escape would jeopardize their safety. His only hope of rescue lay with Harley Stafford, and Harley was more than seven hundred miles away, without the slightest idea as to where Nathan might be. How long, he wondered, before a slug from a Winchester became more tolerable than imprisonment and endless days of slave labor?

Nathan had silently vowed not to antagonize Quivado again, for he suspected a second bout with the whip would be fatal. But he had no control over Quivado's brutal, sadistic nature, and he believed it was but a matter of time until Quivado came after him again. Nathan and three of his companions were preparing to drop a heavy ponderosa log into a hole, where it would become an upright for the dam. Nathan's foot slipped, and without his support, his three companions were unable to control the log. It fell, and went tumbling down the slope, toward the river.

"Damn you," Quivado shouted. Dropping his Winchester, he came after Nathan with the deadly whip.

But Nathan caught the lash with his left hand, and with a mighty heave, tore it out of Quivado's grasp. Quivado went for the Colt at his hip, but he was slow. Even the leg irons didn't stop Nathan. He threw himself to the ground and rolled, going after the Winchester Quivado had dropped. Quivado fired twice, the slugs kicking up dust, but before he could fire a third time, Nathan had his hands on the Winchester. He fired once, twice, three times, sending Quivado sprawling in the dirt. But there was the roar of a second Winchester, and Nathan was struck in the back. He fell belly-down and lay still. Sanchez, the second guard, approached. He prodded Nathan with the toe of his boot, without response. Kneeling, he felt for a pulse. The man was still alive. This was a situation that needed a bit more authority than he possessed, and since he couldn't leave these laborers to seek the sheriff, they must all go together.

"Rutledge," said Sanchez, "bring my horse."

The horse was near enough not to be a temptation to Rutledge, and when he brought the animal, Sanchez pointed to another of the prisoners.

"You, Haynes, help Rutledge get Stone across the saddle."

The two men lifted Nathan to the saddle, turning him belly-down.

"Now," said Sanchez, "we're all going to take a walk to Judge Ponder's office. Stone is their responsibility, since he's unable to work. Rutledge, you lead the horse."

While it was more than a mile to town, to Ponder's office, nobody complained. Every man secretly hoped Nathan Stone lived. Hadn't he rid them of the sadistic, evil Quivado? Somebody saw them coming, and by the time they reached the dusty main street, Sheriff Hondo was waiting.

"Sanchez, what'n hell . . ."

"Stone shoot Quivado, I shoot Stone," said Sanchez. "I cannot leave these hombres by themselves. What could I do but bring them with me?"

Sheriff Hondo had no logical argument, so he said nothing. Instead, he took Nathan's wrist, seeking a pulse. It was there, and he sighed with relief. Stone could still recover in time for the exchange Judge Ponder had in mind.

"Wait here, Sanchez," Sheriff Hondo said. "I'll talk to Judge Ponder."

Judge Ponder listened. Finally he spoke.

"Take Stone to the saloon. Tell Mallet I said patch him up, bed him down somewhere, and pour the whiskey down him. Then I want you to go with Sanchez, and get those men back to work. For the rest of the day, you'll replace Quivado."

"By God, I'm the sheriff," Hondo bawled.

"For the rest of today, and until I say otherwise, you're Quivado," said Ponder.

Nathan awoke, uncertain as to where he was, recalling only that he had been shot. He could hear the clink of glasses and the distant hum of voices, evidence enough that he was in the back of a saloon. On a table beside his bunk sat a whiskey bottle and a pitcher of water. He raised himself on one elbow and drank thirstily from the pitcher. The whiskey accounted for his thundering headache, but it had evidently rid him of fever, for he was sweating. Suddenly a curtain was drawn aside, and Sheriff Hondo stood there looking at him.

"Well, you're alive," said Hondo. "Soon as you're able to be up and about, the judge wants to see you."

"I can understand that," Nathan said. "He wants to look me in the eye while he adds another five years to my sentence."

"Oh, I don't think he aims to do that," said Hondo. "He's a compassionate man."

Pueblo, Colorado. March 20, 1877

Barely on his feet from the shooting, Harley Stafford had taken sick and was confined to bed for another two weeks. He was frantic.

"Harley," said Vivian, "you heard what the doctor said. You got up too soon, and in your weakened condition, you had a setback. He's promised you can get up tomorrow."

Harley said nothing. His mind was on Nathan Stone, and he silently cursed his rotten luck. He imagined he could hear a ticking clock, and with every stroke of the pendulum, time was running out for Nathan. . . .

*   *   *

The twenty-fifth of March, Nathan was again taken before Judge Ponder. Sheriff Hondo was the only other person present.

"Mr. Stone," said Ponder, "in light of your recent conduct, I have found it necessary to evaluate and amend your sentence. Your first day in our town, you shot a man. Since you had no record, I took that into consideration. Now, however, you stand accused of a second killing. On the sixteenth of April, you will be taken to the territorial prison in Yuma, where you will spend the rest of your natural life. Until then, you will be confined to a cell."

Nathan said nothing. He was shocked but not surprised. He had three weeks to gain his freedom. He had no doubt that if the formidable gates of Yuma prison closed behind him, he would die there. The night came, and sitting in his cell, he could hear the distant wail of coyotes. Then, somewhere much nearer, there was an answering cry. It was the mournful howl of a dog, harkening him back to that dismal night in Virginia, when Cotton Blossom had howled over the grave of old Malachi. Somewhere on a distant hill, Empty waited, his cry sending chills up Nathan's spine. Empty howled again, and as the mournful sound faded away to silence, it seemed more and more like a harbinger of death. . . .

Days passed, and Nathan knew only one thing for sure. Escape from the outlaw town was out of the question, for his leg irons were never removed, nor was he allowed out of his cell. While he had no idea how long would be the ride to Yuma, he believed it would be his only hope of escape. Various guards had visited the jail, and Nathan had overheard their conversations with Sheriff Hondo. Two men would be selected to escort Nathan Stone to Yuma territorial prison, each man to be paid a hundred dollars, and there apparently was some competition among the outlaws. Time dragged on, and the day before the fateful journey was to begin, Judge Ponder invited the chosen men to his office. Their names—probably not their own—were Hiram Doss and Rum Tasby.

"Sit down," Judge Ponder ordered.

The two sat, not in the least intimidated. They were burly, bearded, and in addition to a thonged-down Colt, each had a second weapon slipped under his belt. Rawhide thongs about their necks attested to Bowie knives down their backs. Their clothing consisted of worn Levi's, sweaty flannel shirts, scuffed, runover boots, and sweat-stained hats.

"Both of you have done this before," said Judge Ponder, "so I don't have to tell you what is expected of you. Moreover, I shouldn't have to remind you of the consequences, should you fail. Should there be an attempt to escape, you are to shoot to wound, not to kill. Have I made myself clear?"

"Yeah," the pair said, in a single voice.

"I can't hear you," Ponder snapped.

"Yes, sir," they replied, irritated.

"No questions?"

"No, sir," they said.

"Good," said Ponder. "Now get out of here, and be ready to ride at first light."

Nathan was taken from his cell at dawn. The work crews were being marched from the mess hall, and for just a moment, Nathan's eyes met those of Strong and Rutledge, the men who had worked beside Nathan. In that brief look, Nathan tried to convey the fury that threatened to engulf him, to impart to them some spark of hope. Silently, he promised himself that the terrible gates of Yuma prison would never close behind him. He would go free or he would die. If he escaped—if God allowed him to live—he vowed he would return to and destroy this outlaw stronghold.

"Mr. Stone," said Judge Ponder. "Hiram Doss and Rum Tasby will be your escorts to Yuma. I regret that I cannot say it's been a pleasure knowing you."

Nathan Stone said nothing, for if he spoke, he feared he might betray his intentions. Instead, he allowed his eyes to meet those of the pseudo-judge, and Ponder involuntarily shuddered. Where he had expected hatred, there was only grim, fiery determination, and a promise of eye-for-an-eye retribution. Doss removed Nathan's leg irons and manacled his wrists.

"Mount up," said Doss.

The horse, to Nathan's surprise, was the grulla on which he had ridden in to Ponder's town. Nathan mounted, paying attention to the weapons of his captors. Each had a

tied-down Colt with a second under the waistband, and a
Winchester in his saddle boot. The rawhide thongs about
their necks suggested hidden Bowie knives. They rode out,
the sun at their backs, and many residents of the outlaw
town watched them go.

"Time to rest the horses," said Tasby, when they had
ridden a little more than an hour. "Git down and stretch
your legs, and if you're needin' water, belly-down."

Nathan dismounted, and stretching his manacled hands
out awkwardly before him, he drank from the spring runoff.
He struggled to his feet and turned toward some bushes.

"Hold it," Doss snapped.

"I'm tired of holding it," said Nathan. "This is private.
Do you mind?"

"Yeah," Tasby said. "We mind. Do whatever you got
to do where you stand. Nothin' you got in mind is gonna
shock us."

The pair laughed at the crude humor. Nathan remained
where he was. His need to go to the bushes wasn't as great
as his need to know if Empty was following him. His heart
leaped when he saw the faithful hound peering at him from
the brush. He turned back to face his captors, lest they
discover his ace in the hole. When they mounted up and
rode on, Nathan's mind worked feverishly, seeking some
means of escape. Common sense told him he must wait
until they were far from Ponder's town. Otherwise, Doss
and Tasby had only to alert Ponder, and a hundred men
would take Nathan's trail. Each time they paused to rest
the horses, Nathan's sharp eyes searched for Empty, and
he was always there. The dog was careful not to be seen
by Doss and Tasby, and that was essential to Nathan's plan
of escape. When the time came, the surprise must be total.

"Just so's you don't git no ideas," Doss said, when they
had stopped for the night, "you'll be sleepin' in leg irons."

It was no less than Nathan had expected. Obviously, they
believed when he was riding ahead of them, he was less
likely to make a run for it. That told him that the pair of
them would be more than ready for just such an attempt,
and he abandoned the idea. Instead, he determined to
make his break after he had dismounted, but before the
leg irons had been replaced. Before the end of the first
day's ride, they reached a river, and began following it west.

"We're stoppin' here for the night," Tasby finally said. "Step down."

Nathan dismounted, and while Tasby stood out of Nathan's reach, Doss again locked the leg irons in place.

"Now don't try nothin' foolish," Tasby said. "I'll be watchin' you while Doss rustles up some grub."

Nathan eyed the swift-running river. He was still too near Ponder's town to make his break, and as they traveled westward, the river should deepen. The evening of the third day he would make his move.

"Time to secure you for the night," said Doss, when supper was finished. He unlocked one side of Nathan's leg irons. "Set facin' that pine, with one leg on either side of it."

Nathan did as he was ordered, and Doss secured the manacle he had removed. Nathan was then able to stand, sit, or lie down, but he could not escape. It suited him, because it wasn't necessary for Doss and Tasby to constantly watch him. Sometime during the night, he knew Empty would come to him, and Doss or Tasby might shoot the dog.

Far into the night, when Doss and Tasby were snoring, Nathan was awakened by a cold nose on his cheek. He sat up, ruffling the dog's ears, and Empty whined deep in his throat. While Nathan might hold his own against one of his guards, the other might shoot him, without some distraction. While Empty would readily attack a man about to shoot Nathan, there was no assurance that the dog would be near enough when Nathan made his desperate move. It was a chance he would have to take, and time was running out.

When Nathan awoke near first light, Empty was gone. Instinctively he knew Doss and Tasby were hostile to him, as they were to Nathan. While he didn't know the reason for them, he understood the chains that imprisoned Nathan, and the two had been through enough together that the dog would be expecting a break for freedom. After a second day on the trail, Nathan felt Empty's presence, and during the night, the dog again visited him. With or without Empty's help, Nathan vowed to make his escape the next evening just before dark, before he was locked in the leg irons. . . .

The third day passed as uneventfully as had the first two. Nathan kept an eye on the river, aware that it flowed wider and deeper. When they reined up near the end of the day, there was what appeared to be a natural campsite near the river. A heavy stand of pines dissipated the heat of the evening sun, while there was plenty of graze for the three horses. Nathan rode the grulla as near the river as he dared, before he was given the order to dismount.*

"Git down," said Tasby, taking the leg irons that hung from his saddle horn.

Nathan dismounted, and for just a moment, Tasby's horse was in Doss's line of fire. Nathan seized the startled Tasby and the two of them went over the bank and into the river. Nathan's hands were manacled, but his legs were free. He brought up both hands, slamming the manacles on his wrists against the underside of Tasby's chin.

Doss had his Colt out, awaiting a chance to shoot, when Empty came after him. The dog didn't growl or bark, and when Doss became aware of him, it was too late. Seizing the gunman's arm in his powerful jaws, Empty hung on, forcing Doss to drop the Colt. Doss went after the gun with his left hand, only to have Empty loose his grip and seize the left hand. The dog bit down hard, and Doss screamed.

Nathan did his best to hold Tasby's head under the water, but the man was heavier than Nathan. He broke Nathan's grip, coming up with his Colt, and Nathan seized his arm in both his hands. But Tasby had a free hand, and was driving his fist into Nathan's neck. Only when Nathan drove a knee into Tasby's groin did he drop the Colt. Nathan took full advantage of the brief respite, kicking free and allowing the swift current to take him away. Looking back, he could see Tasby struggling to free himself from the river. While he had lost his Colt, he still had a Winchester in his saddle boot. Aware that the second antagonist was returning, Empty retreated into the brush and trotted along the river. Doss grabbed his Colt and ran along the riverbank, firing at Nathan. But the bank was grown up in briars and thorns, and Doss soon gave up the chase.

*The Gila River, which flows across southern Arizona.

"Mount up, damn it," Tasby shouted. "We'll ride him down."

Drawing their Winchesters from saddle boots, they rode out, but found the riverbank a mass of underbrush. The water had cut a deeper path and the banks were higher, denying them a clear look at the water. They rode on, and by the time they were able to reach the bank for an unobstructed view, there was no sign of Nathan. They looked at each other in frustration.

"By God," said Tasby, "if we don't find him, our hides won't hold shucks. What'n hell was you doin' while I was wrasslin' him in the water?"

"A wolf lept out of the brush an' damn near tore my arm off," Doss said. "I dropped my Colt, and when I went after it with my other hand, the bastard chomped down on it. It feels like some bones is broke."

"It'll be dark in a few more minutes," said Tasby. "We ain't got a chance of findin' him today. He's got to come out of that river sometime. We'll search both banks, and when we find his trail, we'll ride him down."

But all Nathan's luck hadn't been good. One of Doss's shots had struck him in the upper arm, above his left elbow. While the slug had gone on through, he was bleeding to the extent that he must somehow plug the wound. Aware that Tasby and Doss would take their horses and come after him, he dared not leave the river until darkness concealed him. Reaching a bend in the river, he fought his way close enough to the bank that he was caught behind a huge stone upthrust that extended into the water. There it was shallow, and he was able to stand. He could use mud to ease the bleeding, but with manacles on his wrists, he was unable to reach the wound with his hands. Cupping his hands, he sloshed water against the riverbank, creating mud. He then leaned his wounded arm against the muddy surface, seeking to slick over the wound. While the pressure hurt, he kept adding new coats of mud until the bleeding stopped. Finally, when he judged it was dark enough, he climbed out on to the riverbank. Almost immediately Empty was there, and when Nathan leaned over to ruffle the dog's ears, he almost fell on his face. He straightened up, his head spinning. He was weak. Was it from loss of blood, or from having had nothing to eat since the skimpy breakfast many long hours ago?

The wind had risen, and while Arizona days were hot, the nights were cold. Nathan's teeth were chattering, and his only thought was to escape the wind, allowing his sodden body to dry. The best he was able to find was a cluster of rock, and he settled down on the lee side, thankful to be out of the wind. Empty lay down beside him, knowing all was not well, but excited that they were together again.

Nathan slept, only to be awakened by the pain in his arm and shoulder. Empty was there, having nothing to offer but his presence. Nathan knew that with the dawn, Doss and Tasby would come looking for him. If he was weak and light-headed now, his condition would only worsen during the night. He thought of the trails he had ridden, of those whose lives had touched his, who were now gone. The more he thought, the more it all seemed to fall into place. It seemed he had lived his life by the seasons. The hell of the war and his capture by the Yankees had been winter. Reaching Virginia and finding all his family had been murdered, he had ridden west. Thus the spring of his youth had begun with the dawn of fury, from which he had never escaped. He had found no lasting joy in the summertime of his life, for it had become a killing season, a time to kill or be killed. Now it seemed that autumn was fast approaching, that this might be his last trail. Come the morning, he would struggle on, enough of a gambler to know that someday he must draw the black ace. The past rustled across his mind like dead autumn leaves, and he had the feeling—much as had Wild Bill Hickok—that it might be a premonition of his own death. Far above, in the purple heavens, twinkled a star, and Nathan fixed his eyes upon it. Despite his precarious position, he felt a kind of peace, a hope, and he spoke as much to the star as to the dog.

"Tomorrow, Empty, I'll face up to whatever comes, if it's the autumn of the gun. . . ."

EPILOGUE

March 19, 1873, Lampasas, Texas. Tom, Mart, and Sam Horrell, accompanied by Clint Barkley—a brother-in-law—shot and killed three of four Texas lawmen seeking to arrest Barkley.

June 3, 1873, Wichita, Kansas. Edward T. Beard, owner of a dance hall, shot two soldiers. Two days later, a group of solders burned Beard's dance hall to the ground.

August 15, 1873, Ellsworth, Kansas. Ben Thompson was running a game of monte in Joe Brennan's saloon. Involving himself in Ben's argument over a gambling debt, Ben's brother Billy killed Sheriff C.B. Whitney with a shotgun.

December 1, 1873, Lincoln, New Mexico. Benjamin Horrell was killed, and his three brothers—Martin, Samuel, and Thomas—returned to Texas. Clint Barkley, outlaw and brother-in-law to Merritt Horrell, disappeared.

January 7, 1874, Colfax County, New Mexico. After an argument over a horse race, Clay Allison and Chunk Colbert had dinner together. During the course of the meal, Colbert drew his pistol, and Allison shot him dead.

May 26, 1874, Comanche County, Texas. In a saloon, Hardin had words with Deputy Sheriff Charles Webb. Both men went for their guns. Hardin was wounded in the side, while Webb was shot in the head. Hardin's two companions also shot the lawman.

January 1, 1875, Dallas, Texas. Doc Holliday lost his temper and shot up a saloon. He departed in anger, but nobody was hurt.

April 1, 1875, Bastrop County, Texas. Wild Bill Longley shotgunned Wilson Anderson, who had killed Longley's cousin. It was this murder that resulted in Bill Longley being hanged three years later.

May, 1875, St. Louis, Chicago, and Milwaukee. The whiskey ring was a conspiracy devised to defraud the Federal government of whiskey taxes. Large distillers bribed government officials high and low, retaining the tax proceeds.

U.S. Secretary of the Treasury B.H. Bristow assigned special investigators outside the treasury department to secure evidence. Bristow struck suddenly, seizing the distilleries involved and arresting the persons involved. Three million dollars in taxes were recovered, and of the 176 persons indicted, 110 were convicted.

November, 1875, Bell County, Texas. Wild Bill Longley engaged in a running gun battle with a man called Lew Sawyer. After Sawyer had killed Longley's horse, Sawyer fell from his saddle, and the two continued the gunfight on foot. Sawyer, when he finally died, had been shot thirteen times.

January 24, 1876, Mobeetie, Texas. A soldier stormed into a saloon, killing Molly Brennan, a girl with whom Bat Masterson was sitting. Wounded himself, Masterson shot and killed the soldier, the only killing of his long career.

August 2, 1876, Deadwood, Dakota Territory. While playing poker in Saloon Number Ten, Wild Bill Hickok was shot in the back of the head by Jack McCall. Acquitted by a miner's court, McCall was later arrested in Laramie City by a Deputy U.S. Marshal who heard McCall bragging about killing Wild Bill. McCall was taken to Yankton, Dakota Territory, where he was found guilty and sentenced to hang.

September 7, 1876, Northfield, Minnesota. The James and Younger gangs, seeking to rob the bank, were met with a hail of lead. While Frank and Jesse escaped, the Youngers weren't so fortunate. James, Robert, and Cole were captured.

December 21, 1876, Las Animas, Colorado. Clay Allison and his brother John were on a drunken spree in the Olympic Saloon. Charles Faber, a deputy sheriff, went after them. After Faber had wounded John with a shotgun, Clay Allison gunned down Faber.

December 25, 1876, Zavala County, Texas. An enraged King Fisher gunned down a cowboy, William Dunovan.

December 25, 1876, Austin, Texas. Ben Thompson shot and killed Mark Wilson in a variety theater, following an argument.

June through July, 1877, Lampasas, Texas. There were numerous clashes between the Horrell-Higgins clans. While nobody was killed, many were wounded.

August 17, 1877, Fort Grant Arizona. In George Adkins's saloon, seventeen-year-old Henry McCarty (aka William Bonney and Billy the Kid) had a quarrel with F.P. Cahill. Cahill slapped the kid's face and threw him to the floor. Billy pulled a revolver and shot Cahill, who died the next day. A coroner's jury indicted Billy for criminal and unjustifiable murder.

August 23, 1877, Pensacola, Florida. Texas Ranger John Armstrong arrested John Wesley Hardin aboard a train. When Hardin drew his gun from his waistband, it caught on his suspenders. By then, Armstrong had his own weapon out, and clubbed Hardin senseless. He was returned to Texas. Convicted, he did time in Huntsville prison.

September 25, 1877, Dodge City, Kansas. Sheriff Bat Masterson and Deputy Ed Masterson exchanged fire with a drunken cowboy. The fray ended when the cowboy ran for his horse and galloped away.

November 5, 1877, Dodge City, Kansas. In the afternoon, a quarrel broke out in the Lone Star Dance Hall, owned by Texas Dick Moore and Bob Shaw. Shaw was firing at Moore, when Deputy Marshal Ed Masterson arrived. He clubbed Shaw on the head with the butt of his gun, but Shaw whirled and began firing at the marshal. Masterson was hit in the chest, paralyzing his arm, causing him to drop his pistol. Masterson fell to the floor, and seizing his revolver, shot Shaw twice.

April through July 1878, Lincoln County, New Mexico. Gunfights involving Charlie Bowdre, Richard Brewer, Henry Brown, Frank and George Coe, and Billy the Kid. These events led up to the Lincoln County War.

April 9, 1878, Dodge City, Kansas. Marshal Ed Masterson was shot and killed by a drunken cowboy.

July 26, 1878, Dodge City, Kansas. At three o'clock in the morning, lawmen Wyatt Earp and Jim Masterson engaged in a gunfight with drunken Texas cowboys. George Hoy, a Texan, was hit in the arm, and died from infection.

June 9, 1879, Dodge City, Kansas. Sheriff Jim Masterson, attempting to enforce a gun ordinance, engaged in a gunfight with drunken Texas cowboys, one of whom was shot in the leg.

July 19, 1879, Las Vegas, New Mexico. Doc Holliday and Mike Gordon engaged in a shootout, after Gordon began shooting up a saloon partly owned by Holliday. After Gordon had fired two shots, Holliday felled him with one shot.

November 20, 1879, Las Vegas, New Mexico. Constable Dave Mather was taking some drunken soldiers to jail, when one of them attempted to escape. One of the soldiers was wounded.

Ready to find
your next great read?

Let us help.

Visit prh.com/nextread

Penguin
Random
House